Shelley Rivers is a Bournemouth girl, who spent most of her childhood reading. Married with a family, she now splits most of her time between reading, writing, and pandering to the whims of her hilarious greyhound. Her hobbies include lopsided sewing, holey knitting, and collecting old stuff that no one else sees the beauty in.

Born and raised just outside Toronto, Ontario, **Amy Ruttan** fled the big city to settle down with the country boy of her dreams. After the birth of her second child Amy was lucky enough to realise her lifelong dream of becoming a romance author. When she's not furiously typing away at her computer she's mum to three wonderful children, who use her as a personal taxi and chef.

REUNITED BY HER TWIN REVELATION

SHELLEY RIVERS

FALLING FOR HIS RUNAWAY NURSE

AMY RUTTAN

MILLS & BOON

First Published in Great Britain 2021
by Mills & Boon, an imprint of HarperCollins*Publishers* Ltd,
1 London Bridge Street, London, SE1 9GF

www.harpercollins.co.uk

HarperCollins*Publishers*
1st Floor, Watermarque Building,
Ringsend Road, Dublin 4, Ireland

Reunited by Her Twin Revelation © 2021 by Shelley Rivers

Falling for His Runaway Nurse © 2021 by Amy Ruttan

ISBN: 978-0-263-29777-5

09/21

MIX
Paper from
responsible sources
FSC™ C007454

Printed and bound in Spain
by CPI, Barcelona

REUNITED BY HER TWIN REVELATION

SHELLEY RIVERS

MILLS & BOON

To C, with love.

And special thanks to paramedic Graham Woolcott, for his expert help during the writing of this story.

CHAPTER ONE

'So you are really leaving us?'

Dr Logan Fox glanced up from studying the computer screen and smiled at the old man waiting his turn in the busy waiting room. Several small children sat reading books on the tiled floor, and a group of mothers stood beside the small babies' play area at the far end of the room, whispering and laughing as they waited to be called for their appointments.

With a smile of thanks to the receptionist, Logan wove his way over to the local man who'd become a good friend during his months while working on the island of Malta. The man who had helped him through many a long, lonely night, as they jointly put the world to rights in the crowded surroundings of a local bar.

'I am indeed, Matthew. In less than two hours I shall be on a plane to England. My taxi is due to arrive within the hour to take me to the airport.'

'Have we driven you away with all our sunshine and steep, narrow streets?' the old man joked, shooting Logan a toothy grin. His left hand clutched a brown wooden walking stick—a stick it had taken Logan weeks to convince him to use.

Logan smiled and shook his head. 'No, it's time I went home and tied up the last of my father's estate.

Retrieved the few belongings I wish to keep before the house and everything inside it is sold. I've put it off long enough, but the solicitors are threatening to send over a team of mercenaries to kidnap me and take me back to England if I don't return this coming week. Worse still, they insist they'll charge me for the trouble.'

Matthew chuckled, the deep, strong sound at odds with the man's small and wizened stature. Logan had learnt while treating his friend after his last health scare that he had great stamina, and his mind was as strong and as sharp as a teenager's—and just as crafty.

'Well, just make sure you come back to us,' Matthew insisted. 'Old Doc isn't going to last much longer. I swear the man was ancient when I was a boy, running through the countryside with nothing but merriment and mischief on my mind.'

Logan chuckled. 'Between you and me, I think the man intends to continue working until the next millennium. Anyway, you'll be far too busy to miss me as I hear you're looking for another wife. Though surely five is enough for any man's lifetime?'

Matthew tutted and removed his cream Havana hat. 'Any man who is tired of women should be rotting in the grave, my dear friend. Is it my fault that women keep leaving me? Inconvenient, it is. You just get used to one and then she either ruins things by croaking it or she runs off. Besides, I'm still looking for *her*.'

'Her?' Logan repeated curiously.

'Yes—you know, the special one. The one who is supposed to fill your heart with everything your soul requires. I've come close with each of my wives, but never quite got it right. Good, but not perfect.'

'Then why marry at all?' Logan quizzed the man,

who had a reputation in town for being a long-time rogue and charmer.

Matthew grinned again, and this time a rakish twinkle lit up his ageing eyes. 'A man has to pass the time somehow while he's waiting for "the one", Logan. It can get lonely and boring otherwise. And kissing the wrong women has many, many sweet advantages.'

Logan laughed and patted his friend on the shoulder. 'I guess you're right.'

With a final farewell, Logan left the building and stepped out on to the old narrow street. Passing small bars and tiny shops crammed full of goods to buy, he walked the short distance to the traditional Maltese house he shared with a male nurse from the same health practice. With luck he would have the place to himself while he finished packing his suitcase. He and the other members of staff had said their goodbyes the night before, when they'd all shared a meal and several bottles of the local wine at Old Doc's house. Now he just wanted to slip away without any fuss.

Strolling down a second narrow street, he continued on until he came to a small courtyard concealed from the main busy thoroughfare. Built from the local limestone, three-storey buildings rose around Logan, cocooning him within their rough, golden weathered walls. Passing an open gate, he could smell freshly baked bread, garlic and the local culinary speciality of rabbit stew filling the air. With a glance inside he observed groups of locals and tourists, tucking into mouth-watering plates of food courtesy of the hidden backstreet restaurant.

Moving on, he ignored the tantalising and tempting aromas that called to his empty stomach and teased his appetite, disappointed not to have time to enjoy one last meal before leaving. But he'd made up his mind to travel today and it was too late to change his plans.

In the far corner of the courtyard a small child ran up a flight of stone steps, singing a nursery rhyme. Nearby, his doting grandmother sat on a stool, watching.

Logan waved to the old woman, but headed for the traditional blue arched door in the opposite corner. Purple tube-shaped flowers spilled down from the black wrought-iron balcony just above it, the sprawling lower leaves brushing the top of his head as he unlocked the door. The familiar sensation brought a moment of pleasure to his restless soul.

Letting himself into the building, he climbed the narrow steps to his bedroom, glad to reach it without encountering anyone. He just wanted to pack and leave. Say goodbye to the island the same way he'd arrived. Without fuss or fanfare. Malta had become his refuge after his failed engagement, and leaving it arose mixed feelings he refused to examine or dissect. If not for the solicitor's insistence that he return to England, he wouldn't be going home at all.

Entering his bedroom, Logan let his gaze fall immediately on the half-packed suitcase lying open on the double bed. Glancing around, he checked over the rest of the furniture for any remaining belongings, his eyes eventually landing on the folded letter on the dressing table.

It was a letter he'd spent the last few months ignoring, after discarding it there following one single read. He was refusing to deal with the reality of what lay folded inside the envelope and his feelings towards the people it concerned.

Reluctantly, he walked over to the dressing table and picked it up. A thin layer of dust now covered it. Blowing off the worst, he slowly turned it over, staring down at the thick paper, not eager to confront the strange jumble of emotions it triggered inside him.

The words printed within informed him of several facts he would have preferred never to discover. The main one being that Victor Fox, the man Logan had believed was his father, did not, in truth, share one particle of DNA with him.

Which meant that for thirty-five years every single person in Logan's so-called family had lied to him. Each one guilty of deception by choosing to keep the loathsome truth a secret.

Apparently everyone had known his mother's dirty little lie—except for him. The person it concerned the most. The individual who'd been fed a dishonest fairy tale, only to discover a sordid tangle of falsehoods.

Nausea rotated in Logan's stomach, but he ignored it and forced himself to list the uncomfortable truths mentally. His beloved late mother had indulged in a long-term love affair at some time during her twenty-year marriage to Victor. An affair which resulted in a child—him. Facts he'd only discovered after reading this letter from Victor's solicitor. Precise, impersonal words, disclosing the ugly facts and the information his so-called family had purposely chosen to keep from him. Telling him that Logan could use the Fox name, but that not one drop of genuine Fox blood flowed through his veins, making him null and void as the man's assumed son and heir.

Making Logan's presence in the family entirely irrelevant now Victor no longer lived.

The aching tightness in Logan's chest had nothing to do with the light cold he'd picked up a few days ago. No, the pain spreading out from the area around his heart originated from the callous reality that betrayal and treachery stained his whole existence. That, despite believing differently, Logan actually had no true family other than an estranged half-brother.

Was this destiny's sick joke? A way to knock him off his complacent perch and show him that trust was nothing but a foolish hope? Something people liked to offer and declare, but rarely executed for the benefit of others?

With each breath, the ache in Logan's chest increased. The constant thick tension that had begun the day news of Victor's death had reached him. News only forwarded after the man's funeral in England had already taken place. Exactly the way Victor had desired it, according to Bellman, his faithful solicitor.

No bedside farewells or last-minute explanations for him. Just these blunt and impersonal words on a piece of paper that shattered and destroyed everything Logan had thought true. An abrupt statement proclaiming his mother's adultery and Victor's swift and brutal renouncement of Logan as his true son. No other explanation or justification given.

One night he had gone to sleep a son but awoken the following day as no one.

Logan's fingers tightened around the letter. Everything he'd been raised to believe in had been harshly ripped away without care or thought for his feelings. Leaving him cast aside like one of Victor's flawed business deals. Cold-heartedly disconnected from the birthright he'd assumed was his to claim.

Who knew why Victor had chosen to reveal the truth after so many years pretending? The man's thought process had always at best bordered on complicated, so there was no point in trying to decipher this last action.

Victor's vast fortune would be distributed through various charities and associations. Gifts to good causes— another out-of-character act from the old man. Logan didn't need or care about the money, or the ridiculously large house in Salisbury where he'd grown up. None of the material possessions mattered—only the bitter truth that the man he'd always believed cared for him had mercilessly rejected any familial connection linking them once he no longer had use for Logan. Once he no longer required a son.

After years of sharing what Logan had believed was a strong, close father-and-son relationship, Victor had discarded both his affection and his presence in the family with soul-obliterating and ruthless ease.

All Logan's life Victor had drummed home a mantra of discipline, hard work and family loyalty. He'd pushed Logan to be the best at everything and to reject failure. When Logan had gone to university Victor had chosen which one, and what career Logan would pursue. As he'd had a natural ability for science and excelled in tests, he'd decided on medicine. Not a general doctor, though. No, Victor had expected Logan to become the best in his field. Always the greatest. Because any less would be neither allowed nor contemplated.

Thankfully Logan had also wished to pursue medicine. He'd loved working with patients and finding ways to heal them, so there'd been no hardship in following Victor's wishes. Not when they had also been his own.

The only time Logan had witnessed the old man's anger and disappointment had occurred on the day he'd informed Victor that he planned to go to Malta, after calling off his six-month engagement to the daughter of a family friend. Then he'd seen something in Victor's eyes that had unsettled him. Some emotion that made sense to him now.

Tugging off his black-framed glasses, Logan tucked them into his shirt pocket and headed in the direction of the bed. Throwing the letter inside the suitcase, he reached for the lid, then paused. After a second's hesitation, he snatched the letter out again. With one final look, he scrunched it into a messy ball and walked over to the wastepaper bin. Dropping it inside, he glared at the crumpled letter for a moment longer before turning away.

He had no need to keep it when the words were already burnt into his memory. Singed into his brain with no chance of his forgetting. Not now he understood how little he'd meant to the man he'd spent years calling Dad. A loving term it turned out he'd had no right to use.

The sudden blast of a car horn interrupted Logan's heavy and grave thoughts. Strolling over to the French doors, he pushed back the sheer net curtains and turned the key in the lock. Stepping out on to the narrow balcony, he let the warm sunshine and the smells from the restaurant float to him once again, dispelling some of the bleakness of his mood.

Leaning over the lush trailing plants and the railing, he waved to the driver in the taxi below.

Time to return to England and finish with the past for good. To track down the one person who might know the truth concerning the whole deplorable situation surrounding his birth. The older sibling Logan hadn't seen for years. Maddox, his elusive half-brother.

'Those babies need a father.'

Thurza Bow rolled her eyes and lifted the four-pack of super-soft toilet rolls out of the cardboard box, fighting the urge to throw the item at her cousin's head. Sometimes the itch to be wicked took hold when she was in Rachel's company. A dreadful but unfortunate truth.

Just for once Thurza ached to throw respect, good manners and decency to one side and give her nagging cousin the shock of her life. Besides, the toilet rolls were soft—it said so on the purple wrapping. So they wouldn't hurt...much.

'What you really need is to call the twins' father to account and force him to do his part in parenting. Don't you think it's time Daddy took a turn?'

Thurza placed another pack of toilet paper on to the shelf. 'He's not interested.'

'He's their father. He gets no choice. It's not right how he gets to walk away and leave you with the consequences of your joint sexual pleasure.'

Thurza glanced at her cousin. 'It's my choice to keep him out of our lives.'

'You're lying,' Rachel replied bluntly. 'You may tell yourself that nonsense, but I know you're hiding something.'

Thurza frowned, wondering if her cousin had resumed learning witchcraft. Lately, she had an uncanny knack of being right over most things. It was most annoying. 'I'm not lying. The man is unsuitable father material.'

Rachel scoffed. 'Didn't stop you sleeping with him.'

'At the time I wasn't considering him as a prospective father. I just sought a night of uncomplicated sex.'

Rachel sighed and shook her head. 'More lies. You don't do one-night stands, so the reason the twins' father tempted you into breaking your normal code of behaviour must be more than you're admitting to.'

Thurza slammed the final toilet roll pack down on

to the shelf and retrieved the empty cardboard box. She hated how her cousin knew her so well.

Making her way towards the rear storeroom, she asked, 'Do you have everything you need today?'

'As you don't sell cousins with sense, I guess so,' Rachel returned sarcastically.

Thurza threw the box into the back room, hoping Rachel would leave, so she could resume shelf-filling and daydreaming about the one man she wasn't supposed to dream about. The man they were unfortunately discussing. A man who was truly forbidden and lost to her. Who had turned out to be the worst kind of jerk after their long illicit night together.

Rachel took her time picking up her bag of shopping. 'At least think about joining one of those dating sites I sent you the links for the other day. I'm sure even with your picky taste you can find someone. You do still have that list I gave you of local men with potential, don't you?'

'Somewhere…' Thurza hedged, not about to admit that she'd deleted both the links and the list from her phone five minutes after her cousin had sent them.

'You're a good-looking woman with that Viking female warrior vibe you're rocking. God, why did I have to take after my mother?' Rachel complained. 'Who wants little Miss Mousy Hair?'

'At least your mother lives close by,' Thurza pointed out.

Her father had died ten years before and her Swedish mother had left England not long after, to go and live in France with a French film director she'd met on a singles' mountain-climbing holiday.

Rachel scoffed. 'At least yours comes with the bonus

of a holiday in France whenever you fancy it. Anyway, think about what I said.'

Thurza sighed. 'The boys and I are fine as we are. I'm twenty-seven years old, Rachel. I can manage my life on my own, thanks.'

'Yeah, right... You managed to leave this town and what happened? You returned, having left a very good nursing job, four months pregnant with no willing man to help. Let's not even touch the subject of contraception, Nurse Bow. Something, dear cousin, you apparently forgot the second your knickers hit the floor.'

Warmth flooded Thurza's cheeks. 'It was an unexpected encounter and we used contraception. My mistake came from trusting it to work.'

Rachel snorted and headed for the exit. 'You're the type of person who will always be in that unlucky two per cent failure rate, I'm afraid.'

The words stung, but Thurza refused to react. She had already accepted her mistake in giving in to the man's charms, without her cousin rubbing it in because the contraception they'd used had failed.

Letting out a sigh of relief when Rachel finally left the shop and jumped into a small white van with the local chemist's logo on the side, Thurza reluctantly considered her cousin's suggestion.

Should she encourage a man into her and the boys' lives? She closed her eyes and shook her head. No, she didn't want a man hanging around, getting in the way and disrupting her calm and normality. The encounter with the twins' father had been nothing but one foolish moment of yielding to basic physical needs and ignoring the sensible inner voice that had warned her of the risk. For one night she'd given in to the irrational urge to be *seen* by a sexy doctor. A special evening when she'd become as attractive and as sexy as all the other nurses who worked at the hospital, instead of the shy woman people hardly noticed.

That out-of-character night had resulted in her becoming a mother to two beautiful baby boys.

She didn't regret her sons. Right from the moment she'd found out she was expecting them something had clicked and finally made sense in her life, had given her a true purpose.

She'd tried to let the man know about the pregnancy. Sent letter after letter to his flat during it. Once she'd even turned up on his doorstep, eight months pregnant, to be told by his cleaner that he had gone away for a while and she wasn't sure when he would be back.

She'd even sent a card after the twins' first smiles, when an attack of sadness had hit her at all the man was missing. Just like her letters, it had gone unanswered.

Yes, Dr Logan Fox's interest had vanished almost as quickly as his attraction to her. One night of lovemaking and then all those pretty sweet words he'd whispered in her ear as he'd taken her to a place she'd never dreamt existed between a man and woman had disappeared quicker than a twig dropped into the centre of a scorching hot fire.

She'd not received one answer or acknowledgement from him. Not a phone call, a note—not a single thing except a telling silence.

She could have pursued the legal option, but she refused to force a man into having a relationship with his offspring when he'd made it clear he didn't want one. She just wished he'd told her to her face, so she could live without the occasional qualm or doubt.

Thurza reached for another large container full of toilet rolls. No, she didn't need the man or his reluctant help. The twins deserved better than an uninterested father. She'd quite like some spare hours in the day, and a new washing machine that didn't sound as though it was on the verge of taking off every time she used it. But both were impossible wishes, so Thurza did what every other single parent did and sucked it up with a smile.

Because her boys were her happiness and they fulfilled her life. She just wished her cousin would one day understand that.

Logan pulled into a space in the garage's parking area, relieved to finally be in Dorset and close to where his half-brother Maddox lived. Soon he would be able to get the answers he'd come here for. The answers that would finally settle everything from the past and allow him to move on from it for good.

Gripping the hire car's steering wheel, he sighed. After years of no contact, he had to talk to his estranged half-brother. The half-brother who'd walked out of the family home on his twenty-first birthday and never returned. The sibling Logan had always believed he could trust, despite their lack of communication over the years.

Logan wanted to stare into his face and hear the whole and complete story. Not hostile statements parroted through a dead man's solicitor's letter. A full explanation from someone Logan suspected knew everything. He wanted to see with his own eyes the moment when his half-brother realised that he knew of their mother's long-ago infidelity, and then watch him try and squirm out of answering Logan's questions. Because he had many.

His so-called family—the people who were supposed to support and care for him, to love him, even—had all lied to him. Individuals who'd regularly over the years lectured him on loyalty had shown him none. For them the trait had become unimportant and insignificant when compared to the hope of one day gaining favour and eventually a decent share of Victor's wealth. A selfish goal that not one of them had actually achieved.

In the Fox family a person accepted and played their role. For him it had required being the perfect son. The one who'd achieved more than the disappointing older sibling. He'd had to do what Victor expected, when it was required. And Logan had done just that for years, without resentment or complaint, because he had cared about the man.

But now he refused to be disregarded or ignored. In the next few hours his dear half-brother was going to spill the truth whether he wanted to or not. He owed Logan. Even if he had to wring it out of Maddox syllable by drawn-out syllable.

Reaching for his phone where it lay on the passenger's seat, next to an empty takeaway coffee cup, a half-eaten ham sandwich and an unused paper napkin, Logan flicked through the long list of contacts until he found his half-brother's name and punched the button.

He'd discovered Maddox's whereabouts after finding a postcard amongst the wad of papers the solicitor had handed him when he'd collected his belongings from the family house in Salisbury. Sent over a year ago, it had Maddox's address and phone number scribbled on it. Nothing else—no greeting or comment—just his name, address and mobile number.

The solicitor had found it while sorting through Victor's study. Hidden at the back of a drawer in the old man's desk, as though he hadn't been able to bring himself to throw it away, but hadn't wanted anyone else to see it either.

Drumming his fingertips against the leather steering wheel, Logan waited as unanswered rings purred in his ear.

After at least twenty rings, his half-brother's voice finally growled down the line. 'What?'

'How do I get to your place?' Logan demanded, too irritated to care about pleasantries or polite greetings. This close to getting his answers, he'd given up any pretence of patience or manners.

Removing his glasses, he rubbed the bridge of his nose, and pushed back the weariness that hovered close.

Tense silence answered his demand.

'I said, *brother*, how do I get to your home?' he repeated, biting out the words with icy firmness.

If Maddox imagined he could put him off, then he intended to prove differently. Wherever the man resided in this godforsaken seaside town, Logan would find him and force him to have a long overdue conversation.

'Logan?' Maddox barked. 'What the hell do you want?'

After years of no contact, Logan wasn't offended by his sibling's less than friendly greeting. 'I'm in Dorset, in the town where you live, and I'm not leaving until we talk.'

Silence returned, before a heavy sigh came from his half-brother. 'What's happened?'

'Victor's dead.'

'When?'

'Ten weeks ago.'

Logan forced away the flood of sentimental emotion saying the words pulled from his heart. The man had lied to him his whole life, and only when he knew he wouldn't face the consequences of that deception had he made certain that his fake son discovered the truth. When he'd no longer needed Logan to ease his old age loneliness Victor had cut him off. Thrown Logan and his love away like redundant, useless objects he no longer wished to possess. The man didn't deserve his grief or his tears, and he refused to give in to either.

'The old man told you, didn't he?' said Maddox.

Logan's fingers tightened around the phone. The small pathetic hope that his half-brother might not know the truth withered and died. His instinct had been sadly right once again.

'In a way. He left instructions with his solicitor to inform me of the truth regarding my parentage after his death.'

Further silence settled between them, before Maddox sighed again. 'I guess you'd better come to the farm.'

Logan grabbed the napkin from the passenger seat and pulled a pen from his shirt pocket. In silence, he wrote down the instructions Maddox gave him.

Finishing the call, Logan decided he might as well get some fuel while he was there, and drove round to the fuel pumps. He glanced out through the windscreen at his surroundings. A large plastic kangaroo tied to the garage's shop roof bobbed around in the breeze. The sight was an apt reflection of the sensations inside him.

Replacing his glasses, Logan opened the car door. The ache in his chest refused to ease and continued to grow and intensify. Damn emotions. Why couldn't they just stay stuffed down where he'd shoved them? He didn't have the time or the inclination to deal with them.

After his conversation with his half-brother, he intended never to think about Victor again. He planned to cut his last remaining ties with England and fly out before the end of the week. Whether he'd return to Malta or head somewhere new he didn't know.

His eyes shifted to the shop, his gaze drawn towards the large window and the woman who stood inside. A strange, unfamiliar tingling surfaced from the deep recesses of his stomach, slowly prickling and twisting through his whole body.

Staring harder at the woman, he took in her appearance, slowly moving his gaze over the mustard-yellow top she was wearing to rest on her long blonde hair and strong Nordic features. She looked familiar. Like someone he'd once briefly known—in the physical sense, anyway. A woman who'd tempted him to do unfamiliar and sinful things he'd never tried before. Someone whose sweet, gorgeous body he'd explored intimately during one long night.

Someone whose sweet, kissable and frankly too enticing mouth he still dreamt about all these months later.

Logan swallowed hard, unable to pull his gaze away. His heart kicked up its pace until it banged painfully against his chest. The woman didn't just resemble the woman from that night—he was pretty certain it really was her.

Turning away, he ran a palm over his face while his mind raced. Focusing on the petrol pump, he grabbed the nozzle and filled the car's tank. Wasting time as he tried to make sense of the situation.

Okay, play it cool, Fox. Go inside, pay and leave. Pretend you don't recognise her. If she tries to drag you into conversation or tries to get reacquainted, leave fast. You've more important things to do than revisiting an ex-lover, even if she did provide the best night of lovemaking you've ever known.

She was the only woman he'd ever shared a one-night stand with. The woman he'd taken to bed mere days after calling off his doomed engagement, only to wake up and find her gone the next morning, leaving him with nothing but the scent of her fading perfume on his love-wrinkled bed sheets and a heart full of regrets.

Was some higher figure messing with him as punishment for a crime he didn't recall? First Victor's death, his painful rejection, and now an awkward meetup with a past lover. Together with the upcoming meeting with his half-brother, these last few months were rounding off to be a blinder.

Sliding the pump back into its rest, Logan replaced the car's fuel cap and glanced again at the woman inside the building.

Bite the bullet, Fox, and face her.

With a deep breath, he wiped his damp palms against his trousers and took a step towards the building and his one lapse of sanity. The thudding of his heartbeat echoed loudly in his ears with each step closer to the woman he'd done his best to forget.

Not that he'd succeeded. For eighteen months this woman and their time together had repeatedly taunted him on those nights when the clock had ticked sluggishly through the dark night hours and he'd been alone in a huge bed with only his frustrated thoughts and memories to keep him company.

A goddess in bed, with skin soft and smooth, and a sweet naughty mouth which had taught him some moves he'd never known before. Hair like a Viking queen's and an accent that had rocked between low Dorset tones and a faint sexy Swedish lilt.

That night he'd recognised her from the corridors in the hospital where they'd both worked. Her wonderful fresh eagerness for the job had yet to be dimmed by long, endless shifts and the never-ending conveyor belt of patients.

What he'd discovered once he'd taken her home was that beneath her clothes was a body made to entrance and seduce a man. In that ultimate, exquisite moment when their bodies had joined, he knew he'd experienced heaven for the first time.

Or maybe he'd just imagined it. Envisaged the memory of her sweet soft moans and angelic gasps to make his dented confidence feel better. So that despite all the turmoil in his life at that time, the woman in his bed had really wanted him as much as he'd wanted her.

His gaze returned to the window, his unease increasing when he noted her expression. Was that horror on her face? Really?

Unexpected disappointment rushed through him at the same time as a loud, high-pitched scream sounded across the forecourt, freezing him to the spot.

Twisting in the direction of the scream, he spotted another vehicle with two squabbling young boys and a woman standing next to it. After a moment, the woman picked up one child and put him into the rear seat of the car.

'Let me see,' she instructed the remaining boy, who stood clutching his right eye while screaming at the top of his voice. 'What did Troy stab you with?'

'His toy screwdriver!'

With all thoughts of the woman inside the building and her lack of welcome on pause, Logan walked purposefully towards the injured boy. Facing the complications of his past could wait. Right now a child needed his medical expertise, and that took priority over everything.

CHAPTER TWO

THURZA GULPED AS her one past mistake walked away from the building and headed in the direction of the mother and child beside the second car on the forecourt. Gripping the blue cloth she was using to wipe a dirty smudge from the windowpane, she briefly tussled between whether to run out through the back door and away from the complications the man's unexpected arrival represented, or head outside and help the six-foot-two bulge of hard muscle and inflated ego she'd once stupidly shared an unforgettable night with.

Glancing at her shaking hands, she drew in a deep breath and went to grab the first aid kit. She was a nurse. She would do whatever was needed to help the child and ignore the man now striding across the forecourt.

But what if Logan Fox recognised her? Not an impossibility. Not really. Considering they'd once shared a night together. After all, he'd explored and tasted intimate areas of her body no other man ever had. But she'd prefer he didn't. Then she could return to forgetting him—which wasn't easy considering she lived with two small reminders who were his image, and also her constant and unfortunate habit of daydreaming about him.

But imagine having to explain to her sons in future years that, yes, she had seen their father again, but sadly, he hadn't recognised her, and had instead stared blankly into her face as though she were a stranger. Crushing— not only for her own self-confidence—and hardly the candy heart stuff of happy families that children hoped to hear where their parents were concerned.

She pushed the door open and a cold breeze greeted her, causing a full-body shiver to join her internal shaking. Great. By the time she joined the group she'd probably be a mass of quivers inside and out.

Swallowing the dryness from her mouth, and with slow, reluctant steps, she walked towards the trio. Mass fluttering swelled inside her stomach as she approached, her eyes skimming hesitantly over the man's white shirt and dark trousers, before working their way back up the line of his spine to linger for a traitorous second or two on his wide shoulders.

Fighting her natural nursing instinct, which was clamouring to push in and take over treating the still yelling child, Thurza stopped a few paces away from the group. 'Er…excuse me? Can I help?'

She waited for a reply, but all she obtained was a distracted glance from the boy's mother, before the woman returned her attention to the man now softly talking to the boy.

After a moment, Thurza gave in to the inevitable and crouched beside Logan, accidentally bumping his arm as she bent. *Oh, fiddles.* It felt as firm as she remembered. All hard muscle and solid tissue. Pulling back from the unexpected contact, she swallowed hard and tried to ignore the sizzling impression it had left on her own body. Inappropriate reactions and thoughts were not wanted right now.

'It's okay,' she said gently to the boy, forcing herself to concentrate on the injured child and not the brief moment of physical connection she'd just experienced. 'We're here to help you feel better. What's your name?'

'Fr-Fr-Freddie,' the boy stuttered out in between wails.

'Hello, Freddie. I've brought our first aid kit so we can help you,' said Thurza. Logan continued trying to soothe the hysterical child, not glancing her way. 'What happened?' she asked Logan, also keeping her eyes firmly focused on Freddie.

'Thank you for bringing the kit. This young man has sustained an injury to his eye, and it needs to be stabilised until he can get to a hospital for further investigation.'

'Will he be all right?' demanded the mother, who was on Logan's other side. 'One moment they were laughing and singing, the next he was screaming his head off.'

'Let's concentrate on saving your son's eyesight, shall we?' Logan replied gently. 'Questions can wait for the moment.'

The mother nodded and moved a little closer to her son. Thurza noted the movement had also brought her closer to Logan.

'Why don't you tell me what happened, Freddie?' Logan asked, his voice quiet but firm now he'd coaxed the child down from his hysterical wailing.

Sobbing, Freddie said, 'Troy stabbed me with his toy screwdriver.'

Logan winced. 'Ouch, I bet that hurt.'

'It's agony,' the boy answered dramatically. 'I hate him.'

'Did it go right into your eye or just catch your eyelid?' Logan quizzed, ignoring the last part of Freddie's remark.

Thurza hid a smile, though. It was a universal truth

that all siblings hated one another at some point during their childhood years. She doubted this would be the last time the boy thought or uttered those or similar words.

'Right in. It won't stop watering and it hurts bad.'

Thurza opened the box and took out a pair of sterile gloves, offering them to Logan. 'Here. We should have everything you need. I keep it well stocked.'

Logan finally turned to Thurza and met her gaze. The strong flash of recognition shone in his dark blue eyes as they silently searched her face, triggering another quiver to surge through her. Every part of her body, inside and out, throbbed from the power of that look.

'Thank you,' he said.

Breath wedged in her throat like a large roughly peeled raw potato. Thurza found herself unable to look away. The face that had plagued her for months and months had now physically materialised in front of her. All sane thought vanished as she took in the strong jaw, dark cheeks and long, straight nose. When his eyes dropped lower, to rest on her mouth, she noticed his curly lashes and the perfect arch of his eyebrows, gorgeously magnified by his glasses.

No dictionary in the world could possibly hold an adjective to truly describe the male beauty in front of her. The man was physically stunning.

Forcing herself to remember the way he'd used her for one night and ignored her later attempts at contact, she dragged her gaze away and fixed her attention on the contents of the first aid box. Time to stop dithering and do her job. The one she was trained to do.

Falling back on her nursing professionalism, she waited silently as Logan once again spoke to the child.

'Right, Freddie. Please keep your head absolutely

still for me while I take a quick look at your eye. Can you do that?'

Seeing the calm, patient way he dealt with the young boy pulled at her heart. Were there other Fox children running around? Were hers the only ones he'd chosen to ignore? The notion caused another squeeze to her heart, and a new wave of dislike for the male at her side washed over Thurza.

The child nodded, until Thurza reached out and stopped him. With an encouraging smile, she suggested, 'How about we ask your mum to come and stand behind you, so she can hold your head while the doctor has a look?'

She motioned to the mother, who shifted behind her son and did as Thurza directed, gently cupping the sides of Freddie's head with her palms.

'I'm going to move your hand,' Logan encouraged Freddie. 'I won't hurt you. I just need to take a quick look.'

Freddie stood quietly as Logan gently lowered the hand covering the boy's eye and silently studied the child's streaming eyeball before he spoke to Thurza. 'I can't see any visible damage, but it is extremely bloodshot. I think it's best to be cautious and pop to a hospital…get the doctors there to take a proper look.'

'Is it really that bad?' the mother asked.

'Without the proper equipment I can't answer that,' Logan replied honestly. 'To be sure, you'll need someone at a hospital to check him over. They have the right equipment to do a thorough examination of the eyeball.'

The woman sighed and lowered her hands from her son's head. 'I knew we should never have bought that children's tool set. I told my husband it was a bad idea.

The boys are always fighting and doing stupid things like this to each other.'

'Would you mind handing me a sterile pad and a roll of bandaging?' Logan asked Thurza.

Thurza collected a clean pad and a fresh dressing from the first aid box.

Logan took the pad and positioned it gently against Freddie's eye. 'I need you to keep both your eyes still, Freddie. No looking from side to side or rolling them up and down. Just perfectly still. Not only now, but right up until you see a doctor at the hospital. I know it's hard, but if you don't it could cause further damage to your eye.'

With a nod Thurza's way, Logan held the pad, while she efficiently and quickly wrapped the bandage round the child's head to hold the protective wadding in place. Her unsteady fingers brushed Logan's as she made a final loop around Freddie's head. The touch tingled through her, but she shook it away and focused on her task. The sooner it was completed, the quicker they could all pile back into their vehicles and leave.

Happy that both the bandage and pad were secure, she tied off the dressing and returned the remaining bandage to the box. Once again, she glanced at the good-looking man at her side. Why did God make some men handsome, but also complete and utter jackasses, too? Was it some devious test to see how many women weakened and succumbed to the effects of a roguish smile? Well, she'd failed dismally, having surrendered to this man's smile and more.

To think she'd once kissed those cheeks during their brief romp together. Kissed most of his body. And licked it. Goodness, how she had licked and explored inches of his smooth skin.

Concentrate, Bow. You're a trained nurse and this is a medical emergency. Nothing to do with a man or an ex-lover. He means nothing to you, and you definitely do not still find any part of Dr Logan Fox attractive. Stop the naughty thoughts right this second.

Picking up the box, she straightened at the same time as Logan. Why was he in town? Had he finally grown a conscience after months of silence and decided that he needed to see her and the boys? Or, worse, had he suddenly concluded that he wanted to be in their lives?

Dr Logan Fox in her life permanently? A different kind of shudder leapt through her body, chilling her bones to the very marrow. Oh, no, that was not a good idea. Not after he'd kept his distance for so long.

She pushed away the disturbing thought and pulled her mobile from her trouser pocket. She waved it and asked Freddie's mother, 'Shall I phone for an ambulance?'

Logan also focused on the mother, both his gaze and his silence expectant.

'No, I'll take him,' the woman replied, placing a reassuring arm around her son's shoulders. 'It will probably be quicker than waiting for one to arrive. Plus, I have my other kids in the car.'

Logan nodded. 'Good sight is a precious gift. I would hate your child to lose any of his through a silly squabble with his brother.'

'Thank you for your help,' Freddie's mother said. 'Both of you. Thank you.'

In silence, Thurza and Logan watched the mother help Freddie into the back seat of the car and then drive off in the direction of the closest hospital.

'Do you think he'll be okay?' Thurza asked, not knowing what else to say now they were alone. He'd made no verbal indication to confirm that he definitely recognised her, but a tautness hummed between them. As though their bodies had silently identified one another, despite their efforts to pretend differently.

'I think so. No doubt the child who caused the injury and the father who bought the tool set will suffer an earful later.'

Thurza nodded, hesitantly pointing to the building behind them. 'Well, I need to fill out an incident report.'

Logan rolled off the gloves and dumped them in a nearby bin. 'I need to pay for my fuel.'

'Oh, you can do that at the pump with your card,' Thurza said in a moment of panic, and then she lied. 'The tills are down inside. Sorry.'

Her heart racing, she scurried back towards the building, hoping Logan would do as she suggested. She wanted the man gone. Away from the garage, away from Dorset and, more importantly, far away from her baby sons.

Thurza let out a heavy sigh and waved goodbye to her boss. Wrapping her cream hand-knitted scarf around her neck, she shoved her hands into her coat pockets and headed for home. Turning in the direction of the cottage she rented, she hurried along the poorly lit country road.

Hopefully, she would have a chance to warm the house through before her cousin arrived with the twins. As much as Rachel drove her mad, Thurza wouldn't be able to manage without her help in collecting the boys from day care twice a week and her frequent offers to babysit.

When Thurza had returned home pregnant, Rachel's disappointment had been her main concern. But her cousin had taken one look at Thurza's obvious baby bump, rolled her eyes the way she always did when she concluded that Thurza was beyond help then dragged her into a big hug which had left them both crying on the doorstep.

Thurza had needed that hug more than anything. Sometimes she still did.

Thurza smiled, feeling a whoosh of love for her cousin and her sons. The boys hadn't been planned, but she loved them with every part of her being. From the moment she'd discovered they were growing inside her, she'd sworn to give her children the best home possible and oodles of love.

Which brought her back to the question that had been constantly revolving through her mind since the earlier incident at the garage. Prodding at her consciousness until it left her with a thumping headache. Why was Dr Logan Fox in town? What had brought him to this part of Dorset? Was he just visiting, passing through, or did he have another motive for his unexpected arrival? One that involved her and the boys? One she unquestionably wasn't going to like?

Though he hadn't said anything to confirm that he remembered her, she'd seen it in his gaze when he'd turned and spoken to her. Those blue eyes had given their own confirmation. Speech was unnecessary when their bodies instinctively did the communicating for them.

On the other hand, he'd also got back in his car and left after paying for his fuel. So maybe his arrival in town was nothing to worry over. Just an unplanned momentary glitch in both their lives. One best forgotten.

Not for a second did Thurza see Logan Fox as a fan of Dorset's autumnal countryside. White Caribbean sands and fruity cocktails handed out by accommodating staff were more his style. Definitely more Monaco or the Bahamas than Dorset beaches and earthy leaf-covered forests. No wet Sunday afternoon walks or muddy boots for him.

Yet here he was, in a town which took less than ten minutes to drive through and over twenty-five minutes to find on a map. They had a beautiful coast and an award-winning farm shop and tea rooms, but agriculture remained the main economy in the area, not tourism.

The question remained unanswered. Why had Logan Fox arrived in Dorset? Had he left now or was he still hanging around somewhere while he figured out his next move? Did his presence indicate a wish to make contact after all the letters Thurza had sent to him? Letters she'd initially poured her heart into, until it had become clear he wasn't interested in her or her progressing pregnancy. If so, why hadn't he mentioned them while at the garage? Why hadn't he enquired after the boys? Was he waiting for the right moment to offer her money and forget his connection to their sons, or perhaps he intended to find out more about her life first?

But why would he want to do that?

She frowned and dug her hands deeper into her coat pockets. Was he in town because he hoped to discover some terrible local scandal which involved her, so that he could steal her babies and then try to cut her out of their lives?

She stumbled on a broken piece of Tarmac, barely noticing the pain shooting through her toes as that last thought vibrated through her heart. She gasped as the idea grew, feeling her body tense as her imagination flew. Was that it? Did he hope to take her children away? Was he plotting right this minute to use his wealth and reputation to remove them from her care?

Closing her eyes, she sucked in a deep breath of cold night air and shook her head. Coerced her sickening thoughts back into calm, rational ones. Her unruly imaginings were a strong overreaction, thanks to the man's appearance in town. It was probably nothing more than a horrible coincidence. One best disregarded. Rather like their long-ago night together. No point in hysterics when there was probably no reason for them.

But the small niggle of doubt refused to be hushed completely. The man had definitely recognised her. No matter how much she wished differently. That clear flicker of awareness had shone too brightly between them to ignore or deny. So why hadn't he said something?

Her mind bouncing up and down like a set of old-fashioned out-of-control scales, she scolded herself for pondering over Logan Fox at all. The man didn't deserve her time, or the effort of her agitated thoughts. She'd done her best to let him know about the boys. How much more was she supposed to do? It was he who had snubbed her efforts and refused to include himself in their children's lives, not the other way around.

After all, they were practically strangers, despite the fact she'd given birth to his children. But nobody in town knew that, and she intended to make certain it stayed her secret.

Thurza turned into the narrow lane that led to her home. Originally they had been staff cottages, attached to the large country estate where a B-movie actress from the 1970s now resided. The local council had purchased them over twenty years ago and now rented them out to locals.

She'd suffered through hours of labour without

Logan Fox's help. He'd not rubbed her aching back on those nights when sleep had refused to come because unborn twins took up a lot of room inside a woman's body. No, he'd done nothing to help her. To him she was just a woman he'd slept with. Interesting and attractive for a few hours, but no more.

And what was he to her? Well, he'd been nothing but a convenient sexual partner for a single night. Pretty mediocre sex, too. At least that was what she told herself on the nights when she woke up feeling hot and achy from dreaming about him. Hating herself for twisting and turning beneath her duvet for a man who hadn't cared once he'd had his enjoyment.

Logan Fox had ignored her letters informing him about his impending fatherhood and carried on with his life. And today he driven away, making it obvious that he regarded her and their sons as insignificant. And for that, more than anything, she truly hated him.

With a heavy sigh she pulled her house keys from her pocket and let herself into the dark cottage. If Logan Fox did choose to bring a fight to her door, then he'd find her no easy pushover. She loved her children too much to ever be fooled by him and his charm again.

Lips, kissable and willing. Lips he ached to slowly nibble and suck. To learn their divine taste and enjoy their softness. Lips he prayed to feel pressing light, feather-soft caresses all over his hot, sensitive skin. Starting at the curve of his shoulder before slowly, eagerly, gliding across his chest and lower, to the spot where her kisses felt so very good...

The sound of ridiculously loud music dragged Logan from the wonderful sensations and ruined his concentration on what he hoped the woman in his dream would do next. He desperately grasped for the ebbing sweetness, anxious to return to that delightful unconscious state where wondrous warm pleasure lifted his mood and put his world upright.

The music grew louder.

What the heck was going on?

Reluctantly, Logan opened his eyes and slowly focused on the unfamiliar surroundings. An ugly brass-and-wood ceiling light filled his vision, and there was the smell of fried chips cooked in lard. *Gross.*

'What the hell...?' he groaned, rubbing a hand across his forehead as thankfully the music was turned off. He took in the large black flat-screen television, a wooden coffee table scattered with sports magazines, an array of used coffee mugs and numerous remote controls. Wherever this messy hell was, it certainly wasn't his home. Being close to this much disorder made his skin itch.

He moaned once more and tried to sit up, to get his bearings and clear his head.

'Finally!' a familiar voice boomed from somewhere behind him.

The past twenty-four hours came back and hit Logan with the force of a tumbling log. The flight back to England, the solicitor in Salisbury, the drive to Dorset and finally Maddox. There was something else, too, there on his mental horizon, just out of reach but tantalising all the same. Something important but disinclined to come forward. If only he could remember what or who it was...

Shifting on the sofa, Logan sat up. Rubbing his eyes, he used the time to get his thoughts straight before he started demanding answers from his sibling.

He groaned as the image of a pair of female lips flittered through his mind. God, could he not link several words into a sentence without her sweet mouth penetrating his thoughts?

The thing he struggled to recall hovered once again on the edges of his memory, but still refused to materialise. He could swear it was major and significant. Definitely something crucial.

Maddox appeared in front of him. Six foot and with all the packed muscles of an ex-soldier turned farmer. He wore a faded grey T-shirt and a dirty pair of khaki trousers. Other than a few extra wrinkles and grey strands running through his dark curls, his much older half-brother looked to be the same arrogant bonehead he remembered.

'I suppose you're here to tell me the old man left you everything?' he said.

Logan almost laughed. If only it were that simple.

'No, I'm here because I want answers, and as Mum's no longer around to give them, you're the only one I can ask. Is it true? Am I really the result of an affair she had with one of Victor's business partners?'

Maddox froze. 'What? I thought he just told you about the affair…not the rest.'

Logan cringed at his choice of words. 'The rest'? Was that a summary of his existence? Was he nothing but the human evidence of others' past actions and happenings, without real meaning or significance?

After several seconds, Maddox asked, 'Did you never wonder why you don't resemble Victor? You don't look much like Mum or me either. Yeah, we both inherited her dark colouring, but I take after my Italian father, whereas you could walk into any Bollywood film set and be offered the male starring role.'

Maddox had a point, but Logan had always figured his colouring stemmed from some long-forgotten relative no one recollected, but whose genes showed up every few generations.

'How long have you known?'

Maddox dropped on to a nearby armchair. 'From the moment I found her crying on the day she discovered she'd conceived you.'

Logan swallowed hard, his heart twingeing at the words. Crying didn't sound good. Crying indicated disappointment and unhappiness. Regret. 'Didn't she want me?'

'Of course she did,' Maddox snapped. 'You and your father—the real one—but she knew if she tried to leave Victor he'd have enjoyed destroying her and your dad's lives. She worried that he'd turn his anger on us as well. You know what a petty mean-minded man Victor became when he was crossed. She was too scared to risk ruining our lives. But she loved your father. Even as a spotty teenager I understood that.'

'Why didn't you tell me?' Logan asked. Out of everyone, he'd always believed Maddox could be trusted. Yet, it appeared his half-brother had taken part in the charade and the lies as much as the rest of the family.

'Not for me to say. And when you were born Victor acted smitten with you. Carried you everywhere. Showed you off like one of those fancy business awards he won. I figured he didn't know the truth and thought it best to leave that particular family skeleton alone. If Mum had wanted you to know she would have told you when she became ill. I think in the end she found it easier to continue the fantasy she'd formed over the years to keep everyone she loved safe.'

Logan rose from the sofa, wobbling slightly as he tried to keep both his balance and his temper. He understood Maddox's desire to protect their mother—they'd always been close—but what about him? Didn't his feelings count?

'You all lied to me, Maddox. I had a right to know the truth.'

'And Mum had a right to her secrets. Look, if I'd realised Victor was biding his time, waiting to get even, then I'd have told you,' Maddox said. 'But I honestly thought he cared about you.'

Logan snorted. Yeah, he'd stupidly thought Victor cared, too. The pathetic truth was that nobody really had. They might have told themselves they were protecting him, but hadn't it been more the case that they'd wanted to protect themselves and hide their past indiscretions?

Logan believed his half-brother. He didn't want to, but the sincerity in Maddox's voice and eyes convinced him. He didn't forgive him, but he did believe him. It still hurt, though. To think that all the people he'd grown up around and put faith in had continually lied. That there wasn't one family member he could stare in the face and know he could trust their word.

If he ever fathered a child Logan would never lie to it. He'd be in its life no matter what. But after the mistakes he'd made in the past—nearly marrying a woman he didn't love, walking away from another for reasons he'd never fully understood—he doubted it would happen. Love and relationships were not his forte. He didn't believe in the former and had created a pig's ear of the latter.

'It's good to see you anyway,' Logan said, realising he meant it. They might not be close now, but Maddox was still his half-brother and he'd missed him. 'We should keep in touch better.'

'Yeah, we should.' Maddox nodded.

Again, there was that hazy lurking sensation that refused to come to mind, that tiptoed out of reach. Like a whispered secret spoken just beyond his hearing. Compelling and thrilling, but frustratingly unknown. No matter how he tried to coax it, it refused his repeated beckoning.

'I'm sorry about Victor,' Maddox said. 'Nothing but a twisted son of a she-devil. But I know you loved him. Shame the man didn't appreciate the fact.'

Logan nodded, wanting to shut out everything. If he closed his eyes and breathed deeply perhaps it would all disappear for a while.

A too-familiar set of lips drifted into his subconscious once again, but with practised ease he mentally pushed them away and...

That was it!

He straightened, the memory that had refused to materialise finally coming to him. It was her. The woman who had haunted his dreams for over a year. She was here. Not in Maddox's house, but working at the local garage. She'd helped him treat the boy with the eye injury.

Rubbing a hand over his chest, he felt the unwelcome attraction he'd hoped he'd finally buried while living in Malta stir and re-emerge with fresh potency. All the feelings he'd struggled for months to submerge and deny flared with renewed enthusiasm and vigour.

Closing his eyes, Logan purposely slammed a figurative door between him and the reactions the woman evoked. He'd stay for a couple of weeks to reconnect with Maddox, and then leave for somewhere new. Somewhere no one knew him and he could start over. A warm location, far away from the woman and her persistent memory.

What he and Thurza Bow had once shared was best left alone. Their lives had been linked for a short time, before parting again. One day, with luck and willpower, he'd finally stop thinking about her. Maybe find some other woman to fill his head.

God knew he yearned for the day when he could close his eyes without that woman drifting into his dreams…

CHAPTER THREE

THURZA WAVED GOODBYE to Mr Blakeman's daughter and left the large Edwardian house where she'd finished visiting one of the surgery's terminally ill patients. The illness that was taking over Alfred Blakeman's body might curtail some of his day-to-day abilities and enjoyment, but Thurza hoped that, together with the aid of her colleagues at the local doctor's surgery, who shared his care, she could make the man's twilight days as pain-free as possible.

Passing a row of traditional cottages that led to the seafront, Thurza felt her stomach growl longingly for the two slices of toast she planned to devour once she reached the surgery. Since starting that morning she had carried out five home visits, and was ready for a reviving late breakfast and a cup of tea before her shift ended at midday.

Thankfully all her visits that morning had been within walking distance of the doctor's surgery. On the days she needed to travel outside of town she borrowed Rachel's car. It was cheaper for them to car-share—especially as her cousin had use of her firm's work van during the day.

Heading towards the beach promenade, rather than walking through the town, Thurza quickened her footsteps. With luck, she would catch the local lifeboat crew going through one of their weekly training sessions.

The sight of the boat skimming and crashing over the waves, especially at this time of year, aroused bitter-sweet memories in Thurza. Happy days from her child-hood, when she would rush down to the beach before school and sit on the pebbles to watch. Smiling and waving when she spotted her father amongst the crew members.

On grey mornings like today she missed those happy days. Missed seeing her father's smile. Longed for the comfort and warmth it had always surrounded her with. She still craved one last chance to talk to him about everything and nothing, content simply to be in his company.

But on a similar morning, when the silver-toned grim sea had blended with the dark, overcast sky, her father had gone out with the crew on a rescue and never returned. A large wave had caught the vessel they'd rushed to help and turned it over, snatching her father into the watery depths at the same time. They'd recovered his lifeless body further along the coast several hours later. A freak accident, the coroner had called it. One that would probably never occur again.

Closing her eyes, Thurza held back the tears that still came, despite the loss being over ten years ago. She'd loved her father. Still loved him. He'd been her world and each day she grieved for him. An all too familiar emptiness sat inside her heart for all the memories they shared and for those that fate had robbed them from making. Although the pain of her father's death had faded over the years, the loneliness left behind hadn't.

What would he think of her now, as an adult? Working two jobs to keep herself and her two babies? If there really was a heaven, and he was watching from above, would he be proud of the person she'd grown into? Or disappointed by some of her choices? Would he love her sons as much as she did and see them as a precious gift? Or would he feel, as her mother did, that babies should come with a marriage certificate and old-fashioned respectability?

Would her father be disappointed with her for not only failing to keep the promise she'd once made him, but also for allowing fear to dictate that decision? Or would he understand that sometimes decisions in life weren't always clear-cut and simple? That emotions and experiences often ruled a person's choices, and that sometimes those other considerations took precedence over previously made vows?

With a heavy sigh, Thurza turned, pushing the sad memories and the heart-aching questions away. Tormenting herself over what her father would think was a waste of time. Her choices were hers to live with. Hers to justify to no one but herself. She just hoped that one day it would get easier, living with the knowledge that she had let him down.

Logan rolled over for the umpteenth time on the too-small sofa, slamming a cushion against his right ear in the hope of blocking out the sound of his older sibling's loud and irritating snoring.

Turning on to his back, he gave up on sleep and gripped the cushion against his chest. His eyes fixed on the early-morning shadows playing across the ceiling, and his thoughts returned to the previous day's events.

Being around Maddox after all this time had felt strange and oddly comforting.

Logan had come to Dorset for answers and now he finally had them. Enough to satisfy his curiosity anyway.

His mother had foolishly indulged in a doomed love affair with a man she could never have been with. Had she ever thought about her lover after she'd let him go? The man she'd saved from her husband's wrath and retribution? Had she really pushed him and their affair from her mind? Or had the sight of her child through the subsequent years traumatised her with memories of the ex-lover she could never be with and Logan would never know?

And the man? Did he ever consider the child he'd walked away from? Or was Logan's existence just a long-ago mistake in the man's life? One he no longer considered or recalled?

He sighed and stared at the ugly multicoloured material on the back of the sofa. After the initial shock of hearing that his mother had committed adultery, he'd tried hard not to dissect the information too deeply. He might know the facts and easily envisage the reasons why she'd sought physical comfort from another man, but he didn't want to examine it further. Was his mother's love life any of his business anyway?

And the man whom his mother had tried to protect? Did Logan want to know about the male who'd sired him and then walked away? Who had allowed a woman to stay in an unhappy marriage to save his own skin?

No, he carried no desire to find out more about the mysterious figure who had made the decision to stay out of Logan's life. A man not strong enough to fight for the woman who loved him or to put her happiness above everything else, even his own security.

Logan forced his fingers to loosen on the cushion and closed his eyes. He could only guess at what his mother had felt for the man she'd given up and her reasons for doing so.

Perhaps Maddox was wrong, and their mother had viewed the affair as nothing but a sexual folly with someone different and affectionate. Living with Victor might have included wealth and luxuries, but emotionally he'd starved the people around him. Except for Logan. Out of everyone in the family, Victor had shown him more warmth and affection than anyone.

That was why his rejection hurt so much. Despite Victor's many faults, Logan had truly believed he'd held affection for him.

Victor had raised him as his son. Attended every school play, parents' evening and sports event. When Logan had experienced a phase of bullying at the expensive private school he'd attended Victor had patiently listened to his complaints and then given advice on how to deal with the culprits over teacakes and glasses of lemonade. He'd encouraged and believed in Logan. Had always been there for him, far more than his mother ever had.

Then with his death everything had changed.

Instead of taking the unpleasant truth to the grave with him, Victor had chosen to destroy and ruin everything he and Logan had shared throughout the years. His decision to have his solicitor inform Logan of the truth had been not only cruel, but cowardly.

And that was what hurt the most. Not content for Logan only to find out the truth, he'd deprived him of the chance to confront him, making it clear how little he'd really meant to him.

Standing, Logan slipped on his shoes and grabbed his suit jacket from the end of the sofa, where he'd left it the previous night. Nabbing a stale iced bun from the breakfast bar, he bit into it with an appreciative moan. He needed to clear his head and stretch his legs before he faced another day around Maddox.

A crisp morning frost sent a shiver over Logan's skin as he stepped out of the warm house and closed the door. Buttoning his jacket, he made his way down the gravel path towards the large wooden gate leading on to the country lane. Maddox had mentioned that the short lane led straight to the seafront. Apparently, the town wasn't big, but it was friendly and had everything a person required.

Shoving the last piece of bun into his mouth, Logan put his hands into his trouser pockets and quickened his pace. A few days ago he'd walked in the Maltese sunshine—now he strolled along a damp leaf-covered lane, dodging shiny brown conkers and their spiky green shells, wishing he'd grabbed a jumper from his car to keep out the autumn chill.

He didn't care how friendly the local residents were, or not. He was only going to be in the area for a few weeks. Enough time to catch up with his brother, but not long enough to form friendships. If he took on some local locum work it would give him a chance to sort out the sale of his flat and then find another position abroad. England no longer held any reason for him to stay. He'd occasionally missed it while living in Malta, but now nothing but disappointment tainted the place for him. The country was no longer important now there was no one left in his life who required his consideration or attendance.

An image floated into his thoughts, but as usual he pushed it away. The woman from the garage meant nothing to him. An error in his past—hardly worth one thought, let alone the many his brain insisted on wasting on her. Unexpectedly seeing her again had just brought it all back. Nothing more. Looking into her beautiful eyes had simply reminded him of what they'd once shared.

He'd heard via a friend that she'd left the hospital they'd both worked at a few months after their night together. Perhaps she'd met someone after their fleeting interlude. Someone important to her. Someone who wasn't him.

He breathed in a lungful of crisp air, not sure why the idea of her moving on bothered him. Too late now for doubts and recriminations. Better to go forward than ponder over missed opportunities like a soppy fool. Better to put all his energy into forgetting her for good. Exactly the way he was determined to.

He didn't care any more that she'd left his flat the following morning without a word of goodbye. Nope, he wasn't interested in her reasons for sneaking away. Evidently she'd just wanted a night of lovemaking and nothing more.

Only...

Only something about Thurza Bow had told him that wasn't her way. The awkward way she'd first acted when they'd reached his bedroom that night... Her flushed cheeks as he'd peeled off her clothes and watched the colour in her face deepen when she did the same to him... It had caused him to wonder if she'd ever spent a night with someone before.

Kicking a conker in frustration, he crushed the uninvited speculations. What they'd shared no longer mattered. Two weeks and then he'd leave. Fourteen days of visiting his brother, and then he'd get started on the future. One that did not involve a green-eyed temptress or a phoney family of liars.

Coming to the seafront, he crossed the road that ran along the promenade—and immediately came face to face with the one woman he'd just bitterly sworn to avoid.

'You!'

Thurza stared at Logan, silently cursing her bad luck. Twice in two days was suspicious and in no way a fluke. Was he spying on her? Tracking her around town? Stalking her?

'Excuse me.'

She tried to move past Logan, figuring it better not to acknowledge the man any further, but he stepped the same way and prevented her.

'I know who you are. We were too busy yesterday to talk, and I'd made arrangements to see my brother, but I do remember you,' he declared, taking another step towards her. His gaze held a mixture of purpose with a faint trace of annoyance.

Thurza instinctively backed away, not in the mood for dealing with an ex-lover who plainly didn't appreciate seeing her again. She raised her hand to stop him coming closer, forgetting how their fleeting touch yesterday had left her restless for hours afterwards.

'I don't know who you think I am, but—' She broke off, suddenly distracted by the way he was watching her. How had she forgotten the unusual blue shade of his eyes? Or the serious intensity of his gaze? Perhaps she'd simply refused to remember, finding it easier to forget.

Yesterday a hurt child's needs had occupied him, but now he was focusing his full attention on her, for longer than a few moments.

'I know who you are,' he repeated, his tone grave,

as though she was to blame for this unexpected meeting and he resented her appearance.

'Really?' she quizzed, not believing him. The likelihood of him actually recalling her name after all this time seemed pretty slim. Deciding to test her theory, she asked, 'What's my name, then?'

'Thurza Bow,' he said without a pause.

Pants, she cursed silently, narrowing her eyes. She honestly hadn't thought he'd remember.

Opting for indifference, she shook her head. 'Excuse me, but I have to go.'

He ignored her and said, 'We both worked at St Maria's hospital, though I left just after we met. And your name is like your mouth. Sweet and bow-shaped.'

Her resolve dwindled at the unexpectedly romantic and sweet words. Then reality and common sense returned, and a harsh reminder that for eighteen months this man had callously ignored her and their sons. Logan Fox might spout charming words and phrases, but that was as far as it went. He used women for sex, and when there were consequences—two, in her case—he ignored all attempts at contact.

'I've no idea what you're talking about,' she said, determined to continue with her act of ignorance. Because what other option was there now she'd started? 'Are you ill? Lost? Confused?'

His gorgeous eyes narrowed and his mouth tightened, causing small lines to appear on each side. 'No, I'm not. You are Thurza Bow and we once spent a night together, making frantic, exciting love.'

'Shh!' she hissed, glancing around to see if anyone had heard. The man who ran the small cafe situated on the beachfront looked their way, but more with casual curiosity than outright shock. 'Keep your voice down,' she said. 'I don't think the people out in the bay heard you.'

'Then stop pretending you don't recognise me,' he warned. 'Perhaps I should ask that man outside the cafe if he knows your name?'

He moved to go past her, but Thurza grabbed his arm to stop him, aware that if he did the fragile fabrication of her denial would disintegrate and collapse.

'You're crazy,' she told him.

'And you're lying,' he accused. 'Though I'm not sure why. Especially as our night together was fun.'

'Fun!' she squealed. *'Fun?'*

Their night together had been many things, but 'fun' wasn't one of them. Erotic, exciting and passionate. Hot and satisfying. But not fun. Fun indicated something frivolous and unimportant. A brief moment of pleasure, but nothing more.

Deciding to end the conversation before he irritated her further, Thurza glared at him. 'I need to get to work.'

'I only want to talk to you,' Logan said.

Which was exactly the last thing she cared to do. Months ago, perhaps—but not now. Too much disappointment and ill feeling had developed inside her heart for Thurza to give him an easy time. Did he really expect her to smile and be friendly? To welcome him like a long-lost friend she was pleased to see again after the cold way he'd turned his back on her and the boys? Well, no, she wasn't happy to see him, and she would rather not spend time with him. Not even for five minutes.

Digging up some of her long pent-up resentment, she snapped, 'Well, I'm afraid I don't want to speak to *you*. Especially considering you displayed no eagerness or desire to talk to me yesterday at the garage. In fact,

I'm pretty sure you drove off, after paying for your fuel, without bothering with even a second glance.'

She knew this was true because, like a stupid idiot, she'd watched him go and then spent the rest of the afternoon dwelling on it.

Logan rubbed the back of his neck. 'I'm sorry, but I didn't have time yesterday to—'

She sniffed at his words, not the slightest bit interested in his reasons. No doubt the man figured his life was more important than other people's. 'Well, *I* don't have time now. I need to get to the surgery.'

'Look, yesterday I needed to see my brother. It was important.'

More important than asking after your babies?

The unspoken question sat on the end of her tongue like a stack of foul-tasting copper pennies.

Logan removed his glasses and said, 'I am curious as to why you'd rather not speak to me, though.'

Stunned by his question, she retorted, 'Do me a favour, Dr Fox, and forget we shared a night together. I have.'

'Really?' he asked with disbelief. 'You never think about it—ever?'

She shrugged, not about to admit anything to him. She owed him nothing—especially not the secrets inside her heart. Stupid, useless ones she hated keeping. Secrets she did her best not to acknowledge too often. Secrets she had sworn to one day crush for good.

'It was hardly memorable.'

His whole body stiffened, but he asked, 'Are you saying you—'

With a quick shake of her head, Thurza again moved to go by him. 'I have to get to work. I don't have time to talk to you.'

'I don't understand why you're acting so angry and resentful,' Logan said. 'If anyone should feel peeved, it's me.'

Thurza took a step back at this latest audacity. 'You?'

He nodded and, still keeping his voice low, so no passers-by could hear, said, 'Yes, you're the one who disappeared and left me feeling used the next morning.'

Thurza's mouth fell open at his criticism. Yes, she had left his flat before he'd woken up—but only because she'd been ashamed and uncertain what the etiquette was after a one-night stand. She'd figured he would prefer her gone, to save them both the embarrassment and discomfort of the dreaded morning-after scenario.

'Used? I did no such thing,' she denied hotly.

He raised an eyebrow. 'Oh, I see. You think it's all right for you to use my body for sexual gratification, then sneak out without even a polite thank-you the following morning. I had planned to cook you breakfast.'

'I was being considerate,' she choked, then said mockingly, 'I didn't realise your ego required stroking and bowing to. Were you hoping I would kneel at your feet and thank you kindly for the night?'

'It had nothing to do with my ego,' he dismissed stiffly. 'Surely you can see it's all about good manners.'

'Manners?' Thurza repeated, confused by his attitude. Was there some protocol that nobody talked about concerning casual sex? Some social etiquette she had unknowingly broken by sneaking away?

He nodded in confirmation. 'Yes, good manners.'

Shaking her head, she shifted away from the man and his bewildering complaints, not sure how to respond considering the fact that he'd ignored their sons' existence for so long. Squabbling over manners seemed inconsequential and ridiculous.

'Where are you going?' he asked.

'To work,' she replied.

Where life was normal and no one acted crazy. Where hypocritical males didn't give speeches on politeness when in reality they were guilty of lacking in common decency themselves.

This man had ignored every single letter she'd sent concerning their children, and now he had the two-faced nerve to lecture her on courtesy and manners. Yes, she was going to leave—before she gave in to the unpardonable and deplorable urge to throw that very knowledge right in the man's insolent face. Because a public beach was the last place for that type of confrontation.

'I thought you worked at the garage,' he called after her.

She stopped and turned back to him. 'Not that it's any of your concern, but I have two jobs. One of which I need to get to as I have a patient requiring a blood test in half an hour.'

'But—'

Whatever Logan Fox had intended to say was forgotten when Maddox raced past them without stopping.

'What the…?' Logan's gaze followed Maddox as he headed towards the small building at the far end of the promenade. 'Maddox! What's wrong?'

Although determined to leave, curiosity caused Thurza to wander back to where Logan stood. 'There must be an emergency call. How do you know Maddox?'

Distracted, Logan answered, 'He's my brother.'

'Brother?' she gasped. 'Maddox?'

Logan nodded and pointed to the wooden building his brother and several other people had just disappeared into. 'What *is* that place?'

'It's the lifeboat station,' Thurza answered. 'It's

where they store the boat and all the equipment for sea rescues.'

Logan started to walk towards the building, which was more like an oversized beach hut.

'Where are you going?' Thurza asked.

Logan didn't answer straight away, his focus fixed on the small lifeboat as it exited the building and launched into the sea. Finally, he said, 'To see if I can help, of course.'

CHAPTER FOUR

THURZA WALKED AWAY for a second time, intent on not turning back. What Logan chose to do with his time was his business and absolutely not her concern. But her scruples and her medical schooling slowed her footsteps to a drag, and before she could argue with herself she twisted to stare at the sea. Searching the grim horizon, she sighted the lifeboat, bopping on the waves to the east.

What a mess.

What a horrible nightmare of a predicament.

Logan not only remembered her, but he wanted to talk, too. As if they really had anything to say to each other after all this time. Especially as he'd shown no eagerness to converse over the reason why he'd ignored their sons for so long, and she certainly wasn't interested in hearing any excuses.

She sighed and rotated further, until her gaze fell upon the annoying man who now stood on the beach in front of the lifeboat station. Why did he have to appear, like a huge bad memory, seemingly determined to get reacquainted? Even a selfish jerk would see she wasn't interested. How clear did she have to be? Wasn't pretending not to recognise him a pretty obvious sign?

But no, he'd disregarded all said indications and concerned himself only with his own wishes.

Months ago she might have reacted differently—then she would have welcomed his interest. But not after all this time. Eighteen months, for goodness' sake. Where had he been when she'd suffered hours of labour? Had he helped pay for the boys' clothes and a second-hand pushchair when she'd barely been able to pay her bills? No, he'd ignored her letters and carried on with his single, independent and free life.

She closed her eyes, the sting of his rejection still tender and raw. Oh, she hadn't expected flowers and declarations of all-consuming love. But a little respect and a show of interest in the boys hadn't been too much to expect, had it? She certainly hadn't daydreamed romantic visions about them becoming a family, but an acknowledgement of responsibility and support would have meant something—more than the uncaring silence she'd received.

But Logan Fox had offered nothing. He'd stayed out of their lives when she'd needed him. And she refused to let him think he could just walk in and invade it now on—what? A whim?

She'd cried enough useless tears over the man and his heartless dismissal of their sons. On the night she'd given birth to the twins she'd sworn in the darkness, while the boys had been sleeping in their hospital cots, that she'd never shed another tear over him and his rejection.

Dragging her gaze from the male who'd caused so much turmoil in her life, she glanced at her watch. Her patient would be arriving at the surgery soon. The lifeboat crew could deal with the emergency—after all, they were highly trained and capable.

Decision made, she swivelled on the spot and headed towards town. But something stopped her after a few paces, and before she could change her mind again Thurza turned in the direction of the man her instinct warned was trouble and undependable. A man she suspected was set to bring nothing but problems into her life.

Logan stood on the pebble beach and watched his brother and the rest of the lifeboat team rescue the early-morning swimmer who'd drifted out to sea. The smell of seawater filled his every sense and salt coated his lips like an invisible balm.

A strong wind blew off the choppy grey water, buffeting him and the odd dog walker insane enough to brave a stroll along the beach on such a cold, blustery day. Where only minutes ago he and Thurza had shared an awkward encounter, and where he now stood alone.

Thurza. So much for avoiding her. It seemed that every time he resolved to forget the woman for good, fate pushed her back under his nose. Not that she'd acted any happier over seeing *him*. Their brief conversation had exposed how clearly she would rather he left town and stayed away.

Well, she'd get her wish soon. Two weeks and then he'd be gone—and she could go back to living her life without fear of having to face an ex-inamorato.

The sight of the lifeboat returning halted any further thoughts over Thurza. Letting out a long, relieved sigh, Logan hurried over once the boat hit the shore, the medic inside him desperate to help. Concern for the rescued swimmer and any possible consequences after spending prolonged time in the freezing water crammed his head, and his unease increased when he noted the casualty's advanced age.

'How's he doing?' he asked, as Maddox and another crew member helped the swimmer off the boat. Although a thermal blanket covered his shoulders and torso, violent shaking rocked through the man's body, causing him to stumble as his feet touched the pebbles. 'Has anyone checked him over yet?'

'He's refusing to let us. Insists he's okay,' Maddox answered, his tone making it clear what he thought of the man's reluctance to accept medical help.

Before anyone else could say anything, the man clutched his chest and gasped. 'Pain... My chest...it hurts.'

Logan jumped into action, unconcerned as to whether the lifeboat crew required his expertise. The man needed his help. A speedy diagnosis was all that mattered right now.

'Hello, sir. My name is Logan Fox. I'm a doctor. Let's sit here on the beach for a moment, shall we? It's not very comfortable, but I just want to ask a few questions and check you over.'

Logan, with Maddox's help, carefully lowered the old man down on to the sea-smoothed grey, yellow and white pebbles.

'It's okay,' Maddox assured the other men and women around them. 'My brother really is a doctor and he knows his stuff.'

Logan fixed his whole attention on the swimmer, taking in the blue tinge to his lips and his pale colouring. 'Okay, my friend. I guess you're feeling a little rough, and sitting on these stones probably isn't helping, but we'll soon have you feeling better.'

'Where am I?' the old man wheezed. 'Please…my chest hurts…and my arm.'

Alarm bells rang in Logan's head. Clues and signs immediately clicked together. These symptoms pointed to the probability that the man was suffering a heart attack and possible hypothermia, hence his confusion.

'You're on the beach and…'

Logan sensed movement on the man's other side and glanced up to find Thurza on her knees, staring across at him with concern in her green eyes.

'Need help?' she asked.

Logan nodded, surprised to see her. 'Always welcome, Nurse Bow. I'm pretty certain we're dealing with a—'

Thurza dumped her nurse's bag to one side and unwound her long woollen scarf, placing it on the pebbles behind the swimmer. Still listening, she addressed the old man. 'Why don't you lie back?' she urged.

Suddenly the swimmer let out a groan and collapsed into unconsciousness. Luckily his head landed in the centre of Thurza's scarf.

'Damn,' Logan swore, immediately placing the casualty into a flat position. 'He's passed out. What's his pulse like?'

Thurza already held the man's wrist. 'Weak, but still there.'

Logan tilted the man's head to clear his airways and check his breathing. 'Okay, my friend… You just relax and let us do our job.'

When no response came from the man, Logan clipped out, 'Right, I suspect our swimmer has suffered a heart attack. Let's start CPR.'

'On it,' Thurza said, placing her hands one on top of

the other in the centre of the man's chest, over his breast-bone. Her whole attention was focused on their patient.

Maddox crouched at Logan's side and handed him a plastic face shield. Grateful, Logan took it and positioned it over the casualty's mouth. 'Any chance of an AED?'

Maddox lifted a familiar green case containing the requested defibrillator. 'Ambulance is on its way. Anything I can do?'

'Just let Nurse Bow and I do our magic,' he replied, glancing at Thurza. The swimmer's life and care took priority over personal matters, and right now he was grateful for her assistance.

Taking the case from his brother, Logan opened it and switched on the defibrillator. On the other side of the patient Thurza continued to carry out chest compressions, before switching to blow two breaths into the man's mouth.

Someone handed Logan a towel and he quickly dried the swimmer's upper body so he could attach the AED. Left wet, the pads wouldn't stick to him.

Removing two pads from the sealed pack, Logan pulled off the backing paper and fixed each one to the swimmer's chest, then called, 'Move back.'

Both Thurza and Logan leaned away from the casualty, not wanting to interfere with the machine as it analysed the swimmer's heart rhythm. After a few seconds the machine gave them the information they needed.

'No shock required,' Logan stated, moving near again. 'Let's continue CPR.'

Thurza repeated another set of chest compressions. Several long strands of her hair swung around her face as she concentrated on the job of keeping the swimmer alive. After a quick look in Logan's direction, she continued to work with him. They were a team. Neither of them about to give up on the man they were determined to save.

'How long until the ambulance gets here?' Logan asked the group around them, watching them work.

As if his words had conjured up the emergency vehicle, a loud, familiar siren filled the morning air. Logan glanced up to see it slowly making its way along the promenade, avoiding several groups of bystanders observing the action on the beach.

Moments later two paramedics hurried across the pebbles to join them. Logan quickly filled in the pair and then stepped back to allow them to take over. Within minutes they'd transported the swimmer on to a stretcher and into the back of the ambulance. Accompanied by a second whirl of sirens, they drove away.

Letting out a heavy sigh of relief, Logan turned to Thurza. 'Thanks for the help.'

She bent and grabbed her bag and scarf. With a distracted smile, she said, 'You're welcome.'

'Hey, Thurza!' Maddox greeted her brightly as he joined them. He'd changed out of his foul-weather gear and once more wore everyday clothes. 'How are the twins doing?'

Thurza shot Logan an uncomfortable glance and then looked back at his brother. Her fingers gripped the bag's woven strap tightly before she answered, 'They're fine, thanks.'

Logan's eyes narrowed as she said goodbye and then scurried away. Twins? Thurza had twins? Since when?

Curious, he turned to his brother and asked, 'Thurza Bow has twins?'

Maddox nodded. 'Yeah, sweet babies. Must be nine months old by now. Funny, though… Out of all the women in town, I'd never have pegged Thurza to return home as a single mum after working in the city. Never known her to go on a date or have a boyfriend the whole time I've lived here. Do you know her?'

'We used to work at the same hospital,' Logan said, his gaze following the woman hurrying away from them along the promenade. 'Different departments, but the same building.'

He'd kissed her smart, prickly mouth many times during that one night. Explored her sexy body and captured her seductive moans. It was the reason he'd found it so hard to push her from his mind for months. Why all his determination to avoid her while in town had evaporated the second he saw her again. Not even the fear of being hit by a meteorite would have moved him from that spot when she'd turned away from the sea and looked up at him.

He rubbed at the collar of his shirt and pushed his glasses further up on to the bridge of his nose. Thurza had infused his memory and his flesh like a recurring infection without any known or effective long-term cure. Not one *he'd* managed to discover, anyway.

All those times he'd seen Thurza walking around St Maria's, something about her had always made him glance twice whenever she'd passed by. But he'd been in a relationship, and dismissed it as nothing but a natural male attraction to a pretty female...

Nine months old? Had Maddox said Thurza's twins were nine months old?

He swallowed as his mind quickly did the maths. Nine months pregnant. Nine months old. Eighteen months since their night together.

His breath hitched hard in his chest while his mind

rejected the total he'd arrived at. No way. They couldn't be his. They'd used protection. He'd worn a condom.

Had he checked it afterwards, though? Damn, he couldn't remember. It had been his first one-night stand so he might not have done. But that was basic stuff, surely? He *must* have checked it. He was a doctor, for goodness' sake. Why was he able to recall how her lips tasted, yet not whether the condom they'd used had failed?

Frowning, he forced his rushing mind to slow down and calmly analyse the probability of an unplanned pregnancy. The chance of that night resulting in one would be something like a couple of percent, surely?

She must have met someone else after their night. Someone she hadn't used protection with.

He swallowed again, trying to clear the bitter, uncomfortable taste burning his throat. But it refused to shift. Could Thurza have given birth to his children and then hidden the truth? What was *wrong* with people? Did he carry a sign on his back that stated, *Screw this man over*? Or *Hide the truth from him on every occasion*?

No, he was reading too much into the fact that her children just happened to be nine months old.

But the way she'd wriggled so uneasily when Maddox had asked about her children set off a loud warning in Logan's logical mind. Was fear that he would uncover her secret the real reason why she didn't want to talk to him? Why she acted so offhand and nervous when in his company? Was she terrified he would discover she'd given birth to his children without the courtesy of letting him know? If that was true, then how *dared* she rob him of the chance to be involved?

No. The whole idea was so outrageous and inconceivable it had to be wrong. They'd used a condom.

Yeah, but everyone knew that method of contraception wasn't foolproof, and he had no idea if she had been using any other form of protection against pregnancy.

'Boys or girls?' Logan asked his brother as they left the beach and walked back along the country road towards his brother's property.

'What?'

'Thurza's twins. Boys or girls?'

'Oh, boys,' Maddox answered. 'Are you okay? You look a little sick.'

'I'm fine,' he said, though it was a lie.

No matter how much he wished he could forget the maths, his always sharp mind yelled that there was a huge chance that, unknowingly, in the past year he had become a father.

And if that was true, what right did Thurza Bow think she had to keep that news from him?

CHAPTER FIVE

THURZA CLOSED THE front door, glad to be finally home. Her shift at the surgery had dragged after she'd left the beach.

Thanks to Maddox's appearance, she'd succeeded in leaving without further interaction with Logan. Though he still afflicted her thoughts even now, several hours later. When Maddox had enquired after the twins, she'd thought Logan was going to say something. Instead he'd just stared at her with a slightly confused expression. As if the news that she was the mother of twins surprised him. Well, the man might think he could act and pretend ignorance, but she knew better.

And Maddox was his brother!

Did Maddox know Logan was the twins' father?

Had he secretly watched her and reported back to his brother? Had the two of them been secretly plotting and gathering so-called evidence against her?

What evidence, exactly, she didn't know, but the idea angered and unsettled her. Did they stand in judgement, waiting and assessing every single thing she did? Condemn her for working two jobs and not being a stay-at-home mother? Well, she didn't have the luxury of choice—not with two children to feed and clothe.

Staring around the narrow hallway, Thurza absently

twisted a plait around her fingertip. The cottage she rented wasn't much, but it was home. A comfortable and safe place she'd created for her family. A place to raise the boys. It wasn't fancy and filled with all the latest gadgets, like the ones she'd noticed in Logan's flat the morning she'd sneaked out, but she loved it. Yes, most of the furniture was second-hand—okay, *all* the furniture. But it was clean and tidy, and after a fresh coat of paint to give it a 'shabby chic' appearance, it looked good. She'd done her best to make it a snug bubble of love for the boys. One she alone had provided. She didn't care if it wasn't extravagant or elegant. It was home. *Their* home.

But now Logan's appearance threatened to upend the serenity she'd worked consistently to provide for her sons since their birth. Demanding her time and reminding her of things she would rather forget.

With a snort, she retrieved the basket full of newly washed baby clothes left on the floor and walked down the hall to the kitchen. Her anger with Logan and the situation she'd spent the last few hours trying to ignore was still cramming her mind above everything else.

When the rattle of the letter box sounded, it barely penetrated her jumbled thoughts. Only when the noise became more insistent did she leave the kitchen and trudge back to the front door.

She cursed silently when she opened it, for not thinking to slip on the chain first. Staring at the man she wished would instantly evaporate on her doorstep, she sighed. 'You, again.'

She saw Logan's gaze move over her body in one long optical sweep. Far too intimately for a man who'd made it very clear he wanted nothing to do with her or their children.

She stiffened and folded her arms. The movement was a mixture of protection and defiance. She had no wish to spend more time in his company, and the sooner he understood that, the better for them both.

Raising an eyebrow, she said, 'Yes?'

'Why don't you tell me about your twin boys?' Logan demanded, not bothering with pleasant greetings or any explanations as to why he stood, uninvited, outside her home.

Thurza's cheeks warmed when she met his gaze. He was making her feel like a guilty kid, caught doing something naughty. 'Why would I do that?'

Logan stepped closer, the silent battle in his eyes plain to read. 'Because, Thurza Bow, eighteen months ago you and I spent the night together, and now I hear you have nine-month-old twins.'

She swallowed, but refused to back down from the challenge in his gaze. 'So?'

He leaned closer, his eyes once again lowering to run over her, before returning to meet her gaze. 'So I'd really like to know if I'm their daddy.'

I'd really like to know if I'm their daddy?

Thurza tried to resist the reaction slipping through her body both at his intense look and his confrontational puzzling words. Anger? Annoyance? Attraction? Please, no—not the last one. One mistake with this man equalled a forgivable human failing. Two made her a mammoth idiot.

'How dare you turn up at my home and demand answers from me?' she said, tempted to slam the door in his face.

Logan shot her a glare and said, 'I'll happily leave you alone once you answer my question. That's all I want. One answer to one very simple but important question. I'm no Einstein, but the maths I'm doing is adding up to an interesting total. I'll ask you again, Nurse Bow. Are your twin sons also mine?'

She stiffened at his question and at his attitude. If he cared about the boys, why take so long to show any interest in them? No, this whole sudden curiosity about her family smacked of trickery. And why the pretence of not knowing already? It didn't make sense and it increased her misgivings over what game Dr Fox was actually playing by coming here with his demand for answers.

What hidden agenda did he have? And how was it going to impact her and the twins?

She grabbed the door handle, her fingers squeezing around it for support. 'Other than goodbye, Dr Fox, I have nothing to say to you.'

'According to my brother, you have two babies. That might well be my concern. Is it?'

Thurza decided to ignore his question and asked one of her own. 'How did you find out where I live? Did Maddox tell you?'

He shook his head. 'The woman at the cake shop in town was very helpful when I explained that I'm an old friend of yours.'

She flicked a loose strand of hair away from her face and flashed him her best indifferent expression, determined to distract him from asking further questions about the twins. 'If you're hoping to reconnect for a few hours, then forget it. Some experiences, especially like the one we shared, are best forgotten.'

He tensed at her words and shifted on the doorstep. 'You're still saying that, are you? What's that old saying about the lady protesting too much...?'

Trust the man to be more concerned with a slur on

his sexual prowess than with the children he'd supposedly sought her out to discuss. No doubt women usually fawned over him, treating him like a god. Whereas she'd just prefer him to go away and leave her alone.

'Can you even remember that night?' she asked.

She'd learnt a very good lesson after their time together. One she refused to overlook. Mostly never to mix sex with a work crush. Far too messy and disappointing to be worth the resulting turmoil.

'Or are you just confusing me with the nights you've shared with other women?'

He straightened and crossed his arms. 'Just to set you straight, I do not sleep around and I resent the implication that I do.'

'Yeah, right,' she said, not believing him.

She'd grown out of trusting in fairy tales after their liaison. Did he really expect her to believe a man as gorgeous and sexy as he was didn't attract female attention with ease? She'd seen how nurses and doctors swarmed around him like dying bees, desperate for a taste of his own special nectar, when they'd worked at the same hospital. She wasn't the only staff member who'd experienced the hots for him.

Logan took a deep breath and insisted, 'It's true. I do not jump into bed with just anyone. I'm choosy over who I sleep with.'

'You slept with *me*,' she reminded him.

He shocked her by grinning. 'Yes, I did.'

Not sure she wanted to continue with this dangerous diversion in the conversation, she frowned and grabbed the door tighter. 'This conversation is both boring and over. Goodbye, Dr Fox.'

Logan shook his head. 'I'm not leaving until you

answer my question,' he insisted. 'I'm staying in town until you give me the information I want. If you wish me to leave then just give me an answer and I'll go.'

'I really don't appreciate your bossy tone,' she complained, stalling.

The spicy scent of his aftershave and the saltiness of the sea clung to his clothes and his body, twirling like an invisible caress through the air, swirling its heady mingled fragrance over her already sensitive nerves and making her all too aware of how close he stood.

'Let's act like grown-ups, shall we?' Logan suggested softly. 'All I want is for you to tell me the truth. Am I the father of your twin sons?'

She lowered her head and sighed, desperate for a break from him and his distracting company. For months she and the boys had happily tootled along, facing each new day with a smile, confident and cheerful in the easy routine they lived by. Now, though, Logan loomed in their lives, threatening that serenity with his questions and demands.

Resigned, she asked, 'You're really not going away until I do, are you?'

He shoved his hands into his trouser pockets and shook his head. 'Nope.'

'What if I don't *want* to answer your questions?' she asked stubbornly.

Her answers had the potential to change everything she had built since the boys' birth. She lifted her head and unwillingly took in his features. The man was tongue-meltingly good-looking. Not the pretty-boy kind of handsome, but something more honest and real. A fusion between nerdy cool and academic hotness.

'Then I'll stay here until you do,' he warned, staring back at her.

His blue gaze let her know he meant it. He wasn't going anywhere. Not until he had his answers. And then what? What would he do then?

All the frantic concerns of the last two days returned and simmered and gurgled inside her.

Lowering her eyes to his lips, she let her gaze settle there. Her mind became engrossed in the curve of the lower one. Though it looked innocent, Thurza knew how wicked and naughty his mouth could be to a woman's body. How it liked to torture and excite. Tease and please.

Pushing those thoughts away, she reluctantly motioned for Logan to come in, rather than continue their conversation on the doorstep. She showed him into her small sitting room. Lowering himself on to her floral sofa, he looked as out of place as a dirty weathered boulder dropped into an old lady's chintz-and-lace-decorated parlour.

She frowned. 'I don't understand why you keep asking me the question when you already know the answer.'

'But I don't,' he insisted.

'Yes, you do,' she replied. 'I sent several letters to your flat. When you never answered, or contacted me, I figured you didn't want to know. I even visited one day. Your cleaner said you'd gone abroad, and refused to give me any more information or a forwarding address.'

'Ah...' he murmured, suddenly looking uncomfortable. 'I've been working in Malta for over a year. I haven't visited the flat since I left. My cleaner goes in every few weeks to dust and check up on everything. I only recently returned to England, because my...my father died.'

'Your father died?' Thurza asked, reluctant compassion springing awake inside her. She might dislike the man in front of her, but she understood the pain of losing a parent. The way he'd stumbled over the word 'father' pinched at her heart. Grief, no doubt, still overwhelmed him. 'Recently?'

'Ten weeks ago.'

No wonder Logan had travelled to Dorset to see his brother. He was probably seeking comfort in his sibling's company. As an only child, Thurza had always regretted not having that option. No one person who understood her pain and loss in the same way a brother or sister might have.

She sighed and wrapped her arms around her waist—mostly to stop herself from giving in to the urge to console him with a hug. Losing a parent was hard at any age and any time in a person's life.

'I'm sorry for your loss,' she said.

'Thank you.'

A strange, traitorous warmth, something like hope, floated through her, but she squashed it down flat. Safer to stick to facts and not emotions. The one time she'd behaved the other way around she'd ended up having his children.

'Are you saying you haven't read the letters I sent to your flat?'

He nodded his head in confirmation. 'They must be piled up there. But if you wrote to me, I guess you had a reason to do so.'

Another thought struck Thurza, stopping her from answering. 'If you've never read my letters then why do you think the boys are yours?'

Logan sighed. 'I asked my brother how old your children are.'

'Oh,' she said, before her eyes widened with horror. 'You didn't tell Maddox about our night together, did you?'

'No.'

'Good.' She didn't want anyone to know about their connection until she'd worked out what the man was up to. His explanation of working abroad and not visiting his flat seemed plausible, but she still didn't trust him.

'Are you going to answer my question?' Logan asked, returning her attention to the reason he was in her home. 'I simply want to know if your children are also my children.'

Something inside Thurza twisted at the unexpected expression in his eyes. Was it hope? Yearning? Did he want the answer to be positive? Or was he secretly longing for it to be negative so he could walk away?

Giving in, while wishing she didn't have to, preferring her life to be uncomplicated and straightforward, she forced out the words she doubted anyone had ever used before when dealing with the man in front of her. 'Yes, Logan, they are. You are their father.'

In reply, Logan let out a long, heartfelt sigh. But his expression immediately became closed, giving her no clue to his real feelings on hearing the news.

'What are their names?' he asked.

Thurza hesitated, still reluctant to let him deeper into her private life. But if the man was telling the truth, and he hadn't read her letters, then she couldn't continue to hate him for not getting in touch, could she?

'Tyler and Axel.'

Logan's eyes widened, but he didn't say a word.

She stiffened at his unspoken disapproval of the boys' names—names she'd picked alone, because no one else in her life had cared enough to raise an argument, or pull a face like the one he was doing right now.

'They're lovely names,' she said.

He frowned. 'They're different... When can I meet them?'

She glanced at the clock on the wall, aware they wouldn't be home for hours. 'They're with my aunt and cousin and won't be back until teatime.'

'It must be hard, caring for and providing for two babies,' he remarked after several moments.

She huffed. 'My children are worth it. Look, I have chores to do, so you really need to leave.'

'My name won't be on their birth certificates?' Logan asked suddenly.

Thurza shook her head. 'No, not without your agreement. I sent so many letters informing you about my pregnancy and asking you to get in touch. When I didn't receive a reply I figured you didn't want any contact and definitely didn't want to provide towards the boys' upbringing.'

He nodded, but disappointment etched his face, and for the first time in months Thurza suspected she might have judged Dr Logan Fox unfairly.

Perhaps she should have tried harder to get in touch with the man she'd long believed didn't care.

CHAPTER SIX

DID THE FATES get fun out of messing with his life? Logan glared at the moody charcoal sky and dared the rain to increase. How was a man supposed to make a good impression on the mother of his yet-to-be-seen children if he resembled a drowned rat after a hard night partying.

Not that he wished to make *any* impression on Thurza other than in the respectable father stakes. He certainly wasn't hoping to rekindle the flare of attraction that had led to their night together. A night she'd lied about not enjoying.

He remembered how her body had sung and sighed beneath his fingertips. Oh, yes, Thurza lied, indeed. Each word nothing but a forgery. What he'd yet to understand was why.

Removing his glasses, he rubbed away the rain spots with a handkerchief before putting them back on. His vision was now less spotted, but his thoughts were still focused on Thurza.

Just stop with the musings, Fox. You're here to meet her from work—not fantasise about her pretty body or the sweet noises she makes when aroused.

The less he reflected on that the quicker his mind would settle on the important stuff—like their children. They were all that concerned him...all that mattered in his life.

The maddening woman who'd unknowingly haunted his days for over a year had now given him the ideal opportunity to exorcise her from his head for good. The twins were one thing, but his craving for Thurza was a separate issue. One he intended to rid himself of completely. If they spent time together it was bound to happen. Familiarity bred contempt and all that. Once they got to know one another properly she'd become just another woman. The mother of his sons and nothing else. A friend for life—or at least until the boys turned eighteen and could make their own decisions with regard to seeing and spending time with him.

'Hello.'

Startled out of his ponderings, Logan stared at Thurza, instantly noting the wariness lining her face. A feeling he guessed had arisen from his unexpected appearance outside the doctor's surgery.

He hated witnessing it. Somehow they needed to resolve things between them so they could build an amicable relationship. A relationship for the boys' sake, and absolutely nothing to do with rekindling anything between them. The past couldn't be changed, but the future—theirs and their sons'—would be simpler if they kept everything platonic, set aside any remaining physical desire and concentrated only on the two babies they'd created.

'Hi—' His normally deep voice had shifted skywards in its pitch. Gulping, he tried again, hoping for the return of his usual baritone. After a sharp cough, he croaked, 'All finished?'

'Yes. You?'

Logan nodded. He'd applied to work as a locum at

the same surgery after seeing an advert online. Today he'd worked his first morning shift, and had thought he'd take advantage of their same finishing time.

Thurza frowned and shifted her handbag further on to her shoulder. The guardedness in her green gaze had turned to full-on distrust. 'Is there something you want, Dr Fox?'

'Logan,' he corrected. He'd imagined her pleasure at his appearance when she came out, not this uneasy awkwardness. 'I thought I'd walk you home.'

She tilted her head and studied him with the same intensity he might allot to a complicated medical case. Unspoken worries clouded her anxious eyes and her caginess increased.

'Why?'

A perfectly reasonable query, and one he unfortunately had no logical answer for. He'd stood waiting in the rain because his thoughts continually circled around this woman and how to make things right between them. He and Thurza had created a family, yet they hardly knew each other. Where did they go from here? How did they create a stable relationship in which they could both raise their children?

He didn't want to start pushing into her life, throwing his opinion around like a boxer throwing sharp jabs. But he also refused to stand on the side like an undesirable family member, grateful for any crumb tossed in his direction. He was a father, and he longed to be a good one. And that meant being involved in his children's lives.

Thurza started walking out of the surgery car park. 'You don't need to. I've managed to find my way home many times without help. I have my own internal satnav.'

'I thought…' Logan began. What? That after one conversation they would be able to put the past to rest?

That Thurza would accept his excuses for not being involved with their children sooner and become his best friend overnight?

Not going to happen when he suspected she still viewed him as the kind of man who walked away from his responsibilities and shirked his duties. Even though the truth was the opposite. If he'd known about the boys he would never have left England and stayed away. He would have shadowed her, every step of the pregnancy, and offered his help and support any time she'd requested it.

When he'd seen Thurza that night at the bar he'd recently called off his six-month engagement. Despite liking his fiancée, he'd come to realise that *liking* someone didn't make him eager to slip a gold band on her finger and utter the words *I do*. He'd realised he didn't love the woman. Not the way she deserved to be loved. The terrible truth was that he'd seen their union as a relationship based on family friendship, cold rationality and desperation. A marriage to please others, with little thought for himself or his needs.

His ex-fiancée was perfect—clever and beautiful. But take away the friendship and Logan had come to see there was little else. No deep soul connection or solid bond. No heart-thudding attraction.

The feelings and desire between them just hadn't been strong enough. Not in the way Valentine's cards declared they should be. Or in the way romantic films dramatised them. It had been just an empty relationship formed between two people who had seen time passing without having ticked the marriage box. A decision based on common sense instead of that mystical sentiment called love.

They'd drifted into a relationship—one that had

never felt right—because everyone had told them it was a good match. Not really understanding the relationship thing, for a while Logan had figured if two people got on and had similar interests it would be enough for a marriage. But as the weeks had gone by a voice in his heart had kept insisting he was wrong.

So he'd ended the engagement and then he'd seen Thurza that night, laughing with a group of friends, and for the first time in his life something concerning a woman had felt right. He'd craved it. He'd given in to his selfish hunger to be with her. He'd hankered for a pair of warm arms to find comfort in and hide from the mess of his life, and Thurza was the woman who had provided them. That part he didn't regret. His passionate, wonderful night with Thurza was worth everything.

'I thought we could get to know each other a little better,' he explained now. They had to start somewhere, otherwise they'd be raising the boys in silence and polite disquiet.

Thurza hesitated, confirming his fears that her opinion of him hung around ground level.

'I think I know enough concerning you, thanks,' she said.

Shaking his head, he stepped into her path. 'No, you don't. That's the problem we have, isn't it? I don't blame you for thinking badly of me for not contacting you— though I truly didn't know about your pregnancy. If I had, I swear things would have been different. But none of that is important right now. You and I have created twin sons, and I hope you might try and see that we need to come to some kind of truce and learn to get along. Despite what you might think, I don't regret our night together.'

'You don't?' she asked. 'Even though the twins are

the result of it? Babies you didn't plan on becoming a father to?'

He shook his head, sending the raindrops clinging to the ends of his hair flying. 'No regrets at all, Thurza. So may I walk you home?'

He waited for her decision, determined not to give any hint of the eagerness running through him. She needed to learn to trust him, and he sensed it would take time. Thurza's misgivings were completely understandable, and only time and patience would banish them.

She shrugged and then, like a Viking queen bestowing a rare honour on a mere Christian mortal grovelling at her majestic feet, said, 'I suppose so. If you really wish to.'

Keen to accept the offer, despite her grudging agreement, Logan walked at her side, searching his mind for a safe subject to start a conversation with. Again, the unwelcome notion of raising the boys in silence came to him.

'Tell me something few people know about you, Thurza Bow.'

She hesitated for a moment, before answering, 'My family has lived in this town since the seventeen hundreds.'

He shot her a glance and raised an eyebrow. 'Long time to stay in one place.'

She nodded and smiled. 'Yes, it is.'

Logan tugged up the zip on his jacket. 'Thurza's an unusual name. Does it have local origins?'

'No. My father named me after a great-great-grandmother. She raised thirteen children and ran a business with her husband.'

He grinned. 'Not selling early forms of contraception, I'm guessing?'

She laughed and shook her head, stepping to one side as an elderly couple passed them. 'No. Fish.'

'Fish?' he repeated.

Thurza smiled and nodded towards the bay in the distance. The glistening water and the end of the pier were visible from where they stood. 'They lived near the sea. What else would they sell?'

'Do you hope for more children?' Logan asked, picturing the woman walking at his side in the centre of a family of infants.

He found he liked the image. He'd never really experienced a close and loving family. Any real show of affection had stopped after his mother had passed away. Victor had always been too busy with his business deals to care about Logan's emotional requirements.

'The two babies I have already keep me busy, thanks.'

He nodded and glanced her way. 'Two I've yet to meet.'

For a few moments they walked in comfortable silence. Strange... Generally people liked to fill quiet moments with words and noise, yet Thurza appeared content to just walk beside him. As if they were a couple who'd known each other for years instead of the loose acquaintances they really were.

'What are they like?' he finally asked, breaking the silence.

He'd asked Maddox the same question, but he'd just said they looked like all babies—not much hair and lots of dribble. He hadn't pushed for more information, not wanting to raise his brother's curiosity. He'd tell him later on...once he got used to the notion of being a father.

Logan tried to picture each baby. Were they identical twins or not? Did they favour their mother's fair complexion? Or perhaps they'd inherited his darker colouring? Black hair like his, or blonde like Thurza's? What eye colour did they have? Green? Blue? One of each?

'Who?' Thurza asked.

'Our sons,' he answered, and then repeated, 'What are they like?'

'Wonderful,' she replied, her face softening with love.

A flash of jealousy shot through him. One that both shocked and embarrassed him. He couldn't blame her for the fact he'd left the country and missed the chance to know about her pregnancy and meet his own children. She'd tried to give him the opportunity, but he'd run away from his life in England. He had not been willing to deal with Victor's anger and disappointment over his broken engagement…with his guilt over hurting a friend and his unanticipated surge of feeling towards Thurza after their brief hours together.

Without leaving an address for his post to be forwarded to, he'd closed off all opportunity for things to turn out differently between them. And while he'd left behind his old life she had grown two new ones, and experienced nausea and joy in doing so. Through his own actions, he'd missed out on it all.

Thurza owned those memories of her pregnancy and the boys' early days. They were hers alone. While he had tended the medical needs of strangers, she'd witnessed their sons' developmental firsts. Their first yawn, their first smile. Even their first dirty nappies. He'd missed it all. Every last thing. He envied her that time and experience.

'Why did you leave St Maria's?' he asked, curious as to why she'd returned to this town during her pregnancy. What had brought her back here after living in the city? From what he'd seen it was just like every other seaside town, only smaller.

Thurza stilled, fiddling with the pink scarf around her neck. 'My cousin and her parents are here.'

'What about your own parents?'

She shook her head and glanced away. 'My father died when I was seventeen and my mother remarried not long after. She lives in France now. She wanted me to go with her, but our relationship became tense after my father's death, so I stayed and moved in with my aunt and uncle. I came back here because I was pregnant and alone and this town is home. It's where I belong.'

Home. The way she uttered the modest word revealed how special and important this place was to her. Between boarding school and university, Logan had never felt any real connection to a place. He'd always been able to adapt to his surroundings wherever they were. Especially after his mother's death, when the big house in Salisbury had lost the little warmth she'd created with the scent of her Italian cooking and the rowdy songs she'd loved to sing.

The rain started to increase. Thurza pulled a red-and-white-spotted umbrella from her handbag. She didn't speak again until she'd opened it and lifted it over their heads.

Noting the height difference between them, she offered him the handle with a wry smile. 'Here, you'd better hold it. I'd hate to accidentally give you bruises or stab your eyes out.'

Logan reached for the handle, their hands brushing as he took it from her. Heat zoomed into his fingers and along his arms, reminding him of all the reasons a platonic relationship between them made sense and why he shouldn't want to change that. But his mouth had dried at the contact, and flashes of their night together pitched through his mind. Tantalising shadowy reminders of those passion-filled hours.

His gaze flicked to her face and then her lips. Pretty pink lips that he suddenly yearned to kiss, to see if she tasted as good as he recalled. But that would be a mistake. And this time he was determined, when dealing with this woman, that he would listen to his brain and not other unreliable parts of his body.

Romance of any kind had no place in this relationship. And that was the rational, level-headed decision he intended to stick to, no matter how much his body wished otherwise.

Thurza slowed to a stop outside a small farmhouse with a thatched roof. A huge hanging basket packed with variegated ivy and orange pansies hung by the pink front door. Fortunately, the rain had eased, and now only heavy sullen-looking clouds filled the sky.

'Why have we stopped?' Logan asked curiously.

He recognised the road as the same one his brother lived on. Though Maddox's rambling farmhouse dwarfed this tiny cottage easily. The building's simple and somewhat crude architecture indicated that it was probably one of the original houses in the area.

'This is where my cousin Rachel lives,' Thurza replied. 'The boys are here. I won't be long.'

Moving away, she'd almost disappeared around the tall privet hedge surrounding the property before Logan reached out and stopped her. Gently easing her backwards, he asked, 'Shall I come with you?'

Clearly startled by his suggestion, Thurza struggled not to show her lack of enthusiasm for the idea. Then, with a sharp but decisive shake of her head, she said,

'It's best if you stay here. I'll run in and grab the boys. Be out in a few minutes. Five at the most. Honestly, I won't be long. Why don't you shelter behind this nice thick hedge and wait? Yes, that's a good idea. Just stay here.'

Firmly manoeuvring Logan backwards, she practically shoved him into the large shrub before hurrying off in the direction of the cottage, the heels of her shoes echoing in the quiet air.

Stunned, Logan straightened and tried to make sense of Thurza's actions. Anyone would think she preferred to hide him from both the house and the person inside. Was she ashamed of him? Did she not want her cousin to see them together? Perhaps she hoped to keep him as some sort of dirty secret?

Straightening, Logan pushed his shoulders back and stretched his neck. He refused to be hidden away. The whole idea that they'd done something wrong or shameful burnt like caustic liquid. Was that how she saw their night together? Their sons?

Marching to the end of the hedge, he peeked round the dense vegetation, nearly stabbing his nose on a sharp twig that was sticking out. Narrowing his eyes, he considered his options. If he stopped hiding and instead waited on the doorstep would Thurza open the door and pretend to her cousin that she didn't know him, the way she had when they'd bumped into each other the other morning on the beach? Or would she slam the door in his face and rush out through the rear entrance?

He was tempted to march up the path and plant himself on the doorstep just to find out. But he wouldn't, because he didn't plan on upsetting Thurza and he wouldn't have any rights until his name was put on the boys' birth certificates. And the last thing he was going to suggest now was having a DNA test carried out to prove his paternity. Not yet—if ever.

He sought to become Thurza's friend, not her enemy. Although perhaps it wasn't him she was concerned about, but her cousin's reaction. How bad could this Rachel be? From what little Thurza had said, it was obvious the two women were close. But did that mean the woman interfered in Thurza's life? Or maybe someone else was inside with the cousin? Someone Thurza didn't want him to meet?

Of course, her family must all hate him for leaving Thurza to cope with her pregnancy and the twins' arrival alone. Was she concerned about their response to him? What if she had painted him as so bad and inconsiderate that she was now worried about her family's reaction to his unexpected arrival?

Or was there a man Thurza would rather didn't learn that Logan was in town? Someone she was dating? Maddox didn't know her well enough to know if she was or wasn't seeing someone, did he?

A noise from the house drew Logan out of his deliberations. Shifting back out of sight, thanks to a thin patch in the evergreen bush's growth, he viewed the cottage's front entrance.

Thurza stood in the open doorway, manoeuvring a black double buggy over the threshold. Two baby boys, dressed in matching blue-and-red Fair Isle patterned hats and blue snowsuits, leaned forward in their seats as she pushed the buggy over the wide stone step and on to the gravel path.

Logan's heart stalled at the sight of the two small identical faces and the dark hair poking out from beneath the rims of each hat—the same shade as his own, from what he could tell. Chubby cheeks and matching mischievous sweet smiles sent his heart melting into a puddle of gooey, manly father love.

These angelic babies were his children. His sons. His true family members. Other than Maddox, they were his only real family in the whole world.

Swallowing hard to dislodge the sudden thick lump in his throat, he continued to take them in. These two small human beings were his babies and no one could steal that fact from him. Or deny it. Because even with a few feet between them he could see those faces were small images of his own. His very own little family.

Oh, dear God, look what he'd done! Times two.

A surge of overwhelming emotion gripped him and refused to loosen its unrelenting grasp. He couldn't be a father. Not now, not ever. A doctor and an ex-son, yes. An ex-fiancé, come to that. No matter how he viewed it, he always ended up being an ex-something. But a father? No, he didn't want to fail in this and become an ex-daddy, too.

His life had always centred around medicine and achievement. Helping people with their illnesses and physical problems. But a father? The dreams he and Victor had concocted over the years had never included two boys with adorable heart-shaped faces and kissable plump baby cheeks.

Wiping at the sudden moisture in his eyes, he stepped away to steady his breathing. Grasping the prickly hedge to steady his wobbly legs and keep himself upright, he stopped trying to hold back the sentiments the sight of these two small boys had instantly sparked in his heart. A heart he'd secretly feared too battered to react. But thankfully it had. He truly was a father. Not just in words or in hope. He was a dad to two flesh-and-blood children. His very own sons.

Logan's gaze met Thurza's as she and the pushchair appeared around the hedge, and he struggled between wanting to grab her in a big hug and scatter kisses all over her face or being furious with the fates for denying him his children from the very beginning of their precious lives.

He let go of the bush and then crouched beside the pushchair, coming face to face with his boys. His and Thurza's. The babies they had created together. And now he'd seen them he refused to be one of those fathers who said hi and then bye. It didn't matter what his panicked inner voice said. These little boys deserved the best of fathers and he promised to be that, no matter what.

He would never throw their love away as though it was nothing. The way his father had his. He would take these boys' hands and guide them and love them.

With resolve calming his thoughts he drew in a determined breath. For the next eighteen years he and Thurza would share the connection of their sons and do it civilly and respectfully. Working together as friends, not rivals. No way would he walk away and ignore the twins' existence. These boys were his and he was theirs for the rest of his days.

God, they were cute.

Thurza stepped forward and expertly undid the clasp surrounding the child next to her. Lifting her son into her arms, she spoke softly to him, before turning to face Logan. 'This is Axel.'

Unable to resist the pull any longer, Logan touched the boy's arm. His fingers were shaking as they stroked over the material of the snowsuit. 'Hey, there, little man. How's it going?'

Thurza snuggled Axel and grinned. 'He's a bundle

of mischief and trouble. I swear he'll be an explorer when he's older.'

A disgruntled squawk from the pushchair drew their attention downward. This time Logan undid the strap, his fingers fumbling over the simple task until finally he managed to move the sections apart and pull his son into his arms.

'Hey, there, little man number two. How are you doing? You must be Tyler.'

'That's right,' Thurza said. 'And this young man is mostly content to let his brother get into mishaps alone and play with his toys instead. But don't be fooled. He's just as much of a rascal as his twin brother—just a little less rowdy while being so.'

The baby reached out and grabbed Logan's face, diving forward to bite his nose.

'Tyler, no,' Thurza scolded gently, putting her hand between her son's mouth and Logan's nose. 'Be nice to…'

'Daddy,' Logan supplied swiftly, determined to start his relationship with his children with the complete truth and nothing else. No relegating him to his first name or some pretend title of 'uncle'—not even for a short time. He never wanted the boys to doubt his commitment to them. Now he knew about their existence he wasn't going away. And it was best that everyone, especially their mother, understood that.

'Daddy,' Thurza repeated softly. After a moment, she offered, 'Why don't you come back to our house and spend the afternoon getting used to your new role?'

Logan grinned at the child in his arms, pleased that Thurza had made the offer so willingly. Placing his palm nervously against Tyler's soft cheek, he said,

'Sounds great. What do you think, Tyler? Do you want your daddy to come over and play?'

Tyler giggled and gave Logan a bright smile that melted his heart all over again.

'I think that's a yes,' Thurza murmured gently.

CHAPTER SEVEN

'JUST PUT AXEL in the playpen,' Thurza directed, moments after they'd entered her cottage.

Slipping off her red coat and her scarf, she hung both on the hall stand, indicating for Logan to do the same with his brown leather jacket. With a quick smile, she disappeared into the kitchen.

Logan watched her go before turning his attention to the baby in his arms. Baby shampoo and another scent drifted around him as he cradled his son to his side. It was an aroma completely unique to small babies and reminded him of pure, unadulterated sweetness and wholesome innocence.

This infant and his twin brother depended on Thurza for everything. For too long they had been Thurza's sole concern, from the day she'd discovered she was expecting them. Had she cried over their existence the way his mother supposedly had? Regretted the predicament she'd found herself in?

How she must have hated him for not being around to support them all…for leaving her to face a future without the boost of his financial and emotional support. How had she managed to afford everything two babies required? Even basic baby paraphernalia added up, without multiplying it by two.

And how had she survived the endless sleepless nights every new parent talked about with resigned loving dread. Weeks and weeks of constantly tending to two babies' needs. Caring for one almost broke most new parents during the first tough weeks and months of their child's life—but two? And doing it all alone with no one to lean on except her cousin Rachel.

Logan shook his head in awe and smiled at his son. Thurza Bow must be one strong woman. Not only beautiful, but capable, too.

A sharp squeal from Tyler, still strapped in the pushchair, penetrated Logan's thoughts. Setting Axel down into the large playpen that occupied a good portion of the lounge floor, he turned to give Tyler the attention he demanded.

'Hey, there, buddy boy,' Logan murmured softly as he cradled his second son in his arms, loving the unaccustomed huggable weight of his child pressed into his hip.

Despite being a completely new feeling, it felt comforting and right. A perfect match. An absent piece he hadn't even recognised was missing now returned to its right place.

'I'm your daddy and I'm very happy to be so. It's important you understand how much.'

'Are you?' a voice asked from behind them.

Logan spun round and smiled at Thurza, who stood in the doorway. Her hair now sat in a messy bundle at the back of her head and she wore a purple apron over faded well-washed jeans and a cream jumper. While he and the boys had been getting acquainted, she'd changed out of her work uniform and into everyday home clothes.

With no reason to lie, he nodded. 'Yes. I'm very happy.'

She seemed pleased by his answer and, with a sharp nod in return, said, 'Good.'

'When you first realised you were pregnant,' he asked, eager to know, even though he risked not liking her answer, 'were you upset?'

The question came out awkward and blunt, but it was too late to soften it. Until he'd actually uttered the words he hadn't realised how important her answer was to him. He hated the idea of the unplanned pregnancy being something she regretted. An event in her life she would change if given the chance. Oh, she loved the boys now—he could see that—but back then had she cursed the failure of the contraception they'd used? Had she blamed and resented him?

Thurza folded her arms and frowned. 'No, I was worried at first, about how I would cope, but when I got used to it, I was happy.'

Relief and lightness extinguished his private fears. No regrets or heartache for this woman, then. No tears cried over the conception of their children. No secret disappointments. Nothing she wished could be changed. No, she'd wanted their sons, and the knowledge filled him with a strange and unexpected joy.

'You were? Really?'

She smiled. 'Yes—very happy.'

Pleasure at her honesty warmed and thawed his heart, soaking into areas he'd believed dead and frozen after Victor's death. 'You weren't angry?'

'No,' she said, slipping her hands into the apron's large front pocket. 'I guess the universe figured my life required a double shaking up.'

He smiled. 'Yeah, mine, too. I just wish...'

'Yes?' she probed, lifting her chin a couple of inches higher as she waited for him to continue.

The self-conscious movement indicated that she anticipated some form of criticism or disapproval from him. Thurza might be amazing in the mother stakes, but it was clear after their dealings over the last few days that the woman still questioned his motives and was reluctant to wholly let go of her undercurrent of suspicion in regard to him. It was as though she expected him to say or do something unkind or critical.

Glancing at the baby in his arms, he went on, 'I just wish that I'd helped you from the start…through the pregnancy and everything. All those days and weeks I missed out on.'

She chuckled softly and admitted, 'Well, it's a good thing you did miss some bits. Morning sickness—yuck! I suffered a full three and a half months of it. All day long. I doubt you'd have wanted much part of that.'

'Bad? I'm sorry you had to go through that alone.'

'Horrendous,' she admitted. 'And from the fifth month I took on the appearance of a large house, minus the chimneys. Mind, if you'd turned me on my head you may not have thought so. I'm sure in a low light and from afar my legs could easily have resembled two Victorian chimney pots.'

'I bet you looked beautiful,' Logan said, not believing her. Thurza's natural beauty would have been enhanced during pregnancy.

The idea of her swollen with his children stirred something primitive. Something he figured was best kept to himself. Otherwise he had a feeling he'd be marched back out through the door for daring to utter it.

'Only someone who never saw me would say so,' Thurza declared. 'My cousin insisted I stay away from zoos in case the elephants mistook me for one of their own and I triggered a stampede.'

He chuckled and pushed his glasses up on to the bridge of his nose. 'I think you're exaggerating.'

She sighed heavily and shook her head. 'I'm not. I was truly huge. Mammoth, even. People crossed the street when I went out, for fear of getting knocked over by my baby bump as they moved past me.'

He looked once again at Tyler, who seemed happy to stare back at him. His eyes were blue, just like Logan's. Curiosity twinkled in their depths. Warm, instant love for the infant seeped from his heart. This young boy was his son. *His.* It still felt like a dream. A good dream. No, better than that. A fantastic dream. One he never wanted to disappear, lose or wake up from.

With a self-conscious cough, he glanced back at Thurza. 'How did you manage?'

She shrugged and blew a loose strand of hair that had fallen from the hair clasp back from her face. 'I just did. I concentrated on these two babies I had to care for and provide for. Taking it a day at a time. I simply did my best. What other choice did I have?'

'I'm sorry I left,' he said, meaning his words. 'If I'd realised the condom had failed I would never have—'

'It's in the past,' she said, with a dismissive wave of her hand. Her tone suggested she didn't hold any grudge against him now she knew the reason why he'd never contacted her. 'No point fretting over what's done and gone.'

Logan agreed, but if destiny had tapped him on the shoulder right that minute and offered him the chance to travel in time, back to when Thurza had first discovered her pregnancy, he'd have grasped hold of it and agreed to any condition or clause issued, just to experience every step with her. To be able to hold her hand during those hours while she gave birth. To cradle his sons in his arms moments after they'd taken their first breath. To thank Thurza for the gift she'd given him on the day she did it.

But wishing for the impossible was a waste of hope and time, just as Thurza had said. All he could do was help from today onwards. Be a father in the way no man had ever bothered to be to him. A good father. A loving father who'd make the winners of those 'Father of the Year' competitions look like bumbling amateurs. Bestow upon his sons a sincere and honest love and endless affection.

Logan watched Thurza disappear back to the kitchen, a trace of regret and disappointment still lingering in his soul. He'd left her with no choice but to survive and bring their children into the world alone, while he'd run off hoping to forget the muddle he'd made of his own life. A state *he'd* caused by believing he could organise and control everything—including getting engaged to a woman he didn't love.

What a fool he was. Life and fate couldn't be controlled or manipulated. Neither could people and relationships. Both deserved better attention than he'd given either one.

No wonder his engagement had ended in chaos and bad feeling. Long-time family friendships had been stained forever by his thoughtlessness and actions. Life couldn't be placed into neat squares that suited only him and his requirements. He'd given a ring to the wrong woman, when he should have waited for his own 'special one' to step into his world.

He wasn't like his elderly patient Matthew back in Malta. He didn't need to fill his days and years with 'almost perfect' women to pass the time. Thank God he'd understood that before he'd walked down the aisle to 'The Wedding March'.

But right at this moment the sour taste of remorse coated his conscience. A feeling far more potent and disappointing than any shame over his botched engagement. Unknowingly, the decisions he'd taken back then had caused him to fail three very important people. Thurza, Axel and Tyler.

Because he had a horrible feeling that when he'd left England all those long months ago he'd walked away from the one woman who might have become his own 'special one'.

And he'd stayed away too long to ever know if that could have been true.

After a late lunch, Logan followed Thurza out into the back garden. The autumn sun was for once warm enough to enjoy. Carrying their mugs of tea and a plastic container of mini chocolate muffins outside, they headed to the floral swing seat at the end of the garden.

With full tummies, the twins had fallen asleep in their high chairs, and were now both stretched out in their matching light blue cots for an afternoon nap.

Joining Thurza on the seat, Logan kept a respectable gap between them. Without the twins to distract them, this was the perfect opportunity for getting to know each other better and discussing the twins. No disruptions, no babies, no patients to tend—just the two of them.

Logan settled back, glancing briefly at the woman beside him. Thurza intrigued him. The woman was beautiful, so it was no great mystery how they'd ended up making love. But she possessed more than just sex appeal. She was straight-talking, honest and seemingly not impressed by him at all—she fascinated him.

He'd never struggled to attract female attention, but this woman acted as though she viewed him as just another man in the world—and, strangely, he found he hated it. Although he had no plans to form anything with her other than a relationship shaped around and solely for their children. A family circle, but not living together as involved partners who were in love with each other, but as friends.

Unfortunately, his stupid inner male kept envisaging the idea of something more. Something he was adamant would never happen. He refused to ruin things between them because he couldn't control his sex drive.

Dragging the heel of his shoe along the grass and through a thick trail of spilt sand from the red plastic sandpit shaped like a clam, he half turned towards her. His eyes ran over her hair and face, stopping at the curve of her neck. 'I want to apologise again.'

She raised an eyebrow and enquired, 'What for?'

He twisted fully on the seat until he faced her. 'For not being around during your pregnancy and the birth. I failed you by not contacting you to double-check there were no repercussions from that night. It was a mistake. And it's no excuse, but I am sorry.'

'I never gave you my phone number,' she pointed out, taking a sip of her tea. 'All I had was your address.'

Logan took a gulp of his own drink. The tea was just the way he preferred it. Strong and sugarless. Resting the green mug on his leg, he asked, 'Why did you leave that morning before I woke up?'

It had bothered him at the time, making him wonder if he'd done something wrong during that night. Something that had left her uncomfortable and caused her to leave without a word. Or perhaps he'd said something thoughtless and upset her?

'Why did you sneak out? Did I do something to offend you, or...?'

'Is that what you think?' she asked with surprise.

He shrugged, still not sure, just conscious of how it had left him feeling. As if he'd failed or messed up in some way.

'I thought...' His words trailed off. Secretly, a stupid part of him had imagined that they would wake up the next morning and spend the day together. Get to know one another a little bit better.

'Logan?' she coaxed.

He sighed and admitted, 'Look, I don't know what I thought—but I meant what I said the other day. I would have made you breakfast, at least. I certainly would have satisfied your hunger.'

Her green gaze searched his face and one corner of her mouth twitched. 'Truly?'

'Food hunger, that is. Not—' He broke off, seeing that his words could be taken another way. 'Yes.'

Ripping the top off the plastic container, she offered him a chocolate muffin. 'Did I really make you feel used?'

He took a muffin, glancing away for a second before answering, 'Yes, I guess you did. I know some men might not care much over spending a night with a woman, but I'd never... You were... Hell, Thurza, you were the first woman I'd ever shared a night with in that way. It's not who I am. Yes, I've had lovers, but I don't sleep around with just anyone.'

She smiled softly, as though his admission pleased her. Shyly, she reached out and touched his chin, her fingers fluttering over his skin lightly like a fairy's footsteps. 'Good, because if we're confessing soul-wrenching truths, then you should know that I had never spent a night like that with a man either. You were my first and I suspect my last one-night encounter. I was just as much a novice as you. And the reason I left before you woke up was because I was embarrassed, and I'd heard other women say that men hated the unease and gaucheness of the following morning, so I thought I was doing the right thing by going.'

He chuckled and captured her hand, rubbing his thumb lightly over her skin. 'I wish you'd stayed.'

She tilted her head, her eyes thoughtful. 'You do?'

He smiled, conscious of her long, elegant fingers against his own. The touch and connection was totally innocent, yet heat warmed his cheeks and he feared he was blushing like a stupid kid.

'We're a pair, aren't we?' he mused, lowering their joined hands until they rested on the cushioned seat between them.

He was secretly relieved when she didn't pull away from his hold or tell him to let go. He liked the feel of her hand in his. Just as when he'd held the twins, it felt as though it belonged there. And friends could touch, couldn't they? As long as they didn't go any further. And they wouldn't.

She smiled, lifting her mug to take another sip of her drink. 'We seem to be. May I ask you a personal question?'

'Yes.'

'Why did you leave St Maria's? I recall hearing rumours about a failed relationship or something concerning a woman.'

His heart twisted, but he wasn't overly surprised by the question. Hospitals were a hotbed of gossip and rumour, so it was only natural she would have heard about it after he'd left England. He just wished he didn't have to admit to being such a fool.

'I was engaged for a short time,' he said. 'Six months.'

'Engaged?' Thurza echoed.

He nodded, before confessing, 'To a woman I didn't really love.'

'You didn't?' she repeated. 'Why not?'

'Because for a long while I mistook close friendship for love. We'd been friends since we were children and our families were keen on the match. But as soon as people started to talk about the wedding I realised that it wasn't what I wanted. It was all my fault, and my ex-fiancée is a lovely woman who thankfully has moved on. I hear she's happy with a new man. They plan to marry next year, I believe. Though I doubt I'll be invited to the wedding. Nor should I be.'

'Oh…' Thurza said thoughtfully. 'No regrets?'

'Only that I hurt and embarrassed her in front of our families and friends. She deserved better from me. It was disrespectful.'

She nodded and remarked, 'It would have been worse if you'd married her and only understood your true feelings after the confetti had dropped out of your hair.'

'You're right,' he agreed, deciding they'd talked enough about the past. Where relationships were concerned, the last couple of years had not been his greatest triumph. He squeezed her hand, glad once more that she didn't break the connection, and said, 'You and I need to get to know one another better. For Tyler's and Axel's sake, of course.'

Thurza shifted on the padded seat. An unexpected twinkle of mischief was brightening her eyes, turning them from their usual sea green to almost jade. 'How well do you want to know me, Logan Fox? So well you can tell what I'm thinking?'

'Yes,' he answered immediately.

The notion of discovering her intimate thoughts and desires suddenly intrigued him. What did she really think of their situation? Of him? Did she like him any better than she had yesterday? Or was she still undecided as to whether to let him into her family fully? Perhaps she figured he would eventually grow bored? Fade into the background and rarely visit? He hoped she wasn't clinging to the latter, because she'd be disappointed. He intended to stay right here in town until they'd settled things between them and he'd got to know his children.

'Why?' she asked.

'Because we should try to get along,' he replied. He was determined to prove they could deal maturely with both the circumstances and each other. 'Don't you think?'

Her eyes became serious and held his. 'Do you know what I'm thinking right now?'

He scanned her face, searching for hints or clues, a telling shadow of her thoughts. After a few seconds, he admitted, 'I have no idea, but I wish I did.'

Without another word, she leaned back and closed her eyes, a faint smile playing around her mouth. Her silence signified that whatever her thoughts were, she meant to keep them to herself...tease him with the unknown.

Pushing the seat into a gentle rocking motion, she offered, 'I have the evening off. Would you like to stay for dinner? It won't be anything fancy, but it will be edible.'

'I'd love to,' he replied, searching her face again for

the smallest inkling as to her thoughts. The woman appeared nothing but serene and relaxed.

'Tell me about your cousin,' he said, eager to keep their conversation going.

Thurza opened her eyes and frowned. 'Rachel?'

He nodded. 'You're close?'

'Very. She's extremely bossy, and loves to tell me how to live my life, but we grew up and lived together after my father died, when my aunt and uncle offered me a home.'

Logan wavered between curiosity and respect for her privacy. Was it too soon for sharing further personal information? But, then again, she had asked about his engagement. Finally, simple nosiness won over tact.

'How exactly did your father die?'

Thurza let out a soft, sad sigh that expressed more than any words could. Suddenly he regretted asking, and wished he could take the question back. Obviously, the man's death still hurt her.

'He was a volunteer for the local lifeboat,' she said quietly.

'Like Maddox?' he murmured.

She nodded. 'Dad was in charge of the crew. One morning they went out on a call to save a vessel in difficulty and…well, he never returned home. The weather turned rough and Dad fell over the side at the same time the ship they were rescuing turned over, sucking him under. A strange fluke, they called it. The way it occurred would probably never happen again. But on that day, with the sea as fierce as it was, unfortunately it did. Worse, he wasn't supposed to be on duty that week—he was covering for a colleague who was off sick. If not for that he might still be alive.'

Logan reached out and touched the lone tear that had

suddenly appeared at the corner of her right eye, hating to see the pain clouding her gaze as she silently relived the past. A cruel and significant event that had robbed her of a loved one. 'I'm sorry, Thurza.'

'Don't be. It's not often I talk about him to anyone. Rachel and her parents always become uncomfortable whenever I mention Dad. It's too painful for them to remember. The loss still haunts them. The sea is in my family's blood. They'd worked as fishermen and volunteers for the lifeboat for generations until Dad's death. It was their playground, if you like. My mum never understood that. She hated the sea. Resented its importance to Dad. Detested his loyalty to the crew. Considered the job dangerous and selfish, where loved ones are swallowed by the waves and lost for good. They argued a lot over Dad's need to volunteer. She never comprehended how he felt compelled to give back to the men and the association who'd saved his father's and his uncle's lives before him.'

'He sounds like a good man.'

Her smile this time was wobbly, but a shimmer of light returned to clear the tearful mistiness from her eyes. 'He was. He always hoped I would join. When I was a little girl, I promised him that I would do my turn.'

'Did you want to?'

Thurza was silent for a moment, before declaring, 'I did, but I also wanted to do it for him. Especially after his death. It wasn't as if I'd ever be able to do anything else, was it? And even as a small child I knew how important it was to him.'

Logan shifted, resting his arm along the back of the seat. Sensing the importance of what Thurza was saying, he asked, 'So did you?'

She stared down into the half-filled mug resting on her lap and shook her head. 'No.'

'What stopped you?' he coaxed, sensing the reason behind Thurza not keeping her promise was important.

She hesitated before answering. 'My aunt encouraged me to train as a nurse first. Said it would be a good career to fall back on. She and my uncle took me in when I was seventeen and they hated the idea of me joining the lifeboat. They'd lost Dad and didn't want to lose another member of the family.' She hesitated again, then continued, 'The month before I found out I was pregnant I'd decided to send in my application. I'd enjoyed working at the hospital, but I missed home.'

Logan quickly put together the parts Thurza had left out. Her pregnancy had stopped her plan to follow her dream and keep her promise to her father. Guilt burnt like a rich, corrosive fluid throughout him. Another reason for her to dislike him. Without his meaning it to, his presence in her life, even for a short time, had generated so much change and disruption.

He searched his mind for some way to make it up to her. 'Perhaps you can volunteer now the twins are here?'

She shook her head, her expression becoming firm and stubborn. 'I've experienced the heartbreak of losing a parent to the sea. I won't do the same to the boys. They need me.'

'But if you want—'

'No, it's better to forget my promise,' she insisted, not letting him continue. 'The boys come first. My father would have understood. I'm happy with the way things are.'

But was she really happy? Logan wondered at the truth of her claim. Thurza might tell herself that she was happy, but her uncertainty and regret at not being able to follow her dream and keep her pledge to her father flickered deep in her eyes.

'And that's the only reason?' he asked gently. Intuition was telling him there was something else preventing her from keeping the promise. Something she'd failed or preferred not to mention.

She met his gaze for a second, and then looked away. 'Of course it is. What else would it be?'

He opened his mouth to reply, but the sound of whimpering coming through the baby monitor at Thurza's side stopped him. They both stared down at it.

'One of the boys must be awake,' she said distractedly. Picking up the monitor, she listened as the sound became a full cry.

He let go of her hand and offered, 'Would you like me to go and check? Only right I start doing my bit! If you're comfortable with me doing so.'

She smiled and nodded. 'Thank you.'

Logan stood and started across the small lawn to the cottage. At the back door, he glanced over his shoulder. Thurza still sat where he'd left her, eyes closed, face tilted to the sun. His heart flipped at the sight of her beauty, but he ignored it. Somehow he was going to make life easier for Thurza Bow. Because he suspected that if he won her friendship it would be the best relationship he'd ever formed.

CHAPTER EIGHT

'MORNING, THURZA!'

The greeting from a teenage boy as she walked through the surgery's unusually quiet and empty waiting room the following morning surprised and concerned Thurza.

Smiling, she walked towards Mickey Russell, who was sitting with his grandmother. Thurza's eyes immediately spotted the small wet towel wrapped around the old lady's right arm.

'Good morning. What brings you to the surgery?'

Mickey pointed to his grandmother's covered arm, worry etching his young features. 'She's burnt herself again.'

Nannette Russell—or Nan, as everyone called her—fidgeted on the waiting room seat and sent Thurza a sheepish glance. Her straight white hair hung to her shoulders, held back from her face by a black hairband. Her pale freckled complexion appeared whiter than usual, and one of her wrinkled hands played with the edge of the towel.

Thurza took a seat beside her and gently asked, 'What's happened this time, Nan?'

'It's nothing, really,' the old lady insisted, sounding more apologetic than hurt and upset. 'I wasn't going to come down here and bother a doctor, but Mickey kept on until I agreed. He frets over me, you know.'

Thurza did know. This was their fourth visit in as many months. Nan's frequent accidents were becoming a concern, and something she intended to keep a close watch on. At fourteen years old, Mickey's role in his grandmother's life was slowly shifting from grandson to carer, and she was determined to make certain he received all the help possible to make things easier for them both.

'That's because he loves you,' Thurza said, spotting Logan strolling towards them. Dressed in black trousers and a plain dark blue shirt, he made Thurza's mouth water. 'Which doctor do you have an appointment with?'

'A Dr Fox,' Mickey answered. 'Gran's never seen him before. Is he new?'

Hearing the worry in the young boy's voice, Thurza hurried to reassure him. 'Logan is our new locum, Mickey. And he's very good.'

'Mrs Russell?' Logan enquired, coming to a stop next to them. After a quick glance Thurza's way, he switched his attention back to his patient.

'Call me Nan,' the old woman said, getting to her feet. 'Locum, huh? Thought maybe Thurza had found herself a boyfriend.'

Thurza gasped, heat flooding her face and neck at the old lady's saucy remark. 'I already have two men in my life, Nan. They're enough for me.'

Logan chuckled, his interest on his patient and not Thurza. 'If you'd follow me, please?'

Thurza turned to Mickey as they walked away. 'Logan will deal with your gran's burn. Do you want to go with them or would you rather wait here?'

The boy gave Logan a sceptical once-over, before retaking his seat. 'Is it possible for *you* to go with her?'

Thurza turned to see Logan busy directing Nan through the set of glass double doors that led to the consultation rooms. Mentally running through the rest of her appointments, she nodded, eager to ease the boy's worry. 'My next patient isn't due to arrive for another fifteen minutes, so I can ask if Logan minds if I stay with your grandmother while he treats her.'

Mickey nodded and let out a relieved sigh. 'She's all I have, Thurza. I'd be in some children's home if it wasn't for her taking me in after my mother abandoned me to go off with that bloke. She fought the social workers, Mum *and* the courts to keep me with her. Making sure she's safe and well is the least I can do for her.'

With a reassuring nod, Thurza said, 'I know, Mickey. I promise Logan will treat her arm and have it sorted in no time. Don't worry.'

Hurrying after the other two, Thurza caught up with them just as they were about to enter the consultation room Logan was using. She hoped what she was going to ask didn't cause any offence. She knew some doctors would see the request as a possible slur on their ability and professionalism and dislike her asking. Hopefully Logan wasn't one of them.

Waiting until Nan had entered the room, Thurza pulled Logan to one side and asked, 'Would you mind if I join you while you see Nan? I promised her grandson I would. They've dealt with a lot of family problems over the last couple of years, and Mickey's become very protective of his grandmother.'

'Of course,' Logan said without concern. 'Perhaps he would prefer to join us?'

Thurza shook her head. 'He's happy to wait in Reception. He just asked if I would mind coming.'

Logan nodded and stood back so she could enter the room before following her inside. 'I don't mind your presence at all, Thurza. After all, who knows what else Nan may say to send your cheeks such an interesting shade of pink?'

After guiding Nan over to a chair, Logan took his own seat behind the large desk. He'd run through the old lady's notes before going to fetch her from the waiting room, and other than a recent run of burns she suffered no real health concerns. Surprising and pleasing for a woman of her age.

'Right, Nan. Let's take a look at your arm, shall we? I'm just going to examine the burn before deciding on the best treatment, okay?'

'Don't suppose you can prescribe a bottle of *you* to perk up my spirits?' Nan joked. 'I promise to enjoy a good daily dose.'

Logan smiled, but shook his head. 'I'm afraid not, Nan. Besides, I suspect the effect would soon wear off.'

Thurza moved behind Nan's chair and gently squeezed her bony shoulder.

Nan glanced up at her and enquired, 'Mickey sent you in, did he?'

Thurza laughed and nodded. 'He's a good boy to be concerned. This is your fourth burn.'

Logan carefully unwrapped the damp towel from around Nan's arm and inspected the burn, relieved to see no trace of butter or any other old wives' concoction her generation were apt to use to treat scalds and burns. No matter how many times people were advised not to do it, they still struggled to let go of the home-made cures learnt in their childhoods from their parents.

He studied the wound thoughtfully, relieved to see it was only a first-degree burn. Nothing too concerning. 'Painful. How did you do it?'

'Caught the saucepan while making Mickey's porridge. He likes a bowl when he comes in from doing his morning paper round. Warms his stomach lovely on the colder mornings at this time of the year.'

'Did you run it under cold water for ten minutes?' Thurza asked, moving from behind the chair to take a closer look. She crouched down in the small space between Logan and Nan.

Logan's fingers faltered and his pulse kicked up several paces at the unaccustomed sensation of Thurza's body so close to his own. The scent of floral-perfumed soap powder and warm feminine body crowded his senses, drying his throat as his body tingled from her proximity.

'Yes. I remembered you told me to do that when I burnt my elbow last month,' Nan answered.

Pulled from his distracted musings, Logan forced his attention back to the old lady and her burn. Thurza's body and its intoxicating scent were not his concern. His body just had to remember that.

As though to torment him further, Thurza rested a hand on Logan's shoulder to balance as she straightened. Her touch burned through the thin layer of his shirt to the suddenly responsive skin beneath.

'Were you wearing your glasses?' Thurza asked, dropping her hand and stepping back. She folded her arms and stared down at the old lady.

'Yes, but they need changing. I'm struggling to see

out of them,' Nan admitted with a weary smile. 'It's no fun getting old.'

Thurza nodded. 'I think maybe you should make an appointment with the opticians this week. All of your accidents in these last few months have been caused because you're struggling to see and are misjudging distances.'

'Do you really think it will make a difference?' Nan frowned. 'Spectacles can cost an awful lot of money. I wouldn't want to spend out unnecessarily.'

Thurza smiled and reassured her. 'Yes, Nan, I do. At least have a test done and see what the opticians think. They'll be able to tell you if your glasses aren't strong enough.'

Logan stood, forcing Thurza to return to her original position behind Nan's chair. Grabbing medical supplies and a small white tray, he carried the items back and set them down on his desk.

'Well, it doesn't seem too bad,' he said. 'I think it will heal fine if left alone. I'll dress it with a bandage to keep it clean, but I'm pretty confident your body can deal with this without major interference from me.'

Nan lifted a hand to the delicate gold cross around her neck. 'Thank goodness. Mickey will be pleased. So how long are you going to be in town?'

Glancing at Thurza, he answered, 'I'm not sure what my plans are. I'm staying with my brother Maddox at the moment.'

How long he stayed would depend on how things progressed between Thurza and him. But for now he was happy to stay in Dorset.

Nan's mouth dropped open. 'You're Maddox's brother? Him with the farm up Lilly Lane?'

Logan nodded, not surprised that Nan knew his

brother. So far nearly everyone who'd entered his consultation room over the last few days knew Maddox and Logan's connection to his brother. 'I'm afraid so.'

Nan's regard increased a level. Her eyes slowly wandering over him. 'You don't resemble each other much.'

Logan's smile wavered as he reached for a roll of bandaging. 'He carries my mother's looks and I my... my father's.'

Well, he guessed he did. Whoever his father was, he must resemble him genetically. He certainly didn't look like anyone else in his family.

Nan frowned and asked, 'Are you married?'

'No.'

Nan glanced at Thurza and raised her eyebrows. 'Not married, eh?'

Logan concentrated his efforts on dressing Nan's burn, hoping it would prevent her from asking any further personal questions. Before she attempted to pull every last secret from him.

Once finished, he said, 'Keep the bandage clean and dry. The burn fortunately doesn't require a hospital visit and should heal completely in a few weeks. And I agree with Thurza over having your eyes tested, Nan. It won't hurt to make sure.'

Nan smiled at him. 'Well, if *you* think it's a good idea then I'll phone the opticians once I get home. Thank you, Logan.'

She held up her bandaged arm for Thurza to inspect. 'What do you think? Will Mickey be satisfied?'

Thurza smiled and nodded. 'Nice work, Doctor.'

Logan smiled. How polite and professional she sounded. As if they were two strangers working together for the first time. What would Nan say if she discovered that Thurza's children were his sons, too?

He imagined the resulting gossip would certainly wake up this sleepy seaside town for several days.

'Thank you, Nurse Bow. I'm glad you approve.'

Thurza helped Nan up from her seat. 'Any problems—make another appointment. Don't leave it, hoping it will sort itself out.'

Nan glanced at Logan. 'She's bossy, but she's a very good nurse, you know.'

Logan grinned and nodded. 'I know. I think she's superb.'

Logan stretched out on the rug, elbow bent and head resting in his palm, full of joyous contentment. It started deep within him and filled every crevice, curve and gap until it reached his heart.

Happiness. True and unadulterated happiness.

It was an emotion he'd never truly experienced before. Not with his family or with his ex. And though the truth shamed, shocked and saddened him, it also gave him a real appreciation for the wonder of his new unexpected family.

His eyes never moved from the two babies lying on the light blue padded blanket beside him. Both were stretched out and fast asleep, wearing matching white dragon-printed pyjamas, snoring softly in the quietness of the cottage. His heart turned over with a rush of overwhelming love for these two boys, who in truth he hardly knew, but who now formed the centre of his life and whom he planned to get to know in every single way.

Thurza had accepted his offer to babysit while she nipped to her cousin's house to retrieve a toy, leaving him in sole charge of their sons, whose every whim and requirement now concerned him. At first, he'd seesawed from pleased to scared and then to excited. He'd never babysat anything before—let alone two small babies. But Thurza trusted him, even though he lacked any proper 'father training' or experience. And that show of complete belief, to be trusted by a woman who had every right to question and doubt him, meant everything to him.

Trained for nothing but medicine and doctoring, he now needed to learn how to do the biggest, most terrifying job of all. Being a parent. Someone for the twins to look up to and admire. Someone completely different from the two men who had claimed the role in his own life. One father who'd lied to him for years and the other one who'd walked away without a fight—turned his back on Logan without a care or regret.

To his thinking, if that man had borne any regrets during the preceding years then he would have tried to make contact with Logan—especially once he'd reached adulthood. The cold reality that he'd stayed away told Logan everything in regard to how the man felt.

Two selfish men, with no loyalty or affection for the innocent son stuck in the middle of the mess they and Logan's mother had jointly created. Had either of them cared about his feelings over the years? Had they wondered or lost sleep over the wrongs they'd done to him by not telling him the truth while they were alive?

He doubted Victor had. And his biological father had failed the moment he'd allowed his mother to keep Logan from him. Logan had loved his mother, but she'd had no right to make that decision. She'd robbed him of a relationship. Unlike Thurza, who'd tried to include him in their children's lives even though she'd received no reply to her letters and the evidence had made it appear as though he didn't care or want to know. She had tried repeatedly to build a link between him and their children.

During the last couple of days he and Thurza had formed a loose routine, spending time with the boys and each other when either of them wasn't working. Tonight, though, thanks to Thurza's invitation, issued before she'd hurried out of the house, he was spending the evening here.

He smiled, transfixed by the way each child's chest rose and fell with every breath. Small human miracles. Amazing. Just like their mother. She'd taken what fate had handed her and created a good life for her family. Not only was she good-looking and clever, but incredible and resourceful, too.

Letting out a contented sigh, he pillowed his head further into his arm. Yes, Thurza was wonderful. An impeccable mother to the boys. The kind of woman a man might picture keeping in his life long-term. The sort of woman a man could effortlessly fall in love with…

Logan blinked, then swallowed hard. Sitting up, he stared unseeingly at his surroundings while his thoughts raced back and forth. Dragging his fingers through his hair, he pondered that last notion.

Fall in love with Thurza? Now, that would be a bad idea. A really terrible one.

But…

Maybe it was the happiness budding inside his heart that had pushed his mind in that irrational and unwise direction. Sent him pondering over concepts involving commitment and love. But he didn't do love, and it was clear Thurza wasn't interested in him that way. Not once had she shown or indicated that she saw him as anything other than the twins' father.

The sound of the front door opening and closing drew his attention from his wild reflections. Getting to his feet, he met her at the lounge door.

'Hey,' he greeted her, shoving his hands into his jeans pockets. Mindful of the jumbled feelings still rolling through him, he tried to act relaxed. Did his thoughts show on his face for her to see? Noticeable like a guilty secret? 'Did you get Tyler's toy?'

Her bright smile set his heart into an aching backflip. She held up a small teddy bear in answer and waved it. 'Yeah. Any problems?'

'No, the boys haven't woken,' he said, noting the large glass jar circled with a purple ribbon and with a floral label in her other hand. 'That's a lot of honey.'

'Rachel keeps bees,' she said offhandedly. 'How about a cup of tea?'

'Can do,' he said, following her into the kitchen.

Desperate for a distraction to the thoughts in his head, he tried to concentrate on something else.

Thurza pointed to his laptop, though only the back of the machine faced her. 'Busy working? Or playing computer games?'

'A little of both,' he admitted.

'There's a games console in the cupboard under the television, if you get bored any time,' she said. 'It's not new, but the games are pretty good.'

Surprised, he leaned against a kitchen cupboard and regarded her. How many more surprises did this woman have hidden? 'I never took you for a gamer.'

She shrugged and flicked on the kettle. 'I used to play on the nights I struggled to sleep, thanks to the twins wanting to play kick-about inside me. Of course, they may have just been kicking each other and I received the effects. I'm pretty good.'

Not bad himself, Logan asked, 'Any of those games for two players?'

'I think so. Fancy being slaughtered, do you?' she dared him with a grin.

He shook his head arrogantly. 'Won't happen—but if you're confident enough to try and prove differently, then how about we make something to eat and afterwards play a game or two? We can keep the volume low, so it doesn't disturb the boys.'

She laughed and retrieved two clean cups from a cupboard. 'Trust me, they can sleep through any noise.'

He chuckled. 'I guess they must get it from me. How about it? You fancy taking me on?'

She grinned and met his gaze. Her eyes were sparkling with something more than just competitiveness. 'Oh, just try and stop me, Logan Fox.'

She meant it. Every single word.

Thurza sliced through thick bread that squashed down the moment the knife touched the crunchy outside crust. She'd take on the man and all he had to offer if he indicated that he wanted the same. The idea didn't repel her at all. She found Logan attractive, and the time they'd spent together had forced her to face the fact that, although she'd done her best to hide from the knowledge, she rather liked Logan Fox.

Actually, she more than liked him. She ached to talk to him about everything and nothing, to discover what he thought and believed. The way any woman would with a man she was attracted to.

Her cousin was annoyingly correct in her insistence that Thurza wasn't a one-night kind of woman. Many women happily shared brief moments of no real connection with a stranger, their target and desire being

nothing more than a night of exciting and uncomplicated sex. No expectations. No ties. Just sex.

But not her. Her personality was far too emotionally
open and needy for such a commitment-free physical
interlude with another person. She sought a man who
not only satisfied her physically while sharing her bed
sheets, but also wished to develop a stable and long-term
emotional relationship. Someone seriously into her and
not afraid of commitment and family.

Yet with Logan all her beliefs had disappeared, and
every day since they'd parted she'd wondered what had
really caused her to sleep with him that night.

Yes, he was handsome, and at times funny. He also
owned a serious side she found endearing, and he was
the kind of man a woman could tell all her worries to
and be sure he'd help her work through them…see her
problems as theirs to sort, not just hers. A man able to
view any woman he formed a relationship with as a
partner and not a possession. Though his honesty over
his reasons for getting engaged indicated that his skills
for bonding with a woman still required work.

Would he act differently with someone he loved?
Someone special who owned his heart?

Thurza's parents' relationship had culminated in a
battle of wills. They'd rarely tried to compromise. But
she suspected that beneath the shine and polish of Dr
Fox lay a thoughtful and compassionate male. His expression when he'd first met the twins melted her heart
every time she recalled it. In that precious moment he'd
looked like a man who'd finally found his true meaning
in the world. As though a great internal mystery had finally been resolved for him and he adored the solution.

It had comforted her, and frankly she'd found it sexy.
Behind the sheen of successful, capable doctor, the real

Logan Fox appeared to be a decent, kind and considerate man. A good role model for the twins. A good person to have at her side in a positive capacity. A man she could care for.

But what did he think of her? Did he regret sleeping with her? Did he secretly wish another woman had given birth to his boys? Someone well off and more his kind? Not a small-town woman who worked at two jobs just to pay the bills and rarely spent money on anything new if she could find it cheaper second-hand?

She sprinkled grated cheese over the slices of bread and let out a short sigh. Thinking this way was dangerous and a waste of energy. They were co-parents and nothing more. Their relationship would stay completely non-sexual forever. No naughty carry-ons would occur once the twins were in bed. There would be no sneaky kisses when they sat next to each other. No touching each other's hands by accident. Fingers playing with hair would never happen. Nothing but conversation and friendship would take place. Simple and non-complicated. A loving, stable family circle without all the complex relationship stuff.

Never becoming something more than friends…

It was sensible and practical, if…rather boring.

Staring down at the half-made cheese on toast, she frowned. What if Logan decided to introduce a girlfriend or a new partner into their family? She closed her eyes and refused to deal with those thoughts. When exactly had she started to view them as a family unit, anyway?

She shook her head at her deliberations. No point jumping six steps forward. The future and its problems and concerns would soon arrive. Instead, she would finish their meal and then beat the smug devil at whatever game he'd chosen. For a couple of hours she would enjoy being surrounded by her sons and their father and try to not think about what her silly heart might quietly dream.

Because dreams rarely came true—especially when they were hers.

CHAPTER NINE

LOGAN LAUGHED AS Thurza swung Tyler through the air while attempting to sound like an aeroplane. One whose engine sounded on the verge of failing or catching fire.

Pushing Axel gently back and forth on a baby swing, he smiled at the giggles coming from his son. It was a sound Logan was learning to love each time he was fortunate enough to hear it. It filled him with joy and pride.

Despite it being early in the afternoon, the play park thirty minutes from Thurza's home was deserted except for them. Obviously the locals preferred to stay indoors rather than enjoy the wishy-washy sun of an autumn day.

However, Thurza had decided, after a morning working at the surgery, to wrap the boys up in their snowsuits, hats and mittens and take a long walk around the edges of town before stopping off at this neighbourhood park.

'Having fun?' Thurza asked, as she slid Tyler into the baby swing next to his brother and gave it a small shove that sent Tyler's arms flapping like a panicking baby bird.

'I am,' Logan said, meaning it.

Spending time with Thurza and the boys filled him with pleasure in a new and unfamiliar way. It wasn't just enjoyment from their company, but a peacefulness, too. A sense of being part of a group. *Their* group. Part of something important. He fitted in, instead of standing to one side waiting to be included—or, worse, being compelled to feel he had to earn his place.

Glancing around the park, he took in the five oak trees that lined one side. Their large, aged, weathered and gnarled trunks were wider in circumference than the width of both his arms linked together. An old-fashioned bandstand stood in pride of place close to a large expanse of grass, and it didn't take much to imagine a small brass band playing well-known tunes from the past during the warm weeks of summer, for the enjoyment of the listening public sprawled out on rugs or sitting on deckchairs while enjoying a picnic.

'This place is beautiful,' he said.

'It was first built in the Victorian period, after the land was donated to local residents by someone in the royal family,' Thurza informed him. 'A past queen mother, I think. I can recall playing on the original swings and slides as a child. The council removed them years ago, but you can still see clues of the park's Victorian beginnings if you look carefully at the railings and the gate at the entrance.'

They lifted the babies out of the swings and put them in their pushchair. Logan nodded towards a wooden bench and suggested, 'Shall we sit for a while?'

Thurza nodded, waiting while Logan brushed several dried leaves that had blown off the nearby trees from the slats.

'There you go.'

She smiled and sat down. 'Thank you, kind sir.'

Their eyes met once again, causing a fizz to spiral through Logan. His original plan of spending time with Thurza to stop his feelings growing for her wasn't working. If anything, they were becoming stronger, and he didn't know how to deal with them. It wasn't easy to continue to tell himself to ignore the feelings when something as simple as her smile set off sparks of awareness inside him.

To distract himself from the woman beside him, Logan forced his gaze to move over the scenery once again, taking in the muted orange, brown and green seasonal colours. A light wind danced over the park, shaking the odd cluster of dying leaves still vigilantly clinging to the otherwise bare branches of the oak trees, before their final drop to the ground below to rot and decay into a fresh layer of earth.

Logan had never imagined a small seaside town in Dorset could interest him. But his brother had developed a home and a living in this small town. Same as Thurza. She'd returned to a place she regarded as home. A safe location to raise their sons. It was a sentiment completely unfamiliar in Logan's own life. Yet over the last few weeks he'd started to view this place as more than just the town where his brother resided.

Did a home and roots in a place really bring happiness? Both Maddox and Thurza looked to have found contentment here. But what about him? If he settled in Dorset permanently would he discover the same? Or was true happiness shaped by the people a person surrounded themselves with?

If he stayed in this town with Thurza and the boys would he eventually feel the same way they did? See it as a shelter for his heart and solace for his spirit? Or would he eventually yearn for distant shores, unfamiliar green spaces and polluted city streets? Somewhere different and new? Would he come to resent the ties that rooted him here?

Thurza's affection for the town was deep. He couldn't imagine her being happy living somewhere else. She had relations, friends and patients here. Her memories of her father were here. Would she ever consider upping sticks and living somewhere unfamiliar? But perhaps she would love the idea of leaving this town for good. Would be open to the opportunity to move someplace new, where she could forget the past and refocus on a different future. Or would the ghosts of her previous family generations keep her here?

He suspected not keeping her promise to her father troubled her, despite her denials. If she applied to become a member of the lifeboat crew, even for a short time, would it soothe her conscience and lay to rest the ghost of her long-ago promise? Would it make her happy?

Yes, the job was dangerous, and every part of him struggled against warning her of the risks, but he refused to do that. Thurza more than anyone knew the dangers being a volunteer held. She'd faced and lived with the consequences of those dangers. Accidents happened, no matter how carefully people tried to make sure they didn't. But not fulfilling her dream and not keeping her word to her father was silently eating at her. He understood those emotions that called to a person and refused to leave them in peace. He'd heard similar ones once concerning medicine.

And if she did apply, and was offered a position, then his place belonged on land, caring for their sons so she could do the job free from worry or concerns surrounding her family. He'd be exactly where he wanted to be. So perhaps it wasn't this town that soothed a person, but this woman and the children whose appearance in his life fulfilled him.

Thurza nudged him with her leg. 'Tell me a secret, Logan. You know a little of my past—reveal something of yours.'

He let out a long heavy sigh, already knowing what he was going to confess, but struggling with how to say the words. 'A few months ago I discovered the man who raised me wasn't actually my biological father.'

Thurza gasped, whipping her head round to stare at him. 'What?'

His gaze moved to the twins, happily jabbering to each other in their pushchair. He couldn't imagine any reason or event big or painful enough to cause him to turn away from those boys. Or imagine carrying a vengeful desire to purposely hurt them in some cruel way.

'My mother indulged in an affair during their marriage and I am the result.'

'Oh, Logan,' Thurza said softly. 'That must be hard to take in.'

He continued as though she hadn't spoken, preferring to get it all out in one go. Ignoring it for months had felt a lot easier than confronting it did. But maybe it was time to pierce the festering wound and lance the venom from it.

'The information was only revealed after Victor— the man who raised me—had died and the funeral had taken place. And it was given to me through a formal solicitor's letter.'

'What?' Thurza gasped again. 'A letter? Not face to face?'

He shrugged, soothed by her indignation. 'Evidently

a fake son doesn't deserve the respect of hearing the truth from the person who raised him.'

'Do I have this right?' she asked. 'The man who raised you as his own left you a letter telling you that you weren't his real son and didn't allow you to attend his funeral?'

'Yep.' Logan nodded. 'He instructed his solicitor to inform me of my mother's infidelity and my true parentage.'

Thurza shifted on the bench and lifted a hand to cup his cheek. Her bare fingers, though cool against his skin, gave him a measure of comfort. Her lack of self-consciousness when touching him eased a smidgeon of the anguish reliving it all brought.

'This man... Victor?' she asked, pausing to check she had the right name.

Logan nodded.

'Did he treat you as his son?'

'Yes,' Logan said. 'Not once can I recall him acting as though I wasn't. He always introduced me to his friends or business associates as his son.'

Thurza stroked his skin, her eyes troubled. 'Then why would he allow you to find out the truth in such a cruel way? Why didn't he tell you himself?'

He almost smiled at the outrage in her tone. 'I don't know the answer to that. I presume I was just a pawn in Victor Fox's long and manipulative game of revenge on my mother.'

She continued to rub her fingers against his cheek as though her touch could soothe away his hurt. He ached to move her hand and place it against his heart.

'Maddox believes that by not telling me, my mother hoped to protect me from Victor's anger, but I'll never know for sure. The fact is they all lied, and it's not a

pleasant feeling to realise not one person cared enough
to tell me the truth. Their silence left me open to Victor's unexpected malice at the same time I was grieving his death.'

Thurza continued to caress his jaw. 'Why do people
make relationships so complicated?' she asked. 'Why
can't they just be nice?'

Logan chuckled, turning his head slightly to kiss the
centre of her palm. The urge was too strong to resist
and ignore. Suddenly he didn't want to talk about the
mess of his family or contemplate the questions he'd
asked himself many times over.

'Who knows? What I do know is how much I love
your hair. It's very pretty and unusual. Especially the
plaits.'

She smiled, lowering her hand before giving him
a knowing look. 'Thanks—but don't think you can
change the subject with corny compliments.'

Without another word Logan slipped his fingers into
the thick blonde strands, pushing her hair tenderly away
from her face. His gaze ran slowly over her suddenly
flushed face. 'They're not corny. I mean every word.
You're incredibly beautiful, Thurza. Surely you realise?'

'And *you're* avoiding talking about your family,' she
whispered, tilting her head back as his fingers started to
stroke through her hair. Her lips tilted into a soft smile,
indicating how much she enjoyed his touch.

'I'm trying to,' he admitted. 'But only because it's
all very boring and you are far more interesting than
my family's imperfections.'

She laughed. 'Smooth, Dr Fox. An obvious avoid-
ance tactic, but smooth. I'm sure a lot of women would
fall for such flattery and drop the subject—just as you'd
like me to do.'

'But you're not going to, are you?' he queried, already knowing the answer. Reluctantly, he slowly removed his hands from her hair and sat back.

'Nah—not me,' she agreed. 'So, how do you really feel now you know the truth about your parents?'

He stretched out his legs and crossed them at the ankles, reluctant to search his feelings deeper, but aware that the woman beside him wasn't willing to cut him any slack. 'Why? Does it matter how I feel? It all happened a long time ago. Shouldn't I just forget it?'

She nudged his foot with her welly-covered one. 'Yes, of course it matters. The affair may have occurred years ago, but your knowledge of it is only recent. And I want to know because I'm nosy.'

He smirked, and for a long while pondered her question. For the last few months he'd purposely refused to confront any of it, only doing so once he was back in England and able to get answers. But even then he'd sidestepped exploring his own feelings too closely. Maybe by talking it out with Thurza he could make sense of it all and then forget it for good.

'I think the overriding emotion I feel is stupid.' Until he said the words he hadn't considered that aspect. But it was true. No matter how he looked at the evidence, it left him feeling a fool.

Thurza regarded him. 'Why?'

'How did I not realise?' he said. 'How did I not see that Victor and I shared not one physical resemblance? I mean most kids are a mixture of their parents, aren't they? So how did I not see—'

'Not always, they aren't,' Thurza interrupted, nodding to the twins still jabbering to each other. 'The boys are the image of you, Logan. There is nothing of me in them. Not yet, anyway. It might change as they grow

older, or maybe parts of me will show in their person-
alities, but then again maybe not. Besides, I look nothing like my father.'

Logan rubbed his jaw. 'I always figured I took after
a past relation—someone way back in the genealogy
line. But I never really questioned it. Why would I?
I was raised to believe Victor was my father. I never
thought to question the truth of it. I wonder why I never
once doubted it.'

'Why would you?' Thurza asked. 'You trusted your
family to be honest with you. If they never gave you
any cause to mistrust them, then why would you suspect differently?'

'I can't get rid of the feeling I should have picked up
on something, though.'

'Were you close?' she asked. 'You and Victor?'

Logan leaned forward on the bench, linking his
hands in the space between his knees. 'I thought so. We
spent every holiday together. Right up until two years
ago, just before his health started to fail. We went fishing for trout in Scotland. I honestly believed we were
friends more than anything. Closer than most fathers
and sons. He wasn't an easy man, but we made our relationship work. At least I thought we did. But he died
and left instructions for me to be informed of the truth
by letter and denied the chance to attend his funeral. I
marvel at how good an actor he was. Either that or I'm
nothing but a gullible fool.'

'He doesn't sound like a very nice man,' Thurza murmured, leaning her shoulder against his. 'And you're
not a fool—or stupid. You're a good, decent man who
trusted the people you thought were your family.'

Logan gave her a rueful look. 'Victor wasn't a terribly affectionate or loving human being. But he always

treated me as though he cared. Now I see it was all a lie while he waited to get his final revenge on my mother and her memory.'

'I pity him, then,' Thurza said softly. 'Because if that was what he was doing all those years, then he didn't deserve you or your love. And *he* was the foolish and stupid one for not realising what a wonderful son he had. Blood connection does not make a father and son, Logan. Not always. Love does that. That can be stronger than a physical bond.'

'I never said I loved him,' he replied, suddenly uncomfortable.

'But you did and you still do. That's why it hurts so much. He should have treasured your relationship and your love. It's his loss. Because I know whoever you choose to love in your life will be very lucky and blessed.'

Logan placed his hand over hers where it lay on his lower arm and gently squeezed it. 'Complicated families, huh?'

She snorted and shot him an amused glance. 'Yes, they can be. Look at me and the promise I made to my father. You know, when we talked about him the other day it was the anniversary of his death, and not one person remembered. Not one. Thanks for listening to me.'

Logan slipped his arm around her and tugged her close to his side. 'Thanks for listening to me. Funny, but I feel better for it.'

She glanced away, but not quickly enough that he didn't catch the slight tremor of her lips. 'You feel foolish about not seeing the clues about your real heritage and your father, whereas I live with the burden of letting mine down.'

Logan pulled her closer into his embrace, desperate to ease some of her distress. He sighed. 'Thurza…'

'I want to believe he would understand why I didn't keep my promise and keep up the family tradition, but sometimes I wonder if he would be disappointed in me.'

Logan kissed her forehead. His own problems and disappointments were forgotten while he soaked in Thurza's own regrets and pain. 'I think your father would be proud of you. You're a wonderful person and a fabulous mother. Any man would be proud to father a child like you. I'm proud of you. It probably means nothing, but it's true. You amaze me.'

A tear rolled from the corner of her eye to trail down her cheek. A moment later a sniff followed it. 'But I feel as though I've let him down, Logan, and I hate it. It was the only thing he ever asked, and since his death I've put it off and tried to pretend it isn't important. But it's always there at the back of my mind. Constantly waiting to jump out and fill me with guilt.'

'The boys—'

'Are just a convenient excuse,' she said. 'The same way agreeing to train as a nurse was an excuse. My aunt wished it and I pretended to be against it for a while, but I wasn't really. A huge part of me was relieved to be able to delay keeping my promise. The truth is I'm scared to go out on the water in case the same thing happens to me as it did to my father. It's a feeling that has become stronger since I've had the boys. The worry is constantly there. That I'll go out one morning after kissing my children and never come home again. The same way my father did. That my favourite jacket will hang on the peg in the hall for months before finally being thrown into a charity bag and lost for good. That my boys will sit on a lonely beach day after day, praying for my return, even though in their hearts they know that it will never happen. That they'll never hear my voice or my laughter again. That it will be an eternal loss that will never leave them, just as it has never left me.'

Logan's arm tightened around her, his heart aching at the grief in Thurza's voice. 'The job comes with danger. I'm sure your father would have understood your resistance and your reasons.'

'Doesn't nursing, too?' she countered. 'Every day medical staff are attacked by members of the public. Is the danger found out at sea and the danger in a medical centre or hospital so dissimilar?'

'Only you can decide that,' Logan said. 'But I think at some point you will need to make a decision and then find your peace with it. Because you shouldn't live the rest of your life fretting or feeling guilty. It's not right and it's certainly not fair.'

Thurza nodded, her attention drawn away by a squirming Axel, who'd grown bored sitting in his pushchair.

With a grateful smile, she left Logan's side and murmured, 'Our son calls.' Standing, she glanced down at him, a frown creasing her brow. 'I'm not sure I can make that decision yet, though.'

Logan clasped her hand and lightly kissed the back of it. 'You will. When your heart says it's time, you'll make it then.'

She nodded, her attention now fully on their son. Logan smiled as she bent down and kissed Axel's cheek.

Glancing up, she caught Logan's gaze and mouthed, *Thank you.*

His smile grew and he whispered back, 'My pleasure.'

Because it was. He'd do whatever he could to ease the burdens of this beautiful woman he was slowly coming to adore, and he wanted her to know that.

CHAPTER TEN

'GOOD MORNING, ALFRED.' Thurza stepped into her patient's bedroom and smiled at the elderly gentleman propped up in bed. 'How are you feeling today?'

Alfred Blakeman sighed, his fingers tapping against the floral quilt and the knitted blanket that covered him. Signs of tiredness lined his face, but his brown eyes held their usual lively glimmer. 'I'm a bit cross today, I'm afraid.'

Thurza quickly checked through Alfred's medical notes and then asked, 'Any particular reason? Or did you just wake up feeling that way.'

With another sigh, Alfred glanced at the closed door. 'It's my daughter, Judy. She keeps wandering in every ten minutes and fussing. Good grief, anyone would think I was at risk of vanishing from this bed instead of dying in it.'

'Perhaps Judy just feels like spoiling you,' Thurza reasoned neutrally.

Walking closer to the bed, she gently picked up Alfred's wrist and checked his pulse. Unfortunately the gentleman's illness was terminal, but despite the doctor's original prognosis of less than six months, the old man appeared set on making sure he stayed around longer, just to prove them wrong.

'Yes, but sometimes a man needs a period of quiet time. A chance to have a wallow in peace. To think deep thoughts without interruption by mundane conversations about the weather, or if I'd like another cup of tea. I swear the girl is determined to drown me with beverages. How am I supposed to contemplate the mysteries of the next life if my daughter keeps coming in and disturbing me with questions concerning tea?'

Thurza chuckled and shook her head. Alfred's daughter was struggling with the prospect of losing her father. The two were very close and the only family they each had left.

People reacted to losing a loved one in various ways. Some, when faced with the reality of time running out, coped by pretending it wasn't real, or clinging to the hope of a different outcome. Others, like Judy, struggled against the confusion of mixed feelings. Although she hated to see her father so ill, she didn't want to lose him for good.

There was no right or wrong way to deal with loss. Grief and loss were as individual as the person enduring them.

'Would you like me to sort out your pillows so you can do your wallowing more comfortably?' Thurza asked with a smile. 'Might also help with this new habit you've developed of slouching to one side.'

'If you'd be so kind, my dear.' He gave her a conspiratorial glance, before whispering, 'Between you and I, sometimes when Judy does it I end up feeling like I've been shuffled and battered by a rugby player. She's always been a bit heavy-handed. Her mother was the same, bless her heart.'

'I'm sure Judy does her best,' Thurza said, plumping

the pillows and gently helping the elderly gentleman to sit back. 'Any pain today?'

'Just a bit—but I took the medication the doctor prescribed. Nothing too bad. Tell me, how are those babies of yours?'

'They're as gorgeous as ever,' Thurza said with pride. 'Shall I take a look at the wound on your leg before we talk some more?'

'If you must—'

A knock on the door stopped their conversation and they both turned towards the unexpected interruption.

Logan, dressed in an expensive dark suit and holding a black leather doctor's case, pushed the door wider and stepped into the room. Musky aftershave with hints of tangy orange followed him in, tickling Thurza's nostrils with pleasing aromatic notes. Lately, she'd started to notice the same scent clinging to the boys' clothes, too. And she often found herself taking sneaky appreciative sniffs whenever Logan wasn't around to catch her.

But the man now entering the room wasn't the relaxed and teasing Logan she'd played computer games with, or the father who'd rocked their sons to sleep after playing at the park. This Logan Fox was the professional doctor she dealt with at the surgery. All charm, patience and capability.

Flashing a practised smile, he greeted their patient. 'Good morning, Mr Blakeman.'

Bright, confident and friendly, his smile was no doubt supposed to instil confidence in the person it was directed at. For Thurza it sent her heartbeat thudding and her stomach fluttering, as if she was a silly girl with an enormous crush.

'Logan... Dr Fox...' Thurza stammered, shooting their unexpected visitor a surprised glance. Did he want to speak to her, or was he here in a professional capacity? His smart clothes and his manner hinted at the second likelihood.

Logan sent her a reassuring glance, before turning to the man in the bed. 'I should introduce myself. I'm Dr Logan Fox. Dr Watts at the practice has asked me to pop in and let you know that for the next few weeks I'll be stepping in and taking over as your doctor. As I was passing, I thought I'd stop in and introduce myself.'

'Nice to meet you, Dr Fox,' Mr Blakeman said, waving Logan over to the empty chair next to the bed. 'Please call me Alfred. Though I don't expect I'll see that much of you. I suppose you know Thurza?'

This time Logan avoided looking in her direction and instead placed his bag on the chair. 'Yes, we share a couple of common interests.'

Thurza busily pulled on a pair of rubber gloves and folded back the bedding at the end of the bed to check Alfred's leg wound. Because of his illness, it was taking its time to heal.

Expertly removing the dressing, she spent several minutes checking the wound over, glad to have something to occupy her mind with Logan in the room. Lately, the sight of the man caused her thoughts to wander and her concentration to drift.

When she could dither no longer, she declared, 'Well, this appears to be healing nicely.'

Logan glanced over the folded bedding and also inspected the wound. With a nod, he turned his attention back to the patient. 'How are you feeling today, Alfred?'

'I was in a grump until Thurza arrived,' the old man told him. 'She always cheers me up. Known her since she was a small girl. Used to work with her father on the local lifeboat. Such a tragic day when we lost him.

Real tragedy. Used to tell anyone listening how one day Thurza would become our first female member. Of course that was a long time ago. We've had a couple of female crew members since then. Ah, things change and life happens, I suppose...'

Thurza purposely closed her ears to the conversation and, after applying cream, re-dressed the wound with new coverings. Replacing the blanket and duvet over the old man's legs, she said brightly, 'I'll just get rid of these used dressings and have a quick chat with Judy.'

Leaving the room, she headed for the kitchen, glad for a breather, away from Logan's presence and Alfred's talk about her father. She was not in the mood right now for either.

Opening up to each other at the park the other day, sharing their hurts, had changed something between them. The tangles she'd so determinedly tried to avoid were slowly knotting around them, taking them from casual acquaintances to friends with every deep secret they revealed to each other, leaving Thurza unsure of what she was feeling or where they were heading.

She'd weakened over Logan once before, but now every decision she made and every deed she committed affected two small boys. She refused to jeopardise their happiness and the calm life she'd worked so hard to build for them.

Logan Fox was a risk, wasn't he? And not one she was convinced she should take.

Logan stared at the door after Thurza closed it. The sound of her soft humming as she travelled through the house distracted him and lifted his mood. The woman, even on a chilly autumn day, evoked an impression of sunshine and joy in the atmosphere.

'She's a lovely woman,' Alfred Blakeman said, studying him carefully.

Uncomfortable with the old man's close attention, Logan refocused on the reason for his visit. With another smile, he suggested, 'How about I give you a quick check-over while I'm here?'

'I suppose you'd better,' Alfred conceded with a sigh. 'It is your job, after all.'

The old man waited for Logan to retrieve his stethoscope from his case and place it on his chest before saying, 'Her father was a good man. Thurza was his only child and he doted on her. They were always close.'

Logan nodded. 'Yes, she mentioned that.'

Alfred continued, 'Thurza was always a sensitive child, and I think his death hit her harder than most people realised. She was only a teenager. At a time in a young person's life when they require the steady hand of their parents, I always think. Her mother leaving and remarrying so soon didn't help.'

'It must have been tough for Thurza,' Logan murmured, only half listening as he concentrated on the sounds in the man's lungs.

'It was. Poor girl withdrew into herself for a long time. Stopped smiling as much as she used to. Of course, that's changed since she had her twin boys. Haven't seen her so happy and contented in years. Have you met them?'

Logan shifted and placed the stethoscope against Alfred's back, glad not to be hearing anything concerning or unanticipated. 'Yes, I have. They're great.'

'I believe Thurza regained what she'd lost when she had those children.'

Intrigued, Logan helped the gentleman sit back against the pillows. 'And what was that?' he asked.

'A family. It's what we all need and hope for, isn't it? If we're really honest with ourselves. We all want a family to fall back on. People around us who care. People who love you and support you. Thurza has her aunt and uncle and her cousin Rachel, of course. But it's not the same as your own close loved ones. I was raised in an orphanage until I was fifteen. Met my darling wife at the age of seventeen and grabbed hold of everything she offered. I may have been young, but I was no nincompoop. Man finds a good woman, he doesn't let her go.'

Logan turned away from the bed with Alfred's words echoing in his ears. *Family.* The very thing he'd recently believed he had, only to have it ripped away until Thurza came back into his life.

'Do you have a family, Logan?' Mr Blakeman asked. 'People dear to you?'

Automatically Logan opened his mouth to mention his brother, when a vision of Axel and Tyler floated into his consciousness. Yes, he did have a family. Those two small boys were his family. No matter what happened in the future, he was their father and always would be.

And Thurza? Was she part of that family? Could they make their situation work not just for a few months but for years? Could they build on their new relationship and continue to share raising their sons, or would time bring complications? What if Thurza met someone and wanted to get married? What would he do then? Where would he fit into that scenario? Would she be so keen to include him then?

The notion of some man living in the cottage with his sons disturbed him. Some faceless male he would end up having to share the boys and Thurza with. A man who would sleep at Thurza's side every night while he lived someplace else, alone and missing his family.

And he would have to witness Thurza's love for the man each time he collected the twins for a weekend visit or day trip.

How would he face that when he was in love with her himself?

In love with Thurza?

Was that true?

Was he guilty of lying to himself for all this time?

Was the real reason he hadn't been able to forget her in all those months more than just infatuation?

Finally finding the courage to face the truth he'd spent so long avoiding, Logan searched his heart. He didn't understand how it had happened, and he had tried to pretend it hadn't, refusing to believe in love at first kiss. He had done his damnedest these last few weeks to prevent it from developing, while continually telling himself it wasn't appropriate or right.

The motive behind his desperation to leave England hadn't been just his broken engagement, but because at some point during that night he had fallen completely and wholly in love, and the strength of those unfamiliar feelings had terrified him. Their evening together hadn't just resulted in the boys. It had also been the night he'd secretly, unknowingly, handed the woman in his bed his whole defenceless heart.

Coming to Dorset and meeting her again, spending time with her, had just confirmed what his scared heart had always known.

He was in love with Thurza Bow and he didn't know what to do.

Now that he'd acknowledged it, he couldn't deny it, or pretend it didn't matter. Because it did.

Remembering where he was, Logan pulled the stethoscope out of his ears and answered the old man's question. 'Yes, sir. I have two young sons.'

'How lovely. What are their ages?' Alfred asked.

Logan dropped the stethoscope into his bag and turned to continue with his examination. 'Just over ten months. They're twins.'

Alfred laughed and slapped the bedcovers. 'What a coincidence. Just like Thurza's.'

'Yes,' Logan said, turning as the woman in question stepped back into the room. 'Just like Thurza's.'

'Have you ever thought about dating?'

Thurza's heart turned over and she stared at Logan, who was wiping potato and mango splodges from Tyler's cheeks. They had just finished eating their evening meal and were in the process of clearing away.

'Er…no,' she said. 'I'm too busy.'

'I don't mean anything heavy,' he went on, giving Tyler's face one last wipe. 'I just wondered if you'd consider going out on the occasional date.'

Thurza spun around and plunged her hands into the bowl of hot washing-up water, glaring at the froth of bubbles as her mind tried to understand why Logan was asking. Why the sudden urge to discuss dating? Was he trying to suss out how she felt about the subject? Perhaps he had met some woman in town and this was his tactless way of letting her know? Hinting around the subject before slamming her with the news.

'Thurza?'

She shook her head and concentrated on her chore. Logan was a single man without any romantic ties. They weren't involved or partners. Who he saw and what he chose to do was none of her business.

Even thinking the words hurt. Struck at her heart like

a brutal weapon intent on imposing agony. Who was this woman he was interested in? Did she know her? Was she suitable dating material? What if it was someone she didn't like? Oh, God, now she was starting to sound like her cousin. But how dared the man enter her life, insert himself into her daily routine, make her weaken and start to like him, only to sniff around some other woman within weeks. It was wrong, embarrassing—and plain hurtful.

'Honestly,' she said, slamming a china bowl down on to the draining board, 'I'd rather learn Italian than date.'

'Really?' Logan asked. 'Well, I can teach you, if you want.'

She glanced over her shoulder at him, not missing his pleased and rather smug grin. Her annoyance hiked up a level. 'You speak Italian?'

'Yes, my mother was Italian. I'll have you fluent in the language of love in no time. We'll need to practise. A lot.'

Confused, Thurza turned back to the sink. He had definitely sounded flirty when he'd said that last part. Or perhaps she was hearing what she hoped to hear.

Remembering his mention of dating, she asked, 'Are you trying to tell me that I'm boring and need to get out more?'

'"Boring" is a word that's impossible to link with you,' he assured her, coming to stand next to her. 'No, I'm simply curious over how you feel about dating.'

She frowned and thumped a plate down next to the bowl. Ignoring the shard of china that flicked off it and wrinkling her nose, she asked, 'Do you have someone in mind.'

'Yes.'

Thurza's heart dropped and she prepared herself not

to be offended by whatever man he cited. No doubt it
would be someone awful. Mouth dry, she waited for
him to continue, already thinking up excuses to reject
this mystery man.

'Me.'

She blinked down at the bowl of water, the degree
of tension consuming her body reducing slightly. She
glanced at him and repeated, 'You?'

'Yes.'

'You think we should date?' she asked, half relieved
and half shocked by what he was suggesting. She
reached for the tea towel on the worktop and dried her
hands. 'You and me?'

He dropped the mango-stained cloth into the sink.
'Yes.'

'As in go out and spend grown-up time together?
Meals, walks, lots of talking and occasional drinking?'

Logan laughed. 'Yes, all those and more.'

She glanced at the babies in their food-splattered
high chairs. 'Aren't we a little advanced for that step?'

He shrugged and reached for the tea towel she still
held. His large hands rested over hers, trapping them in
the cotton folds. 'Does it matter if we manage our relationship in a different sequence to the norm? I think
dating will be good for us. And that surely will benefit the boys.'

She silently considered him, not sure what to say.
Part of her was tempted by the idea. She didn't want to
be too scared to try a relationship, and she was sick with
living in fear of something going wrong—but this was
Logan, and whatever they did would involve their children, who would end up being hurt if it did all go wrong.

'You do?'

'I'd like to give it a go. Unless you think it's a terrible idea.'

'I'm not sure,' she answered, stalling. 'Let's be honest—if you hadn't come to visit your brother and found out about the boys, I'd never have heard from you again.'

'You know that's only because I never read the letters you sent. I would have been on your doorstep a long time ago otherwise.'

Which definitely meant that without the tie of their sons she would never have seen Logan again.

The sensual female inside her raged against the idea that her main attraction was the twins. That Logan viewed her and the boys as a package, and her as a mother rather than a hot-blooded woman with sensual needs…a woman he couldn't live without.

Occasionally she allowed herself to fantasise over what it would be like to be closer to Logan, but the idea of changing their relationship worried her. Right now, they got on. Really well. What if that changed?

Logan shifted closer, as if he could hear her silent debate. 'Truth is, I haven't stopped thinking about you since we parted. You're in my thoughts all the time. Persistent, like a recurring dream. Taunting me with the memory of how good we were together. Night after night while I was in Malta I dreamt about you in the darkest hours and I swear I heard your voice whispering to me.'

Her green eyes wide, she joked, 'You may want to talk to a doctor about that.'

His eyes never shifted from hers as he continued to confess. 'Thurza, I desired more with you long before I learnt about the twins' existence. And since meeting you again, and finding out that I'm their father, I want you even more.'

'How can you be certain that it's not just the boys you want?' she asked. 'That your enjoyment of spending time with them isn't blurring your feelings towards me?'

One of his hands slipped under the material of the tea towel and found hers. 'Trust me, Thurza. I want you every bit as much. What you stir inside me is quite separate to what I feel about the boys. Don't ever doubt that.'

Licking her lips, Thurza stared into his face and faltered at the temptation he was offering with this talk of dating and desire. Should she agree and chance the possibility of heartache if it all went wrong?

Which it probably would. After all, he was Dr Logan Fox. He'd achieved his dream of being a doctor and he'd missed the birth of their sons because he'd been working abroad, helping others. She was a nurse, working two jobs and raising her children single-handed. She came from an ordinary family. She rarely saw her mother, because she couldn't forgive Thurza for staying in Dorset and not relocating to France with her and her new husband.

Would Logan be the same once he grew bored with the town and yearned for more exciting surroundings? Once the novelty of being a father and playing dad wore off, would he leave them? Or was she going to be brave, the way she craved to be, the way Logan made her want to be, and grasp hold of all he proposed and do what her heart urged instead of letting her head take over? The same way she had on that night long ago when he'd asked her to go back to his flat and stay the night.

'Tell me what you want,' Logan coaxed. 'Tell me and I'll do it. Just don't ask me to leave. Because I won't.

Even if you want nothing to do with me, or think us dating is a terrible idea, I refuse to leave the boys.'

'I'm not sure…' she started, uncertain how to explain her remaining reservations. The main one being not wanting to ruin the friendship they now shared.

Logan placed a hand to her face. 'I realise it's a lot to ask, but it's worth considering. All I'm asking for is that you think it over.'

She forced a smile and nodded. She could do that. She was an expert at thinking. Often, she thought so much she felt as though her brain would explode. She would sit down somewhere quiet and go through the pros and cons rationally.

'Okay. I will.'

Logan smiled and stepped away, leaving Thurza suddenly crushed and disappointed in herself. Why didn't she just say yes? Throw her arms around the man's neck and agree to the suggestion? Do a happy dance around the kitchen as a show of delight?

Because, as much as she wanted to be brave and say, *Yes, Logan. Let's date*, she wasn't confident that if it all went wrong she would be able to put all the pieces of herself back together again. Not for a second time, anyway.

CHAPTER ELEVEN

THURZA WASN'T SURE if it was the teddy bear lying in the centre of Logan's chest or the sight of the man stretched out on the floor in the narrow space between the two cots, fast asleep, that melted her heart into a slushy pool.

Standing just outside the twins' bedroom, she silently took in the sweet scene before her, not making a sound in case she woke any of the three occupants inside the room.

She and Logan had spent another pleasant evening together, but by the time the boys had gone to bed it had been late, and a storm had been raging outside, so Thurza had offered Logan the sofa to sleep on rather than get drenched walking home.

The dark shadows in the room suggested the time now must be around six o'clock in the morning. Too early to risk waking the boys after such a long and fitful night.

Normally they stuck to a good routine and she was loath to disrupt it. However, last night both boys had woken in the early hours. First Tyler, disturbed by the wind and rain hitting the bedroom window. He had refused to settle again, preferring to stay awake and be grumpy. Soon after, Axel had joined in the late-night gathering, rousing Logan from his sleep downstairs. At around four o'clock both babies, exhausted from their late-night get-together, had finally fallen back to sleep.

The last thing Thurza recalled was Logan guiding her back to her own room, with a promise to call her if the twins woke again.

A light snore from the male on the floor made Thurza smile. She tugged the scalloped edges of the patchwork throw she'd wrapped around her pyjama-covered body closer together. A nip clung to the air, searching out any gap or nook to fill with its iciness.

She frowned at the half-dressed man before her. Was he cold down there on the floor? Was a draught roaming over his body, ready to leave him stiff and aching to the bones when he eventually woke up?

Silently, she pushed away from the door frame and tiptoed over to where Logan slept. Careful not to bump the cots at her sides, she squeezed into the sliver of a gap and pulled the cover from around her shoulders. Leaning over Logan, she slowly and gently draped it over him.

Starting from his bare feet, moving up his unclothed legs and over his black boxers, she didn't stop until the patchwork cover swathed his T-shirt-clad torso. Letting go of the cover, she stared down at Logan, taking the opportunity to study him.

Oh, the man was utterly delectable. Truly gorgeous. His dark hair was ruffled and sticking up in places. Its untidiness added to his appeal. Despite what she liked to tell him, their night together had been far from disappointing. 'Hot' described it perfectly. Completely satisfying and utterly memorable. Her traitorous body hummed at the memory, but her sensible, cautious mind refused to dwell too long.

A second snore came from Logan, along with a

throaty grunt. Thurza bit her lips to stop a giggle from escaping. Though she had to admit that even the man's snoring was attractive.

Unable to resist the urge, Thurza bent down and fiddled with the top of the blanket, gently tucking it closer around Logan's body. Her fingers itched to reach higher and touch the morning shadow that showed on his cheeks. To skim the pad of her thumb over the rough-looking dark bristles just to experience how they felt.

If she lightly traced the outline of his mouth with her finger, would it feel warm and soft, like a plump cushion? If she leaned over and kissed it would he wake up? Or sleep through it the way he had on that morning months ago when she'd left his flat?

Warmth rushed over her at the thought, and shivers sprinted like silver flashes all over her body. She'd kissed him secretly back then to say goodbye. Now she wanted to kiss him and beg him to stay.

Forcing herself to back away from the temptation Logan's sleeping form provoked, she'd shuffled several inches away when Logan muttered, 'Thank you.'

His deep gravelly tone increased the quivers sparking along her skin. Sexy and sleepy. Delicious. Just like him.

'I'm sorry,' she whispered, inching near again. 'I didn't mean to wake you. I thought you might be cold.'

'Don't be sorry,' he growled. 'You can fuss over me any time you wish. I like it.'

She softened at his sleepy words. She suspected Logan hadn't experienced much fussing in his life. It saddened her to picture him as a child, growing up enjoying few hugs and cuddles. Those were the basics every child deserved from their parents.

'I'm not sure that's a good idea,' she murmured. 'You might get used to it.'

'I'll certainly try.'

She leaned forward, her hair falling around her face. 'Why are you sleeping here? Wouldn't the sofa downstairs be more comfortable?'

'I wanted to be close in case one of the boys woke again. I owe you where sleepless nights are concerned, remember?'

'I guess...' she said, touched that he was willing to let her rest so he could take his turn in caring for the twins. It was a luxury she wasn't used to.

'Besides,' he added, not opening his eyes, though he sent her a sleepy smile, 'no offence, but your sofa is a tad small for me, and after sleeping on Maddox's torturous one this floor is heaven. This is my first decent sleep since arriving in Dorset. My back will be grateful forever.'

'I'm glad,' she said.

Even with the barrier of the blanket between them she could feel the heat rising from his body, calling her own to recline into its comforting warmth and melt into his body.

'Go back to sleep,' she urged. 'It's still early.'

This time she shuffled completely away from the enticement of Logan. Before she gave in and took that forbidden step into the unknown. He might want to try dating, but did he really expect it to lead anywhere? Because Logan might admit to fancying her, but that didn't mean he wanted more. Didn't mean he wanted her and a future.

Despite what he said, if it wasn't for the boys she doubted he would still be in Dorset. He might claim to have thought about her constantly, but he'd stayed away and made no effort to look for her. If it hadn't been for his father dying they would never have met again.

So Logan Fox was a no-go zone. In fact, it would be best from now on to keep her hands off any part of his tantalising body.

'You can stay and share my blanket if you want,' Logan offered. 'I don't mind.'

Thurza licked her lips at the notion of resting into his body while the comforting weight of his arm encircled her back. While his naked muscular thighs pressed and moulded to her own softer clothed curves. She'd be wrapped around him like a human vine. Supported in his protective and wonderful embrace. Nice… Very nice to imagine. But far too dangerous to try.

Resisting every impulse silently beseeching her to push sensibility away and accept his wicked and tantalising offer, she continued to withdraw. She might long for Logan Fox, but she required serious commitment from a man. Would he be willing to offer her that or was dating all that was on offer?

'We don't have that sort of relationship,' she reminded him from the doorway.

Logan smiled and then sighed. 'A man can always hope for the impossible, though, can't he?'

Hope.

An innocent four-letter word, yet sometimes impossible. An impossible expectation or optimism for something a person longed for or aspired to.

Listening to her close her bedroom door, further down the hall, Logan silently acknowledged that it described exactly how he felt every time he spent time with Thurza. Nothing else counted but the woman in his company and his happiness at just being with her.

He rolled on to his side with another heavy sigh. That cliché about a person taking another person's breath away expressed totally how she left him. Breathless and aching—not just physically, but with a stronger, deeper and more spiritual hunger. As though their connection was more intense than anything he'd felt before.

This gorgeous woman lit him up and left him whole and contented. She gave him hope again. Real hope that wasn't stained with the blackness of deceptions and lies but held a simple, clean and amazing honesty.

She'd helped him to believe in the future once more. Despite their shaky start, he now regarded the upcoming days, weeks and years of raising their children with enthusiasm and optimism. Things he'd not felt in such a long time. For years all his life had entailed was work and further work. Now it centred around an incredible woman and two amazing boys.

After Victor's death and betrayal he'd imagined that the anger that had first consumed him would grow and expand, but instead a heavy and weighty numbness had settled in its place. Everything he'd trusted and thought true in his life had been wiped out without warning by a single letter. The good and bad memories, the infrequent family gatherings—all of it ruined and defiled by an old man who hadn't been able to find it in his heart to take some of the blame for his wife's infidelity. Who'd refused to bestow forgiveness upon a dead woman. His mother, whose memory Victor's hate and bitterness had tarnished forever for Logan.

He pulled the blanket surrounding him higher, sinking his nose into the soft, comforting fabric. Thurza's scent instantly filled his nostrils. The aroma was soothing to his serious reflections. He would never understand Victor's actions, but the pain wasn't as strong any more.

So, yes, he had hope. Only this time he wasn't going to allow anyone or anything to rob him of it. To steal away the thrilling expectancy building in his gut. Thurza was his and he was hers. And somehow he was going to convince her to give him a chance to prove it.

Because he loved the woman—he just didn't know how to tell her so.

Logan set Axel down in the sandpit and then placed Tyler on the grass. With two babies' needs to be concerned with, he had learnt to keep them both near, as they generally chose to do everything ten-month-olds shouldn't at precisely the same time.

Straightening, he glanced at the cottage and the left-hand upstairs window. Thurza still slept, but when the twins had woken he'd left his makeshift bed on the boys' bedroom floor and carried them downstairs for breakfast. That had consisted of two jars of pre-prepared food he'd found in a cupboard. He figured it wasn't often that they ate roast chicken and apple sauce for breakfast, but neither child had complained.

Checking that both twins played happily in their separate areas, Logan sat on the garden seat and flicked through his phone messages. Most related to work, except for one from Maddox, demanding an update on his whereabouts. Logan smiled at his brother's belated attempt at the caring older sibling role. It was years too late, but weirdly he appreciated the sentiment.

With another glance at the twins, he answered a text from a former work colleague asking if he was interested in a position overseas. Did he want to go abroad again? Would Thurza prefer him as a part-time father?

He glanced at the boys, his heart wrenching at the thought of leaving them. He didn't want to go anywhere.

Every day the boys changed and learnt new things, and he didn't want to miss out on any of it. Yes, he could fly back to England regularly, but he'd still be a stranger who popped in and out of their lives.

And what about Thurza? They were slowly finding level ground in their dealings with each other. Progressing from ex-lovers to something deeper than friends. They'd talked of dating. Thurza had agreed to consider it. If he left, they would need to repeat the process of getting closer every time he returned. No, he wanted to stay with Thurza and the boys permanently. How could he romance the woman if they were in different countries?

His thumb hovered over his reply before he finally pressed Send. The second it went, a new calmness settled through him. No regrets whispered in his ear. No indecision or doubts. One decision made and many more left to work through, but together he and Thurza would do it.

The sound of a strangled gasp jerked Logan from his musings. Flicking his gaze first to Axel and then to Tyler, he felt cold fear wash over him as he took in his small son's pale face and faintly blue lips.

Shooting off the seat, Logan swooped Tyler into his arms. His brain sprinted through a series of medical checks, before landing on the frightening conclusion that his boy was choking.

Flipping Tyler over to rest along his arm, so that his hand could support his head, Logan let his medical training take over, despite the petrified new parent side of him fighting to take control.

He slapped the heel of his hand down in the centre of Tyler's back, then repeated the action an extra four times. Turning Tyler over on to his back, Logan checked his son's mouth with his fingertips, flipping the baby back over when he failed to find any obstruction.

Silently counting, Logan slapped his hand down once again on his son's back. Biting back the cold fear attempting to push in, he forced his mind to focus. Repeating another set of four blows, Logan almost cheered when whatever had been blocking his son's windpipe was finally dislodged and flew out of his mouth.

Swinging Tyler upwards, Logan checked his mouth, breathing and colour, before hugging his small precious body to his chest. A mixture of fear, shock and relief sent him to his knees, still clutching his treasured baby to him.

'Thank God… You're okay…' Softly murmuring comforting words in his son's ear, he swallowed the jagged, smothering lump in his own throat, and gasped, 'It's okay, darling. It's okay, little man. Daddy's got you.'

'Logan?'

Glancing up, he found Thurza at his side. Dressed in her dressing gown, hair damp from a shower, she crouched beside him and wrapped her arms around them both. Her green eyes were full of concern.

'Is he all right? My God, when I stepped outside and saw you slap him…'

'He was choking…'

God, what must she have thought? Had she thought he was harming Tyler?

Thurza checked Tyler over, reassuring herself that he was okay and kissing him before stroking Logan's face with shaky fingers. 'I know you would never hurt him. I realised something was wrong by the way you held him.'

'We could have lost him,' Logan declared, the fearful words that had been crammed inside his head tumbling from his mouth as Thurza went to pick up Axel from the sandpit.

Why hadn't he watched Tyler better? Why had he allowed thoughts of work and Thurza to hold his attention instead of making certain his baby was safe? This was all his fault. *His.* What kind of parent was he that he couldn't keep his mind on his child and the possible dangers surrounding him? A terrible one—that was what he was. One who had no right to look after his children or any children.

Shaking, he turned to Thurza. 'Dear God, he might have di—'

'Don't!' Thurza begged. 'Please, don't say it. You saved him. It's over. It's done.'

Done? It didn't feel done. The terror in his chest still compressed his heart and shook every part of his body. Tyler was crying right now in his arms because he'd neglected to keep him safe.

'It's my fault. If I'd concentrated on the boys and not my phone I would have seen him put it in his... He never would have... I—' He sucked in a wavering breath, shaking his head, barely able to speak as the cold reality of what might have happened poured through him once again. Because of his selfish neglect and distraction his child might have choked. 'God, if I'd never heard him gasp and looked up—'

'Stop it!' Thurza scolded. 'Things like this happen, Logan. We both know that.'

'Yes, but I should have—'

'No more,' she insisted. 'What was it, anyway? Did you see?'

He shook his head and clutched Tyler closer, needing the comforting reassurance of his small form close.

Needing to hear his son's loud crying and feel the warm, regular temperature of his skin.

'I'm not sure. A stone?'

Thurza kissed Axel's head before searching the grass for the hateful item. Bending, she frowned. 'Ugh... gross, Tyler.'

Holding out her palm, she showed Logan a saliva-covered snail's shell.

'Maybe wait until you're older before you start trying foreign delicacies—hey, sweetheart?'

'A snail?' Logan stroked a hand over Tyler's head. 'He must have found it in the grass.'

Thurza inspected it more closely. 'Thankfully, it's just the shell. Mr Snail might have received a nasty shock and an unexpected wash if not.'

Tyler tried to seize the shell back, but Thurza closed her fingers over it and moved her hand out of grabbing distance. 'Let's get you a drink to wash your mouth out.'

'A snail...' Logan repeated, still feeling sick to his stomach as his heart rate slowly returned to its normal beat.

His son had tried to swallow a snail. A snail's shell could have destroyed their family and broken their lives forever. Robbed Axel of his brother and twin, leaving him feeling incomplete forever. Stolen from Thurza the child she adored and loved. Ripped his son away when Logan had only just found him.

'It could have shattered and cut his throat. What if—'

Thurza stroked his arm and pleaded, 'Don't do this. It's over. Those things did not happen. You stopped it from developing into something worse. You're a doctor. It's what you do. You're also a father, and I know you'll always protect the boys. Logan, your quick thinking saved our son. Let's just be thankful and count our blessings.'

'This time.'

He sighed, dark thoughts flooding in and replacing his initial distress. Pushing out all reason and sense. This time he had saved his child, but what if another incident happened, thanks to his lack of adequate care and concentration? What if next time the situation was worse and he didn't react quickly enough? What if he was too late or didn't see the danger…?

A new wave of nausea rose up and burnt his throat. He gasped. 'But what if next time—'

'You can't think like that,' she dismissed crossly. 'None of us can. We're parents, not psychics. We can protect our children as much as possible from hurt and harm, but we're also human, and occasionally things occur no matter how careful we are. Say a prayer of thanks and let it go. The same way you do when it's a patient you've saved.'

'But he's not a patient.' Logan shook his head, still too shaken to listen to her practical reasoning. Tilting his face to Tyler's, he inhaled his soothing baby scent. 'He's my child, Thurza. I should have done better.'

'You did what we all do, Logan. Your best. You're not to blame for the fact that our son has a curious mind and likes to put everything in his mouth.'

Logan slowly headed into the house, with Thurza and Axel following behind. She put Axel in the play-pen and he handed Tyler over to her and stepped away from them both.

Everything Thurza had said made sense, but he couldn't get the sight of Tyler choking out of his head… his blue lips and the sound of his gasping breath as he'd struggled for life. Although in real time it had played out in only seconds, in his head it ran at a slower speed, over and over again, his memory seeing it all on gut-wrenching repeat.

Stomach rolling again, and unable to deal with logic thanks to the swirl of emotions still seizing every part of him, Logan continued to back away. A few seconds' delay and the outcome would have been different. Tragedy had been just seconds away from occurring. And if it had Thurza wouldn't be thanking him. She would be shouting at him for his negligence. Hating him for failing their son. And she would be right.

It was all his fault. No one else's. He wasn't fit to be a father. No more than his own fathers had been. Wasn't it better to leave now, before his sons were seriously hurt? Before he ruined their lives and the safety Thurza had worked so hard to give them? They deserved better than a careless father.

Shaking his head, he stammered, 'I—I need to leave.'

'Please, Logan, don't,' Thurza begged. 'Please, stay and—'

He didn't trust himself around this astonishing woman and their beloved two boys any longer. 'I'm sorry, but I need to go. I'm sorry…'

He stumbled away and left the house, shutting out the cries of each boy and Thurza's continued appeals to stay. He needed to think…to process everything. One second was all it took. One stupid moment was all it required to lose a child forever. Was this a sign that he wasn't cut out to be a parent? One he shouldn't ignore? Would his new family be safer without him in their lives?

Thurza pushed the double pushchair along the lane towards the beach. It was the one place she had yet to search. If she didn't find Logan soon she would have to give up and return home. The boys were due a feed and the weather had turned cold and misty.

Rolling off the pavement and on to the promenade, she scanned the area for the sight of a familiar male. The man who had left her house several hours ago, upset and full of needless remorse and guilt.

In the distance, despite the mist coming in off the sea, Thurza could just make out the end of the Victorian pier on the east side of the beach. At this time of year the council closed it to the public to save money, so it stood abandoned, with neither visitors nor local fishermen.

Other than seagulls and a lone weathered wooden boat, long abandoned by its owner, nothing littered this stretch of shore.

Her gaze shifted to the sea and then back to the pebbled beach. Having already checked Maddox's farm and the doctors' surgery, on the off-chance that Logan might have gone to either, she found her list of possible places to search shrinking. The man was more elusive than a ghost during daylight hours. She understood his need to be alone after the incident with Tyler and the snail, but the way Logan had left, and the state he'd been in, worried her.

She completely understood his reaction. Their jobs involved caring for strangers, but when your own loved one needed care the balance tilted into uncomfortable and unfamiliar territory. Just because they were medically trained, it didn't mean that when faced with a critical situation involving the life of their own child it didn't reduce them to feeling the same terrifying alarm any other parent would experience.

But the expert way Logan had dislodged the snail shell and then comforted their frightened, crying son sent goosebumps of pride and fear all over Thurza each time she recalled it. The moment he'd hugged Tyler with relief, before the self-recrimination had taken hold, would stay with her forever. That display of love for his child had been stronger than any words or deed. That act of love had given her the courage to make a decision of her own that would affect all their futures.

The man believed he'd failed their child, whereas she viewed him as a hero. *Their* hero. Hers and the boys'.

She hated the idea of Logan beating himself up over what happened. She ached to comfort him the same way he had her at the park. He hadn't criticised her or pushed her to make a decision over the promise to her father. Hadn't called her a coward when she'd admitted her own fears. No, he'd held her and let her know he understood. And now she wanted... Well, she wanted to ease his distress and help him in every possible way.

She'd loved their playful conversation that morning. His dubious offer to share the patchwork throw and snuggle into him had lifted her heart like a butterfly hovering in the air, leaving her deliberating over whether taking a chance on a real relationship with Logan would be worth the gamble.

But deep down she already knew the answer. A relationship required more than just sex to grow strong and solid. It required time, friendship, common interests and...love.

Love.

Yes, she'd dilly-dallied over accepting how she really felt. But after the incident with the snail's shell she'd finally opened her heart and searched its depths and accepted the truth in all its glorious colours. The truth that made her yearn to shout with joy.

She loved Logan. Not because of the boys, but because of him. Everything felt right whenever he was close. She was ready to accept his offer to date and to leave the future to unfold itself without worrying over how it would end.

But did Logan still want her?

Oh, he'd accepted his children, and his affection and love for them was obvious, but what about her? Did he still want them to date? Or had this morning's events scared him off? Had his concern over his so-called inability to protect his children changed his mind? Did he want them to be a family? A real one? Did he want her?

Perhaps he intended to return to work overseas and become a now-and-then father after all. One who sent postcards and letters and visited on holidays and birthdays. The 'guilt days', as she tended to think of them. Like her own mother after she'd married her second husband. Dutiful visits carried out mainly to ease her conscience.

Would the episode with the snail send Logan back to Malta? Back to his life as a single man, without responsibilities to a family he had never intended to form?

Thurza's footsteps slowed as she recognised the male figure alone on a bench several feet away. *Thank goodness.* Pushing the buggy towards Logan, she didn't stop until she reached the other end of the bench. Parking the boys between them, she took a seat and stared out at the sea. Though not much of it was visible thanks to the mist.

'Thurza…' Logan began, but she shook her head to stop him. He could talk after she'd said what she'd come here to say.

'I'd really appreciate it if you'd let me speak first,' she said, still not looking his way, finding it easier to speak without facing him. If he did plan to leave, she didn't want to see it on his face—not before she'd said her words.

He shifted on the bench but stayed silent. The lapping of the waves against the pebbled shore was the only sound in the air.

'I would have loved having you at my side during my pregnancy. Even just as a co-parent and nothing else. I felt so alone and uncertain about how I was going to cope with everything. From the birth, to caring for the boys and earning enough money to keep us.'

'I know. I wish I had been here,' he murmured.

She nodded and continued, 'When I first took the twins home I was terrified. A nurse, with all my training and knowledge, frightened by the reality that I was solely in charge of these two very small and vulnerable babies. Their little bodies seemed so small and delicate... And then they liked to wake at the same time and be fed at the same time. They also cried together, and I swear they did it just to see who could scream the loudest. Long, tiresome nights...but I dealt with every single one and managed to get through each day. Honestly, I'm not sure how. Rachel stepped in so I could grab extra sleep. She's so good to me, and she helps with the twins when I work, but honestly it's not the same as being able to turn to someone special...someone close who is there in the middle of the night and prepared to jump in when I need an extra hand or a moment just to take a breath. Like you did last night, Logan.'

She sensed him shift again, but he didn't speak. He was giving her the time she'd asked for to say what she needed to.

'Over the last few weeks,' she continued, 'you've helped me, and I am grateful. But it's also made me realise how much I like having you around. I enjoy your company, Logan. Very much.'

'I like being with you, too,' he admitted.

Finally, she turned to him, taking in the stress etched across his features. Licking the mist from her lips, she said, 'What happened earlier was just one of those things. It's life. It's being a parent. You're a human being, not a superhero. Though to me you come pretty close. But you have to stop expecting to be a perfect parent, because they don't exist. Every single parent is just doing the best they can. Babies are quick, and curious, and they will do things that scare us. That will continue as they get older, and all we can do is stand to one side and try to stop the situation from becoming scary while allowing our children to learn how to be independent.'

Logan sighed heavily. 'I know you're right. It's just…'

She slid closer to him, smiling as she reached for his cold hand, hopeful that he wasn't going to leave. *Please, don't let him leave.*

Wrapping her fingers around his chilled skin, she said, 'I know. It's hard to admit that we can't always be in control of life. It's similar to how I feel about volunteering for the lifeboat. It's the fear of the unknown. And instead of facing it I've permitted it to become a huge blot in my life, to the point where it has grown and grown until it's controlled me. But you'll be happy to hear I've made a decision.'

'And…?'

Hesitantly, she took an envelope from her coat pocket and showed him the address written on the front. 'I've filled out an application form. All I have to do is post it.'

Logan squeezed her hand, the action both supportive

and reassuring. She'd decided it was time to stop faffing around and letting fear dictate her life. She would send the form. And if she made it through the training and was offered a position on the team then it would be for *her*. Not because of a promise to her father, and not because of guilt. But because she was Thurza Bow and she wanted to do her turn for her family. Because she refused to let fear dictate her actions and her life.

She looked up at Logan and said, 'And if they accept me...'

'Then you'll take it,' he said instantly. 'Worry less about what you can't control. You need to do this. Until you do, I don't think you'll ever be able to let the past rest. Grieving is natural, but yours is mingled with remorse, and I'm certain your father wouldn't have wanted that.'

'What if one day I go out into a storm and the rescue goes wrong, the way it did with my dad, and I never come home again. What about the twins?' She glanced at the man beside her. *What about you? Will your heart grieve for me? Will you step in and raise our babies alone?*

'Like I said—stop fretting. It's useless to try and second-guess what tomorrow has planned. I'm here for the boys forever—you know that, don't you?'

Deep down, she did—though she still couldn't ignore that he'd only mentioned the twins and not her. 'Yes.'

'I think the question is whether you're ready to send that form. Ask yourself what you want, Thurza. Deep in your heart, what do *you* want? Yes, things may go wrong, but we can say that about all situations in life. A person can start a normal day that within a few hours can change them forever. As a nurse, you're aware of that as much as I am.' He gave a wry laugh and shook his head. 'Tyler's antics this morning demonstrated that perfectly, didn't they?'

'It was the prod I needed to make my decision.' She stared at him, searching his face, and asked, 'Are you all right now?'

He nodded. 'Yeah, sitting here has helped to put everything into perspective. I'm sorry if I upset you by rushing off the way I did.'

Reaching into her pocket again, she dismissed his concern, relieved that he wasn't planning on leaving them. Silently, she handed him a scrap of paper and waited while he unfolded it and read the telephone number written across it.

'What's this?' he asked, confused.

'It's the number for the local registrar's office. I thought we could ring them and enquire about adding your name to the boys' birth certificates.'

Tears entered Logan's eyes and he glanced at the number on the piece of paper again. With a cough, he asked, 'You're happy to do that? I mean, it's what you want?'

She smiled and nodded. 'It is. It's only right that your name is on the documents along with mine. We're both Tyler and Axel's parents, after all.'

'We are.'

She met his gaze again, sucking in a quick breath at the tenderness and happiness shining in the blue depths. The anxiety and guilt of that morning were nothing but an ugly memory.

'Can I kiss you, Thurza?' Logan asked seriously.

Her eyes widened at the question. Her heart still fluttering at the sight of the emotions in his gaze, she tilted her head to one side. 'Are you propositioning me on the promenade, Dr Fox?'

A rakish grin tilted his mouth. 'Yes, I think I am.'

'Then you'd best get on with it. I need to get going and send off my application.'

He laughed, and on the misty, deserted beach, in front of a lone squawking seagull and not much else, he kissed her.

And then, to Thurza's absolute delight, he kissed her some more.

CHAPTER TWELVE

SEVENTEEN TIMES HE'D tried to talk to her. Seventeen. He knew the exact number because he'd counted each and every attempt. Logan gripped his bottle of beer and watched the woman people insisted on speaking to lift yet another large pumpkin off the ground and into a mud-coated wheelbarrow.

In a fit of genius, Maddox had invited all his friends and neighbours over to the farm to help gather in his vast pumpkin and squash crop. In return he'd handed out mugs of tomato soup, foil-wrapped cheese-sprinkled baked potatoes, cooked in his outdoor brick oven, and sparkler fireworks.

And it seemed as though every person who'd turned up to help wanted to speak to Thurza at exactly the same time Logan did. Every single one.

Taking a swig from the bottle, he sighed as yet another person sought out the woman who distorted every sane thought and emotion in his head. Thurza, whose letters, written and posted long ago, he'd finally read after he'd asked his cleaner to pack them all into an envelope and forward them to him.

The letters had broken his heart on reading them, and left him once again wishing the past could be rewound.

Those words on floral lined paper had started off

apologetic and embarrassed in tone, as she'd politely informed him that she was pregnant with his child. Later the letters had become chattier, as she'd recounted the various stages of her pregnancy and her shock and excitement at discovering she was carrying twins. In one letter she'd even included the time and place of a scan, in case he wanted to join her at the appointment.

Unsurprisingly, the last few letters had turned cold and crisp, matter-of-fact in manner, as she'd accepted his lack of interest and promised not to bother him again. Her disappointment in him pulsed from every word and pen stroke on the page.

But the letters, although despondent, had given him faith in their future. And renewed his hope.

With a heavy sigh, he took another gulp of his beer, softly growling when yet another person called out to Thurza.

Perhaps if he dragged her into the farmhouse and up to the bathroom he could lock the door and barricade them inside by stacking towels and the large clothes basket against it. Then he might finally get the opportunity to say the words that rambled through his mind. The words keeping him awake at night and thoughtful all day. Words he was half terrified to say out loud and half dreaded her reaction to. But he knew deep inside that it was time for them to be said.

Since their heart-to-heart on the promenade he'd practised, rehearsed and edited the declaration bubbling and vibrating in his heart. Shifting and sorting his thoughts and feelings into a comprehensive pronouncement until he knew it by memory. With one chance of getting this right, and hopefully getting the result he desired, the pressure increased with each passing day he kept his thoughts to himself.

'But what if she says no?' he muttered softly. What would he do then to convince her that they should be a family in the true sense? That they belonged together.

'Why would she?' Maddox demanded at his side.

Logan jumped, not realising his brother stood nearby. His already stretched nerves increased with his sibling's company. 'How long have you been there?'

'Long enough for my stomach to turn at the soppy way you're staring at the woman,' Maddox complained. 'Look, you're perfect together. Like bread and butter. Cheese and chocolate. Just stop with the mooning expressions, will you?'

'But does she feel the same way?' Logan muttered.

Maddox shrugged and tugged off his worn leather gardening gloves. 'Too much deep thinking for me, bro. But she must do, seeing as she gave birth to your children. The only way to get an answer to that question is to ask. Now, stop staring at Thurza like a lovesick moron—you're scaring the children and it's embarrassing, watching you pining. Do I need to drag you over to her like an embarrassed teenager with his first serious case of the hots?'

Logan huffed and shook his head as yet another person stopped to speak to Thurza. 'There's no point. I can't get a chance to talk to her alone with everyone else determined to beat me to it.'

'Well, in that case,' Maddox said, placing his arm around Logan's shoulders and giving him a hard squeeze, 'let me make a suggestion—'

'No!' Whatever his brother was going to suggest

he'd ignore. He could mess up his life without Maddox's help.

Maddox squeezed him harder. 'Trust me, will you?'

'Why should I?' Logan asked, already certain that whatever Maddox proposed to do would be a disaster. Relationship advice and his brother did not go together.

Maddox grinned. The light of mischief in his eyes was almost frightening. 'Because I'm your big brother and I always triumph with the ladies.'

Logan snorted. 'You're lying.'

Maddox chuckled. 'Like I said...just trust me.'

Logan wasn't sure he could, but right at that minute he was a desperate man.

'Sorry to interrupt, but I need you.'

Logan smiled politely at the older lady talking to Thurza, before slipping an arm around the woman he loved and guiding her away from the squash-gathering throng and over to a dark corner of the pumpkin field.

'Is something wrong with the boys?' Thurza asked, concerned. 'I thought Rachel—'

'The boys are fine,' Logan soothed. 'But I am not.'

'Is Rachel still glaring at you?' Thurza asked, concerned. 'Because if she is I'll talk to h—'

Logan laughed. 'No, she has turned her attention to finding ways to keep the boys from Maddox. Apparently, the idea of having to share them with an uncle is too much for her to absorb.'

'So why do you need me?' Thurza quizzed.

Logan drew in a deep breath, grasping the opportunity to finally talk to Thurza. But saying the words now he had her attention wasn't going to be easy. 'It's my chest.'

'You're feeling ill?' she asked with a concerned frown. 'Why didn't you say so? Doctors make the worst patients.'

'No, I mean it's my heart,' Logan stated, tugging her towards a bulldozer.

Its large bucket was raised a foot off the ground, and several thick padded cushions she recognised from the garden chairs scattered around the property rested inside, forming a makeshift seat.

'Your heart?' Thurza repeated.

'Yes,' Logan said, pulling her down on to the cushions. 'Let me show you.'

'What are you doing?' she asked, as the bulldozer's engine suddenly roared to life.

A second later Logan's arms slid around her waist and he yelled, 'Take her up!'

'Logan!' Thurza grabbed hold of his jumper and clung to him as the bulldozer's bucket slowly started to rise into the air.

He grinned at her startled expression and leaned back, happy to protect her. 'I'll stop you from falling. Rest into me and I'll keep you safe.'

'Why is this thing moving?' she demanded, closing her eyes when the top of a nearby tree came into view. 'I'm not sure I like it.'

'Imagine you're on a fairground ride. Don't worry— we're not going anywhere. I would simply like to talk to you without everyone interrupting us.'

Concern wrinkled her brow. 'You want to talk?'

'Yes,' he said, trying to recall exactly what he wanted to say. His stupid brain had frozen and stolen the words away. Instead, he said, 'Stop it.'

Confused, she stared at him. 'What? I'm waiting for you to speak. You're the one who wants to talk.'

'I know, but you staring at me with those big green eyes just makes me want to kiss you.'

She smiled and glanced away. 'You're a man with a weakness for kisses, aren't you?'

'Only yours,' he said. 'They're perfect and sweet-tasting.'

'Thank you,' she said, glancing back at him. 'Now, confess—what's wrong with your heart?'

'You,' he stated.

'Me?' she repeated, raising both her eyebrows in surprise.

'And the boys,' he added, not forgetting the other two most important people in his life. The sons who for a while he hadn't known, but who now filled his days.

'The boys?' she repeated slowly. 'And me?'

He nodded. 'Me, too.'

She laughed and shook her head. 'All four of us, then?'

'Yes,' he said, then sighed and dropped his head on to her shoulder, breathing deeply as his mind struggled to find the right words. The ones he'd so carefully composed. 'I'm messing this up, aren't I?'

She giggled. 'I'm not sure what "this" is, so I can't say. I *am* confused, though.'

He lifted his head and stared into her eyes. 'All right, here goes. Thurza Bow, you are an amazing woman and a fantastic mother. If I searched all over the world I'd never find anyone like you. You are uniquely magnificent.'

She waited for him to continue. The lowering darkness and the shadows around them made the moment extra intimate. Up here, away from the people on the ground, it was just the two of them.

'You're delightful,' he said.

'Like my kisses?' she teased shyly.

'Precisely.' He nodded. 'And I think... No... I *know* that I love...'

'Love?' she whispered.

He took the surprise on her face as a good omen and pushed on. 'I love having you in my life. You and the boys are a gift, and I want to ask…'

'Yes?'

He reached out for her hand and rested it against his chest. The heat from her palm radiated through his green jumper to warm his heart. An organ that had always functioned well enough, but until he'd met Thurza hadn't known what true passion and affection felt like.

'Can you feel my heart, beating like a runner's during a race?'

She nodded, spreading her fingers out where they lay on his chest.

'This is what you do to me, Thurza. You make me nervous and excited and desperate to be with you. I've never experienced these emotions before. With you I don't think or plan. I just feel. You make me want a future—one with you and the boys. One where we're a real family. The four of us and any other children who may or may not arrive. Thurza, I love you, and I want to make it official. I want to be in your life from this day until my last. I yearn to sit with you on your garden seat and watch our children grow. I want to watch you smile first thing in the morning and to kiss your sweet lips late at night. I want to sing to you on your birthday and present you with ridiculous anniversary gifts that make no sense to anyone but us. I want to be your—'

'I want to hold your hand the first day our boys go to school and cry on your shoulder as they wave goodbye,' Thurza said, taking over from him. 'To peel mountains of vegetables with you on Christmas morning and then collapse on the sofa together and sleep the afternoon away. To cry at your side when the days are tough and laugh on happier ones. But mostly I want to be your—'

'Husband.'

'Wife.' She finished a second after him.

'How's it going up there? Do you want to come down yet?'

Logan grimaced at his brother's untimely interruption. Without pause, he shouted, 'No! Go away!'

'We're getting married!' Thurza called out laughingly, desperate to yell the news to the world.

He loved her. He'd said the words and her heart knew he meant them. Just as she did. No more worrying over whether to take a chance on a relationship. They were already in one. The day he had demanded to know if her sons were his, their destiny had been set.

'Are you sure you don't want me to lower the bucket?' Maddox yelled up.

'No!' she answered. 'There's things we still need to discuss.'

Logan's happy expression dimmed at her comment, and a worried frown creased his forehead. 'Such as…?'

Shuffling closer, she gently grabbed the sides of his face and said, 'I think we should practise our kisses. It requires a lot of work to maintain such an important skill.'

Eyes shining with happiness, he grinned. 'I agree.'

Moving nearer, she whispered, 'Kiss me, Logan Fox. Kiss me until we hit the stars above us and bang our heads on the moon. Let's go for a whirl around the Milky Way, and Venus, too.'

'Why not?' he agreed. 'I already feel like I'm in the heavens whenever I'm with you.'

* * *

Without another word, he did as she'd asked, happy to take orders if it meant kissing this beautiful, sweet woman, because he loved her. Truly and completely. Forever.

And this time he wasn't running away because he was scared of the feelings she awakened inside him. He intended to stay and enjoy them all.

EPILOGUE

THURZA LET OUT a relieved breath as they finally located the surfer, desperately clinging to his surfboard in the grim swirling sea. After bumping over the waves for ten minutes without any sign of the teenager, she'd started to worry they were too late.

Wiping the rain out of her eyes, she pushed back the strands of hair stuck to her cheeks and leaned over the side as her boss carefully manoeuvred the lifeboat closer to the surfer.

'It's okay!' she called out to the exhausted boy, still clutching his board. His fingers and knuckles were white with fear and the cold. 'We've got you now.'

'I'm so sorry...' the teenager gasped out. Seawater splashed into his face as he struggled to hold on.

Thurza leaned forward and slipped her arm under the teenager's armpit. With the help of a colleague, she pulled the surfer out of the water and into the lifeboat. A second later his board joined him.

'It's our job and we love doing it.'

'Thank you,' the surfer said. 'The weather changed so quickly.'

Thurza nodded and glanced up at the heavy sky. Not great weather for much, but to her the rain didn't matter, because the day was already perfect.

'Your mum contacted the station when you didn't arrive back on the beach at the time you'd agreed. You're safe now.'

'Th-thank you,' the boy stammered, just as a large wave hit the side of the boat, spraying them with water.

Thurza grinned and wrapped a blanket around the teenager. 'Best hold on. The way my boss drives this boat, the ride back may be a little rough and hairy.'

'I heard that,' her boss complained from where he steered the boat. 'Best we get back quick—in case Logan decides to leg it.'

Thurza laughed and shook her head, confident that her man was going to be exactly where she'd left him.

Returning her attention to the teenager, she crouched at his side and said, 'Congratulations. You're officially my fifth rescue.'

'Really?' the teenager asked.

Thurza nodded.

With Logan's support, she'd crushed her fears and was now a member of the town's lifeboat team. She loved the job and, although keeping the promise to her father was important, she had fulfilled her own dream.

Her colleague Fred pointed to the beach. 'Someone's keen.'

Thurza twisted round and searched the shore until she found Logan, her husband of less than two hours, patiently waiting, holding a twin in each arm. Dressed in a black tux and a sky blue shirt, Logan defined the word 'sexy'. The man owned his style and confidence, and his understanding smile as the boat returned to the station just topped off his gorgeousness.

She loved him. He and their sons were the reason she woke every morning and said thanks to the universe before she closed her eyes every night.

Climbing out of the boat, still in her all-weather gear, she waved to the other crew members and headed over to Logan. 'I'm so sorry.'

'Don't apologise,' Logan said. 'You stayed long enough to say *I do*. I asked for no more. It's legal and there's no backing out, Mrs Fox. You're finally my wife.'

An emergency call had come in seconds after the vicar had pronounced them husband and wife. A surfer in difficulty. And, as the newest member of the life-boat team, Thurza had kissed Logan at the altar and then rushed off with several of their guests, still wearing her ivory wedding dress—which she now needed to change back into.

Logan handed over Axel, and then pulled Thurza close against him, circling his now free arm around her waist, not the slightest bit concerned about getting his clothes wet.

Her waist was slowly thickening, thanks to their new baby growing inside her. Soon their group of four would become five, and their happiness and excitement grew with each day. This time Logan would experience the pregnancy with her. This time he would be an involved expectant dad.

In the last few months their lives had changed in several ways. They'd moved into a new home and Logan had become a partner at the surgery where they both worked. Every plan they made concerned their long-term future. One they intended to share together. After so much time apart, fate had brought them back together, and they were determined to relish every precious moment.

'Have I told you how beautiful you are?' Logan asked.

Smiling brightly, she nodded. 'Yes—just before I rushed off and left you at the altar.'

'You returned, though.'

She brushed a hand over his cheek. 'I'll always come back to you, Logan,' she promised. 'You and the boys are home to me.'

He kissed her then, and the wolf whistles from her colleagues already on their way back to the reception and the meal that waited for them all didn't stop them from showing how much love flowed in their hearts.

Somehow, despite everything, fate had chosen to lead them back to each other, and this time they were going to stay together and make it work. Together as a family. Together as lovers. Together for always.

'Let's go and rejoin our guests. We've a married life to start enjoying.'

She smiled and kissed him once again, her heart full of love for the man who held her and for the two small boys resting on their hips. 'You say the best things, husband. You really do.'

* * * * *

FALLING FOR HIS
RUNAWAY NURSE

AMY RUTTAN

MILLS & BOON

In memory of my mother-in-law
and her dream trip to Alaska.

We miss you, Barb.

CHAPTER ONE

"WELL, WE DO need a nurse…"

Lacey smiled and nodded. She knew that the recruitment officer was staring at her—not that she really could blame her—but tried to stay positive. It was a bit of an odd situation, even for her. Well, it was completely odd to her. Lacey didn't particularly like taking risks. She didn't like change or waste.

Things usually ran smoothly in her life, especially when it came to her career.

She planned everything she could.

Like her wedding and that expensive cake that she had shelled out for.

What a waste.

She didn't even get to taste it.

That's because you ran out on your wedding.

Lacey shook that thought away and smiled brightly, smoothing out the tulle on her dress. Not that smoothing it over would diminish its volume, but the sensation of running her hands over the fabric calmed her and stopped her leg from nervously tapping under the table.

"I know my dress is a bit of a surprise."

The human resources woman pushed her glasses back up the bridge of her nose and smiled politely. "You can call me Deb and, I'll be honest, it *is* unusual. After all, it's not often that we have candidates come to an interview in a wedding dress."

Lacey blushed. "It's a long story. I was in something of a hurry to get here."

That was an understatement. When she had walked in on her fiancé in a compromising position with her maid of honor, she had needed to make a run for it.

So she did. She bolted, completely unprepared for what came next, which was so unlike her.

"I can see that." Deb cleared her throat. "Well, your credentials are outstanding, and everything you've provided checked out. We're also in a bind as we urgently need a nurse practitioner for this three-week cruise—though the placement is four weeks in total for staff as they come back with the ship. Not sure we'll need your midwife certification, but you never know."

Lacey smiled nervously. "Well, I do love babies."

She did, but when she'd moved to Vancouver five years ago, there had only been a job in the emergency room, so she became a trauma nurse and put her midwife career on the back burner. She missed it so much.

It was in the ER that she had met Will. He told her she was a great trauma nurse. He told her that the emergency room needed her.

That he needed her.

Lacey swallowed the lump in her throat.

"Welcome aboard, Ms. Greenwood. I'm so very glad that you're able to sail with us this afternoon, though I do hope we don't have any babies born on ship," Deb said, interrupting Lacey's thoughts.

Lacey breathed out a sigh of relief. "Thank you!"

"If you'll follow me, we'll board, and I'll show you the medical facilities. We do provide a uniform and scrubs, but I presume you have other clothes in that suitcase. I know it's summer, but Alaska still has its nippy days."

Lacey glanced back at her suitcase—the one she had packed for her honeymoon—but instead of feeling sad about the honeymoon she wasn't going to get, she just felt anger and a bit of distance. But most of all, disappointment that she had been duped.

Again.

When it came to love, she was cursed. She always picked the wrong guy. Ones who left her, cheated on her—and one time, one who stole most of her clothing. It was hard to trust men when they had a habit of always breaking her heart.

Just like her fiancé. Or rather, her ex-fiancé.

She was angry at herself for not seeing the signs earlier. She didn't want to believe that once again, she'd got it wrong. That she had—foolishly—almost walked down the aisle and gotten married to a man who lied and had cheated on her.

Will had seemed like a stable guy. Someone she could settle down with, who was just as much of a workaholic as she was.

She had thought he was a safe bet. Someone who could make her *feel* safe for one moment in her life.

Did you?

Lacey shook that thought away. She knew she had been stagnating in her work, happy to go along with Will's plans to stay in Vancouver and maintain the status quo. But there had always been a small part of her that had wanted change. She had thought marriage would be that change.

Apparently, that wasn't meant to be.

Before Vancouver Lacey had spent so many years

of her life bouncing from one place to the other, making her crave stability.

Or so she'd thought.

She liked Will well enough and thought what they had was enough for a successful marriage.

Their relationship was comfortable. It wasn't needy. They both agreed that work came first.

It was okay.

And so she had asked him to marry her. It seemed like the right thing to do. The natural progression. None of her previous relationships had lasted that long before. She'd never stayed put for so long.

And wasn't marriage the step that everyone took eventually?

Being settled with Will was the only time in her life she'd had a sense of stability and peace since her family had lived in Yellowknife when she was younger. When she'd had a real best friend.

Carol.

Another lump formed in her throat as she blinked back tears. Carol had been like family, but she'd died last year just before Lacey got engaged. Lacey had been devastated, and had been grateful that she had the wedding to focus on to help her get through her grief.

She'd had Will.

Now she didn't.

She should've trusted her gut.

On a whim, she'd decided to see him before the ceremony, because she didn't really believe in that silly custom of the groom not seeing the bride before the wedding. That's when she caught him in the act, with her friend Beth.

It brought to the surface all those signs she'd been ignoring because she thought Will was perfect for her. Stable.

She'd wanted that stability so badly.

Did you?

She'd been blind, and seeing Will with Beth was a wake-up call.

Instead of waiting to hear all the same excuses she'd heard from others in the past, she marched out of the room, grabbed her suitcase and caught the first taxi she could to take her as far away from Will as possible.

The taxi driver drove her around for an hour as she figured out what she wanted to do—all she knew was she needed an escape—and as the cab passed the docks, she saw all the waiting cruise ships. Lacey remembered there had been an opening for a nurse practitioner on one of them. She had only been casually looking at the postings—though she realized now it hadn't actually been all that casual—and it had caught her eye.

When she showed it to Will, he'd scoffed. He didn't see the point.

"Why would you want to do that?" he'd asked.

"Why not? It's an adventure. We can use a break, and heading north to Alaska sounds exciting."

Will had made a face. "North? Exciting? Those two words don't go together."

"Sure they do. I lived in Yellowknife. It's wonderful."

Will had shaken his head and ended the discussion with a firm, "No. Not at this time. We're busy. Things are good here."

Lacey had agreed—Will was right. Vancouver was safer—but there was a part of her, one she'd tried hard to suppress, that still wanted to go. She wanted to travel up north again.

It called to her.

The one time when she'd been truly settled as a child had been when her father had been stationed in Yellowknife.

She'd never stayed long enough in one place to have a best friend before, but this time they did, and she'd met Carol. That had been the happiest time in her life.

Alaska was far from Yellowknife, but it was an escape.

Right then, an escape was exactly what she needed. Time for herself and to figure out what she really wanted. She was going nowhere in her career. She missed midwifery. The emergency room kept her busy, but all she did was work, and obviously her personal life was doing the same. She was stuck in a rut.

Lacey wasn't sure what she wanted anymore, but she knew what she needed—adventure. And fast.

Applying for a job on a month-long Alaskan cruise seemed like the right thing to do.

In theory.

She pulled herself back to the present, realizing Deb was still waiting on an answer.

"I have clothes, Deb. Don't worry." There was no point in getting into the details about her canceled honeymoon, and she had everything she needed to get by. She'd already texted her dad and asked him to get her stuff from Will's place, so there was nothing holding her back from disappearing for a few weeks.

She was free, and it was a bit unnerving. In fact, she was shaking, her heart was racing, and she was already beginning to second-guess this decision.

"Oh, good, because I do have to warn you that Dr. Bell probably won't take too kindly to the outfit."

Lacey noticed Deb kind of winced, but still had a smile on her face, which Lacey could only deduce meant one thing. Dr. Bell was most likely a bit of a stubborn mule.

Lacey could deal with a doctor like that.

She had a lot of experience dealing with grumpy surgeons.

Her father was a Royal Canadian Mounted Police officer, and he'd taught her how to be strong. As they'd moved from place to place all over Canada for his work, she had learned how to grow a thick skin. She'd also learned to live in some of the most remote places in the north, and if it didn't faze her as a kid she wasn't going to start letting it bother her now.

She could handle this.

There was nothing to be nervous about. This temporary job was just a chance to clear her head and decide what to do when she returned to Vancouver, because she already knew that she wasn't leaving Vancouver just because Will had betrayed her.

Her parents were there.

They were her only roots now.

Lacey pulled her suitcase behind her as she followed Deb out of the office and up a gangway that led onto the ship. It was a staff entrance and didn't have the same fanfare as the main gangway that would soon be full of tourists embarking on a dream cruise. There were no crew greeting her, no free drinks and warm reception. Just a narrow hall and busy crew members getting everything ready for departure.

She knew this cruise was work—her means to escape the reality she was now facing and the fact her life had gone so wrong—but she had to admit that a free drink would really hit the spot right now.

"I'll take you to the clinic so you can meet the doctor. I still have to figure out your room assignment, though, and get you identification so you can open doors only accessed by staff," Deb said over her shoulder as they made their way through the maze of hallways.

As far as Lacey was concerned, the sooner they left, the better, even though right now her nerves were shot and her stomach seemed to be doing backflips in her abdomen.

Lacey just wanted to get to work and forget this whole day had ever happened.

She wanted to forget the shock of finding Will and Beth together. She wanted to forget how foolish she felt to have missed the signs that she and Will were not actually compatible.

She was hurt, angry and numb.

Finally they arrived at the infirmary.

"This is where you'll be working with Dr. Bell." Deb knocked, but didn't wait for anyone to answer as she walked in. "Dr. Bell, I have a replacement nurse for you."

Dr. Bell came out of an exam room, ducking because he was at least six foot and the doorway was not. His dark gray eyes were stormy, he was scowling and his ginger hair was a bit mussed, like he'd been raking his fingers through it in frustration. The white uniform suited him, and before she could help herself, she found she was checking him out from head to toe.

What are you doing?

Her cheeks grew hot in embarrassment. She had no idea what had come over her. All she could think of was how frazzled she felt—her heart was racing and her blood was heated. She just hoped she wasn't blushing.

This was so silly.

She'd just walked out on a wedding. Now was not the time to be admiring her new boss.

Still, Lacey was zapped with a rush of something she hadn't felt in a long time. In fact, she couldn't recall ever feeling or experiencing this kind of visceral reaction before. It seemed right and was mixed with a sense of familiarity too. As though she'd seen him before.

She couldn't quite put her finger on it, but she felt as if she knew him.

Get a grip.

It didn't matter where she'd seen him before.

She was here to work and figure out why she kept falling for men who cheated on her. Whatever momentary attraction she'd felt for Dr. Bell was wrong.

Even if he was very dashing, he was her boss, and she was fresh off an almost-marriage.

That was a recipe for disaster.

In a British accent, he began, "It's about bloody time..." He paused when he saw her, and his lips pursed together. "I asked for a nurse, Deb, not a wife!"

This was not what he was expecting.

Thatcher had been worried he wouldn't have a nurse on this trip. He'd felt so flustered about potentially not having support staff that he'd answered a call from his brother.

Something he never did.

Thatcher had been annoyed with himself, especially when it was clear Michael was angry, spending several minutes grousing over the fact he'd had to hire a private investigator to locate him. A fact that made Thatcher livid.

So instead of a normal conversation, Thatcher had to endure a thirty-minute guilt session on how he'd abandoned the family and the title and that their father was ill. So now more than ever he needed to get married and produce heirs. Thatcher tried that once. It didn't work.

He didn't want the title. And harsh as it sounded, he didn't want to see his father. All Thatcher wanted was his medical career, to stay and settle in Canada and to do so without his father's help.

It had always been his goal to make his own way, buy some land in the Yukon and set up a practice in a small community where no one knew his father was the Duke of Weymouth and that he was next in line to inherit the estate and title.

A place where no one would eventually call him "Your Grace."

That was his dream.

The cruise ship gig was just a job to get him the funds so that he could purchase the land—the means to the end—and after this cruise, he would have all he needed to live out his dream. As long as nothing screwed it up, that is. He just needed this to be a smooth and uneventful trip.

And then Michael had called and nagged him about not settling down and taking up his birthright. As if being married and procreating was all that he was good for to his family. Were they stuck in some kind of Regency-era book?

It wasn't for lack of trying that Thatcher wasn't married. A wife and kids were things he'd always wanted. The kind of loving family he'd never had growing up.

He'd been close once, but it turned out Kathleen didn't want *him*. All she wanted was to be a duchess.

Thatcher didn't want to be the duke if it meant turning out like his father.

Distant.

Cold.

Uncaring.

When his mother was sick and dying, the most compassionate, kindest person had been her physician. His father wasn't there, but the doctor was.

And that was why Thatcher had wanted to become a doctor. He wanted to save lives.

Only, Kathleen didn't share in that dream.

She wanted the aristocracy and the money that went along with it.

She didn't love him, and when it became clear he was serious about moving to Canada, she left him. After that, he'd moved, changed his name to his mother's surname and avoided women altogether.

Thatcher fell in love with the Yukon and Canada and convinced himself it was easier to live out his dream single.

Except you're lonely.

He shook that thought away. Even though he'd always longed for a family, a wife, he couldn't trust a woman to want him for him.

So he gave up on all that.

Now here he was, staring down a bride. And a beautiful one at that.

Was this some kind of cruel twist of fate or karma or whatever?

"I'm Lacey Greenwood. Your new nurse." She smiled brightly and stuck out her hand.

Thatcher looked her up and down.

She was enchanting.

He couldn't deny that. Her honey-blond hair was done up in a bun with a few loose strands. Her blue eyes twinkled and her lips were full, pink. They were made for kissing.

Don't.

He was shocked that she was standing there in a wedding dress. Was she fresh from her wedding ceremony? Was she a jilted bride?

She didn't look all that heartbroken.

There were no red splotches on her creamy skin, no puffy eyes to hint that she'd been crying. And while she wore an engagement ring, there was no wedding ring on her finger.

Maybe she was the jilter?

"Are you indeed?" he finally said, breaking the silence, but not taking her hand. "What qualifications and experience do you have?"

The smile on her face slipped, and her big blue eyes narrowed. He knew he was making Deb uncomfortable too. He hated being an old crank, but he wasn't going to let anything ruin his last cruise.

He just wanted things to go smoothly and calmly.

He didn't need some flighty runaway bride as his nurse.

Especially such an attractive one. He found himself wondering what was under all that tulle…

No, you don't!

"I'm a registered nurse practitioner and certified midwife. Deb has all of my credentials," she stated firmly.

Thatcher raised his eyebrows. She had spirit. He liked that.

No, you don't.

"Dr. Bell, I did my due diligence," Deb started, flustered. "Nurse Greenwood is more than capable."

He felt a pang of guilt for being disrespectful to Deb. He'd honestly forgotten she was there. All he saw was Lacey.

Lacey frowned. "I'm more than qualified, Dr. Bell.

Are you going to be so pigheaded to let something as silly as a wedding dress hold up the cruise? I'm not going into lengthy explanations about why I'm wearing a wedding dress, because that's my business, but I can assure you it won't affect my work."

"Are you lecturing me?" he asked, amused.

No one stood up to him, not usually, and he kind of liked it.

No. You. Don't, that inner voice reminded him again. It was setting off danger flares.

Lacey crossed her arms. "I am."

"Fine." He sighed in resignation. He didn't want the cruise postponed, and he was sure Deb had vetted her properly. "You can stay, I suppose."

Deb looked visibly relieved. "Well, now that it's all settled, I'll just take Lacey to meet the captain, get her identification and show her to her quarters."

"I expect you back here at seventeen hundred hours to report for duty, Nurse Greenwood. That's five o'clock, if you're not used to military time."

She screwed up her eyes, and she smiled, saluting him. "Aye, aye."

Thatcher chuckled to himself as Deb led Lacey out of the infirmary and down the hall. He peeked out the door to watch her walk away, pulling her suitcase behind her.

Her tulle skirt took up the entire width, and he smiled again. It was comical.

This is your last cruise. Remember? Focus on that.

He shook his head and shut the door. Thatcher was hoping for smooth sailing, but with Nurse Lacey Greenwood working with him, this would likely be a choppy voyage indeed.

CHAPTER TWO

GRUMPY JERK-FACE.

Lacey opened her suitcase and began packing away her clothes and toiletries in the wardrobe that was in her cabin. She had a very small room, but Deb had told her at least it had its own bathroom and a porthole, unlike the interior cabins, so that was something. And right now, the way she was feeling, she was glad that she wasn't sharing a cabin with anyone.

She needed her own space to think, as she was having a hard time gathering her thoughts. Especially after meeting Dr. Bell.

Lacey slammed her suitcase shut and glanced out her porthole at Vancouver.

It might not be the best view on the ship, but she wasn't here as a tourist, and clearly it wasn't going to be any kind of vacation working with Dr. Thatcher Bell. She was here to work. When he crossed through her mind again, her heart fluttered and warmth crept up her neck.

He made her nervous, and she'd never been this skittery around a boss before.

What was wrong with her? Why was she reacting this way?

She'd been surprised when she heard the British accent. She was a bit of a sucker for a British accent. It always made her heart skip a beat.

You need to stop.

She zipped up her suitcase in frustration.

She had to keep reminding herself to work and figure out her life.

Not indulge an inappropriate attraction to her new boss.

Lacey couldn't remember the last time she had been so struck with instant attraction when she met a man.

With Will, she'd thought he was cute, and after she'd had some disastrous relationships, she liked that he was open and honest—or so she'd thought.

All she'd ever wanted was stability.

Something constant.

She wanted roots and to raise a family. Will had made it clear kids weren't in the plans anytime soon, and so she'd put that thought out of her mind too, even though it was important to her.

She should have taken that for the warning sign it was that her relationship with Will was doomed from the get-go.

Was she so obsessed with safety that she was willing to settle?

Still, she never expected him to cheat on her. Especially not with someone she considered her best friend in Vancouver.

That hurt, but not as much as it should.

And that thought was sobering.

What is wrong with me?

When had she become so numb?

She wasn't a romantic and didn't believe in the whole "one true love and soul mate" nonsense. If she believed in that, she'd go insane. People you loved left you. Or you had to leave them. She knew that better than most.

Her heart ached as she thought of Carol. Will hadn't gone to the funeral, leaving Lacey to face it alone. Another red flag she'd ignored.

The pain of losing Carol had scared her.

It's why she proposed to Will. She wanted a family of her own—a net of security if something happened to her parents, the only family and roots she had left.

When exactly had she stopped believing in the fairy tale and become so pragmatic?

She wasn't sure, but she was sure of one thing…she'd dodged a bullet by not marrying Will. And she was glad she ran when she did.

Although it terrified her. She didn't like the uncertainty of not knowing what her next steps would be. It made her stomach turn. Just like when she was a kid and her dad would talk about a new posting, the uneasiness about the unknown that always settled in the pit of her stomach was back.

Working this Alaska trip and buying herself time to make a plan was exactly what she needed. Even if it meant working for the dishy ginger British doctor.

Just thinking about him and the way he'd looked her up and down caused a shudder of anticipation to run down her spine. It was lust, it was need and it was a level of want that she'd never experienced before.

It was kind of unnerving, and she hated herself for feeling this way. That wasn't why she was here. Only, she couldn't help but think of him and that visceral fire he ignited in her. It was almost like she'd never really seen a man before. It was like she'd been asleep, and now she was awake.

Don't think like that. You're here to work.

She had to keep reminding herself of that.

Alaska was always on her bucket list, and it was a perfectly timed escape when she needed it, but this was a job, and she was a professional. She prided herself on her work, and she was going to make sure that Dr. Thatcher Bell knew she was one of the best nurses there was. She was going to impress him. And then, while she was working, she could figure out what she wanted to do next when she got back to Vancouver.

Not having a plan made her nervous, but she was sure she could figure something out soon.

Lacey finished folding the rest of her clothes and then changed out of the wedding dress, which she shoved into the back of the small closet, behind her suitcase.

She cleaned up a bit, wiping off the wedding makeup and brushing out her hair, opting for a simple bun rather than the intricate updo that had been done for her veil and tiara.

The white dress uniform was a bit weird and different from her usual scrubs, but the entire staff wore it, and she would have to get used to it. She glanced down at her hand, saw the engagement ring there.

Even though she had popped the question to Will, he'd still bought her a simple ring. It had been a romantic gesture, but she was annoyed by it right now because it had obviously meant nothing to him, and now it was even more of a reminder of what a farce the whole wedding idea had been.

Yet she couldn't bring herself to take it off.

There was a knock at the door.

"Come in," Lacey said, straightening her uniform.

Deb opened the door and smiled. "You look much better."

Lacey laughed. "I suppose it would look strange to be walking around the ship in that gown."

"Just a bit. I have your identification tags and some

scrubs. You only have to wear the white uniform when we're in port or in the evening if the captain has his staff at his table."

"Do we eat with the captain every night?" Lacey asked.

"No, not every night. Just when the captain asks his senior staff to join him."

"Am I senior staff?" Lacey asked, puzzled.

"Yes. You and Dr. Bell are the only medical staff on this ship."

"Okay." She had never been referred to as senior staff before. She'd had a promotion and she hadn't even done anything yet.

Deb nodded. "Well, I better go make sure that everything is prepped for sailing. As we leave port, it's expected that everyone goes on deck, but Dr. Bell can guide you. Departure is at five thirty."

"That sounds great. Thank you, Deb."

"No. Thank you for coming and taking on the job so quickly. You've gotten us out of a real bind." Deb left, and Lacey clipped her identification tags on.

There was also a deck map in the pile of documents Debra had handed her, which she really appreciated.

It was going to take her some time to figure out this ship. She glanced at the alarm clock in her room, and as it was getting close to the time she had to report for duty, she grabbed what she needed, checked that her hair was neat and left her quarters.

She studied the map to remind herself where the infirmary was and made her way through the narrow passages to the staff stairwell. The higher she climbed, the more she could hear the happy passengers boarding the ship. She could feel the excitement of travel in the air.

It made her a bit anxious, but in a good way this time.

She couldn't wait until they pulled out of port and she was waving goodbye to Vancouver for the next month.

Then she would be able to breathe easier.

She made her way to the infirmary and took a deep breath before she opened the door. Sure, Dr. Bell might be hard to work with, but she'd dealt with worse. It was the attraction she was feeling toward him that she had to get control of.

That pull.

One she'd never dealt with before, and it was unwelcome and distracting. She wanted none of that.

Don't you?

"Nurse Greenwood reporting for duty, sir." She saluted as he casually turned around to look at her with indifference.

"You don't need to salute. I'm not the captain," he replied stiffly.

"Ah, but you are my commanding officer."

He frowned. "It's fine when the bridge crew is around, but down here I like to keep things informal, like a real clinic."

"Aren't we a real clinic, though?" she asked.

"Are you going to be flippant with me the whole voyage?" he asked despondently.

"Sorry, sir."

"Dr. Bell is fine. Even Thatcher is preferable."

"Okay, if we're going by first names, you can call me Lacey."

A strange expression crossed his face. "It's a strange name, isn't it?"

"What?"

"Lacey. I've never heard of it before."

"No weirder than Thatcher, which I thought was just a surname," she replied.

A smile tugged on the corner of his lips, briefly. "Deb gave me a copy of your curriculum vitae. You have outstanding references and credentials. You walked away from quite the impressive job at Vancouver General. Why?"

She crossed her arms. "I'd rather not get into that."

"Were you fired?"

She tried not to roll her eyes. "You can see I wasn't. I quit."

"Yes. Quite quickly. So, do tell me why you left."

"It's personal," she responded stiffly.

"Oh?" He cocked his eyebrow and leaned against the exam table. "So it has something to do with the wedding."

"Obviously."

His gray eyes landed on her hand. "Well, you're still wearing the engagement ring, so I'm assuming he ended it."

"I don't appreciate you being so flippant. Haven't you ever had your heart broken before?"

A strange look crossed his face. "Yes. You're right. I'm sorry. Please accept my apologies."

"Apology accepted." She stared at him, and once again she could've sworn she'd seen him before. She couldn't take her eyes off him as she tried to figure it out.

"What?" he asked, his back straightening.

"It's nothing. You just look vaguely familiar. That's all."

The moment the words slipped past her lips, his expression hardened and he turned away.

"I don't know what you're talking about," he groused. *It's probably better to drop it.*

The last thing she wanted to do was make things even worse.

"So, what is the first thing we have to do? This is my first voyage, and Deb mentioned something about having to go on deck as the ship leaves port."

He nodded, but still didn't turn around to look at her. "Yes. The captain runs through a safety protocol."

"Okay, well, you'll have to guide me."

He finally turned around. "We'll go up on deck together. We'll have to guide people out. Just stick by me."

"Great. Look, I know the circumstances of how I came to work here are a bit odd, but I'm willing to work hard if you just give me a chance."

That was the understatement of the year.

Still, Thatcher couldn't fault her for the circumstances that brought her on board, and was thankful Deb had found her.

Even if she was tempting. And God knew he didn't need to be tempted. He might be lonely, but he had no intention of ever getting married. He also wasn't a fling sort of person. A one-night stand wasn't for him.

What bothered him was the way she looked at him. It was worrying that she seemed to recognize him. He just hoped that she didn't actually know who he was. Not everyone read the tabloids or kept up with the British aristocracy. Still, when he'd left England, the rumors of his disappearance from the social scene had been rampant, and his picture had been plastered everywhere. Why would an heir to a dukedom just up and leave?

It was five years ago, but he knew he was still appearing in the occasional royal magazine. He was used to showing up in those rags quite a bit when he still had to attend events like the horse races at Royal

Ascot and diplomatic receptions for foreign royals and dignitaries.

When he still wore suits and had the glamorous Kathleen on his arm.

When the whole world watched him simply because of his birthright.

He'd had a few close calls since he moved to Canada and took up this job on the cruise ship—passengers coming close to realizing who he was. Thankfully, though, no one who worked on the ship had recognized him, and he knew that no one would bother him when he was finally able to move onto his own land up north.

He loved the idea of isolation, embracing the hermit lifestyle.

Do you, though?

There was still a small part of him that longed for the family, the love, his mother had provided him. His father might have never been around, but when his mother had been alive, he'd felt part of a family. She'd brought light to his otherwise lonely life.

He missed her. It was a constant ache inside him. One he had learned to live with.

But after what happened with Kathleen, he wasn't going to risk opening his heart again, and there was no point mourning what he'd never had.

It's not meant to be.

He shook the thought away.

Thinking about things that wouldn't happen was distracting him from his task. He grabbed his hat and slammed it on his head, pulling the brim down. Then he pulled out the life jackets and tossed her one.

"Life jackets?" Lacey asked, confused.

He nodded. "It's part of the safety protocol. Put it on.

We'll guide the passengers we're in charge of managing to do the same."

She nodded and put the life jacket on.

"Come on," he said gruffly. "Just follow my lead and you'll be fine."

He walked away from her swiftly, wanting to put some distance between them, but knowing that he couldn't completely leave her behind. She needed to know what to do, and this would help him gauge how she worked on the fly. Not that they got many traumatic injuries on a cruise.

Mostly it was people getting seasick or indigestion, or minor scrapes and injuries from people being a little too adventurous during a shore excursion.

Still, he wanted to see how she did.

Lacey kept up with him as he guided her out onto the deck, where the first officer was explaining the protocol over the speaker system. Thatcher stood on one side of the door, and Lacey took the position across from him.

Lacey didn't need much guidance, which he was impressed with. He closed the doors after everyone was on the deck and was standing in their assigned section.

"Now what?" she asked.

"We stand on the deck, and the ship pulls out. After we clear the port, everyone is free to go. We'll head back to the clinic, and I'll familiarize you with the layout and how I like things."

"Okay."

They stood side by side in the crowd of passengers and other crew members, and Thatcher was suddenly aware of how close she was. He could smell her hair, and it made his stomach knot. It smelled sweet, like honey, just like its color.

What is happening to you, Thatcher? Seriously, man. Get a grip.

It was not like him to wax poetic. What was happening to him? The ship lurched as it began to pull away, and before he could stop himself, he instinctively reached out and caught her, holding her tightly in his arms. He could feel the soft skin on her arms and looked down at her, her big blue eyes looking up at him in surprise and her lips just inches from his.

Big, soft, pink lips that he had the sudden urge to kiss.

Pink tinged her cheeks in embarrassment. "Thanks. I guess I don't have my sea legs yet."

"Not quite," he said gruffly.

Even though he knew that he should let go of her, he couldn't. He just held her there, pressed against him, the life vests the only thing separating them.

The rest of the crowd dispersed, and still he held on to her as they pulled out of Vancouver, heading north up the inside passage toward Alaska.

"I think I'm okay now," she whispered finally, pushing herself away from him.

"Right." He cleared his throat and let her go, taking a step back. What was it about her? Why did he forget himself around her? From the moment he'd met her, when she was standing there in that wedding dress and he felt like it was some kind of weird sign, he'd been drawn to her.

He couldn't stop thinking about her and wondering why she hadn't got married. What had brought her here?

The idea of her being hurt made him feel protective, the same way he'd felt when his mother had been weak, vulnerable and sick.

And then he remembered that it really wasn't his

business. Lacey was a stranger. She was his colleague, that was all. Letting someone—and especially letting Lacey—get too close to him was dangerous. If she got too close, she might discover who he really was. And if she found that out, who was to say others wouldn't also soon discover the truth?

He didn't want everyone to know that he was heir to the Duke of Weymouth. That he would have a seat in the House of Lords, that he had a duty pressing down on him like a thousand-pound weight.

He wasn't like his father. His father relished being the Duke of Weymouth and the attention it drew. The title meant nothing to Thatcher, and he didn't like the attention that came with it. And though his father might have been happy to put his title and duties before his family, Thatcher could never be like that.

His father had not understood why Thatcher didn't want the title, why Thatcher hated the limelight. They'd had so many bitter fights over their differences, leading up to their falling out.

"Come on," he said, breaking the silence that had settled between them. "Let's head back to the clinic so I can show you around."

Lacey nodded. "That sounds great."

They had just turned to walk back to the clinic when an ear-piercing scream stopped them in their tracks.

Thatcher turned around in time to see one of the passengers from the upper deck dangling over the railing before crashing down onto the deck he and Lacey were standing on.

CHAPTER THREE

LACEY HAD HEARD stories of people falling overboard, and there had been a few movies, usually ridiculous comedies, where a character fell from a ship into the ocean and had spiritual revelations with sea life, like dolphins, but she'd never thought she would witness someone falling onto the deck. Especially not on her first day.

Thatcher looked as shocked as she knew she did, so maybe he wasn't used to it either.

"Get a gurney," he shouted to one of the porters who was nearby.

"Should I go?" Lacey asked.

"No. They know where the emergency medical supplies are. You don't. I need your help here."

Lacey nodded and crouched down next to the unconscious man.

"Sir?" Thatcher asked as he began to go over the ABC's of triage. Airway, breathing and, well, they didn't really need to assess his consciousness level as he was obviously *un*conscious. "Sir, can you hear me?"

A porter appeared beside them with a first aid kit. Thatcher cracked it open and pulled on gloves, tossing a pair to Lacey as well.

"Sir, this is Dr. Bell. Can you hear me?" Thatcher asked again.

The man moaned.

"Pupils are reactive," Lacey said. "And he doesn't appear to have any contusions to the back of his head."

"It was lucky he didn't have that far to fall. Still can't rule out a head contusion. He did hit the deck hard," Thatcher muttered.

"What happened?" the man asked, beginning to regain consciousness. "Where am I?"

"On the *Alaskan Princess*. You fell from the upper deck," Lacey said.

"What?" the man asked.

"Harvey?" a frantic woman screeched as she rushed over to where they were crouched over their patient. "Oh, Harvey!"

"Is this your husband?" Thatcher asked.

"Yes. I'm his wife, June." June was frantic, and Lacey knew that she had to help calm her down so that Thatcher could get to work ascertaining what was wrong with Harvey. At least they had a name for him now.

"June, I'm Lacey. Can you tell me what happened? Did he faint before he fell?"

June nodded, but her gaze was still locked on her husband. "He'd been feeling a bit under the weather, but he still wanted to go on this trip, you know? It's been his lifelong dream."

"He wasn't feeling well?" Lacey asked.

"Right, but no fever. Just a bit dizzy, and I thought it might be excitement. We had a long flight yesterday from St. John's. That's in Newfoundland."

Lacey smiled. "Yes."

"Some people think we're from New Brunswick

when I say that," June said, evidently on the edge of beginning to ramble—the last thing that Lacey needed right now.

"June, I need you to focus. He was dizzy, right?"

June nodded. "He was leaning over the side and waving. Then he just kind of slumped, and before I could catch him, he slipped over."

"Could be almost anything," Thatcher said, joining the conversation. "We'll get him on a backboard, take him down to the infirmary and run some tests."

Lacey nodded. "We'll figure out what's going on with Harvey," she said as reassuringly as she could.

June nodded nervously, wringing her hands.

Lacey went back to help Thatcher and the porters.

"Harvey, we're going to strap you to this backboard. Try not to move too much until I can properly examine you," Thatcher said.

Harvey nodded slowly.

The ship's infirmary looked well stocked from the brief glance that Lacey had managed the couple of times she'd been in there, but hopefully Harvey passed out and went over the side of the balcony for a simple reason.

Thankfully, he'd landed near them, and it wasn't a big drop down from the deck above.

She caught Thatcher watching her briefly as they worked together to get Harvey strapped down on the backboard, and her cheeks heated as she thought about being in his arms and how it would affect her.

It unnerved her how safe that short embrace had made her feel. His arms had been so strong, and for a moment she'd forgotten where she was and just let him hold her. She'd certainly never felt that way in Will's arms. Not that they had ever been particularly affectionate.

Thatcher made her feel like everything would be

okay. She didn't know why, but Thatcher's strong arms around her grounded her.

For the first time since she'd arrived, she had relaxed and found she hadn't wanted him to let go.

Then she'd remembered where she was. She had to remind herself that what she'd felt in that moment when she stumbled and fell into Thatcher's arms was nothing.

Today was an unusual day. She was dealing with the fresh hurt of having been burned by Will and Beth and run away from her wedding. Her nerves were all over the place, and she'd just been caught off guard when Thatcher's arms came around her.

That's all it was, and she had to hold on to that fact.

She didn't know Dr. Thatcher Bell well enough to feel anything for him.

She was just glad that he was there to catch her in that moment she'd stumbled.

Lacey was hoping for a quiet first day so she could continue to process everything that had happened to her in the last couple of hours, but obviously that was not meant to be, if medical cases were literally falling from the sky.

They got Harvey into the infirmary and onto the exam table in one of the small rooms, while June hovered nervously outside. The porters left and took the first aid kit and backboard to the spot on deck where they were stashed for emergencies such as that.

"What should we do first?" Lacey asked.

"We need to start an IV. I think Harvey is a bit dehydrated, and by the scent of booze on his breath, he might be intoxicated. First, though, I want to hook him up to an EKG and monitor his blood pressure for the next hour." Thatcher strung his stethoscope around his neck. "If you could tell his wife—"

"June," Lacey interjected.

"Yes, June. Please tell her she should return to her cabin as we don't have a waiting room here, and we'll have her paged when we're ready to let him go."

Lacey nodded and sent June on her way before collecting what was needed to start an intravenous line of fluids.

When she re-entered the small exam room, Thatcher was taking Harvey's blood pressure.

"So, you had a bit to drink today?" Thatcher asked.

"Yes. I was a wee bit nervous, you see," Harvey said sheepishly. "We landed yesterday. We had some oysters down at this seafood place, and the beer was mighty fine. I've never had a problem with seafood before. I'm from Newfoundland and my dad jigged cod for a living."

"Where did you have the oysters?" Lacey asked.

"O'Shanty's," Harvey responded.

Lacey made a face, which Thatcher saw but Harvey didn't as he'd closed his eyes and lay back.

Thatcher motioned for her to step out of the exam room.

"You reacted when the patient said O'Shanty's. Are you familiar with it?" he asked.

"Yes. I wouldn't eat anything there if you paid me a thousand dollars. It's notoriously cheap, but it's also notoriously dirty, and I can only imagine what the oysters would be like. We had a lot of cases of norovirus and hepatitis A come through the emergency room doors, and they were often tourists who'd had a seafood meal at O'Shanty's."

"No locals?"

"The odd one, but most people in Vancouver know to steer clear of O'Shanty's food menu."

Thatcher's lips pursed. "And what is the standard course of treatment for norovirus?"

Lacey tried not to be annoyed. She was used to doctors testing new-to-them nurses like this, so she went along with it.

"It's like any kind of stomach flu. It has to run its course. I didn't notice any jaundice, but we should check to make sure he's had his hepatitis A vaccination. It's too soon to tell if it's that, and I doubt it's vibrio, but it's something to mindful of."

Thatcher raised his eyebrows and smiled. "Well, let's hook him up to an IV and get him some fluids and get the EKG done to check his heart, just in case. I'll report to the captain what happened."

"Of course, Dr. Bell."

Thatcher walked away, and Lacey couldn't help but smile as she watched him. He might be a grump, and she might be strangely drawn to him, but he wasn't going to be hard to work with.

In fact, she was suddenly looking forward to her professional relationship with him. Because that was all she wanted from him.

Liar.

There was a part of her that did want something more. Something physical and primal.

Something intense she'd never felt before.

It was unnerving.

Thatcher made his way up to the bridge to officially report what happened to the captain, though he was sure that the captain would already know someone had fallen over a balcony. Thankfully, the patient was stable and didn't seem to have any fractures. He likely had a mild concussion, though, so some rest would be in order over the next few days while the ship was at sea before they reached their first port.

He dashed up the stairs and entered the main bridge area, which was full of computers and other high-tech nautical equipment, and found Captain Aldridge was at the helm. He turned and looked back at him.

"Ah, Dr. Bell. I heard there was quite the excitement when we were leaving port."

Thatcher saluted and nodded. "Indeed. We had a gentleman faint and fall over a balcony, dropping about ten feet from one deck to another."

"And how is he?"

"He's stable. There were no fractures, but he was quite dizzy, so my nurse and I are monitoring him and trying to ascertain what might have caused him to faint in the first place."

The captain nodded. "I'm glad to hear that he wasn't more seriously hurt and that we don't need to call for an air ambulance to come and remove him from the ship."

"Yes, he was lucky," Thatcher responded.

"Incidentally, how is your new nurse working out?" Captain Aldridge asked. "I'm very glad she was able to come on board at the last minute, even if she was a bit overdressed for the job."

Thatcher chuckled. "Nurse Greenwood is working out quite fine."

"I'll say," the first mate interjected with a snicker.

"Have you even met her?" Thatcher snapped.

"No, but I did see her briefly when she came on board."

Thatcher wasn't the biggest fan of the first officer, Matt Bain, because he didn't like that he was such a cad. His own father had been a bit of a playboy, and Thatcher remembered how much it had hurt his mother.

Matt's interest in Lacey set him on edge.

Why is it bothering you? It's not your business.

"Nurse Greenwood and I will be quite busy on this voyage," Thatcher said stiffly, changing the topic.

The captain looked confused. "Busy? I hope not. I don't want this voyage to be one of the damned, Dr. Bell."

Thatcher smiled. "What I meant is, there's a lot to show her, and she's eager to learn."

Matt sniggered. "I'll bet."

Thatcher glared and clenched his fists.

Captain Aldridge glanced back at Matt and then at Thatcher. "Well, I'll leave you both to it. Keep me updated on the passenger's prognosis or if there's anything they need. I plan to go down and speak to him later."

"I will, Captain. Thank you." Thatcher saluted again and left the bridge.

It had taken every ounce of strength he had not to leap across the bridge and knock that smirk off Matt's face. And he was annoyed because it had to do with Lacey. Why did she bring out this protective side in him?

It's because she's vulnerable. She's a runaway bride.

Still, he didn't know the circumstances of what had brought her on board. So what was it about her that had him ruffled?

He remembered when he'd first met Kathleen. She'd been hurt and vulnerable.

Maybe he just had a soft spot for women who seemed to need him. He'd watched his mother be treated terribly by his father, her heart breaking over and over again, and though Thatcher's heart had ached, he'd been a child, and there was nothing he could've done then. As a man, he vowed to be different.

He wanted to cherish and protect women, but he'd been duped by Kathleen and others before her. They only wanted his title and his money—never him—and so those women had moved on to someone else. It's why he didn't get involved seriously with anyone anymore.

Medicine and saving lives, helping others, were honorable, and what he'd always wanted to do, so that was what he'd focused on these last few years.

But here he was, falling into that trap again, feeling like he needed to protect Lacey.

Well, he could keep her busy so Matt didn't bother her, but he'd keep his distance.

He wasn't going to put his heart on the line again.

Even if you want to?

Yes, there was a part of him that wanted a family and kids, and he hated that Lacey brought those thoughts to the surface. He was going to have to do his best to keep away from her so he didn't get trapped in her snare. Not that Lacey was consciously trying to trap him, but there was something about her that drew him in like a moth to a flame.

Lacey made sure that Harvey was settled and the fluids and antibiotics were running. She didn't want to take the chance that it could be something like vibrio, though it was a rare infection and if it was caught early, it didn't do as much damage. Thankfully, Harvey had his hepatitis A vaccination last year, so they didn't have to worry about liver damage.

When she closed the door to the exam room, where Harvey was stable and napping, she ran smack-dab into Thatcher, who looked a bit flustered and annoyed.

There was a strange energy coming off him.

He was agitated.

"Is everything okay, Dr. Bell?" she asked cautiously.

"I told you, you can call me Thatcher," he said. "And yes. I was just up on the bridge letting the captain know that the patient was stable. How is Harvey?"

"He's doing well. Blood pressure is stable now he's getting some fluids, and I started him on an antibiotic, just in case it's more than food poisoning."

Thatcher nodded and crossed his arms. "And his EKG?"

"Normal."

"Good."

"He may have a mild concussion, but we'll continue to monitor him to be sure."

"I was thinking the same thing. He may have landed feet first like a cat, but he still could have banged his head on the way down. Did you check his legs?"

"No fractures, no swelling. There's some bruising, but nothing alarming. I think that once his course of antibiotics and saline bag is empty, we can send him back to his cabin. He'll need a light diet of crackers and broth for the next couple of days and, to be safe, no seafood or alcohol."

Thatcher smiled briefly. "I agree. You did a good job out there today, Lacey. I was quite impressed with how you jumped right into the fray."

"I'm used to triage situations as I've been a nurse practitioner for some time. I'm not fresh out of school."

"Of course. Still, sometimes in a new job, there's uncertainty, even if you've done the very same thing many times before. And that was certainly an unusual situation."

"You've never had a man fall from one of the decks?"

He smiled, and it went straight to his eyes. It made her feel warm. She liked this smile on him. It was genuine and friendly. Will was all business and never smiled. He didn't have the best bedside manner with his patients.

Thatcher might try to act like a grump, but he had real empathy, and that empathy made her heart skip a beat.

Get a grip, Lacey.

It was not the time to think like this. She'd just gotten out of an obviously bad relationship. The last thing she needed was to have the hots for her new boss.

"I have, but it's not quite the same, and it's never happened right when we left port. That was a first," he said, interrupting her thoughts.

She chuckled. "Well, I guess fate decided to really test me tonight."

An uneasy silence fell between them. Her pulse was racing, and she didn't know what it was about being around him that made her feel this way—uneasy, but not afraid.

It was something else. Something she had never quite felt before.

A feeling she didn't know existed.

That instant animal attraction.

Like she'd been hit with a magnetic bolt.

Her cheeks heated, and she cleared her throat. "Well, I better get rid of this medical waste."

"Right, right," he said nervously. "I'll go check on him. You've had quite the day, so after you clean up, why don't you take the rest of the night off? Get something to eat and rest. I'll expect to see you at zero five hundred hours tomorrow."

"Who covers the night?"

"There's a call button for me. Usually the night is quiet."

"Don't say that," she teased.

"What?"

"Never say it's going to be quiet." She knocked on a wooden doorjamb. "You say that in the emergency room, and inevitably things go wonky."

"It's been a long time since I worked in A&E. I don't remember all the superstitions."

"You don't have superstitions in England?"

"Perhaps, but I don't recall much about my short stint in A&E. I had a private practice on Harley Street."

"Wow, Harley Street. That's quite posh, isn't it? Did you treat any members of the royal family?"

A strange expression crossed his face then.

"Yes. Why this sudden interest in my past?"

"Why the sudden interest in mine earlier?" she clapped back.

"You're new here. I'm not." He got up and walked away from her.

She sighed and collected the medical waste to take down to the incinerator chute. Even though she wasn't tired, she was going to accept his offer and take the rest of the night off.

She still couldn't shake the feeling that she'd seen him somewhere before.

Does it matter?

She realized it didn't. All that mattered was that they kept a good working relationship. There weren't many places to hide on a cruise ship, so whether she liked it or not, they were stuck together for the next month.

CHAPTER FOUR

LACEY TOSSED AND turned all night as rain pattered against the porthole in her room. The ship was rocking back and forth, and she wasn't used to the motion of the waves.

They were sailing up what she'd heard one of the crew refer to as "the inside passage" and knew it wouldn't be as rough as the open sea they'd encounter when they headed further up the coast of Alaska toward the Bering Sea. She needed to prepare herself for the choppier waters still to come.

She also couldn't sleep because she couldn't get Thatcher out of her mind. All she could think about was his arms around her and how safe his embrace had made her feel.

It bothered her.

Only twenty-four hours ago, she was on the edge of getting married, looking forward to stability at last. Instead, her sense of security had been shattered, and now she was on a cruise ship, of all places, trying to clear her head of indecent thoughts about her new boss.

Her stomach twisted in a knot.

What was wrong with her?

Why didn't Will's betrayal affect her more? Why wasn't she crying over him?

Why did she only have thoughts for Thatcher, a man she'd just met?

The phone in her quarters rang, and she reached over to grab it, hoping she didn't groan too much when she answered it.

"Greenwood speaking," she said groggily.

"I didn't wake you, did I?" Thatcher said on the other end of the line.

"No. I wasn't sleeping well." She glanced over at the clock and saw it was two in the morning.

"We've had an influx of seasickness, and I'm hoping that you can come and assist me."

"I'll be right there."

"Thank you."

Lacey hung up the phone and grabbed her scrubs. She might not be able to sleep, and she might be thinking about Thatcher and how he made her heart beat a bit faster when she shouldn't, but at least she could throw herself into her job and forget about all this.

She quickly got ready, tied back her hair, made sure her face was clean and headed straight up to the infirmary.

As she stepped out into the hall, she ran into someone.

"Whoa," the man said, his arms around her.

"I'm so sorry." She glanced up and saw from his uniform that he was one of the crew members from the bridge.

"I'm the first officer, Matthew Bain," he said, smiling. "You can call me Matt."

"Right. I'm Nurse Greenwood." She tried to step back so she could continue down the hall, but he stood in her way, blocking her. "Look, I'm sorry, but…"

"No need to be sorry. Where are you off to in such a rush?" he asked.

"The infirmary. There are a few sick passengers, so if you don't mind…"

"I can walk you there."

She groaned inwardly. This guy couldn't take a hint, could he?

"It's kind of you to offer, but you don't have to."

"I know I don't have to, but it would be my pleasure."

She smiled, but it was forced. "Fine."

She hoped that he would get the hint to leave her alone as she quickly walked down the hall toward the staff stairwells, but instead he followed her.

"You're in quite a rush. It's just seasickness."

"And the doctor is overwhelmed," she said over her shoulder. "It's the middle of the night. I'm not going to leave him in the lurch."

Lacey dashed up the stairs, but Matt kept pace beside her.

"There's not much to do for seasickness. The problem is the passage is choppy. There are some storms, but nothing this ship can't handle, so don't worry."

"I wasn't worried." She stopped in front of the infirmary. "I better go and help the doctor. Thanks for walking with me. Sorry I can't stay and chat more."

He stepped in front of her. "Would you like to meet for a drink tomorrow? There's a great eighties-themed bar on deck twenty. It's a lot of fun."

She was about to turn him down when the door opened and a tired-looking Thatcher peered out. The moment his gaze landed on Matt, his body tensed and his eyes narrowed.

"If you could pull yourself away from flirting, I could really use your help, Nurse Greenwood."

Her cheeks flushed with embarrassment and anger.

"Relax, Dr. Bell. I was just escorting Nurse Greenwood here," Matt said.

She rolled her eyes. "Excuse me."

She pushed past Thatcher and went about getting medicine ready. She assumed that they would visit the passengers' cabins and administer the anti-nausea drugs there.

Lacey really didn't know what was going on in the hallway between Matt and Thatcher, but she also really didn't care.

The door shut, and Thatcher came over to help pack the bags, but said nothing. She could feel that he was annoyed.

"What is wrong with you?" she snapped.

"There's nothing wrong with me. I'm focusing on my work. Unlike some people, I know that's more important than flirting," he said coldly.

"What?" she said in disbelief. "I wasn't flirting."

"Everyone fawns over Matt."

"Well, I'm not everyone."

"I'm sure."

Lacey rolled her eyes. "I was trying to get rid of him. I accidentally bumped into him in the hall and he insisted on following me here. I was almost running and he jogged beside me."

Thatcher snorted, and a smile tugged at the corners of his lips. "Really?"

"Yes. He couldn't quite take the hint that I would not be interested in accompanying him for a drink at an eighties-themed bar."

"Well, it is a fun bar. They have karaoke, and there's lots of neon," Thatcher teased.

"Are we really going to talk about neon at two in the

morning?" she asked, laughing softly as the tension that had been hovering between them melted away.

Which was a relief. It was her emotions running amok given what an unusual day it had been.

In the light of the infirmary, with patients to attend to and work to do, she relaxed.

All she wanted to do was work.

And it was easy to work with Thatcher...so far.

She glanced over at him prepping the bags with medicine, and she felt that rush, that zing, traveling through her body again.

A flush crept over her skin.

What is going on?

She ignored that thought and focused on prepping her kit.

"I'll take the more severe cases, so here's your list of patients. Give them an injection, and leave them with some anti-nausea tablets. You know the drill, I'm sure."

Lacey nodded. "I do."

"Hopefully they'll feel better when the weather improves."

"Let me guess. This hasn't happened before to this extent?"

Thatcher chuckled. "Only once, on the second voyage I did. It happens more when we're closer to the Bering Sea. The inside passage is smooth...usually."

"It's because you said it was going to be quiet," she teased.

He groaned. "I certainly hope word doesn't get out, or people will be calling to put Weymouth's head on a pike—" He stopped himself and clammed up, looking annoyed with himself.

"Who is Weymouth?"

"The town I come from."

"I thought you came from London?" she asked.

"I worked in London, but I was born in Weymouth. Does it matter?"

"It's just that the name rings a bell. My mother is a huge royal follower, so I know that a few years ago, the heir to the Duke of Weymouth just up and left. No one knows where he went. She's read a lot of conspiracy theories about what might have happened."

Something was niggling at her as Thatcher locked up the infirmary, his whole body tense.

"Does she really? Well, I don't know much about the Duke of Weymouth. Like I said, I was born there, and that's about it," he stated.

They walked in silence down the hall and up the stairs. At the deck where she would begin seeing patients, he paused.

"When you're done, report back to the infirmary, and we can go over the roster for the day. I think we'll be done just as our day starts."

"Of course."

She watched as he climbed the steps. What was with him? He ran so hot and cold, she was going to get whiplash if she wasn't careful.

He was kicking himself internally as he attended to the more severe cases of seasickness and one case of what appeared to be morning sickness, which was a first for him on this cruise too.

He made a note in that patient's chart to have Lacey follow up with the soon-to-be mother.

Thatcher had made a huge mistake when he'd been joking with Lacey and referred to himself as Weymouth. It had been quite some time since he'd done that.

Usually no one got it if he let something like that slip, but of course Lacey's mother had to be a royal watcher.

He knew that there were various conspiracy theories about his disappearance, but he didn't want his family correcting what was written in the press and feeding the beast. Thatcher just wanted to be left alone.

Over the years that he'd been working on these cruises and spending his vacation time in Canada, he'd had a few close calls, but he always managed to evade the reporters and photographers.

There was no love lost between Thatcher and the papers. They had plastered his name everywhere when Kathleen left him for another man and showcased his father's extramarital affairs throughout his childhood. He could still perfectly picture the hurt etched on his mother's face whenever she saw the images.

He hated that he had no privacy at home.

It was different here. Here he was anonymous.

Until he'd said the name Weymouth and she'd caught him on his slip.

He had to be more careful. The problem was, he let his guard down around Lacey. It was so easy to talk to her, and he didn't know why.

Maybe because you're lonely?

Thatcher shook that thought away. He had to regain control.

He finished his house calls to the passengers just as the sun was coming up and made his way back down to the infirmary to find Lacey sitting outside the door. He realized she didn't have a set of keys yet. He'd have to make sure she got them soon.

"Sorry," he said quickly. "Were you waiting long?"

"No. I just got here." She stood up.

"I have a pregnant patient for you to follow up on. She just found out." Thatcher handed her the file.

"Oh, how lovely." Lacey flipped through it. "I'll check on her later. If she has extreme morning sickness, I want to make sure she gets enough fluids. Although the weather has turned nicer. I did see the sun through the clouds."

"Yes. It should be a calmer day." He opened the door, and they set their gear down and cleaned up. "Would you like to go get some coffee with me? I'm sure one of the coffee shops on the main deck will be open, and I think we'll need it."

"Yes. I would love that."

Thatcher locked up and posted a sign with his pager number in case anyone needed them. Then they made their way to the main deck.

It was still early in the morning, and most of the passengers were still sleeping, but there were a few milling around as they made their way through the main deck to the upper decks of the ship. The main deck wasn't open to the elements as it would have been on a warm Caribbean cruise. Instead there were domed windows to allow the sunlight in and heat up where everyone congregated, so it felt like you were on a tropical cruise.

There were several couples walking or running the perimeter of the deck—the early bird passengers getting in their exercise as the ship started to come to life for its very first full day at sea.

"Is this your first time on a cruise?" Thatcher asked, trying to make small talk as they stood in the short line for coffee.

"It is. I've always wanted to do something like this. When I was a kid, the most exciting moves were when my father would get postings in the far north. Exciting, but scary. I didn't always enjoy moving around."

"Was your father in the armed forces?"

"No, he was an officer with the Royal Canadian Mounted Police—one of the few officers that ended up finishing off his career in Ottawa, protecting the prime minister. When I was a little girl, he had several postings in the Northwest Territories and Nunavut."

"Did you ever live in the Yukon?"

"Yes." She smiled. "And he had a short posting in Inuvik. That was before the road was built to Tuktoyaktuk. We only lived there for six months. Never got to really experience a winter up that far, but it was still one of my favorite places. It was adventurous."

He smiled and nodded. That adventure was something he'd always craved when he was younger, which was why he was here and why he wanted to stay. He was envious of her childhood. It was so unlike his.

"That sounds like a lot of fun."

"Well, it's just Canada, and when I became older and started traveling on my own, I did a bit of the United States, but I haven't been anywhere truly exciting like Europe or Australia."

"Europe is great, but it's crowded."

"What's wrong with crowds?"

"I like space."

"You're on a cruise ship. There isn't exactly a lot of space here."

"This is only temporary. In fact, this is my last trip. I'll finally have enough."

Her finely arched eyebrows rose, and her blue eyes lit up. "Oh? You'll have enough for what?"

"A piece of land in the Yukon. Preferably near Dawson, somewhere in the mountains." It would be his own land, land he'd worked hard to be able to afford, with no help from his father or the family fortune.

"That sounds wonderful. Are you going to continue practicing medicine?"

"Yes. That's the plan." He ordered them two coffees— free, because they were staff—and they wandered away from the shop and found a couple of chairs out in the sunlight, where it was warm.

He was actually shocked that he'd told her his plan. It was something that he'd kept to himself for so long. The only other person he'd told was Kathleen, and she'd wrinkled her nose in distaste.

"Why would you want to do that?" she'd asked.

"Because it's exciting! Don't you want to have this kind of a chance at something new?"

She'd smiled placatingly. "Yes, but not in the Yukon. I was thinking more of Majorca or somewhere in the Mediterranean, and just for trips. I don't mind taking trips, but to somewhere trendy and fashionable. I mean, you are in line to the British throne."

"A lot of people would have to die for me to become king," he'd said dryly. "And that's something I would never want. I'm not even sure I want to be duke when my father dies."

She'd looked horrified. "What? You can't turn down the title."

"Why not? My brother, Michael, would be an excellent duke. He's more interested in the land and more involved with Parliament. I want to be a doctor, out in the wilds somewhere, helping people and living an adventure."

His father would never agree to it, but with Kathleen at his side, he wouldn't care. They'd make it work.

"I'm sure you'll get over it. You'll spend a week there and you'll change your mind and see sense."

She'd patted his head like he was some kind of petulant child and left.

And still he hadn't seen sense and realized that Kathleen wasn't the one for him.

He'd been so blinded by her beauty and the fact that she kept saying she loved him. And then, when he told her that he was serious about his plans for the Yukon, she'd cheated on him with a wealthier man. One who ran in all the right circles and didn't mind the press. It was demoralizing. Broke his heart, embarrassed him.

It was obvious to Thatcher the people that operated in his father's realm didn't quite get his passion and would never understand him.

It was better to leave. Maybe then his father would stop insisting he take the title.

Which was why he was here. And now he was so close to having everything he'd ever wanted.

Not everything.

Thatcher shook that thought away. He wouldn't think of his lost dreams of family or of a wife.

"Well," she said, "I think the two places out of Canada I would most like to go to are Iceland and Antarctica."

"You really do like the cold then, don't you?" he teased.

"I do. There's just something about the north." She sighed sadly. "I wanted to work in Iqaluit or even further north, in a place like Alert, in Nunavut, but my fiancé, or rather my ex-fiancé, didn't want to go that far. So I stayed in Vancouver."

He got the sense that she hadn't been happy. It was at that moment that he thought maybe he'd pegged her wrong, and he was annoyed at himself for judging her so quickly.

"Is that why you left?" he asked gently. "I know you said you didn't want to talk about why you arrived here in your wedding dress…"

"No, it's fine. Yes, I ran from him. I caught him in the act with my maid of honor."

"Ah." He winced. "I'm sorry."

She shrugged. "It is what it is. I realized as I watched him with my former best friend that I wasn't that hurt that he was cheating on me. I guess part of me expected it since I don't have the best luck with men." Her cheeks flushed pink. "And I don't know why I'm telling you this."

"It's okay, but why marry him if you expected him to cheat?" Thatcher asked.

Lacey shrugged and picked at the corner of the napkin on the table. "It seemed like the logical thing to do at the time. It was safe, or so I thought. I left the church after I caught him in the act, as it were. We both got ready at the church. I thought he'd be alone, and he was not."

"And you don't regret walking out?" he asked.

"Not so far, but it has been exceptionally busy!" She laughed, and he couldn't help but laugh with her.

It was easy to laugh with her.

And that thought scared him. He stared at his empty coffee cup. "Well, we better go and plan out the roster for the day. You know, you should try a couple of the shore excursions if you get the chance."

"I'd like to. I'm very excited that we're going to stop in Skagway. I've always wanted to explore that city. Maybe there will even be time to take the train into the Yukon up the White Pass. That's also on the bucket list."

"I think time can be made for that." He smiled and stood up.

Lacey followed.

They tossed their coffee cups in the trash and walked in silence back to the infirmary. It had been a long time since he sat down and really talked to someone.

It was nice, but he had to remind himself to be careful.

He didn't want to get hurt again, and he didn't want Lacey to be hurt either.

At the end of this cruise, he was going to buy his land in the Yukon and start his local practice. There was no stopping him.

He was going to follow through.

And nothing was going to change his mind.

CHAPTER FIVE

LACEY QUICKLY FELL into a routine on ship as the rough weather settled down and time at sea became more peaceful. She made her rounds to check on those patients who had extreme seasickness that first night and checked in on Harvey, who was recovering well from his food poisoning and minor concussion.

Everything was going really smoothly, and she appreciated that it kept her busy. Busy was good because it meant she didn't have to think about Will or Beth or her failed attempt at marriage.

It was nice to focus just on the work…and Thatcher.

But thinking about Thatcher and how much she'd enjoyed working with him over the past couple of days was distracting.

Lacey tried to keep her distance, but it was hard to do that in a small infirmary, and every time she tried to keep herself occupied with busywork and admin, she'd see emails from Will and Beth in her inbox.

Lacey couldn't bring herself to face the emails. She was mad at herself for being duped and mad at herself for agreeing to marry Will, for not seeing the signs earlier. She didn't need to read some half-hearted explanation of why he'd cheated when she should have known all along that it wasn't to be.

Work always came first for Will. They never talked at the hospital unless they had a brief moment, and then it was quick and to the point.

When she talked to Thatcher, it was different. Easier. But since their coffee a couple of days ago, he himself was acting a bit distant, as if he was keeping her at arm's length. And even though she shouldn't be bothered because she was only here to work, she found she was sad.

You can't get attached.

She wasn't looking for love.

Only a lucky few could find love.

She wasn't one of them.

Maybe it was for the best that he kept his distance, making it easier for her to fight this strange, overpowering attraction that she was feeling for him. When she was around him, she felt able to let go. Usually she was pretty private, but around him, her pulse would race and all those things she kept close to her heart just came pouring out.

It was like she lost all sense around him.

She saw him every day, but Lacey missed chatting with him, like they had the first day of the voyage. It was better that they were professional, but she liked talking with him, and she liked learning more about him. He was so sure about his plans. So focused.

Lacey was a bit envious of that. He had a solid plan for the future, whereas she wasn't sure where she was going. She had learned to roll with the punches and pick up and move wherever her dad got a new posting, but there was always a part of her that longed for roots. Now, once again, she didn't know what she would do next.

She craved having a place to belong, like she did when they lived in Yellowknife. When she'd been her happiest.

You could go back.

It wasn't the first time she'd had the thought, but Carol was gone now.

The people she once knew there were probably gone. It was no longer home.

A lump formed in her throat, and Lacey shook the thought away. This was why she tried to never let herself think of Yellowknife or the fact Carol was gone.

She finished up writing in her patients' charts and started wrapping everything up. She was off duty soon, and she thought she might take advantage of the chance to take a shore excursion—a small boat trip inland and then a kayak journey to an inlet to see grizzlies in a hidden bay. Seeing grizzlies sounded like an experience she shouldn't miss. Of course, she wasn't here to have a vacation—she was here to work and keep her mind off the things she didn't want to think about— but that didn't mean she couldn't also have a bit of fun in her downtime.

"You're off duty soon, aren't you?" Thatcher asked from his office.

She turned and looked back through his open door. "I am."

"What are you going to do?"

"I might do the shore excursion to see the grizzlies."

"I've done that one before. It's really good. You almost finished? The first boat leaves in an hour," Thatcher said, coming out of his office. She noticed that he was back in his officer's white uniform. She hadn't been able to see it when he was sitting behind his desk at his computer, and she couldn't help but admire how good he looked. She'd always had a thing for a man in uniform, and this one fit his muscular body like a glove.

Warmth crept up her cheeks, and she hoped she

wasn't blushing, which she always seemed to do when Thatcher was around. She felt like a young girl who had her first crush.

"Why are you so adamant I go now?" Lacey asked.

He smiled. "It's a once-in-a-lifetime experience."

"Okay. I'm almost done, though, and there are small boats leaving all day. I don't have to be on the very first boat."

"You know, I find the last boat out to the inlet is more magical. The water is so clear, and with the moon and stars, it's like a mirror."

"That's quite poetic," she teased.

He smiled briefly. "Well, I can be poetic when the mood strikes me. Which is not often."

She laughed softly. "That's a shame. You have quite the nice accent to take the stage at Stratford and recite Shakespeare."

"I am not an actor," he groused. "At Eton we often performed Shakespeare, and I didn't have an acting bone in my body. It was shameful. It would always make my father wince at how terrible I was."

"Eton? Wow, I had no idea. So did you go on to Cambridge or Oxford?"

He frowned and looked a bit worried. "Cambridge."

"Sorry, I didn't mean to pry. I know you don't like it when I pry."

"No." He shook his head. "No, it's not that. It's just I don't have very fond memories of my childhood, and I don't like talking about it. I prefer to focus on the future and the plans I'm looking forward to."

"I'm envious of your plans," she muttered, not really wanting to let it out, but unable to stop herself. She didn't know what was going to happen when she got back to Vancouver. All the plans she'd made for herself the last couple years were gone.

"Are you?" he asked, curious.

"See, my childhood was very transient, but happy. I love my parents." She smiled just thinking of them. They had always been there for her, and her father had been the one to help her when she'd run from her wedding.

"He did what?" her father had shouted.

"Don't shout, Dad. It's okay." She'd continued to sort out her suitcase. "I'm not upset. I mean, I am, but right now I've just got to focus on going away from here."

Her father had looked at her, concerned. "Going where?"

"Somewhere to think. I'm not sure I really believe in love, but I know that I don't believe in a relationship founded on unfaithfulness."

Her father had nodded. "You were always quite pragmatic and logical. I just want you to be safe. What do you need me to do?"

She'd hugged her father. "Move my stuff out of his place while I'm gone. I don't have much...you know I'm a minimalist."

Her father had grinned and touched her cheek. "And then?"

"I'll call the hospital and do what I have to, and quit my job. I just need to clear my head and figure out my next steps."

"The whole world is yours," her father had said gently. "I never thanked you for all those times we moved because of my job. I know it was always hard on you and your mother, but you two... I couldn't have done what I did if it wasn't for you and your mom."

She'd kissed her father on his cheek. "I'd be grateful if you could also explain my decision to Mom. I know she's a bit more emotional than us."

"I will. Just be safe."

Her parents were loving and supportive, and she was so thankful for that. She couldn't have done this—taken this leap—without their support and her father's help.

Her father had been right. The whole world was hers, but she didn't know where to go, and she was envious that Thatcher had this plan all thought out.

She wanted roots, but she didn't know where she wanted to live. The world was open, but also closed. It was scary. She felt like she was free-falling.

"I did not have such a tranquil childhood," he muttered. "I am glad you did, though, but don't be envious of me."

"Why not? You have plans. I don't."

He smiled at her. "You have a plan for today. You're going to take a boat up to the Khutzeymateen and see some grizzly bears."

She smiled. "Yes. I suppose I do have that plan."

"Just because it appears that someone has their life together doesn't mean that they do. In fact, they often don't." There was sadness in his voice.

Lacey didn't know what he meant by that, but the moment he said it, she could sense that he wasn't happy, and she couldn't figure out why. For one moment, she wanted to take him in her arms and reassure him that everything would be okay—making him feel safe the same way he had made her feel safe—but how could she comfort him when she wasn't even sure what she was comforting him for? She didn't even know him.

"You should go," Thatcher said. "Go enjoy the bears. It's amazing."

"Why are you trying to push me out the door?"

"I'm not. I'm trying to make sure you don't miss the chance of a lifetime. So go!"

Lacey closed her chart. "I swear I won't miss the chance of a lifetime."

Thatcher smiled the friendly, warm smile that made her heart skip a beat. It was so easy being around him. "Okay, see that you don't, and stop stressing."

Thatcher watched Lacey finish up her paperwork. He didn't know why she was envious of him. There was nothing to be envious about.

He might have plans, but it didn't mean his life was together. Sure, he liked to think he had it all figured out, but then something happened to prove him wrong. Something like his brother calling to let him know their father was seriously ill.

He felt lost.

His father had never been a true and loving father to him, but Thatcher felt bad to learn the duke was sick.

At least Lacey had a happy childhood.

He couldn't say that.

His father had been cruel. He didn't care about his wife or children and was never around, too busy cheating on his wife and breaking her heart over and over again. Thatcher's mother had been loving and caring, but also so sick, and he'd spent a lot of his childhood worried about her.

The only bright spot in his early years was his younger brother, Michael. They had been close once, but Michael had been so hurt when Thatcher walked away from it all, and their bond had been broken. He had never wanted to hurt Michael like that, and it pained him to have his brother angry at him, but Thatcher wanted nothing his father had to offer. He'd really had no choice but to walk away, but he always regretted leaving Michael behind.

Leaving Michael with their father.

But Thatcher had no choice. He had to leave, and he had to live out his dream. It was his life and he owed his father nothing.

Michael liked dealing with the estate and loved politics, but their father refused to let him take over, claiming it was Thatcher's birthright, not Michael's.

So he might have plans, but his life wasn't together yet.

Not in the slightest.

It wouldn't be until this cruise was over and he was moving up to the Yukon to scout out his piece of land and then slowly building his practice while he built his own house. That's what he wanted.

Everything had been so clear in his head. Thatcher knew exactly what he had to do, but now Michael was begging him to come home and make things right.

Thatcher couldn't. He was so close to having everything he wanted, and he just couldn't give it up, his future, couldn't walk away from it.

You walked away from the estate.

That thought made his stomach twist. The estate was a birthright not a commitment.

Medicine was his life. And what he'd wanted to do for so long.

And there was Lacey. The runaway bride who had shown up as his nurse.

He wanted to ignore her, but he was drawn to her.

No matter how many times he told himself that he was going to keep his distance and just remain professional, he couldn't. He would try to work, and he'd catch himself staring at her. She was beautiful, and being around her, he didn't feel so lonely.

She wasn't easy to ignore.

He was a moth and she was the flame.

Are you seriously comparing yourself to a bug right now?

Thatcher laughed at that thought.

He opened up his email and saw that his brother had emailed him again, but he couldn't bring himself to open it.

Instead he glanced out the window of his office and saw Lacey was still there, charting. She hadn't left yet, and he couldn't help but smile when he saw her there.

She was supposed to be off duty and yet she was still working.

It was a quiet day, and she should take a chance to explore like most of the passengers who were off ship, enjoying the shore excursions.

He sighed. At least she was dedicated to her work—that was something to be admired. He opened up the door to his small office. He wouldn't mind her staying here with him all day, but she deserved time to enjoy herself too.

"Lacey, didn't I tell you to leave thirty minutes ago?"

"You did," she said, not looking up at him.

"Would you come in here please?"

She rolled her eyes, closed her chart and came into his office, her arms crossed and an annoyed look on her face.

"If you keep interrupting my work then I can't leave on the shore excursion at all," she stated.

"I'm beginning to suspect that's what you want. You don't know what you're missing." He motioned her to come closer. "I'm going to show you the photos I took when I went on the excursion a couple of years ago."

She rolled her eyes and came to stand beside him. The closer she got, the more he could smell the scent of her shampoo, and it fired his blood. This was the opposite of keeping his distance from her. He wasn't sure what he was doing or what possessed him, but he didn't care. He never showed these pictures to anyone, but right in this moment he wanted to share them with her. Which was strange. Anytime he showed Kathleen a glimpse of these secret dreams of life in the north, she'd whine or ignore him.

And his father had had no interest either.

Thatcher had always had to keep it private, but here was an opportunity to share it without the fear of judgment. The fact that it was Lacey he was sharing it with felt intimate and made his pulse race with anticipation. He wanted to reveal this piece of himself to her.

And her reaction would let him know if he was attracted to the wrong kind of woman again. Did she genuinely love the north or was she just saying she did?

Could she be lying or putting on an act the same way Kathleen did in the beginning of their relationship because she wanted the title of duchess?

Don't think about Kathleen.

"What am I looking at?" Lacey asked.

"The inlet, before you get to the floating lodge that some people travel to stay at."

"A floating lodge?" she asked, leaning over. A strand of her soft honey-blond hair escaped from her tight bun and tickled his neck.

He tried to shift and move away from her, only he couldn't without it seeming obvious that he wanted to put distance between them. So he focused on trying to ignore how close she was to him.

"That looks like an amazing place to stay! Do they get there by boat?"

"They can if it's a flat-bottom boat, but mostly people who stay at the floating lodge take a float plane from Prince Rupert. Our passengers, and you, if you hurry up, take a flat-bottom boat up the inlet, and the lodge provides kayaks for those who want to explore."

"Do you recommend the kayaking?"

"Yes." He clicked on the next picture, which showed some of the rain forest and the bears. Pictures that calmed him. It was experiences like this that had solidified his desire to live in the north.

There was peace here.

For so many years, it felt like his soul was uneasy. Since his mother had died, he was dissatisfied and unhappy— restless. Thatcher had tried to fit into his father's world, but the more he tried to be like the man his father wanted him to be, the more he lost himself.

The more he hated himself.

Then he met Kathleen, and for that short time he was with her, he'd been happy.

He thought she wanted the same things he did. Only she hadn't.

Kathleen had lied to him, broken his heart.

And he'd made a promise to himself not to end up like his mother.

Sad.

Shattered.

Jaded.

Trapped in a loveless marriage.

Here, in nature, and up north, he was who he truly believed he should be.

"I guess I will do the kayak, then," Lacey said, interrupting his thoughts.

"You should. It was one of the best experiences of my time in this job."

She glanced over at him, her lips close to his, and his throat went dry. He could see her neck, slender and long, and he wanted to kiss it. To feel her pulse beneath his lips. His heart was racing, and his body stiffened. She was so close, he would feel her warmth, and he wanted to drown himself in her. To wrap his arms around her and take care of her.

"Doctor?" someone called out. He was relieved at the distraction of a patient.

Lacey started to leave his office, but he reached out and took her hand to stop her.

"You're off duty. I'll take care of this. You stay and look at the photos, convince yourself to go."

She smiled. "Fine."

He got up and left her. It was good to put some distance between them. And fast.

Lacey continued to scroll through the pictures. They were beautiful. She didn't know why she'd been debating going on a shore excursion. It was a great opportunity. It was a change. And maybe the change of scenery would help clear her head, give her the space she needed to process everything.

She really needed to do that.

So why did she feel like she didn't deserve it?

Because you're here to work, not enjoy yourself.

Except she was enjoying herself. She'd been on this cruise for several days, and she'd never enjoyed work this much before. Yes, she'd loved her job at the hospital, but the hospital stayed put. The cruise went somewhere new every day, and she never knew quite what to expect when she looked out the window in the morning.

It had been a long time since she'd felt this way.

She'd tried to put down roots in Vancouver because her parents had, but look how that had turned out.

Maybe she really was meant to be an eternal nomad.

Only the idea of moving constantly made her a bit uneasy. It brought out all those old feelings. It made her stomach twist.

She was confused and didn't know what she wanted.

Lacey could usually keep control of her emotions—it was how she'd avoided getting attached to things as a child—but she could see already she was getting attached to Thatcher. He stirred so many feelings inside her, to the point that she didn't know what she was feeling at all. She had no control.

It scared and thrilled her in equal measure.

As she finished clicking through the pictures, a notification popped up. Though she tried to ignore it, it was large—magnified almost—and ran right across the screen. There was no way for her to avoid it. It was to Thatcher, it was from the Duke of Weymouth and the first line that was previewed read, Dear Son...

CHAPTER SIX

LACEY LEANED OVER the side of the railing on the flat-bottom boat as it made its way slowly up the inlet, but instead of focusing on the beauty around her, all she could think about was that email notification.

She couldn't believe Thatcher was the missing heir. He was going to be the next Duke of Weymouth. Sorry... Edward. Thatcher wasn't even his real name!

Obviously he was in hiding, but why?

When she saw that notification pop up, everything had started to click into place. Eton, Cambridge, his attitude whenever she said he seemed familiar and his attitude about the British aristocracy.

Every time she mentioned those things, he tensed right up, and now she understood all too well why. What she couldn't understand was why he was hiding away.

Why are you *hiding away, Lacey?*

She ignored that thought.

She glanced up at the trees, craning her neck to see the canopy, but she couldn't—as they say—see the forest for the trees. All she could see was Thatcher. And the fact that she didn't know anything about who he really was.

Who are you, *Lacey?*

She didn't know that either.

It bothered her that Thatcher had lied about who he was.

What else was he hiding?

Lacey sighed. Why did she always fall for the wrong man?

The thought made her spine stiffen. She was not falling for Thatcher. She was here to work, not rush into another romance. Not that she would now consider her relationship with Will a great romance...

Her stomach knotted, and she shook her head to clear out all the conflicting thoughts running around in circles in her mind. She should be focusing on the beauty around her. Not on Thatcher and his secrets.

"Enjoying the scenery?"

Lacey glanced over her shoulder, groaning inwardly and trying not to openly show her disdain when she saw it was Matt Bain, the first officer of the *Alaskan Princess*, standing next to her.

He thought he was charming, and maybe he was to the right type of woman, but that wasn't her, and she was annoyed that he was intruding on her thoughts. She'd rather obsess about Thatcher and all the feelings he was stirring up inside her than chat with Matt.

"I am," she said politely. "It's nice and quiet."

She was hoping that Matt would take the hint, but she was dismayed to see that wasn't going to be the case.

"It kind of gets boring after multiple trips. It all blends together, you know?"

"The trips or the trees?" she asked.

"The trips."

She nodded. "You've been doing this for a while, then, I assume?"

"Yes. Waiting to get my own command. Hopefully somewhere warmer." He grinned at her, a grin that was clearly supposed to charm her and make her simper, but didn't. And what was with everyone sharing all the plans they had for their futures with her? It was the last thing she needed when she couldn't get her own life together.

The future was blank to her. At least when she would move around as a kid, she had her parents with her for support.

"That sounds like a good plan." She turned to look back at the trees, hoping that he would leave. She just wanted to be alone with her thoughts.

"You know, if this trip goes smoothly, I'll be able to choose my own crew, and I'll need medical staff."

"I think Dr. Bell has other plans."

"I don't mean him," Matt said with a hint of derision in his voice. "I mean you."

"I'm a newbie here."

"So?" He grinned again and moved a bit closer to her. "I was so impressed with how you handled the situation when that man fell from the balcony."

Lacey really didn't know how to respond to that, so she avoided looking at him and focused on the bow of the barge. It was then that she saw one of the other passengers start to shake. The woman's knees seemed to buckle, but even though she righted herself, it was a red flag to Lacey, and the warning bells began to go off.

She moved away from Matt and walked toward the woman, and as she began to wobble a bit more, Lacey quickened her pace.

"Ma'am?" Lacey called out. Only she was too late. The woman started to fall, and all Lacey could do at that point was try to cushion her landing.

* * *

Thatcher was waiting at the boat launch on the *Alaskan Princess*. He'd gotten word over the radio that one of the barges had to turn back because of a medical emergency. He'd been about to get on another barge to meet the other boat halfway, but then he'd learned that Lacey had been there, and the passenger was stable.

It relieved him to know Lacey had it in hand, but he felt bad that she was going to miss out on the grizzly bears.

If the situation was reversed, you'd have done the same.

Patients first.

Always.

Sort of like how your father put the estate and his title first?

Thatcher ignored that thought. It was different. He was saving lives, and if he was in the position his father had been in, with a wife and children, he'd make time for them.

And he would certainly never cheat on his wife, the way his father had constantly cheated on his mother.

The barge docked, and he climbed aboard to find Lacey had the patient lying down. At least the patient was conscious, even if her color still didn't look good.

"What happened?" Thatcher asked, setting down his medical kit next to them.

Lacey didn't look at him. "Ms. Lawrence here fainted and took a while to come to."

Thatcher cocked an eyebrow. "Her blood pressure?"

"I couldn't take an accurate reading, but it was low and sluggish. It seems to be coming back stronger now."

Thatcher pulled out his blood pressure cuff. "Well, we'll see what it is now."

"This is Dr. Bell, the ship's doctor, and he's going to run some checks on you," Lacey said calmly.

Ms. Lawrence nodded.

"Hello, I'm Dr. Bell. Can you tell me how you're feeling?"

"Better," Ms. Lawrence said shakily.

"Ms. Lawrence said she's a diabetic," Lacey stated.

"I think I didn't have enough to eat this morning," Ms. Lawrence said. "I was so nervous about the bears and being on a smaller boat."

Thatcher smiled at Ms. Lawrence. "That's understandable."

He glanced up at Lacey to find she was staring at him intently. Usually it would cause a physical reaction in him. He liked when their gazes would meet, but this was different.

She was acting odd.

Like she didn't know him. As if he was a stranger to her.

Like she saw him in a new light.

His stomach twisted in worry, and for one fleeting second, he thought she might know who he really was… but that wasn't possible.

Still, there was a pit in his stomach. It gave him pause.

When she left the infirmary to join the shore excursion, something had changed.

He hoped he was wrong and that she didn't know who he was, because that would change everything.

You don't know that.

Except, he sort of did. Everyone who knew he had a title coming to him treated him differently. They weren't genuine.

And when he walked away from it all, all those people who had claimed to care for him turned their backs.

It saddened him to think of Lacey being just like everyone else. It made him anxious.

Focus on the patient.

He didn't have time to worry about Lacey and why she was acting so weird, and he wasn't here to make friends. He took this job five years ago to finance his dream.

To be independent.

Not contemplate a romance.

That was the furthest thing from his mind.

Is it?

"Your blood pressure is better, Ms. Lawrence, but still a little lower than I'd like. You should probably head back to your cabin for now. Nurse Greenwood will accompany you and then come to check on you a bit later, once you've had some food and a rest."

Ms. Lawrence nodded and continued to sip the orange juice one of the crew members had handed her when she and Lacey had docked.

Thatcher packed up his equipment, and Lacey asked him to step away with her for a moment.

"You okay?" he asked stiffly, trying not to worry about her behavior.

"Fine," Lacey said, but she didn't sound fine. He noticed how her eyes darted away, and she wouldn't look at him squarely.

"You don't seem fine."

"How should I be?"

"I would assume annoyed you had to come back," he said.

She smiled, but it was forced. "There is that, but it's my job."

Thatcher smiled back at her, trying to ease the tension. "Well, I'm sorry."

"Don't be. I can always come another time."

"On the next cruise?"

"I haven't decided on that. Although Matt Bain was on the barge and offered me a job on his ship next year."

Thatcher cocked an eyebrow. "His ship?"

"He has big plans too."

He snorted. "I'm sure. Well, good for him."

"To be honest, I'm not sure if I'm going on another cruise or not."

"Can you take care of Ms. Lawrence and report back to me?" he asked.

"Of course." She still refused to look him in the eye.

He stared at her, confused as to what could have come over her.

It's not your concern.

And it wasn't.

When this cruise was all said and done, he'd finally have everything he'd ever wanted. He could disappear into the Yukon and no one would ever know where or who he was.

He'd be happy.

Finally.

Will you?

Lacey took a deep breath and left Ms. Lawrence's cabin to walk back to the infirmary. She wanted to tell Thatcher about that notification she'd seen, and ask him about it. He had been lying to her.

Maybe he wasn't even really a doctor…

She couldn't finish that thought without laughing at herself for even contemplating it.

Of course he is. He knows what he's doing.

At least, that's what she was telling herself. He talked about schooling and a practice on Harley Street, which was where all the posh physicians in London were. She was being silly. Yet he had lied to her about who he was...

She couldn't help but wonder why.

Thatcher was going to be the next Duke of Weymouth. Why hide that? She couldn't exactly recall the reasons the papers had suggested why the heir had up and left, and a large part of her was hoping he could—and would—explain it.

It's not your business.

He didn't know everything about her. Why should she know about this?

She knew that was true, but she also knew she couldn't work with someone she didn't know or trust. She'd been lied to so many times before—heck, she'd almost married a liar!—and yet here she was, completely attracted to one.

He didn't exactly lie. He just didn't tell you about his past.

Either way, they were still strangers.

Still, she wanted him to know she saw the notification. She didn't want to hide that from him, and she hadn't done anything wrong.

Lacey took another deep breath and stared at the closed door of the infirmary. Her anxiety was running away with her. She had to remain calm and focused.

Just ask him and admit you saw it.

If he got mad, he got mad. It wasn't as if she actually read the email...though she did search him on the internet and saw the photos, and it was a bit surreal to know she was working with the missing future duke.

She opened the door and walked into the infirmary.

Thatcher was sitting in his office and glanced up from his desk.

"How is Ms. Lawrence?" he asked.

"Good. She tested her blood sugar and it was low, so she's going to rest, and I'll check on her later."

"I'm sorry you missed the excursion."

"I'm here to work. It's fine." She bit her lip and shut the door to his office behind her.

He frowned. "Is everything okay?"

"I don't like to deceive anyone." Her voice was shaking, and she was sweating.

His brows furrowed. "Neither do I."

"When I was looking at your photos earlier, an email notification popped up on the screen. I didn't click on it, but I saw it. I'm sorry."

His eyes widened. "A notification?"

"Yes." Her heart was pounding and thundering in her ears, and her palms were sweaty.

Thatcher folded his hands on his desk. "Thank you for being forthright about it."

"You're welcome. I don't believe in deception, and I have to trust the person I work with, so I wanted you to know I'm not nosy by nature."

"I appreciate that."

She could hear the edge in his voice, and she knew he was questioning what she might have seen. She'd be doing the same thing if she was in his position, wondering which email he saw and whether she had something she needed to hide.

"I know who you are, Thatcher. Or rather, Edward. And who your father is."

His lips pressed together in a thin line, his eyes sparking. She knew his back was up and she was treading on dangerous ground.

Thatcher didn't respond right away. He just tented his fingers and stared at her.

"Do you?" he finally asked, a bit stiffly.

"You're the missing heir. You'll be the next Duke of Weymouth." Her heart felt like it was in her throat.

She'd seen something personal, something secret about him, and she felt nervous knowing that because she wasn't sure about how she would feel if the situation was reversed. Not that she had any secrets to hide. She was just a private person.

She had never really let anyone in that deeply before.

Not that she was anywhere as interesting as a missing heir.

She just needed him to know that she'd seen the email and she wouldn't betray his trust because it wasn't her business. His secret was safe.

Her conscience would be clear.

Thatcher said nothing. His eyes narrowed. "How much?"

Lacey shook her head, not understanding what he was saying. "How much of the email did I see? I told you, just the notification—who it was from and the first line of the body of the email, which included the word *Son*."

"That is not what I meant," he snapped, standing up and leaning over the desk, staring her down in a way that unnerved her and shook her to her very core. "How. Much?"

"I don't understand," she said back just as fiercely.

Lacey didn't know what he wanted. Did he not believe her that she only saw the notification? Was he insinuating she'd read the actual email? Because she hadn't.

"I mean how much money do you want from me to keep this quiet?"

CHAPTER SEVEN

THATCHER HAD FELT sick to his stomach when Lacey said she saw one of his email notifications. He hoped it was something else she saw, but of course it wasn't. It was the one email he didn't want her—or anyone—to see.

The one from his father. And his father used his actual given name.

Edward.

Which he hated. It was the same name as his father's.

He preferred his middle name of Thatcher. Which his mother gave him. Still, Lacey saw it. There was no denying it, and it made him feel numb.

And now he had to pay her off. Why else would she tell him she knew who he was?

It was blackmail.

Only she seemed quite confused that he was asking her to name her price.

"Why would I want money?" she asked. "Are you insinuating that I'm trying to blackmail you?"

"Isn't that what you're doing?" he asked.

"No. And frankly, I'm insulted you would think that."

"You're insulted?" he asked, surprised.

She crossed her arms and frowned at him. "I am, rather."

"Why did you tell me, then, if you don't want money?" It was now his turn to be confused.

"I felt bad I had seen the notification, and I don't like deception. My ex-fiancé lied to me, cheated on me, so I don't like liars, and I didn't want to pretend I hadn't seen it. I wanted you to know that I knew and that your secret is safe with me. I wouldn't betray your trust."

Thatcher was growing increasingly confused, and he sat back down. He wasn't used to this.

The concept of feeling safe with someone was foreign to him.

The only person he felt safe with had been his late mother. His mother had never lied to him or hurt him, like his father had. She had been his home, and then she'd died, and he'd tried to be that for Michael. Only he couldn't.

Usually people wanted something from him, and he had assumed the same of Lacey. He thought she wanted money.

You don't know her. You can't trust her.

Which was true. He didn't know her, and he didn't feel safe that she had this knowledge about him. For five years he'd been in hiding, and now someone knew who he really was. It was bad enough that Michael had finally tracked him down to guilt him into coming home.

Now Lacey knew who he was.

But she didn't want his money. She said his secret was safe with her. Thatcher wanted to believe her, but couldn't.

"I'd rather just pay you off," he grumbled.

Lacey smiled. "Jeez, you are a jaded one."

He couldn't help but chuckle at that. "It's what I'm used to. So is this why you were acting so weird when you came back on the barge with Ms. Lawrence?"

Lacey's cheeks tinged pink. "Yes. It was weighing

heavy on me, knowing something you obviously didn't want the rest of the world to know."

"Okay. Well, thank you for telling me. I was a bit worried about your behavior."

"I'm sorry for that, but I felt it was right you knew that I knew who you were, Your— What do I call you?"

"Thatcher or Dr. Bell, please. Nothing needs to change, and I don't really enjoy the proper titles."

"Do you also not enjoy being called Edward?" she asked.

"No. I hate that name. It's my father's name. Thatcher is my middle name and my preferred moniker."

Lacey sat down across from him. There was a slight smile on her luscious lips. "So, you're really a physician?"

"Of course I am. I wouldn't have been in this job long if I was faking it."

"I know. I was just joshing. Not many dukes are doctors. None that I'm aware of anyway."

"Well, I am. I do need money to live."

"Your father is wealthy…" she said. "You don't necessarily need to work."

"And that's just it. My father is wealthy. I am not. I needed a job. I didn't want to rely on my father. That was never my style. I wanted to earn my keep. Always."

"Is your brother a doctor too?" she asked.

"No, he manages the estate…and our father. He does the work I technically should be doing as heir. The problem is, I was never really into it. I would've probably been really bad at it if I had given it a go."

"That's all I need to know."

"What? That I'd be a bad land manager? Or that you thought I was a spoiled rich kid pretending to be something I wasn't? This isn't some kind of dramatic novel."

"I know. I'm sorry I asked, and I'm sorry I saw the email notification. I really won't say anything. I promise." She crossed her heart to emphasize her point. "And I don't want your money. That's not why I told you."

He wanted to believe her, but he was having a hard time doing that.

He didn't know her. How could he trust her? He couldn't trust anyone...

His father had made him promises of being more available after his mother passed away, but he wasn't.

Kathleen swore she loved him, but she didn't. She loved the title. The money.

He wanted to believe Lacey, he truly did, but how could he?

The reality was that he was at her mercy, and he'd have to put his faith in her promise. He'd have to trust this complete stranger with a secret that he'd kept to himself for a long time.

"Thank you," he said, breaking the silence. "I appreciate it."

Lacey stood. "Well, I'm going to check on Ms. Lawrence again, and then I'll be back. I'm sure there will be some minor injuries as the barges full of passengers return from kayaking."

"You can almost always count on it." He stood as she moved to leave. "Lacey?"

She turned and looked back. "Yes, Dr. Bell?"

"Would you like to have dinner with me tonight? In my quarters, away from the others, so I can properly thank you and we can talk more about this?"

She smiled, a big, beautiful one that reached her twinkling eyes. His pulse was racing, and he felt like an awkward teen again in that first flush of youth, instead of the jaded, crotchety man he knew he'd become over the years. She was a breath of fresh air, and she made him want to breathe more.

"I'd like that very much," she said.

"Great. Around seven?"

"Sounds good. I'll see you in a bit. We'll meet at the boat launch when the passengers come back and assess the damage from kayaking."

He smiled and chuckled softly. "Okay. Perfect."

She shut his office door, and he sank back down in his chair.

What had he just done?

He hadn't been out on a date with someone since Kathleen.

It's not a date. It's a thank-you-for-not-blabbing dinner.

It had been five years since he'd admitted to anyone who he actually was. Even to himself, if he was honest. He'd put it all out of his mind when he'd left and just focused on his work and his dreams. It was scary having that knowledge—his truth—out there, but a bit freeing too.

He could be himself with Lacey and not have to worry about tripping up.

It almost meant trouble.

He was already fighting a strong attraction to her, and he didn't want this to mess up his tenuous hold on his control. He didn't want to fall for her. He didn't know what she wanted for her life. He didn't know where her heart lay. She'd just gotten out of a relationship and was even still wearing her engagement ring. He doubted she was ready for anything.

This was his last cruise.

He couldn't wait for her.

He had plans.

Nothing was going to stop him from his future and buying his land.

Nothing was going to keep him away from his dream.

Lacey didn't know why she'd agreed to come to his quarters for this private dinner. She should've politely said no, only she couldn't.

Thatcher obviously wanted to talk, and they hadn't had much of a chance when the passengers returned from the shore excursion because, as she had suspected, there were a lot of cuts and scrapes, and a sprain or two.

Thinking about having dinner with him alone later made the butterflies in her stomach do backflips. She was so nervous, and she'd never been this nervous about having dinner with a colleague before.

What was it about Thatcher that made her feel this way?

Excited.

Anxious.

A jumble of emotions.

Why was she letting herself be so affected by him? It wasn't like her to get emotionally attached or invested in people—she was too used to always getting hurt in the end. Every time they left a place when she was a kid, her heart had broken. She was used to being uprooted, but it still hurt to lose all the friends she'd made, knowing they likely wouldn't keep in touch. Only Carol had stayed in her life, but friendships were always different—harder—when they were at a distance.

It's why she locked away all of her emotions and allowed her work to keep her busy through the years.

She knew Thatcher would hurt her in the long run, just like all the others, but she couldn't help but accept his dinner invitation. He wanted to talk to her, to let her in, and she wanted to let him in too.

Her pulse raced as she thought about him, wondering if he might put his arms around her again.

She had to stop thinking about him like that.

Lacey wasn't sure what her future held, and Thatcher had plans practically etched in stone.

Plans that didn't include her.

And he could still go back to the UK and take up his dukedom, or whatever it was called.

The point was that Thatcher had options, and she didn't even know where the heck she was going once the ship docked back in Vancouver. Lacey had to get control over her runaway thoughts and this crazy anxiety that was gripping her. This was just dinner between two colleagues, nothing more. And she needed to keep reminding herself of that.

Still, her hand shook as she knocked on the door of his quarters.

He answered and smiled when he saw her. "Welcome."

He opened the door wider and ushered her in. His quarters were larger than hers, and he had a small enclosed balcony.

"Wow, I guess it pays to be a senior officer."

"You're a senior officer too," he quipped.

"Yes, but my cabin is nothing like this. Of course, I'm new and you've been the ship's doctor for a while, so that probably has something to do with it."

"True."

"Or maybe you're just lucky," she teased.

"I am, I suppose. I also took a slight cut in pay to get a better room, and I never take time off, so the captain assigned me this cabin." He motioned for her to come out onto the enclosed glass balcony.

It was only seven, and as it was late August, it wasn't near dark yet. There was a beautiful glow of a higher-latitude sun on the waters of the inside passage that played well with the green of the forests clinging to the land edging the calm waters.

It was beautiful.

She'd been in Vancouver for five years, but she'd never left it, never traveled north like this to see the landscape beyond the city borders.

Work took priority, and because she'd spent so long traveling around as a child, it had felt good to plant roots when her parents had retired there. She'd settled in, met Will and thought she'd have a stable life. Obviously, it wasn't meant to be. It was weird to be uprooted once again now, but on the flip side, she was being reminded of how much she loved traveling. She hadn't realized she was missing it. Even though she'd hated moving around so much as a kid, constantly feeling as though they were leaving almost as soon as they arrived, there was also another small part of her that had always liked seeing new sights, new landscapes.

She missed the adventure.

She missed the north. Alaska, or at least what she'd seen of it so far, was beautiful. The landscape made her think of Yellowknife, reminded her of that excitement she'd felt when her parents drove along that lonely stretch of highway to a city in the middle of the wilderness.

She missed it.

Vancouver, she didn't miss.

Maybe her father was right, and the world really was hers to make what she wanted of it.

"If you're lucky, we might see a pod of orcas go by," Thatcher remarked, interrupting her thoughts.

"Really? I've never seen them in person."

"Aren't you from Vancouver?"

"No, I was born in Toronto. I've been in Vancouver the last five years, but work takes precedence over sightseeing. I know you can go to an aquarium or sea life park to see them, but frankly I don't want to. I don't like captive whales." She sighed and gazed out over the water. "This is where they belong. Wild and free."

Thatcher smiled, his eyes twinkling. "I absolutely agree."

A blush warmed her cheeks, and she found she was suddenly nervous again.

Get a grip, Lacey.

Thatcher pulled out a chair, and she sat down, laughing nervously. "No one has ever pulled out a chair for me before."

"What? Not even your ex-fiancé?" he asked.

"Nope. We didn't go out together much. We were both too devoted to work to make time for fancy dinner dates."

"Well, us Brits are taught manners," he teased. "Well, some of us."

"Ha ha."

"Would you like a glass of wine?"

"Please."

"I've got rosé, if that's acceptable?"

"Very," she replied.

He brought out the bottle from the chiller, uncorked it and poured her a glass.

"Dinner will be here soon. I mentioned to the captain we were having a staff meeting, but I suspect the first officer doesn't quite believe my intentions are honorable."

Her heart skipped a beat as she took a sip of her drink. "Are they?"

"Perhaps," he teased, pouring himself a glass.

Lacey laughed nervously. "I don't know why I'm here."

"I just wanted to thank you for not blackmailing me."

"I would never do that."

"Also, I wanted to mention that we make port at Skagway tomorrow, and since all the passengers are disembarking, we both can enjoy shore leave."

"Great! I'm looking forward to shore leave and Skagway."

Thatcher cocked an eyebrow. "You're looking forward to Skagway?"

"Yes! It's the gateway to the Yukon and the gold rush."

"Are you going to ride the train?"

"No. Probably not. I wouldn't do it alone."

"Why not?" Thatcher asked.

She shrugged. "I don't know. I haven't ever really played tourist by myself before."

"It might be fun."

"It's more fun with friends, I think, and since I don't have any friends on this cruise, I'll sit it out."

"I'm your friend."

Her heart skipped a beat. "What?"

"I'm your friend." He smiled, his gray eyes sparkling. "Or at least, I could be."

Warmth spread through her body. Tears stung her eyes. She would like Thatcher to be her friend. She wasn't in a place to expect—or accept—more from him, but she could be his friend.

"I'd like that."

"Good. And as your friend, I'll go with you," he offered.

"Really?"

He shrugged. "Why not?"

Before she could respond to his question, there was a knock at the door.

"That must be dinner." He got up to answer the door, and one of the porters wheeled in a cart with their food. She watched him speaking with the porter, stunned and pleased at the thought of being Thatcher's friend.

And nothing more.

Even if there was a part of her that wanted more.

"Thanks, James," Thatcher said, giving the young man a tip.

James smiled. "Just leave it outside when you're done and I'll come by later and get it, Dr. Bell."

The porter left, and Thatcher handed her a covered plate from the room service cart. Whatever was under the cover smelled heavenly—like butter, garlic and cream. All the stuff that was bad for you...and yet tasted so good.

"I think it's shrimp scampi tonight," he said.

"Yum!" She lifted the cover, and after the puff of escaping steam evaporated, she could see that it was indeed shrimp scampi. Her stomach rumbled in appreciation. It was one of her favorite dishes.

"So what were we talking about?" Thatcher asked, sitting down.

"The Yukon and Skagway."

"Right." He smiled. "Not the most riveting of conversations."

She laughed. "I suppose not, but really it was my bad segue into asking you why you decided to settle in the Yukon."

"Because I love it. When I was younger, my father took me on a trip to tour northern Canada, and I was instantly hooked. It was a place I'd always wanted to go, and it surpassed my expectations. You know how you said that the orcas are wild and free? That's how I felt the first time I saw the Yukon."

"You knew right away?"

"I did. I always was fascinated by the north. I read everything I could about it. I was obsessed."

"Why?"

"Why not?" he asked.

"Well, you just come from a completely different world. It's not something I would've expected of a duke."

"Well, I'm not a typical duke. I'm not a duke at all," he teased.

Her heart fluttered again. His smile was so warm, it was dazzling, and his eyes were twinkling again. It made her insides flutter when he smiled at her like that.

It made her weak in the knees.

"No, I suppose you're not," she said softly.

Thatcher laughed. "I think part of what fascinated me about it was influenced by the fact that when my mother was ill, there was this young doctor who was so kind to her. He was from the Yukon, and he'd tell me stories. Impressionable youth and all that, I became obsessed and I read all I could."

"That sounds great. I've never felt such an attachment. I have to admit I'm a bit envious of that. Of course, how could I get attached when I was always on the move?"

Now who's lying?

She loved the north.

The only place that had ever really felt like home had been Yellowknife.

Now she was free. She could go back.

And that thought scared her.

Her freedom scared her.

"You said you liked the north," he prompted her.

"You're right. Some of my happiest memories are from the short time my father was stationed in the Northwest Territories and Yukon. I have to be honest, though. I try not to think about it. It hurts too much." Her voice shook, and she hated being so vulnerable in front of him. She usually always kept tight control of her emotions.

"Have you ever thought about going back?" he asked gently.

"Every day."

It was a shock to admit it out loud. She was over thirty, and she didn't have anything or anyone holding her back from doing what she wanted, going where she wanted.

And it scared her, the uncertainty of her future. She wasn't really sure she could ever go back.

"You should consider going back if Vancouver doesn't hold your heart any longer."

"I guess I could, but…"

"What?" he asked, the softness of his voice causing her heart to flutter.

"I don't know," she said nervously, fidgeting. "Everyone I knew in Yellowknife is probably gone or doesn't remember me anymore. My friend Carol was the only person from that time that I kept in touch with, and she passed away a year ago from cancer."

It wasn't really home anymore.

Nowhere was.

"I'm sorry for the loss of your friend."

Lacey tried to shrug indifferently, but she was fighting back the urge to cry. Tears were stinging her eyes, and she hated that she was being so vulnerable in front of him.

Tears were a sign of weakness in her mind. A weakness for her, anyway.

And then he reached across the table and touched her hand. The brush of his fingers against her knuckles sent a shiver of anticipation through her.

She should pull her hand away, only she couldn't. Thatcher offered comfort, and she took it. She wanted it.

She craved it.

And then his fingers touched her engagement ring. That brought reality crashing back. She pulled her hand away.

"Thanks. You're a good friend."

"And a good friend rides the train with his friend."

"You don't have to."

"Nonsense, we're taking the train tomorrow. It's been decided," Thatcher said.

"Will we be able to see your land from the train?" she teased, glad for the change in subject.

"No. I don't know where in the Yukon I'll be settling. Somewhere will sing to me, I'm sure."

"And eventually you'll head back to England?"

"No," he said firmly. And in that moment, everything about his countenance changed. The spark in his eyes was gone. His back straightened. It was definitely a touchy subject.

"Not even when you eventually become the duke?"

"No." He was quiet, and he took a sip of his wine. She knew this line of questioning was bothering him. Thatcher was the missing heir, so there were obviously issues he wasn't comfortable discussing. But could one just walk away from a title?

She didn't know.

All she knew was she wanted to change the subject, to steer the conversation back to something light and easy.

"So, after dinner, if there are no patients, do you want to go down to that eighties bar?"

"What?" he asked, almost choking on his wine. "Why?"

"I hear it's good."

"I don't dance."

"Don't all rich men who come from money know how to dance?"

"That's a stereotype," he said firmly, but the twinkle was back in his eyes.

"That's a shame. Although I could show you, if you'd like." She smiled slyly.

Thatcher shook his head. "I don't think that's wise."

"Why not?"

"I'm not the most graceful."

"Oh, come on. You're poised. You're strong. I'm sure you can hold your own on the dance floor."

Thatcher cocked an eyebrow. "I assure you, I have no grace when it comes to dancing."

"Look, you've got me going on a train to the Yukon tomorrow, so the least you could do is indulge me for a dance or two."

"So you *are* going to blackmail me after all," he teased.

"Maybe, in this."

Thatcher poured her another glass of wine and rolled his eyes, smiling. "Okay, I guess I have no choice."

"No. You don't," she teased.

"I have managed to keep from going there the last five years. You're breaking my streak."

"Good. It seems like you could use some fun."

She could also use some fun. She couldn't remember the last time she'd gone dancing.

It had been a long, long, long time.

"Hardly," he groused.

"Oh, come on," she teased. "It'll be fun."

"I'm a hermit. I keep a low profile."

"You'll have plenty of time in the Yukon to be a hermit. We're going dancing." She was a bit nervous, but she was excited. She just wanted to move to the music and not think about anything.

He was frowning, but she could tell it was just an act. He might complain, but he would go with her.

It was fun being with Thatcher. He was willing to give it a shot, but Will would've gotten angry and made her feel bad for asking. Not in a million years would Will have ever gone dancing with her.

She really didn't know what she was thinking being with Will. It was becoming clearer every day that she'd made the right decision coming here.

Lacey laughed, and they finished their dinner chatting and teasing each other about nothing in particular.

It was so easy to talk to him, and she couldn't remember the last time she enjoyed herself more. It was refreshing.

The thumping beats of eighties music filled the hallway on the main deck that led toward the nightclub, Spin Me Round. At least Lacey didn't insist they dress up in neon or crimp their hair.

Not that you could crimp his short, wiry, ginger hair.

He really didn't want to go into the club. There was a reason he was avoiding it. A lot of the crew frequented the bar, and a lot of passengers tended to go a bit overboard. Especially in regard to neon and acid-wash jeans.

It was over-the-top, loud, clichéd, and so not his scene, but Lacey was excited, and he couldn't resist her. He was lonely. He hadn't realized how lonely he'd been until he started spending time with Lacey and felt how fun it was to be with her.

She was easy to talk to.

When she came to his door for dinner, his breath had been taken away when he saw her.

Her hair was down, and she was wearing a soft gray sweater that bared one creamy shoulder. Everything about her look was soft, and it was all he could do not to hold her in his arms.

When he'd reached out to take her small, delicate hand over dinner, he hadn't been thinking straight. It was just meant to be an offer of comfort, and he'd thought she'd pull away right away. She hadn't, and it had felt right to hold her hand in his. But then he'd accidentally touched her engagement ring. That was when she had disengaged, and he realized he had pushed it too far.

He had to resist his attraction to her.

Why? the other part of his brain asked. The part that was attracted to Lacey.

The part that wanted to kiss her.

Lacey knew who he truly was. What if she was acting this way because of who his family was? He hated that those thoughts crept into his mind, but he'd been burned that way before and knew he needed to be careful.

Get a grip.

"The music sounds great!" she shouted as they waited outside the club to get in. She was bouncing up and down, and he hadn't ever seen her so animated or excited.

She was adorable.

And even though he didn't want to be here, he was glad he was here with her.

"How can you tell? It's all so loud."

Although he wouldn't admit it, the music was indeed catchy. The atmosphere reminded him of when he was in college and he and his friends would go clubbing.

It was in a themed club like this that he'd first met Kathleen, and maybe that was why he felt some trepidation—a bit of his lived trauma encroaching on the present. When he went to that club all those years ago, he'd felt out of place and awkward, and then Kathleen had approached him from across the dance floor. She was a beautiful woman, and she'd swept him off his feet, but he'd been younger then and not so hardened.

Thatcher hesitated when the line moved, not wanting to go in, and Lacey reached and slipped her hand into his, catching him off guard. This time it was she who was reaching out to comfort him. She pulled him into the club, the touch causing his blood to heat. Her hand was so tiny in his, and it felt right to hold her. It was reassuring. He knew he should take his hand back once they were inside, only he couldn't.

It was nice holding her hand as they walked into the club and made their way to the dance floor. Then all he could do was watch, mesmerized, as she began to dance. He couldn't even hear the music. All he saw was her as she moved to a popular song. All he wanted to do was stand there and stare at her.

He wished he could be as free as she was. She didn't seem to have any inhibitions. There were no protocols she had to follow. No one was watching her like the world watched him. And he was envious of her freedom. He knew what was waiting for him if he went back to his father's world, or if someone found him. Everything would change. What was he talking about? Everything had already changed when she saw that notification.

After she'd told him what she'd seen and left him alone in his office, he had opened the email from his father.

It was the first time he had written to Thatcher since he'd left the UK five years ago, following the worst argument they'd ever had. It was just after Kathleen had broken up with him, when he'd gone to see his father. Instead of finding solace for the betrayal, for the broken heart he was feeling, Thatcher was given a cold rebuff and a lecture about duty. That had been the breaking point.

That was when he'd realized he'd never please his father.

That was when he'd decided to leave.

"It's simple. You find another woman to be your duchess," his father had stated.

"Kathleen would've happily been my duchess."

"Then what's the problem?" his father had asked, confused.

"I don't want to be the duke," Thatcher had snapped.

His father's face had gone red. "What do you mean, you don't want to be the duke? It's not a choice. It's a duty one is born into."

"And it's one I don't want, which is why Kathleen left."

"You have no choice, Edward. Just like I didn't."

"You have two sons. Let Michael have it," Thatcher had said.

His father's eyes had narrowed. "No. It's your duty. You will be the next Duke of Weymouth. That's how it's always been done. Find a new duchess if Kathleen isn't willing to come back."

"Kathleen doesn't love me."

"What does love have to do with anything?"

That question had enraged Thatcher. His mother had loved his father, but it was obvious his father had never truly cared for her.

Thatcher wanted a woman to love him for him.

Even though his father insisted he had no choice in the matter, Thatcher wouldn't settle for a life he didn't want or a loveless marriage.

He had been unsurprised to find that the email didn't say anything new or different. His father hadn't changed.

For five long years, they hadn't communicated, and yet the old man was still going on about Thatcher's duty and his birthright, begging him to come home and do what was right.

His father couldn't understand that what Thatcher was doing *was* right for him. Distracted by his thoughts, Thatcher made his way off the dance floor to grab a drink.

"She is a firecracker!"

Thatcher spun around to see a couple of guys talking appreciatively about Lacey. They were right. She did have a spark and did ignite his blood. From the short time he'd known Lacey, he knew she was confident in her work, and that she was strong and tough, but there was a part of her that she kept hidden and controlled.

Almost like a firework getting ready to explode.

He smiled, finished his drink and headed out onto the dance floor as a ballad started, one of those old heavy metal ones, the lead singer screeching about romance over heavy guitar riffs. It was kind of piercing, but he didn't care. He just wanted her in his arms, and he was feeling brave.

"Can I have this dance?" he asked, bowing slightly at the waist.

"Of course." Her eyes were twinkling as she wrapped her arms around his neck and pulled him close, but she trembled slightly in his arms. His pulse was racing, and it was like he was dancing with a ball of flame that sent a zing through his body.

Making him feel alive again.

He felt every nerve ending in his body.

"See, dancing's not so hard," Lacey whispered in his ear.

He chuckled, pleased. "We'll see."

"Be nice."

"No. I think not." He grinned at her, holding her tight against him. His pulse was thundering between his ears, and he could feel her tremble again in his arms as the music slowed.

No one else was there, or at least no one that he noticed.

It was just the two of them.

It was as though time was standing still, and it took every ounce of his strength not to reach down, touch her face and pull her in for a kiss.

He noticed a pink blush had tinged her cheeks. He loved when she blushed like that. She was so stunningly beautiful. He was enchanted by her.

She smiled as she looked up at him, her fingers tickling the nape of his neck. "Would you like some air?"

"You mean leave? Yes. I would like that."

He wasn't a fan of crowded dance floors, and he wanted her alone.

More than anything.

This time he was the one who took her hand as they walked out of the club, and he led her up a set of stairs to the upper deck that was open. They walked hand in hand as the sun finished slipping down below the horizon and the first stars began to creep out.

Lacey stared up at the sky. "It's so beautiful."

He had to agree, but it wasn't the stars that he was looking at. He didn't care about the night sky.

"Have you ever seen the northern lights?" he asked.

"Yes, but not for some time. I hope we'll see some once we're further north."

"I hope so too." He thought about how magical it would be to kiss her under the aurora borealis.

She was so beautiful, and as they stood there, stargazing, he reached out and touched her cheek. A pink blush crept up her neck, and he felt goose bumps break out over her soft skin. She bit her bottom lip, her big eyes looking up at him through thick lashes.

He couldn't resist. He pulled her into his arms and softly tasted her lips.

His hands went into her hair as she pressed closer, the kiss deepening as he drank her taste in.

What're you doing?

She pushed him away gently.

"I'm sorry," she said breathlessly.

"No. I'm sorry."

He didn't want to rush her into anything. Especially because anything between them would only ever be temporary. He had plans, and she wasn't part of them. He was getting swept up in something. They barely knew each other—she was a stranger. He knew he shouldn't trust her, but he was lonely. Until Lacey came on board, he hadn't realized how isolated he had been in his self-imposed exile.

"I can't, Thatcher. I only just left a man at the altar. I can't… I can't do this."

Lacey dashed away, and he cursed himself under his breath.

He knew she was vulnerable. What had he been thinking, kissing her like that?

Her lips, his body answered back.

Thatcher shook that thought out of his mind. Lacey was off-limits no matter how much he wanted her.

CHAPTER EIGHT

LACEY TOSSED AND turned all night. The feel of Thatcher's lips was still etched on hers, and she touched them in the dark, yearning for more.

She was also kicking herself for leaving.

For one moment she'd almost been swept away. When he took her in his arms and kissed her, her body had melted.

It was like she'd been woken up, like everything that came before had been in black-and-white and suddenly her world was Technicolor.

For a moment she forgot about Will, her wedding... everything.

When it all came rushing back, she'd felt guilty for allowing herself to get caught up in the moment with Thatcher. Like she had betrayed Will or something.

Will cheated on you, though.

And that was true, but she couldn't shake the feeling that *she* had done something wrong.

Will always accused her of being too work-centered and not affectionate enough. She should've seen that as a warning sign, and the more she thought about it, their last fight before she'd caught him cheating on her should've told her what was going to happen next...

"You never pay attention to me," Will had said.

Lacey had looked up from her computer. "What?"

Will had frowned. "Exactly. You work more than me, and I'm a surgeon."

She'd smiled. "I'm sorry. I thought we'd agreed that work came first. You work a lot too, and I just got in the habit of doing the same."

"Well, you barely pay attention to me. You rarely show affection in public," he'd groused.

"Where is this coming from, Will? Why now? You never liked it before."

Will had shaken his head. "I don't know. I mean, our situation together is ideal. I guess this must be a midlife crisis."

"You're not at midlife yet. You're a successful surgeon with a fiancée. Hardly midlife meltdown material."

"That's not funny, Lacey. I have so much more to accomplish," he'd said firmly, but there had been something about the tone of his voice that had made her a bit worried.

"Is it that you're not sure where I fit into all this?" Lacey had asked quietly.

He'd nodded. "Do you fit into the life I planned for myself? I'm not so sure."

Will had walked away, and she'd gone back to work.

If she was honest, Lacey hadn't been sure either. Will had laid out his life for himself, and they were only getting married because it seemed like the logical thing to do. They liked each other, but now, looking back, she wasn't sure she'd ever really been in love with him.

Thatcher's kiss had been amazing and rocked her to her very core, in a way Will's kisses never had.

She didn't know what she wanted. This cruise was supposed to be a chance for her to clear her head. Instead, it confused her all the more.

She didn't know what she wanted.

Except to continue that kiss. That kiss that had fired her senses.

It was right to break things off before they got too heated, though. She wanted to be friends with Thatcher, but nothing more. She couldn't commit to anyone when she didn't know what she wanted.

Are you sure? a tiny voice asked in her head, but she shook that annoying little voice away and got up an hour earlier than she had to. She got dressed and ready for her day in Skagway, even though she wasn't sure she even wanted to go after what had happened. If Thatcher wanted to put off their plan to take the train over the White Pass, then she'd be fine with that.

She didn't want to make him uncomfortable.

They could be friends, right?

She just wanted things to go back to the way they were, before that kiss.

Lacey liked working with Thatcher, and she wanted the rest of this cruise and the trip back to Vancouver to go as smoothly as possible.

After she finished getting ready for the day, she headed out of her quarters and made her way to the infirmary, where she and Thatcher were going to meet. The ship was still and quiet as it had docked in the Skagway port overnight.

Soon the rest of the passengers would be getting up and making their way off the ship to enjoy a long day in Skagway.

To distract herself from the silence, Lacey went over the cruise itinerary in her mind. She knew that after today, the ship would depart in the middle of the night on the way to the next port of call, which was Juneau, to view the glaciers, and then out into the Gulf of Alaska to make its way up to Anchorage, stopping along the coast. After Anchorage, the passengers would depart and fly home after three weeks at sea.

Lacey was grateful for the long break from real life. She needed to get her mind straight.

She needed to think.

She took a deep breath and headed into the infirmary.

Thatcher was working on something, but was casually dressed for his shore leave in jeans and a nice sweater. The deep forest green color suited him, and her heart skipped a beat. He turned when she walked in, and she could feel the awkward tension between them.

"Hi," he said.

"Hey," she responded, wringing her hands.

"Look, about last night…"

"I'm sorry for bolting."

He smiled, looking relieved. "I'm sorry too. I didn't mean to kiss you."

"I think I was kissing you back," she said, laughing nervously.

"Yes."

Lacey laughed again, softly this time. "Look, I just want things to go back to the way they were. I would hate to ruin our professional relationship, and I would hate to ruin a possible friendship."

He nodded. "Agreed. I wasn't sure that you would come today. I bought two tickets for the darn train, and thought I might have to ride it alone."

"You bought two tickets?" she asked. "I can buy my own ticket."

"I expect you to," he teased. "I'm kidding. It's my treat. I got tickets for the first trip. That way, we can get it done first thing and have the rest of the day open. It's actually supposed to be sunny instead of rainy, which is kind of amazing."

Lacey chuckled. "Well, that sounds great. I'm glad we can put this thing behind us and move on."

Thatcher smiled. "Me too. Shall we go? We can disembark with the rest of the passengers."

"That sounds great."

Thatcher grabbed his raincoat. "Do you have a beanie?"

"No. It's August. Should I?" she asked, confused.

"It can get cold on the pass. We'll hit one of the outfitter stores on the walk to the train and get you some warmer outerwear. Besides, they won't let you back into Canada without the right supplies when going over the White Pass." He locked the infirmary, and they headed to the lower deck, where everyone was disembarking into the port.

"What?" she asked.

"Haven't you studied anything about the gold rush era? You needed a certain amount of supplies to head to the Klondike or they'd turn you away. I thought you knew that. You were excited to come to Skagway."

"I know it was the gateway, but I'm sorry that I don't remember the exact list of things that prospectors were required to have to go over the pass."

"They needed to take a ton of supplies to survive the Canadian winters in the Yukon, and if they didn't have the right amount of items at the checkpoint, the Mounties would send them back. Sam Steele and all that. You're the daughter of an RCMP officer and you don't know that? For shame," he teased.

Lacey rolled her eyes. "Sorry. I do remember that it was almost like a human chain, just a constant mass of men going over the pass, and that both horses and men would often fall to their deaths."

"So you pick up on the deaths, but not on the supplies. I have to say, Lacey, that's kind of morbid."

They both laughed, and she thought about how good it felt to laugh with him.

It also felt good to feel that tension from their kiss the night before melting away.

They joined the mass of people funneling out of the ship and down a gangway to the dock.

Once they were off the boat, people began to disperse.

Lacey stared around in wonder at the small bay that was surrounded by not only mountains but also other behemoth cruise ships filling the harbor and towering over the small town.

The main part of town was filled with brightly colored buildings meant to attract tourists, but Lacey closed her eyes and tried to picture what it would have been like when this town was founded on the spoils of the gold rush.

The beach would have been filled with cargo that was brought in off the barges and steamboats. There would have been tents, mud and hope for the gold that could be found over the treacherous White Pass. There would also have been absolute despair from those who had lost everything and now needed to find a way to get back home.

That's if they survived, because until the narrow-gauge train was built, the walk was often gruesome, littered with those who had dropped dead of starvation or disease.

Maybe Thatcher was right, and she was a bit morbid.

They made their way past many tour company booths offering passengers cheap tours for the surrounding area. There were wildlife tours, fishing expeditions, dog mushing, helicopter rides to the glacier and more.

As they followed the general direction of the crowd, they passed one of the first stores in the historic frontier town, which sold everything from T-shirts to diamonds to outerwear. Lacey bought herself a pair of woolen mittens and a beanie, and then they walked over to a bakery.

The shop smelled like coffee, sugar and golden sizzling fat. It made her stomach rumble.

"Two coffees and a fry bread, please," Thatcher ordered.

The woman behind the counter nodded and walked away.

"Just one?" Lacey asked.

"They're huge and full of sugar. One is enough, believe me."

When the woman came back, Lacey's eyes widened. It *was* huge. Thatcher took the coffees and Lacey paid, then picked up the freshly made fry bread. It was warm in her hand, and despite the paper wrapped around it, the powdered sugar was everywhere.

They made their way over to a small table, where Thatcher set down the coffees.

"Go on," he said.

"What?" she asked.

"Take a bite." His eyes were twinkling. "It's your first time. Ladies first and all that."

She took a bite, and a whoosh of powdered sugar puffed out as she bit into the warm, heavenly dough.

She couldn't help but laugh.

"How bad is it?" she asked, grabbing a napkin to wipe.

He was chuckling. "You look like you've stuck your face in a snowbank."

"You knew it would do that!" she accused him, laughing.

"Maybe. This is the only shop that does them like this." Then he reached out and brushed sugar from her nose. The simple act made her pulse race and her breath catch in her throat.

He paused and moved away as if realizing what he'd done.

She blushed and handed him the fry bread. "Well, that was an experience."

"It's good, though, right?"

"It is. It reminds me of a beignet a bit."

He smiled, but there was an awkward tension that settled between them again. She hated that.

"Come on," he said. "We better go or we'll miss the train."

After boarding, they found seats near the back.

"You have the window seat, since this is your first time and all," Thatcher offered.

"Why, thank you." She slid into the seat, and Thatcher sat next to her. She set down her coffee cup in the small cup holder. "How long is this trip, anyway?"

"Are you in a rush?" he teased.

"I do want to visit the Gold Rush Cemetery."

He wrinkled his nose and made a face. "You really are morbid."

She laughed. "I just want to see where Soapy Smith is buried."

"Soapy who?" he asked.

"Okay, now who doesn't know their frontier history?"

"I guess between the two of us, we'll have enough information to be know-it-alls on this trip."

"That sounds like fun. So, are you going to answer my original question?"

"Which was what?"

"How long is the trip?"

"Two hours, almost three round-trip. Of course, we could've said bugger it all to the whole day and taken the eight-hour trip to Lake Bennett and back."

"Ooh, that sounds fun, but probably way more pricey."

"It is, and you need slightly more time than we have."

Lacey settled against the seat as the last of the passengers from the various cruise lines boarded the train, and they waited for the final preparations to be made to start their journey over the winding White Pass to the summit.

Thatcher was absolutely exhausted. After their kiss last night, he couldn't think about anything else. All he did was toss and turn, dreaming about that kiss and what it was like to have her in his arms.

It had felt right in a way it had never felt with Kathleen. Then again, he'd thought what he had with Kathleen had felt right at the time, but he'd been proven wrong in the end.

He barely knew Lacey.

Why did he want to continue whatever this was developing between them? The only reason he could think of was the fact that Lacey actually listened to him. She didn't think his plans were crazy like Kathleen had. She didn't try to convince him to go back and take up his birthright.

It may also have been his loneliness that caused him to act the way he did. He'd been irrational, foolish and swept up in the moment.

She was easy to talk to, and it had felt right, so he'd kissed her. And then she pushed him away. She'd been hurt and vulnerable, and maybe he shouldn't have done that.

He was worried he'd scared her off and hadn't been one hundred percent sure that Lacey was going to show up today. So when she walked into the infirmary, he'd been so relieved.

He'd also been relieved that she wanted to continue their friendship, because that's what he wanted too.

It was nice to have a friend again. He'd worked with many other nurses, but they'd never been interested in forming any kind of friendship, and that didn't bother him in the least. Thatcher wasn't sure what was so different about Lacey, but he wanted to continue to find out. He couldn't stop thinking about her.

And he liked being with her.

For the first time in a long time, he was enjoying himself.

He was glad that they were able to work this out. He was glad there was no awkwardness after his faux pas last night. Not that he thought kissing her was a mistake. He just didn't want to push her away.

The only problem was, the more he was spending time with her, the more he didn't want just a friendship.

He wanted more from her, and he was doing everything in his power not to put his arm around her or hold her hand.

There was a moment in the bakery when he'd forgotten that she wanted to be just friends, and he'd come close to kissing that sugar off her nose. Her lips were sweet, and he wanted to taste them again.

It would have been an incredibly intimate gesture. He'd known he shouldn't do it and had stopped himself just in time.

But he was drawn to her.

It would be hard to say goodbye to her when the cruise was over and they went their separate ways, because that was one thing he wasn't sure about when it came to Lacey.

She didn't know where she was going.

And he did.

He glanced over at her as she rested her chin on her hand, staring out the window as the train slowly climbed up to the White Pass. She was beautiful sitting there, so thoughtful.

"Come on," he said, standing up and holding out his hand.

"What?" she asked, startled.

"You can't experience the climb this way. Let's step outside."

"Outside? Are you crazy?"

"It's safe," he said. "There's a platform between cars. Come on."

Lacey took his hand and hers shook in his, which he found endearing. He led her through the jostling car. They opened the door and stepped out onto the platform that connected the cars. There was a spot for them to stand so she could get a real feel of the way the narrow-gauge train hugged the side of the mountain and see the drop down. They could also see a train that had departed after them slowly starting its ascent.

The trees became thinner as they climbed and clung to the precarious side, and her mouth opened in wonder.

"This is amazing. I can see why they called this Dead Horse Pass."

"You seriously have to stop with the death stuff," he teased.

"Sure, sure," she said.

There was a jostle, and as Lacey cried out, he braced

himself behind her, his arms going around her. "You're okay."

"My heart is racing," she said a bit breathlessly.

"It's an old train, but it's safe, I promise. Look at the trestle bridge. You can see the glacier, which means we're getting closer to the pass."

Lacey craned her head to look over the side, and he held on tight, making sure that she didn't fall. He could smell her hair. It felt so right being this close to her.

"Do they let us out to walk around up there?" she asked.

"We don't have passports."

"I bet I can. I'm Canadian." She smiled smugly, teasing him.

"You still don't have your passport. The ship does."

"Right." She frowned. "I'm a Mountie's daughter. I should be allowed. I mean, my great-grandfather was a Mountie up in the Yukon."

"I highly doubt your great-grandfather worked with Sam Steele," he said dryly.

"No, but we had a dog who was named Sam Steele." Her eyes were twinkling with amusement, and he couldn't help but laugh with her.

"I don't think that will count."

They stood quietly as they went over the trestle bridge and stared down at the maw of forest, rock and water so far down. His pulse was thundering in his ears.

"Here comes a tunnel," she announced, and he knew it was the last tunnel they would go through before the White Pass.

Thatcher just stared at her. His heart was racing, and his body felt like it was on fire. He was burning for her.

For the first time in a long time, he wanted someone

again, but he was scared to open his heart. He wasn't sure that he could do it, even though he wanted to.

Even though he wanted Lacey. Maybe it was because she knew the truth about who he was, and that was incredibly freeing. The tunnel ended and the summit came into view.

There were flagpoles designating the separation of Canada and the US and a small obelisk in memorial for all those pack animals who had died along the route.

The train slowed to a stop, and they waited to make the proper turnaround and head back down.

"This is the boring part," he murmured.

There were a lot of people around him taking pictures, which made him uneasy, and she frowned as she looked up at him, as if reading his thoughts.

"Shall we go back to our seats? There seems to be a crush of people out here all of a sudden."

"I would like that." It was unnerving being in a crowd sometimes. He was always worried that someone would recognize him, and then the press would find him.

They were headed back to their seats when the door from the back of their car was flung open by an out-of-breath conductor.

"Is there a doctor on board?"

Thatcher raised his hand. "I'm a doctor. Is everything okay?"

The conductor was trying to catch his breath and shook his head. "There's a woman in the back car who has gone into labor!"

CHAPTER NINE

LACEY DIDN'T HAVE time to ask why a woman who was nine months pregnant was allowed on a train that climbed to this elevation—she could ask that later. Right now she had to jump into action. As soon as the conductor had announced that a woman was in labor, she took off like a shot, with Thatcher close at her heels.

"I'm a midwife," she said.

"Thank God," the conductor said, still breathless. "Can you follow me?"

"Lead the way, by all means," Thatcher urged.

They followed the conductor, who had clearly checked the other cars for a doctor, as the passengers they went by were abuzz, and all eyes were on them.

She had noticed how uneasy Thatcher had been when there were a bunch of people snapping pictures of the White Pass around them, so she could only imagine how he was feeling now, with all the other passengers staring at them.

The last car was used for the staff, so no other passengers were present, and it was apparent that the woman and her partner had made their way back there for privacy.

"I found a doctor and a midwife," the conductor announced, the relief in his voice palpable.

The woman in labor was panting and in pain, on the floor with a blanket covering her. Lacey grabbed the first aid kit that had been brought out and pulled on a pair of gloves.

"I'm Lacey Greenwood. I'm a nurse practitioner and certified midwife. This is Dr. Bell."

The woman in labor nodded, and her partner smiled shakily. "I'm Sherry, and this is my wife, Robyn. This is our first!"

Lacey smiled encouragingly. "Congratulations."

"What do you need?" Thatcher asked Lacey.

"Water and emergency blankets, for starters. I also don't want this train moving until this baby is delivered."

The conductor left to speak to the engineer.

"I'll be your nurse this time," Thatcher offered.

Lacey nodded and examined Robyn. She was fully dilated, and Lacey could make out the top of the head.

"Okay, Robyn, on your next contraction, I need you to push." Lacey placed her hand on the top of Robyn's abdomen and felt the next contraction building up. "Robyn, I need you to bear down now and push for me."

Robyn pushed with all her might, her wife, Sherry, holding her shoulders and encouraging her.

"Good," Lacey told Robyn. "You're doing so well."

The contraction ended, and Lacey could see the baby was moving and getting ready to turn.

"I knew this was a mistake," Robyn whimpered between contractions.

"What was?" Lacey asked.

"Coming on the train," Sherry said. "We thought

we had time. She's only thirty-five weeks. This was our last hurrah."

Lacey nodded. "Well, babies do have their own time-line."

"Oh, God," Robyn moaned.

"Here comes another contraction. I need you to push, Robyn. Hard. Come on," Lacey urged.

It only took a couple more pushes, and the baby was born, screaming heartily into the world.

"You have a brand-new Canadian," Lacey teased. "It's a boy."

Sherry and Robyn began to cry with joy as Lacey cleared the baby's throat, and the little boy cried even harder.

Thatcher was smiling as he clamped the cord for her.

"Sherry, would you like to cut the cord?" Lacey asked.

Sherry nodded, crying with happiness as Thatcher handed her the scissors. She cut her son's umbilical cord, and Lacey wrapped the baby up and handed him over to his parents. She couldn't help but smile as the new family got to know each other.

Lacey then delivered the placenta and ensured that all looked good.

The conductor entered the carriage. "Is everything all right?"

Lacey nodded. "You can tell the engineer it's safe to head back down now, and if you can arrange for an ambulance to meet the train at the Skagway station, that would be excellent."

The conductor nodded. "I'll do that straightaway."

Lacey cleaned up with Thatcher's help as the train started with a chug, and the conductor got on the speaker to announce the birth of wee little Christopher and to congratulate the new family.

"You did amazing," Thatcher said to Lacey. "I was so glad you were here to do this. It's been a long time since I delivered a baby. It's certainly not something you usually see on a cruise ship."

Lacey laughed. "No. I suppose not. I never thought that particular skill of mine would be used on this trip, if I'm honest."

"Well, usually it's not," he said, and then he smiled at her. "Of course, this has been one for the books."

She chuckled. "It has, hasn't it? I'm glad I was able to help."

She looked back at the happy family. It was such a beautiful scene. She always thought she wanted to have children, but then there was a part of her that didn't think she could have them. Maybe it had never been on her mind because she wasn't sure where she was going to end up for so long.

Will hadn't wanted a family anytime soon.

Another sign she had missed. Why did she ever think that Will had been right for her?

She loved babies.

She loved kids, and looking at Sherry and Robyn holding their brand-new baby, there was a part of her that was envious of their love. There was a part of her that longed to have what they had. Her parents had always given her love. They had been her only constant.

Warmth spread through her. A warmth that she hadn't felt before, or at least hadn't felt in a long time. The warmth she'd felt when she and her family had been settled in Yellowknife. When she had friends and they stayed in one place for a long time.

When it had felt like home.

And then her father got a new posting and she'd had to say goodbye to that home. She'd had to say goodbye to her friends, her teachers, everything she loved about that place. It had broken her heart.

That was when she'd decided never to get too attached to things or people.

It was just easier when you knew you'd eventually have to move on. She hadn't thought about those feelings of connectedness and warmth in a long time, but seeing Robyn and Sherry with their new baby brought it all back. Suddenly it seemed to be the exact thing she wanted.

And for the first time in a long time, she thought about her future and about what she wanted. It made her nervous.

It made her wish for things that she thought were long forgotten.

Things she had thought she'd put aside and buried away, but apparently hadn't. She didn't realize that it was all still simmering, there below the surface.

It was unwelcome.

It was unsettling.

Because she suddenly wanted it so much, and wasn't sure she'd ever get it.

Lacey watched the ambulance take the new family off to the hospital so that the doctors there could check over the newest member of Sherry and Robyn's family.

"You did a good job on that train," Thatcher said, coming up beside her.

"Thanks. I didn't have to do much other than catch," Lacey joked.

"Were they part of the *Alaskan Princess* cruise?"

"No," Lacey said. "I had the paramedics contact their ship. I didn't know what the protocol was in a case like this, but that seemed to make the most sense."

"I don't know either. I haven't had to deal with something like this before."

They walked away from the station and headed back to town. She was still feeling a bit sad and didn't know what to say.

"Are you quite all right?"

"How do you mean?" Lacey asked.

"You've gone quiet. Something changed up there after the baby was born."

Lacey shrugged. "I don't know. I guess I was thinking about how lucky that little family was."

When Will had told her he didn't think kids would happen soon, she'd sort of just buried that desire for a family deep down. After all, she cared for Will and had been with him for two years. Not having a family right away wasn't a reason to walk away from a marriage, was it?

Except it was. She realized that now. When she saw that little baby with his parents, it had made her feel all warm and sparkly on the inside.

She wanted that.

She always had.

"I thought you had a good childhood?" Thatcher asked.

"I did, but we were always on the move, and that birth just made me think of the time when we stayed put for a while. It made me think about how happy I was. I didn't really realize how much I missed it until I saw them. So it made me a little bit..."

"You were reminiscing?"

"Yes." She smiled. "I was. So, sorry if I'm a bit maudlin."

"I know something that will cheer you up."

"It's okay. I don't really need to visit the Gold Rush Cemetery."

"I know, and that's not what I was suggesting," Thatcher said. "I was thinking we could go to a saloon and grab some lunch. One of those really cheesy places with really bad food. What do you say?"

She laughed. "You want to take me to a place that has bad food?"

"No, good food, but bad for you."

"That sounds great." And it did. She was hungry, and she needed to take her mind off everything. She needed to bury those feelings deep down again.

She wasn't sure what her future held, and she didn't want to think about something she probably wouldn't ever have.

Thatcher knew that something had changed with her. She had two great parents, but she was sad too. They were more similar than he'd thought, because seeing that new happy family had also made him long for a family.

A wife and children.

Only that wasn't in his future, and it made him melancholy. One thing was for certain, Lacey did an amazing job helping that mother deliver her baby.

He was so impressed.

He loved working with her, and it was an amazing moment, watching a new life come into the world. That was something he didn't get to see very often.

There was a point in his past when he'd thought about having children with Kathleen, back when he still believed Kathleen loved him. But after Kathleen left him, she took with her all his dreams about having a family. Now it was something he thought he could never have, so he didn't waste time dwelling on it. Instead he focused on the plans for his land and a small practice.

When that little boy was born, though, it had forced him to think about that lost dream he had.

What they both needed to do was have a bite to eat to cheer them up and celebrate the fact that there was a new baby boy in the world. This was shore leave, and it would be their last until they got to Anchorage.

Then, once they were back in Vancouver, he was done. It saddened him to think that his time with Lacey was finite.

This was his last trip. He'd be heading off to the Yukon to start his life over, and Lacey would be off somewhere else too. That thought gave him pause.

The Rusty Saloon was close to the port where all the cruise ships docked, and it was dressed up to be like one of the old-time frontier saloons. He'd never bothered to eat here, but he had kind of wanted to. He'd heard the food was good, and the few times he'd come into Skagway, he'd peeked inside, but never actually grabbed a table for himself as it was always so busy.

A grin broke across Lacey's face as they walked through the swing doors. The sign said to seat yourself, so they found a small booth that was tucked away in the corner with a window that faced out over the pier. They could see the ships, the water and the mountains.

"This is a lot of fun," she said excitedly. "Do you come here every time you're in Skagway?"

"No. This is my first time here."

She frowned. "You said the food was good. I assumed that meant you'd been here before."

"I heard that the food was good, but I never came here on my own. So I guess having lunch here is a good way to finish off my last visit to Skagway."

"You might come back to Skagway again."

"Probably not. I plan to hide myself away in the Yukon."

She cocked her head to one side. "Why hide, though?"

"I think that it's pretty obvious. So I'm not found."

"Your father knows where you are."

He tensed when she mentioned him. Thatcher didn't want to talk about his father. Not now. The email hadn't said anything new. He'd heard it all before.

"He knows the general area where I am. It's no secret, though. He's known my whole life where I wanted to go. It's not just him. It's also everything else I want to hide from and ignore. I don't think that you quite understand the embarrassment of your fiancé cheating on you and finding out via the papers. The whole world watching every single moment of your life. Nothing about my life was private."

Her cheeks flushed pink, and he realized it was the first time he'd mentioned that he'd been cheated on.

"I'm sorry that happened to you," she said quietly.

"Look, I didn't mean to get angry with you. It's just…my situation is unique."

"Is it?" she asked. "We were both cheated on."

"Yes. But in my case, she did it because she only ever wanted me for my title," he whispered. "Whereas I wanted her. She wanted the money and the fame, not me, and my choice to not accept my birthright was her breaking point."

She nodded.

He cocked an eyebrow. "What about you?"

"Honestly, now that I think about it, I should have

known it was coming, but I honestly didn't see the signs. We were together for so long, and marriage seemed like the right next step."

"Sounds like you were going to settle."

He noticed she was fiddling with that engagement ring again. It annoyed him that someone else had given her a ring first.

He was...jealous.

Lacey sighed. "It was...logical. I'm not sure that I believe in romantic love at this point. I've been hurt too many times."

Thatcher was disappointed with that answer. He wasn't sure why, though, as it really didn't affect him. Except...he did believe in love. He'd been blinded by it and burned by it, but he still believed that romantic love existed for some people.

Definitely not for him, but he thought it was sad that she didn't believe in love, especially when she was such a loving, caring healer.

"I still believe in love. Not that it's for everyone," he said, and he saw a strange expression cross her face. Almost like she was disappointed.

"This is awful," she said.

"What?"

"Us. Two jaded, maudlin creatures sitting here in such a fun place with jobs on a cruise ship, doing what we love, and we're complaining about not having or believing in romantic love. It's kind of a bummer."

He chuckled at that. "Yes, it kinda is. So, then, what do we talk about?"

"Well, did you ever email your dad back?"

"My *dad*?" he asked, teasing. "I would never refer to him as Dad. I've always just called him Father."

"Don't be so pedantic, you pelican." There was a

twinkle in her big blue eyes, and it looked like everything that had been bothering her before had melted away.

"That is the first time I've ever been called a pelican as an insult before."

"I couldn't think of anything else." She nodded. "First bird I saw outside, I suppose."

"Is a pelican so bad?" he asked.

"No, except they kind of stink, so maybe." She smiled, laughing slightly.

"Thanks." He sighed. "No, I haven't talked to my father or responded to his email."

"Do you think you should? Maybe he's worried about you."

"He's not worried about me," Thatcher intoned.

"You said he didn't know where you were, but had a general idea. I mean, I know my parents would be worried if they didn't know where I was."

"Remember, our childhoods were completely different."

Which was true. Her parents both loved her, and it seemed as though they made sure she always knew it.

Thatcher understood that his mother had cared for him and Michael, but she died when he was young and Michael was barely more than an infant. As for his father, he was just absent and really had no interest in them until they got older.

Even then, it was all about duty.

It was all about pomp and circumstance.

It was cold and forced.

There was nothing warm or cheery about his childhood. That was why Thatcher had always sworn that if he had children of his own, it would be different.

Except, he wasn't going to have children. It was kind

of hard to plan for a family when you didn't plan on having someone to share your life with.

"What're you going to order?" he asked, trying to read the very large menu, but he was unable to focus on any of the words.

"I'm surprised that they have poutine on here," she murmured. "I'm going to have to try it and see what it's like. You don't often see it outside of Canada."

"Probably because Skagway is so close to the Canadian border. It's only a two-hour drive or so to Whitehorse."

"I didn't realize it was that close. Well, I'll definitely have to taste their poutine, then. See if they do it justice."

"That is something I haven't tried," Thatcher admitted. "I've been in Canada for five years, granted mostly doing cruises, but still haven't tried poutine, and I haven't the faintest idea what is in it."

Her mouth hung open. "Are you crazy? Have you been living under a rock?"

"Sort of. I haven't the time or inclination to pay attention to much except working and planning out the next stage of my life in the Yukon."

Lacey shook her head. "I can't believe you don't know."

"Well, what is it?"

"French fries, gravy and cheese curds."

"That's it?" he asked. "That's what the hype is about?"

"Split a large plate with me and you'll see it lives up to said hype."

Thatcher folded his menu. "Fine. Since you're buying."

Lacey smiled and closed her menu too. The waitress

then came over, and Lacey ordered the largest plate of poutine they had and a couple of pops. She then chatted with him about how different places in Canada sometimes called it *soda* and sometimes called it *pop*. Since her parents were from Toronto, they called it *pop*, and that's what she grew up saying.

It was so great to talk to her about nothing.

It helped him to forget everything else.

And that was a dangerous thing indeed. Dangerous for his heart, because he couldn't deny any longer that he was falling for her.

Even though he had plans and Lacey didn't fit into any of them.

She could, a little voice said in his head, but he didn't want to get his hopes up.

They finished their lunch, and he had to admit that the poutine hadn't been terrible. It was quite good, actually. Lacey admitted that the poutine was good, but not the best she'd had. Apparently it was fairly passable, especially for a restaurant that was outside Canada.

For the rest of the afternoon, he tried not to let his mind wander to the what-ifs when it came to Lacey Greenwood.

He just wanted to enjoy his day with her.

Their last shore excursion. In Juneau they would have to stay on board the ship because it was such a short trip, and then they would head out into the Gulf of Alaska, following the marine highway to finish off the cruise in Anchorage.

At least in Anchorage they could disembark for a day before they headed back to Vancouver. Though he'd been looking forward to it, it suddenly made him sad to think that his last cruise with the *Alaskan Prin-*

cess was coming to an end and that his time with Lacey would soon be over.

Apparently he was a sucker for punishment, falling for a runaway bride.

CHAPTER TEN

THE SHIP HAD left in the middle of the night when it got clearance from the port authorities, but there was a storm as they headed to Juneau from Skagway, and the ship was moving slowly as rain lashed at its sides.

With the rougher weather, some of her original patients were suffering miserably from seasickness again.

Lacey was also feeling a bit miserable, but it wasn't the motion of the ship that was bothering her. The only thing making her sick was the turmoil of her own emotions. She'd had such a brilliant time with Thatcher in Skagway, especially when they had been on the train to the White Pass and he took her out on the little deck that connected the cars so they could stand outside and watch as the train wound its way up the high mountain pass.

It felt like they were on top of the world, and when his arms came around her, she'd felt safe. Thatcher made her feel safe in a way she hadn't in a long time, and she'd wanted to stay in that moment forever.

She could see clearly now that she had loved Will, but it was different. If it had been the two of them on that train ride, neither would've said much besides polite small talk, and he certainly wouldn't have stepped outside to enjoy that moment. Truth be told, he probably would've been bored by the whole thing, whereas Lacey had found it thrilling.

And the fact that she was there with Thatcher and feeling all these things was even more confusing.

The whole day—from the birth of the wee baby to the pretty good poutine at the saloon—had been an experience that she would never forget. The thing terrifying her, though, was that she didn't want her time with Thatcher to end, even though she knew it was going to end sooner rather than later.

He'd made it clear that this was his last trip.

She needed to figure out what to do with her life. Lacey thought that by now she would have some idea of what she wanted after this cruise ended, but she still wasn't sure. The cruise was fun, but she felt a bit lonely, and she missed the hustle and bustle of the hospital. So to carry on cruising didn't seem like the right fit for her.

She also missed delivering babies, and there wasn't much of a demand for that on a ship.

And the main thing holding her back was the fact that she wasn't sure that she could handle an Alaskan cruise without Thatcher working alongside her. It would just bring up all these memories, and it would hurt.

That thought shocked her.

It would be painful when he left, and that concerned her. She didn't want to feel that kind of pain ever again, and yet every day they drew closer to Anchorage and then the voyage back to Vancouver. Where she would have to say goodbye to him.

Lacey shook all these confusing thoughts from her mind as she finished the last of her checks on the patients and made her way back to the infirmary. She hadn't seen Thatcher since last evening when they'd boarded the *Alaskan Princess* as he'd gotten called away to see a patient and she'd headed to her quarters.

She'd done some paperwork but was still ignoring her personal emails.

She wasn't quite ready to read an explanation from Will or Beth.

When she walked into the infirmary, Thatcher was sitting at his desk, and she could see him working on some charts. He didn't look up when she came in.

"How are things?" he asked, continuing with his paperwork.

"Everyone is okay. I handed out some more anti-nausea meds." She set her case down and began to throw out the used items and put away the medicine she had left over.

"Great," was all Thatcher responded.

Something had changed. It bothered her. Gone was the playful man she had spent the day with in Skagway. Now he was distant, and she didn't know what she had done wrong.

Does it matter? You want to keep your distance too.

It would be easier on her heart. It would make it easier to say goodbye.

Maybe starting the separation now meant she wouldn't feel any pain when their friendship ended. There had always been an expiration date on this relationship—not that it was a relationship—and she had to accept that.

Lacey sat down at her small desk and began to make notes in the charts of the various passengers.

She could hear the rain and the water lashing at the side of the bulkhead. It sent an eerie feeling down her spine. Something was off about this whole day, and she wasn't sure what was going on.

The PA system came on.

"Dr. Bell and Nurse Greenwood, please report to the upper deck. Medical emergency."

Lacey leaped up and grabbed emergency gear off the shelves.

Thatcher came out of his office. "Do you have your raincoat?"

"No, why would I?"

He pursed his lips and tossed her a green slicker. "I have extra."

"Thanks."

They quickly gathered everything they'd possibly need, and she pulled on her raincoat. She was worried about what they were going to find. Why did she think that a cruise would be an easy job and she'd have time to think?

Since she'd arrived on board, it had been go, go, go.

Lacey followed Thatcher through the passages as they made their way to the upper deck and out onto the exposed portion. Even though it was August, the rain was cold, and the wind was blowing hard. The ship was rocking a bit, and the rain was coming in sideways. It stung at her face.

Thatcher's lips were pressed together in a firm line. She could feel the worry coming off him, and she could feel it in the pit of her stomach.

Suddenly she was terrified.

He turned and looked at her. "Are you okay?"

"I'm fine."

He nodded, and they continued on their way to the bow of the ship, where there was a crowd of crewmen gathered.

As the crowd parted for Thatcher, her heart sank to the soles of her feet. She saw it was Harvey, the man who had fallen from the upper deck when they had been leaving Vancouver.

"What happened?" Thatcher asked.

"He fell overboard. His wife said he fainted and went over," someone from the crew said.

Lacey knelt down on the other side of Harvey. There were blankets on him, but he was soaking wet and his lips were blue, as were his fingertips.

It didn't look good.

"He's breathing," Thatcher shouted over the rain. "How long was he in the water?"

"A while," the crewman said. "Thankfully, I was on deck and able to drop a GPS sensor when he fell."

"That is fast thinking. You probably helped save his life, Crewman," Thatcher stated.

Lacey worried her bottom lip as she pulled out more blankets from the emergency kit. Thatcher leaned over Harvey, calling his name, but he wasn't responding. He was breathing, but he was unconscious.

"His left pupil is blown." Thatcher cursed under his breath and looked up at her. They needed to get him to a hospital. There was nothing more that they could do for him here, other than keep him stable.

"How far are we away from Juneau?" she asked with trepidation as she cleaned up one of his bleeding head wounds.

"A while still," Thatcher said. He looked up at the crewman. "Get a backboard, and we'll take him in out of the rain. He needs to get warmed. And call in the coast guard. A helicopter can land on the deck. We need to get this passenger to Juneau ASAP."

"It'll be a rough landing," the crewman said. "This storm is dangerous."

"It doesn't matter," Thatcher shouted. "I need to get this man to Juneau or he'll die."

The crewman nodded and left to call the coast guard. This storm was more intense than she originally thought.

Thatcher and Lacey worked to get Harvey stabilized, and once they'd secured him to the backboard, they carried him out of the rain, into the interior of the ship. Lacey was able to start an IV she'd gone to get from the infirmary and get some warm fluids into him.

The crewman who had dropped the GPS device came running back. "The helicopter is on the way. The captain has come to an all stop to wait for the helicopter."

Thatcher nodded and then turned back to Harvey.

"Hold on, Harvey," Lacey whispered.

Thatcher glanced at her, and their gazes locked. He gave her a half smile, but it was grim. She knew, just as he knew, a closed head injury and such a long fall into frigid waters were not good. Harvey needed more medical attention than they could offer him right now.

"I'm going to accompany Harvey to Juneau," Thatcher said. "I want to make sure he's taken care of, so I'll need you to man the infirmary until I get back."

"Of course," Lacey said.

Soon they heard the distinct sound of the helicopter's whirring blades over the rain and thrashing sea.

First Officer Matt Bain and a couple other officers had donned rain gear and everyone went to help load Harvey into the helicopter, while another officer tried to calm Harvey's wife, June. She would have to wait until they docked at Juneau to join her husband at the hospital as Thatcher had to be the one that went on the helicopter with Harvey.

The wind was rough, and Lacey had a sinking feeling in her stomach as the boat swayed in the waves. Even with the stabilizers, the storm was still significantly rocking the boat. It was a strange storm. It was all strange, actually, and that sinking feeling she was experiencing was upsetting. One that she had never experienced before. She was worried for Thatcher going on that helicopter in this storm.

It took every ounce of her strength not to reach out and ask him to be careful like she wanted to do.

She had to remind herself that he wasn't her concern, and the only concern was Harvey, but a lump formed in her throat as they loaded Harvey onto the helicopter and as she watched Thatcher board behind him.

He glanced back at her as the door shut, and she was glad for the rain so that he wouldn't see the tears of her fear rolling down her face. There was a storm, and the helicopter could crash.

She ran back to shelter as the helicopter's blades began to whir again and then lifted it off the deck of the *Alaskan Princess*.

"Do you think he'll be okay?" someone asked, coming up behind her.

"I hope so," Lacey whispered to herself, answering the question, but not turning to look back at whoever asked it.

Although it wasn't Harvey that she was thinking about. She was worried about Thatcher, and that surprised her. She was worried about his safety. This storm was like nothing she had ever seen, and as the helicopter rose into the sky, the wind was blowing it around like it was a leaf.

Her heart stood still, and she held her breath, watching it fly away, worried something would happen to him.

It made her heart hurt thinking that he might be in

danger. She would be worried until they docked in Juneau and Thatcher came back on board the cruise ship.

Thatcher had been trying to keep his distance from Lacey, trying to keep things professional, but when he saw her as the helicopter lifted off, all he could see was the pain on her face. He could see the worry etched in her eyes. As if she was worried about him. Was that possible?

He was kind of anxious about the ride too.

He didn't particularly like helicopters, but they needed to get Harvey to the Juneau hospital as quickly as possible.

It tore at his heart to not be there with Lacey to tell her that he was going to be okay, but he had to tell himself that she wasn't his concern. They weren't in a relationship. They had only kissed once and shared some fun times together. She'd made it clear she wasn't ready for anything more serious, and he respected that.

Yet no matter how much he tried to remind himself of that or remind himself of the heartache that Kathleen had caused him, he was still drawn to Lacey, and when he saw her standing on the deck in the rain, all he'd wanted to do was protect her. Wanted to reassure her that he'd be fine.

Once they got to Juneau and landed on the roof of the hospital, there was a trauma team waiting to greet him. He was able to go over Harvey's history with the team while the patient was taken down for a CT scan, where internal bleeding was found.

They also found a blockage in one of Harvey's arteries, which was the probable cause of his fainting spells.

Thatcher remained in the waiting area while Harvey

was whisked into surgery and the blood was evacuated from his head wound.

When Harvey was stable in the intensive care unit, June arrived and Thatcher explained everything to her, he knew that he could head back to the ship.

The captain was in the waiting room and met Thatcher as he left the intensive care unit.

"How is our patient?" Captain Aldridge asked.

"Stable. The surgery was successful. He's still intubated, but they're taking good care of him. They plan to address the blockage causing all of his fainting issues tomorrow, but they think it will be a straightforward procedure, and he should make a full recovery."

Captain Aldridge smiled. "Good work, Dr. Bell. You handled that well."

"Well, it was lucky for Harvey that there was a crewman close by, and that crewman had the foresight to drop a GPS device into the water."

"I know, and I'm going to promote him. I wish you would stay with us, Bell. You're a good physician."

Thatcher acknowledged the remark with a smile. "I know. It's been an honor serving under you. If you're in the mood to promote people, though, then might I suggest you promote Nurse Greenwood? She's the most exemplary nurse I've ever worked with."

Captain Aldridge nodded. "Noted. Shall we head back to the *Alaskan Princess*?"

Thatcher nodded. "That would be great."

"I would like you and Nurse Greenwood to join me at the captain's table tonight for dinner, and I'll have the crewman who dropped the GPS join us too."

"Thank you, Captain Aldridge."

They walked out of the hospital, where a hired car was waiting to take them back to the ship. He was sure that Lacey was on edge to hear about Harvey as he'd been at the hospital for several hours now.

Most of the passengers were still out exploring Juneau, and Captain Aldridge told him that the ship would leave port a little bit later than scheduled that night. They would make up the time as the weather was clearing up and the Gulf of Alaska was surprisingly calm. No one would miss their flights in Anchorage.

The captain continued to drone on, but Thatcher only half listened. He was exhausted.

What had felt like a matter of minutes was actually hours, and though he didn't much feel like having dinner at the captain's table tonight, he couldn't say no.

All he wanted to do was take a hot shower and a nap, but he knew that he would have to see Lacey first, let her know what happened with Harvey and tell her about the dinner.

He'd been hoping for such a calm last cruise, but this had been the busiest he'd ever had. Maybe Lacey Greenwood was cursed. He smiled thinking that. She'd only cursed his fragile heart.

He cared about her, and he'd miss her.

He shouldn't have gotten so close. It was clear that Lacey wasn't ready as she was still wearing her ring.

He was so jealous of her ex. He wished he had been the one to give her the ring, because she wouldn't have run away. He wouldn't have given her a reason to.

Just as he thought, Lacey was waiting in the infirmary when he walked in. She looked like she hadn't been to sleep either.

"Thatcher!" She moved to give him a hug but then hesitated, which he was half relieved, half disappointed about. Even though he knew he shouldn't encourage it, he wanted a hug from her.

He could definitely use a hug from her. In his five years of sailing on the *Alaskan Princess*, he had never lost a patient. Harvey had been the closest call he'd ever had.

"Harvey made it through his first surgery," Thatcher said, trying not to yawn too much.

"He did?" Lacey sank back down in her office chair. "What was wrong? Do they know why he was fainting?"

"Small arterial blockage. An EKG wouldn't have picked it up. They're going to clear the blockage tomorrow, but he made it through his surgery today. They evacuated the brain bleed and released the pressure from the head trauma. He was stable in the intensive care unit when I left, and June was with him."

"She was so upset," Lacey said.

"You looked upset too."

"What do you mean?"

"When the helicopter was taking off, you looked worried." There was a part of him that was hoping she was worried about him, because then maybe it meant that she cared about him, but there was another part of him that didn't want to hold out hope for that.

"I was worried about that helicopter in the storm." She turned back to her charts, her expression hidden. "I was glad to hear that you...that you both landed safely in Juneau."

"Were you?" he asked softly.

"Yes." Her smile wobbled as she looked back at him. "The weather was so rough."

"It was. I'm okay," he said gently.

"Well, I'm really glad." When she said that, his heart skipped a beat, and he wished he could take her in his arms again. To reassure her.

"Yes. Well, he should be okay. That's the end of their cruise though, unfortunately," he said, then cleared his throat.

Lacey nodded. "A crummy way to end a vacation, but I'm glad he survived going overboard."

"Same."

"You look exhausted. Would you like some coffee?" she asked, getting up and heading to the coffee machine.

"Thanks." He walked into his office and sat down in his chair, leaning back as his eyes began to droop.

"Why don't you head back to your quarters and have a nap?"

"Later," he murmured. "Tell me what happened while I was gone."

"Nothing," she said.

He cocked an eyebrow. "Nothing?"

She shrugged. "Nothing. Should be a quiet night. Go to bed early."

"I can't." He groaned.

"Why?"

"We've been invited to the captain's private table for dinner tonight. He wants to honor us and the crewman for saving Harvey's life."

"Then you need this." Lacey handed him a cup of coffee. She smiled at him sweetly.

"Thanks." He took a sip, but he really didn't want coffee. What he really wanted was sleep.

"So, dress whites tonight?" she asked.

"For me," he murmured. "If you have a formal dress, you can wear that."

"Okay." She turned to leave. "Well, try to get some rest before dinner tonight."

"I will."

She left the room, and he leaned back, clicking on his computer and seeing another email from his father.

A couple, in fact.

Thatcher scrubbed a hand over his face and shut off his computer.

He didn't have the mental energy to deal with the Duke of Weymouth today.

He didn't have the energy for much, not even for keeping Lacey at bay and protecting his heart.

CHAPTER ELEVEN

BEFORE LACEY LEFT the infirmary, she checked on Thatcher and found him asleep at his desk, his hand wrapped around his coffee mug. She couldn't help but smile, watching him sleep, leaning back in his chair. He looked so peaceful. It made her heart flutter.

The ship had left the port of Juneau and was trying to make up time to get out into the Gulf of Alaska and finish the last leg of the cruise. She had been busy making house calls and came back to check on Thatcher. She didn't want to disturb him, but she had to leave to get ready for dinner in the captain's private dining room, and she was sure he had to get ready too.

She knew it was to thank them for helping save Harvey, but really she would rather not have dinner with the captain, and it looked like Thatcher wasn't in any kind of shape to either. She was just so exhausted. Emotionally and physically spent. She'd rather just go to bed.

Thatcher had been gone almost eight hours after the incident happened, and it had turned her stomach to think about how she felt when that helicopter took off in stormy weather—like her heart was firmly lodged in her throat. She had so many fears the helicopter was going to crash that she couldn't breathe in that moment. And she couldn't remember the last time she'd been that worried.

Those eight hours were long, wondering what had happened to him. She'd tried to work, and she'd tried to concentrate on other stuff as the ship made its way to Juneau, but she couldn't stop thinking about Thatcher. She'd kept wondering what was happening and wished she could've been there to help him. It would've put her anxiety at rest, to know he was safe.

It had driven her crazy, which freaked her out. Lacey prided herself on having better control of her emotions. What was it about him that changed her perspective? Why was she letting herself get so attached to him? Especially when she still couldn't even really process what had happened with Will.

In her past relationships, when things ended, she moved on. The same with Will. She caught him in the act with Beth, and it was just like all those other times.

It hurt, but she left.

The idea of leaving Thatcher, on the other hand, physically hurt.

And the only thing she could compare it to was that time when they had to move away from Yellowknife, and she had to say goodbye to her friends, her teachers and the home she loved. When they went to the next posting, she'd moped. She was depressed, and then she saw how it was hurting her parents to see her like that, so she sucked it all in. She learned how to deal, so it wouldn't hurt so much.

Then she met Thatcher, and everything she had learned to deal with—all of her carefully constructed walls—came crashing down. Suddenly she was dealing with a bunch of emotions she didn't know how to deal with.

All she knew was she was falling hard for Thatcher.

Lacey had to get control of these emotions before the end of the cruise. If she was going to move on with her life, she had to learn to be on her own, because she didn't know where her life was heading.

She moved into his office as quietly as she could and gently took the coffee mug from him so that he wouldn't spill it all over his computer.

Thatcher woke with a start. "What time is it?"

"Five. I was going to leave and get ready for dinner now."

Thatcher blinked a couple of times. "Right. Yes. Do that. I should get ready too."

"I was just going to dump your cold coffee. I thought it would be better if I dealt with this rather than have you spill it everywhere."

"Thanks. Well, at least I got a power nap in before tonight." He moaned and scrubbed a hand over his face. "I hate these formal dinners. I hated them when my father would hold them, but usually those were complete black tie affairs and involved members of the royal family. If you think a captain's dinner is bad, then try one with royal protocol. It's exhausting."

"I can imagine. I think I'll pass on that," Lacey said. "I would not do well with rules and protocol. I would definitely say the wrong thing or do the wrong thing and end up in the Tower."

Thatcher laughed. "Go get ready, and I'll see you at the captain's private dining room. I'll be more alert then, I promise."

"Okay."

She left his office, dumped the cold coffee and washed the mug, and put it away. She cleaned up the rest of her stuff and then headed to her quarters.

Whatever tension had been between them when they boarded after Skagway was gone. It felt like it had before and she was relieved.

She just wanted this last half of the trip to go smoothly.

It didn't take too long for her to get to her cabin, and thankfully she had a nice black dress that she had packed for the honeymoon. It was nothing spectacular, but at least it would work for tonight. She took off her scrubs and shoved them in the ship's laundry bag, then headed to the shower. A nice hot shower would help her clear her head.

Her phone rang, surprising her because the last couple of days she hadn't been able to get cell service.

She picked up her phone and saw it was a call from her dad.

"Hey, Dad!" she answered, trying to sound happy, even though she wasn't.

"Lacey! I wasn't sure I would be able to get a hold of you. I kept getting the message that the user wasn't in an area with service."

"Well, that's true. We've been at sea and in some remote spots."

"That sounds like fun!"

"Yeah." It had been fun, but she just couldn't muster real enthusiasm, and her father noticed.

"What's wrong?"

"Nothing. Just tired. It's been a lot busier than I expected it to be. Including a delivery."

"You delivered a baby on the cruise ship?"

Lacey laughed. "No, in Skagway. Not one of our passengers. I was on the train with…a friend."

She didn't know why she didn't just tell him about Thatcher. It wouldn't be strange—Thatcher was her colleague—but she felt guilty.

"Well, it sounds like you're busy enough. I would ask you to tell me about all the interesting cases, but I know you can't because of patient confidentiality and all of that. I just wanted to check in on you. Will said you haven't been responding to his emails."

"I haven't had time to respond to his emails," she said, annoyed. And it surprised her that she was so annoyed.

For the first time since the incident on what was supposed to be her wedding day, she was pissed.

"I know. I'll tell him."

"I'll get to them when I can. I have to go soon, Dad. Dinner is at set times."

"Okay. Be safe, and I'll see you in a couple of weeks."

"Bye, Dad." Lacey ended the call and swallowed past the lump in her throat.

She wasn't sure what was happening to her, but she had to get control over this. She didn't have time to feel these things. What she needed was to focus on her next step and what she wanted after this cruise was over.

You want Thatcher. You just can't have him.

She shook that thought away, mad at herself for thinking about something so foolish...even if it was the truth. She glanced down at her hand again. She was still wearing the ring. It annoyed her.

She didn't want this attachment anymore.

She was done.

Lacey pulled the engagement ring off, set it on the counter and took a deep breath to calm her jangled nerves.

Thatcher was feeling a bit more alert, but not completely recovered. He was still exhausted and was uncomfortable in his white dress uniform.

There were a couple other people who were in the dining room, including the crewman Derek, who had been there when Harvey fell and threw the GPS tracker into the water. Derek looked excited to be here, and Thatcher couldn't blame him.

Derek deserved the accolades, but Thatcher just wanted this dinner over and done with so he could go to bed.

The door opened to the private dining room, and he glanced over his shoulder and saw Lacey walk in. She was absolutely stunning. The only other dress he'd seen her in was her wedding dress, and the way she looked now took his breath away. Suddenly he was very much awake.

She had looked beautiful as a bride, but this little strapless black dress she was wearing was gorgeous. It hugged her curves and left nothing to the imagination. His gaze roved over her hungrily, and his pulse kicked up a notch. His blood heated as he let his gaze linger over her long legs, her hips and her breasts.

Her honey-blond hair wasn't pulled back. Instead it hung down in silky waves over her shoulders.

The only thing on her neck was a simple string of pearls.

There was a pink blush to her cheeks, and when she met his gaze, that pink blush deepened. His heart beat just a little bit faster then.

Lacey walked over to him. "Am I dressed okay?" There was a nervous edge to her voice.

"Why would you ask that?"

"Because there are several people staring at me."

"It's not because you're inappropriately dressed, which you're not. It's because you look amazing."

She dropped her head, and her blush deepened. She

tucked a strand of hair behind her ear. "I didn't have a formal dress. Just this old black velvet thing that I love."

"It suits you." He hoped his voice didn't shake. He couldn't take his eyes off her. "Would you like a drink?"

"I would love one. I'm so nervous, and I have no idea why."

Thatcher smiled, and they walked over to the small bar.

"How can I help you?" the barkeep asked.

"A white wine would be great."

"How about prosecco?" the barkeep suggested.

"That sounds great too," she said.

The barkeep turned to him. "And you, Dr. Bell? What would you like?"

"Whiskey. Neat, please. Thank you."

The barkeep turned to prepare their drinks.

"All this fuss," she murmured. "Just for doing our job."

"I know, but Derek, the crewman, is eating this up. He doesn't know it, but he has a promotion headed his way, and he deserves it. He thought quickly and probably is more responsible for saving Harvey's life than we were. In stormy seas, with how long it can take for a cruise ship this big to stop and turn around to rescue someone…well, it could easily become impossible to find someone in time."

"I never really thought about that."

"No one does. It was actually my first 'man overboard' situation in the five years since I started working on the *Alaskan Princess*. Since you arrived, things have been a bit busier."

Lacey laughed nervously. "I don't think that's a good sign."

"It's fine. It just makes work more interesting."

The barkeep handed them their drinks, and they walked away from the bar as the captain's private waiter made his rounds with hors d'oeuvres.

"So now we're at sea for a week?" she asked.

"Yes. We'll be passing some beautiful sights, though, like Kodiak Island, and we'll be heading out to the Aleutian Islands and be close to the Bering Sea. Really the westerly edge of the Americas."

"That's really neat. Don't those islands have volcanoes?"

"Yes, but we're not in any danger."

They were making small talk, but he couldn't think of anything else to say to her, other than repeatedly telling her how beautiful she was, because that was all he could think about. How absolutely stunning she looked in that dress.

How much he wanted her.

He hated that feeling. He hated the way he burned for her, the way she filled his thoughts, but he couldn't help himself, and he didn't know why he was fighting it at this point.

"This is incredibly stuffy and boring," she whispered.

He chuckled. "Agreed."

Captain Aldridge walked over to them.

"The other two people I wanted to thank personally," Captain Aldridge said.

Lacey smiled brightly at the captain. "Thank you for inviting me, Captain Aldridge."

Captain Aldridge nodded. "Well, of course. You two have been on the go this voyage, and your work has been absolutely exemplary. I have to tell you again, Thatcher, I'm really sorry to see you go."

"I'm sorry to leave too, Captain. I have enjoyed working with you, but it's time to move on," Thatcher said.

"Where are you off to, old man?" another crewman asked.

Thatcher really wasn't interested in talking to anyone. He just wanted to be alone with Lacey. "The Yukon. I'm going to buy some land and open a small practice."

"That sounds...uh...great." The other crewman turned and left the conversation as Lacey tried not to laugh.

"That sounds wonderful. I'm envious, Dr. Bell," Captain Aldridge said.

"I'm looking forward to it," Thatcher said.

"Well, enjoy your evening." Captain Aldridge excused himself to go greet other guests.

"Maybe you'll change your mind and join the first officer's new ship," Lacey teased.

Thatcher rolled his eyes. "No thanks. Besides, he didn't get the Caribbean but a maritime East Coast cruise."

Lacey chuckled behind her hand, and Thatcher couldn't help but snicker a bit.

"Well, so much for his hope of seeing all the ladies in string bikinis," Lacey teased.

"Did he really say that?" he asked in disgust.

"He did. He wanted to 'enjoy the sights.'"

"Especially you." The words slipped out, and he couldn't believe he'd said them.

Pink tinged her cheeks. "What?"

"Oh, come on. You don't think he would appreciate seeing you in a skimpy bikini? I know I would." His blood froze.

Thatcher had been thinking it, but he didn't mean to actually say it out loud.

Though Lacey didn't look offended. She crossed her

arms and cocked one of her finely arched brows. "Really?"

"I'm so sorry."

"No, you're not," she teased.

"I didn't mean to say that."

"I don't mind when you say that," she told him.

His heart skipped a beat, and he just stared at her. She was smiling so sweetly, and she was so close he could smell the honey scent of her shampoo. He recalled how soft her lips were and how good it felt to have her in his arms.

"Lacey," he whispered.

"Dr. Bell!"

He groaned inwardly and spun around to see one of the other officers burst into the dining room, looking around frantically until he found them.

"What's wrong?" Thatcher asked.

"There was an accident while break dancing, and it appears someone actually did break something."

Thatcher groaned inwardly and set down his whiskey.

Lacey sighed, and she set down her drink too.

"We're coming," Thatcher said.

He was glad for the distraction, but not for another accident.

This cruise seemed to be cursed. Like the ship of the damned.

The passenger was groaning in the middle of the floor of the nightclub. The lights were on, and the other passengers had been removed. Thatcher had everything he needed on board to set a broken bone, and he hoped that it was just something simple, or they would have to arrange for another helicopter to come to the ship.

At least this wasn't a life-and-death situation.

Lacey kicked off her heels and knelt down on the floor.

"What happened?" Thatcher asked the few people who were remaining.

"Raymond was showing us some moves he used to do as a teenager, and when it came to the twist on his head, he screamed, and there was a crack," a woman said. "I'm his wife, Loretta."

Thatcher winced. "Well, let's have a look, Raymond."

Raymond nodded, and Thatcher cut off his Relax shirt. The moment that he did, he could see the bump on Raymond's clavicle.

"I think you've broken your clavicle, Raymond. We have to get you to our X-ray." Thatcher motioned and had some staff help him with a backboard.

He and Lacey worked to get Raymond onto the backboard and strapped down.

"Loretta, you can come with us to the infirmary," Lacey said over her shoulder.

Loretta nodded.

Thatcher had to get an X-ray done before he even thought about trying to set anything. He was hoping it was a simple fracture that he could just immobilize and treat with painkillers. Anything worse and they would have to get Raymond off the ship and to a hospital for surgery.

Back in the infirmary, Lacey got the X-ray machine ready, and they put on the draping they needed to protect themselves and Raymond.

It was apparent that Lacey had done this before, because she knew how to drape the patient properly to get films. His last nurse didn't. In fact, if he had that same nurse still on this cruise with all the injuries and what happened with Harvey, Thatcher probably would've gone bonkers. Lacey had obviously worked in trauma and the operating room. She knew how to do so much more than his last nurse, who had worked in a simple clinic before the cruise.

Lacey was more like his right hand. She was a partner.

"Okay, Raymond, I need you to stay still so I can get some clear pictures."

"Okay, Dr. Bell."

Lacey placed the last piece of protective draping and then came behind the screen with Thatcher as he took the X-ray.

The picture came up on the computer instantly. It was definitely a clavicle fracture, but it looked like a hairline fracture and probably wouldn't require surgery. He breathed a sigh of relief when he saw it.

"Well, at least we don't have to call the coast guard to come and get him," Thatcher said. "We'll have to immobilize his arm with a sling and give him a script for painkillers, and when we get to Anchorage in a week, he can get it rechecked."

"We'll just have to keep an eye on him this week at sea. No more break dancing," Lacey said, smiling.

"Not for Raymond, anyways. Do you want to break the news to him?"

Lacey frowned. "That's a terrible pun."

"Yeah, I realized the moment I said it that it sounded bad."

"I'll let him know that his break dancing days aboard this ship are over."

"I'll get a sling."

Lacey nodded and went to deal with the patient while Thatcher grabbed a sling. He was going to have to cut the rest of Raymond's shirt—which was probably one of the original relics from the eighties—off, but it had to be done so he could adjust Raymond's arm.

When he reached the exam room, Lacey had already removed Raymond's shirt, and Loretta was with them. Raymond was clearly starting to feel the effects of the morphine and was relaxing.

"I'll give him some more painkillers, but after a couple of days, he'll just need acetaminophen for the pain. I would avoid ibuprofen," Thatcher said.

Loretta nodded. "Should we get this checked out before we board our flight back to New York in a week?"

"I would," Thatcher said. "It looks like a hairline fracture, but it's such a long flight, it wouldn't hurt to get it checked out. I'll give you my discharge notes and a copy of the X-ray for the doctors in Anchorage."

Loretta smiled. "Thank you, Doctor. He's forty-eight, and I told him he doesn't have to relive his glory days, but he wouldn't listen."

"Relax," Raymond slurred. "Reach out and touch me."

"Those are not the lyrics. Not at all," Thatcher replied dryly. "Sit back and relax, Raymond."

Loretta rolled her eyes, and Lacey chuckled under her breath.

"Sorry I had to ruin your shirt, Raymond," Lacey said. "You can have it sewn back together."

"I would've burned it," Thatcher said.

Loretta and Lacey were laughing, and Raymond just lay there as Thatcher put the X-rays up on the light box and manipulated the arm so it was immobilized against this chest. Then he showed Loretta how to arrange the sling and explained that it needed to be kept tight.

By the time the sling was on, Raymond was dozing on the exam room table.

"I'll get a wheelchair," Lacey offered. "And then I'll push him back to your quarters."

"No, I can do that," Thatcher said. He didn't want Lacey ruining her dress, and he knew he would be able to handle Raymond a bit better. The man wasn't big, but he was tall.

Lacey brought out a wheelchair, and Loretta woke Raymond enough to get in. Thatcher helped them get back to their quarters and settled Raymond into his bed, leaving Loretta with the medication she'd need and his pager number in case Raymond spiked a fever or anything else happened.

He steered the wheelchair back to the infirmary, where Lacey was waiting to clean it with sanitizing wipes.

The rest of the clinic had been cleaned, which was a welcome sight. And then he realized that Lacey was barefoot.

"Where are your shoes?" he asked, confused.

"I kicked them off in the club. One of the waitresses there picked them up for me and left them outside my quarters. I can't kneel down properly in heels. I'm good, but I'm not that good."

"Sorry you didn't get a dinner with the captain in his private dining room. I'm sure he'll make it up to you."

She made a face. "No, that's quite all right. Like I said, it was a bit too stuffy for me. I'm someone who likes simple things like poutine and fry bread."

Me too.

And he loved Lacey for it all the more. She was a breath of fresh air. She wasn't demanding. She didn't ask for anything.

So different from Kathleen.

Still, their lives were going in different directions, and he couldn't give up his dreams, the things he'd been working on for the last five years, for the chance of a romance with Lacey. Especially as Lacey had made it clear when they kissed that it was a one-time thing.

She didn't want a relationship. Not that he could blame her—she had just gotten out of a relationship—but if she wanted him, he would take her with him to the Yukon in a heartbeat.

She didn't know what she wanted out of life, but there was a part of him that wished it was him she wanted.

The two of them working together in the wilderness would be a perfect team. She could add so much to his practice.

And he could see this whole life unfolding in front of him. The life he wanted with her, but not necessarily the life she wanted.

Thatcher knew all about having a life you didn't want forced upon you, and he was never going to do that to Lacey.

No matter how much he wanted to.

CHAPTER TWELVE

LACEY HAD REALLY thought for a moment a couple of days ago that Thatcher was going to kiss her again at the captain's dinner. Of course he hadn't, though, because they'd had to deal with Raymond's accident on the dance floor at the nightclub.

It was also probably for the best that it didn't happen. Especially not in front of the other officers.

Thatcher didn't seem like the type to attempt public displays of affection.

Although she wished he would've.

She couldn't stop thinking about that moment. She saw the way he was looking at her, and she was feeling the same.

She wanted him.

She might not know what she wanted as her next job or what she wanted in her life besides being a nurse practitioner and midwife, but she knew that she wanted Thatcher, and she'd never wanted a man like this before.

Not even Will.

And she couldn't understand now why she was with Will for the last two years, because her relationship with him had been nothing like this.

She had settled for consistency because it was safe.

She'd been so blinded by security that she'd ignored her gut instinct. She had ignored all the red flags.

She'd been a fool.

A lump formed in her throat. She was so annoyed with herself.

The problem was, she didn't want to hold Thatcher back. He might desire her—she had sensed that in his kiss—but he had concrete plans. Plans that he'd been working on since his own heart was broken and he decided to leave his family and title behind.

He had these amazing dreams, and she didn't want to interfere with them. She didn't even know if he wanted her to. What if he just wanted a fling? She wasn't that kind of person, and the uncertainty of it all just gnawed away at her.

And he also didn't know where in the Yukon he wanted to settle. It was all very flighty, and she wasn't comfortable with that.

If only she could figure herself out and figure out what she wanted to do with her life.

The last few days traveling along the Gulf of Alaska had been amazing and quiet. After her checks on a couple of other patients, she walked the deck, trying to work out what she wanted and staring at the vast glaciers and the islands. The forests giving way to tundra and the north. To glaciers and peaks. Stone and sea.

It was beautiful—colder than when they were down in Skagway and Juneau, but it was also very peaceful.

Although the peace wasn't helping her think at all.

This morning, before she made her rounds, there had been a couple more emails from Will, and she still hadn't opened them. She was mad at herself for not facing it, but how could she move forward if she didn't face Will and his infidelity? She couldn't.

She didn't want to hold Thatcher back or hurt him with her uncertainty.

"I thought I'd find you here."

She turned and saw Thatcher walking toward her. Her heart began to beat a bit faster, and she smiled.

"You caught me," she said nervously. "How is Raymond?"

"He's doing good. I don't think he'll need surgery, but he's still going to get himself checked out when we reach Anchorage in a day or so," he said, leaning against the railing beside her.

"I'm glad to hear it." She didn't know what else to say.

She loved being near him, and she resisted the urge to rest her head against his shoulder and watch the world go by.

"I noticed you're not wearing your ring anymore."

Lacey glanced down at her hand. "No, I took it off the night of the captain's dinner."

"You did?"

She blushed. "I did."

Thatcher didn't say anything, and she was disappointed. He cleared his throat. "The captain will be turning around soon, and we'll be heading back to Anchorage. I can't believe this cruise is almost over. These last couple of weeks have flown by."

"They have." She sighed.

"What's wrong?"

"I have a couple of emails from my ex waiting for me in my inbox. I still haven't opened them. My father called me a few days ago and mentioned that my ex was fretting over the fact I hadn't responded."

"What does he expect? He cheated on you."

"Well, he may have actually cheated on me, but how

much did I contribute to that? I wasn't exactly the most affectionate person. Maybe I deserved it. I don't think we were ever suited for each other."

"No one deserves a broken heart," Thatcher said sadly.

"My heart doesn't feel that broken, though."

"Maybe he wants some absolution?" Thatcher offered.

She shrugged. She didn't know, but she didn't want to talk about Will or Beth or anything. She just wanted to savor those last few minutes that they were still gliding west toward Unalaska Island before they turned back along the coast and to Anchorage. Once all the passengers were off, they'd be heading to Vancouver, and she would have to make some hard choices about her life.

"I suppose I need to return his ring. Though I don't want to see him."

"Chuck it overboard," Thatcher teased.

She laughed. "No. I guess I'll have to bite the bullet and face him. I'm not reading his emails or calling him today, though. Today I don't want to think of him."

"How about tonight we have dinner again? Since we didn't get the nice dinner at the captain's table."

The question caught her off guard, but pleased her.

"You're not going to make me dress up again, are you?" she asked.

"No. Actually, I'm not, but the captain is. He's offered us a table in the Upper Deck Restaurant, and it has a dress code."

"Rats, but I guess I can't say no to a dinner that's been offered by Captain Aldridge. Especially if I want to stay in his good graces."

"You've decided to stay on, then?" Thatcher asked.

"No, but I don't want to burn any bridges. Just in case."

"Probably a good idea."

The ship began to slow as the *Alaskan Princess* made its maneuvers to turn around. She caught a last glimpse of Unalaska and, beyond that, the Bering Sea.

The turn of the ship meant a bit of closure, and it made her sad.

"I wish I could go on," she murmured.

"Well, you can. You don't have to stay with this ship. The cruise line has many options. There are cruises that go around the world on even larger ships."

"It's a possibility, but most likely not."

"Well, I have a report to finish. I'll see you at the Upper Deck Restaurant about seven?"

She nodded. "Yes. I'll be there."

He nodded and left.

Lacey sighed and watched as the ship continued its turn. She wasn't the only one watching; most of the ship's passengers were watching the land disappear and the open waters of the Gulf of Alaska take its place.

The sun was starting to set, but it still wouldn't sink below the horizon until about ten at night. The sunlight made her smile.

It was so surreal to see snow and glaciers and have a coat on in August.

She'd forgotten till this trip just how much she loved the north.

She'd forgotten about all those summer nights in Yellowknife. Even the nights when the sun barely set, the nights when the streetlights didn't even have to come on. And she remembered the dark nights of winter, when she and her parents would cuddle up at home as another blizzard howled off Great Slave Lake.

Lacey had locked away all those memories. And as

she let them out of the careful box that she kept them in, a tear slipped down her cheek.

She brushed it away, annoyed that she was allowing herself to cry.

That was something she didn't do. Something she hadn't done in a long time.

She straightened herself up and went back to do the last few rounds of check-ins before dinner tonight.

She had a lot to figure out, and crying was something she didn't have time for.

Reminiscing about or mourning something that she couldn't have was pointless.

It would get her nowhere.

Even though she had to wear her little black dress again, because it was the only one she had, she was slightly disappointed when she walked into the restaurant and saw that Thatcher wasn't wearing his white officer's uniform.

She loved the way he looked in that.

Don't let yourself think of him like that.

Only, she couldn't help herself. Even though he wasn't wearing the officer's uniform that she appreciated so much, he still looked good in a dark, well-tailored suit. She couldn't help but wonder if he wore that suit back in England, when he was still the heir and not missing.

It was a shame that he felt like he needed to hide away.

Aren't you doing the same thing?

Hiding away from Will and what had happened. Hiding away from herself. At least she'd taken off the ring. For one brief moment, when Thatcher had suggested it, she'd contemplated tossing it off the side of the ship.

Only, she couldn't.

It wasn't hers anymore. She should return it.

"You look lovely," he said, standing to greet her.

"You do too."

Thatcher pulled out her chair for her. She sat down, and then he sat down. No one she'd been with before had ever pulled out a chair for her; she kind of liked it. Lacey had always done everything on her own, never asked for anything. She took care of herself.

Which was one of Will's gripes, now that she thought about it, because to him it meant that she never took care of him. He'd suggested she was self-centered. Lacey took offense to that. She wasn't self-centered. She'd just been taught to be self-sufficient and not rely on anything or anyone.

Especially not anyone she might get attached to.

It was a scary prospect, getting attached, but a part of her was dreadfully lonely. She'd even been lonely with Will. She just hadn't realized it. She'd ignored it. Just like all the other signs.

She'd grown attached to Thatcher, and she was going to miss him when this was all over.

"I can't believe it's Anchorage tomorrow and the passengers are leaving. I've gotten used to checking on them."

"I know. It's a bit eerie having nothing to do on the voyage home, but it's relaxing."

"Have you heard anything more about Harvey from the hospital in Juneau?" she asked, thinking about the first patient they had worked on together.

"I did. Harvey is awake and doing well. They were able to clear his blocked artery, and hopefully that will resolve his fainting issues."

"Well, that's great news." She was having a hard time

coming up with what to talk to him about. All these emotions were running around inside her, and she was trying to get control of them. She hated losing control. She hated this feeling of being so vulnerable in front of him, but it was also a freeing prospect to be her true self and not worry about having to hold anything back.

"I know that I've said it before, but this has been the weirdest, busiest trip I've ever done, and the only new variable is you."

Lacey laughed. "I'm sorry about that, but in a way, I was glad it was slightly busy. It kept my mind off things."

"Like those emails? Have you responded?"

"Have you responded to yours?" she queried back.

"Touché."

The waiter interrupted, poured them wine that Thatcher had ordered before she'd arrived, and then left. There was nothing to order as the restaurant offered a set menu. She took a sip of her wine, suddenly very nervous.

Her stomach was swirling and twisting. Her hands were shaking, and she wished Thatcher's arms were around her right now.

"I need to deal with it," she finally said, not looking at him. "I have to decide what I want to do when this cruise ends, because I don't know. At least you have it all figured out."

"Partly," he said gently. "I know the general direction I want to go, but I don't know where I'll be settling and when I'll be able to get my practice up and running or even if the territorial government will let me. I hope they will. I have all my visas, but there's still a process."

Lacey was surprised. "So you're rushing to the Yukon blind and without a backup?"

"I suppose I am," he said.

"That's kind of crazy," she admitted.

"It is, but it's what I've always wanted. I want to make it work. I love Canada, and I love the Yukon territory. It's where I want to be, and I'm willing to do whatever it takes to make it work."

"And what if you have to leave?" she asked.

"It'll break my heart, but I'll deal with it as it comes."

And there it was. She wasn't sure that she could latch onto something or someone with the threat that it might all be lost to her. She'd experienced that pain before, and she wasn't willing to go through it again.

It was better to play it safe.

"I'm not sure I could ever take a risk like that," she admitted.

"Yes, but what is that saying I heard once? There is no growth in a comfort zone."

"Perhaps not, but at least there's safety."

The waiter returned with their food, but Lacey couldn't really focus on it. Her emotions were everywhere, and she wasn't really hungry. It was like the world was spinning, and she just wanted to get off the ride. The food was like a lump of tasteless nothing in her mouth, and it was hard to swallow.

She couldn't breathe. All she could think of was everything she had lost.

And how she'd soon lose Thatcher.

It was too much.

"Lacey?" Thatcher asked. "Are you all right?"

"No. I don't think that I am," she said quietly. "I think I'm having a bit of a panic attack."

Thatcher stood up. "Come on. You need some air."

She stood up, and Thatcher put his arm around her; it was reassuring. They headed out of the restaurant, onto the deck. It was getting dark, but it was still warm since the deck was covered, and they could see outside.

Still, she shivered, and Thatcher pulled her closer.

"Sorry," she said, trying to catch her breath. "I don't know what happened."

"It's okay," he said gently. "You've been through a lot."

"We both have," she said. "I don't know what came over me. It's weird that we're coming to the end of this."

"It's okay, and it is odd. Trust me."

Lacey smiled. "I do, which is a huge thing for me. I don't trust easy, especially those I don't know well. Will isn't the first to have cheated on me. I've been hurt too much. Lost too much."

Thatcher smiled. "Same. Did you actually trust your ex-fiancé, though? Because something tells me that you didn't. Not really."

"You're right. I didn't. I don't even know why I was with him, to be honest." She sighed. "It just seemed like the right thing to do, and when I saw him with the woman I thought was my best friend, I left. But I didn't cry. I…don't know why."

"Because you weren't even angry?"

"I was, but… I didn't say anything. What kind of person doesn't say anything in that situation?" She could feel tears welling in her eyes. "Am I that unfeeling? Am I that uncaring?"

"I don't know," Thatcher said softly. "I questioned myself when my relationship with Kathleen ended. I was crushed. I felt betrayed. She thought I was going to be the duke, and maybe it was shallow, but I wasn't the person she thought I was supposed to be, so maybe in a way I betrayed her too. I don't know."

It touched her heart that he was opening up to her like this.

Why was it that she could be herself with him? Why did she let all these emotions out around him?

What kind of hold did he have on her?

She glanced up at the sky above her and could see stars through the glass. So many stars, just like the sky she'd seen when she was a little girl.

"Wow," she whispered. She'd been so busy on this cruise that at night she just went to bed and slept. She hadn't looked up at the sky since that night after their first kiss. It calmed her. Just like it had done that night.

In Vancouver, Lacey didn't see the sky. On the odd sunny day, she'd look up at the blue, but it had been a long time since she'd paid attention to the night sky.

And suddenly all she could think about was her friend Carol. She remembered them lying in her back-yard in the middle of the night in late August, staring at the sky.

All the stars.

"It's kind of amazing. Another reason I love the north. There is no artificial light drowning out the night sky. I'll never get tired of this."

Lacey nodded. "Yes, I'd forgotten. It's been so long. When I was a little girl, I would spend many nights just staring up at the sky. I turned away from the sky when I moved to Vancouver."

And as if the sky was acknowledging her back, a small ribbon of light wound its way across the stars, faint at first, like ink in water. It was bright green, and she smiled as it moved, rippling and flowing above her.

She could hear other people who were out and about, watching like she was. She could hear their gasps, but she kept silent, watching in awe as that thin little ribbon turned thicker and pushed its way across the sky, erupting into beautiful waves of green stretching up above her.

It had been a long time since she'd seen the aurora borealis.

Too long.

All that anxiety she'd been feeling melted away. All she felt was joy and connection. She'd been living in a fog for too long. It was as though Carol was reaching out to speak to her again.

"I'm so glad we saw them," Thatcher whispered.

"Me too. It's perfect." Lacey looked up at him, his head turned toward the sky as he watched, but then he looked down at her, his gray eyes twinkling.

Just like that night they had shared their first kiss. Lacey wanted to kiss him again. Her body was thrumming with need. She'd wanted him from the moment she first saw him, and she knew that if they kissed this time, she wasn't going to stop. She wouldn't be able to stop. Lacey wanted Thatcher, and even though their journeys in life weren't on the same paths, she was going to experience this time together with him to its fullest.

Thatcher was right. Nothing grew out of a comfort zone, and she was going to take this one small leap, just this one time, and see where it led.

"You are more beautiful than the northern lights," Thatcher said, touching her cheek gently. "I know I shouldn't be saying it, but I can't help myself."

"Why shouldn't you be saying it?" she asked.

"Because neither of us can promise each other something, and you made it clear the first night we kissed that nothing can come of it. I don't want to make you uncomfortable."

"You're not." And then she leaned forward and

kissed him gently. "You're not making me uncomfortable, and I know you can't promise me anything, but
that's okay. I just want tonight."

"Tonight?" he asked, confused.

"Yes. Just tonight. I just want tonight." And then she
kissed him again, letting him know exactly what she
wanted out of tonight.

This time with Thatcher was fleeting.

For one night, under the northern lights, she wanted
to live.

To feel again, with him.

Thatcher wanted her more than anything. It had been
something he'd been fighting for weeks.

He knew she had a lot to deal with, and there was
a part of him that wasn't sure he could really open
his heart to someone again, but he was lonely, and he
wanted her. It burned his soul, his need to have her, but
he didn't want to rush her or push her. That was not his
style, so he'd just desired her from afar. Pined for her,
knowing nothing would probably happen.

And then she kissed him. A kiss that burned him
right down to his very soul. His body yearned for her,
to hold her and kiss her.

To claim her as his own.

Only, he couldn't have her. She wasn't his to claim.
She'd made that clear, and he had plans too, but for tonight, if she wanted, he would happily be with her and
let his desire rule his mind and his heart.

"Lacey," he murmured against her neck.

"Please, Thatcher," she whispered, before kissing
him again. "I know nothing can come from this, but I
also know I want this."

Lacey took his hand and pulled him away from their

dark little corner of the deck, toward the stairway leading down to the staff quarters. If only they had had dinner in his cabin so he could've scooped her up in his arms and carried her to bed.

Getting from above to below deck took forever in his mind, but he knew it would be worth it. His pulse was racing with anticipation, his body reacting to the promise that soon she would be his. Even if only for one night.

His quarters were the closest, so that's where they went. His heart was in his throat, his blood burning as he opened the door.

Once they were on the other side and the door was shut, those kisses that had been controlled up on the deck were let loose.

He pressed her against the wall, his hands in her hair. Devouring her.

He broke the kiss off. "Are you sure, Lacey?"

Even though he was burning for her—desired her, needed her—if she changed her mind, he'd let her go.

He was all in, though.

More than all in. He was close to losing his heart if he wasn't careful.

"I'm sure," she whispered, her voice trembling. She took his hand and pressed it against her chest. He could feel her pulse racing under his fingertips.

Her skin was like satin. Soft. Smooth.

And she burned hot. For him.

He liked that dress she wore, but now he needed her out of it. Thatcher wanted nothing between them. He wanted to run his hands over her, his lips. He wanted to be a part of her.

Lacey nuzzled his neck, the press of her lips against him making a zing of awareness course through his body.

Her fingers worked the buttons of his shirt while he unzipped her dress.

He just wanted her naked and pressed against him.

That's all he wanted.

Just her.

There was no fighting it anymore.

He was lost to her.

Lacey couldn't ever recall being so consumed with passion before.

She'd never had this burning need for someone, but with Thatcher it was a craving. She wanted him. Needed him.

Lacey just wanted to forget about it all.

She couldn't get her clothes off fast enough.

"You're so beautiful," Thatcher said again when it was just her, naked in front of him.

She found she wasn't embarrassed. She pulled him flush against her body.

"Touch me," she murmured, guiding his hand up to her breasts. It made her blood sing, her body come alive for the first time in a long time. And she wanted more as Thatcher pressed her against his bed, his lips branding hot flames against her skin. She arched her back, trying to get closer to him, her body tingling and every nerve seeming to wake back up after a long sleep.

A shiver of anticipation coursed through her.

It was so good.

"I want you, Lacey," he murmured.

"Feel how much I need you." She opened her legs, thrusting her hips up at him.

He growled possessively, his hands hot and heavy on her skin.

Thatcher's hand slipped between her legs, stroking her. She gasped, crying out.

Her body was thrumming with need for him.

"Do you have protection?" she asked.

"I do." He reached over and pulled a condom out of his nightstand drawer.

"Let me help you with that." She tore open the packet and slowly rolled the condom down over his shaft. Thatcher moaned as she stroked him. He was at her mercy.

"Oh, God, Lacey."

"What?" she teased breathlessly. "What're you going to do?"

He grinned, grabbing her hands and pinning her wrists down as he thrust into her, making her cry out.

Thatcher moved slowly, so slowly, and she urged him to go faster. She wanted all of him, and she wanted it now. He thrust hard against her, over and over as a coil of heat unfurled in her belly. Pleasure overtaking her.

She wrapped her legs around him, not wanting him to move or leave her as she came, and it wasn't long before he cried out, coming right after her.

Her body was like a puddle of Jell-O, and it was good to just be in his arms.

It couldn't be forever, but it could be for tonight.

CHAPTER THIRTEEN

WHEN THATCHER WOKE up in the morning, he realized the ship had stopped, and as he rubbed his eyes, he could see the blurry cityscape of Anchorage in the distance through the open drapes.

Lacey was still sleeping soundly, her bottom warm against him, and all he wanted to do was stay snuggled in bed with her. He couldn't remember the last time he'd slept so soundly. In fact, he wasn't sure that he had ever slept like this before.

She made him happy, and he wished they had more time together.

Thatcher gently kissed her cheek. "We're in Anchorage."

Lacey opened her eyes slowly. "We are?"

"Yes. I'm afraid we're going to have to get up and do our job as the passengers disembark in a couple of hours."

Lacey stretched. "I suppose so."

As much as he didn't want to get up, he knew they had to. They weren't the ones on vacation, after all. Lacey climbed out of bed and began gathering up her clothes to get dressed, which was a real shame in Thatcher's opinion.

Lacey finished pulling on her clothes. "I'll see you later?"

"Yes. Make sure you wear your white uniform."

"Oh. Joy." She leaned over and kissed him. "Thank you for last night."

"Thank *you*."

Thatcher pulled her down and kissed her again. She laughed and pushed him away, slipping out of his room.

He lay back and stared up at the ceiling, and all he could do was smile. But then it struck him that soon this would be over, and he'd be on his way to the Yukon.

Alone.

He sighed and got up to get ready, washing up and then dressing in his white uniform to prepare for the departing passengers. Thatcher didn't want to think about Lacey leaving.

She's not leaving. You are.

And he had to keep reminding himself of that. This was only supposed to be a temporary thing. That was it.

He wasn't going to hold Lacey back. The last time he tried to have a woman follow along with his plans, it had gone spectacularly badly and left him brokenhearted.

Lacey isn't Kathleen, though.

Lacey was different.

Still, she had just come out of a serious relationship. She didn't know what she wanted out of life, and she deserved the chance to figure it all out, without him trying to sway her. When they had kissed again and she told him that she wanted him, she told him that it would only be for one night.

And he had to accept that, even if he didn't want to.

He locked up his quarters and made his way along the hall to head to the upper decks. As he passed other members of the crew, they stared at him, which made him uneasy. He smiled, but something was bothering him about the way they were looking at him.

It sent a chill down his spine.

He headed above deck and saw a group of officers mingling by the door where passengers were slowly disembarking. As he approached, he saw Lacey in the crowd, looking distressed. As he waved to passengers leaving, he realized the passengers were looking at him with what he could only describe as awe.

A shiver of dread coursed through his blood, and he stared at the pile of complimentary newspapers that was sitting at the check-in desk of the ship.

On the front cover of the paper was a photo of him… and Lacey.

A photograph of them on the train in Skagway, or rather, a photograph of them on the train at the White Pass, and the headline read, The Missing Heir Has Been Found.

"Thatcher," Lacey said, rushing over.

He picked up a paper in disbelief, just staring at it.

For five years he'd managed to keep his identity secret, but the one time he went back up the White Pass and decided to step outside the train car to enjoy the ride with a woman, someone from the other car had recognized him and snapped a picture.

He was upset.

No, he was livid.

"Your Grace, I had no idea that we had such a celebrity serving on the *Alaskan Princess*. A bit beneath you, isn't it?" Matt said, taking the chance to scoff while the captain wasn't around.

Thatcher saw red, but he wasn't going to lower himself to the first officer's level, so he turned on his heel, storming off.

Lacey followed him.

"Thatcher!"

He couldn't turn around. He had to figure out what to do, and he wasn't sure what that might be. He headed straight for the infirmary to collect his thoughts, and as he stared at the newspaper he saw there was more.

There was information about Lacey—about her jilting her fiancé and leaving him at the altar.

And there was information about Thatcher's father being on his deathbed.

It made his blood run cold. He tossed the paper to the side as Lacey entered the infirmary and shut the door behind her.

He didn't really want to see her, but he knew she was probably reeling from the insinuations made against her, the claims she had jilted her ex for a duke. What the world didn't know was that Lacey didn't know he was a duke when she ran away from her ex. Not that it would matter much if they told anyone.

The world would believe what they wanted to believe.

He was sorry that he ever got involved with Lacey and caused her name to be dragged through the proverbial mud.

"I'm so sorry," Lacey said, staring at the paper.

"Why? It's not your fault. You didn't tell anyone. And they slandered your name too."

"I know," she said quietly. "They can say what they want. My family knows the truth. I didn't leave Will for a duke. And also, you're not a duke."

He gave her a half smile. She was trying to make things lighter, but he didn't feel like making light of the situation.

"My father is ill," he stated.

"Did you know that or is this news?"

"I knew. Michael called me right before we left and told me Father was sick and wanted me to come home. I ignored him."

"And you didn't respond to the email from your father, did you?"

He shook his head. "No."

"What're you going to do?"

"Nothing."

"Nothing?" she asked. "What if your father is actually dying?"

"I don't want to be duke."

"Yeah, but that doesn't change the fact that your father could be dying, and this is your only chance to make things right with him."

"You don't know what you're talking about. You won't even face your ex," he snapped back.

Lacey frowned and crossed her arms. "He's not dying. And I'm headed back to Vancouver next week anyway."

"Lacey, come on. You don't know what you want. Who's to say you won't run away again? You shut people out."

"I'm not the only one running."

"What do you mean?"

"You've been hiding these last five years."

He narrowed his eyes and glared at her. "You have no concept of the life I would have to lead, the life I would have to give up to take my birthright. I don't want that."

"Sometimes we have to do things that we don't want to do."

"Like marrying a man you don't love? Because wasn't that what you were going to do?"

Lacey glared at him. "Why are you turning on me? What have I done to you?"

He ran a hand through his hair. "Nothing. Nothing."

"You're lashing out irrationally."

"It's because I love you."

Her eyes opened wide in shock, and she took a step back. "What?"

"I said that I love you. I want you to stay with me."

She shook her head, looking terrified. "No. No you don't. You can't. We've only known each other for a few weeks. There is no way that you can... You can't love me."

"I do," he said fiercely. "And if I have to face this inevitable fate as a duke, I want you to go with me."

"You're insane."

"Lacey, I want you with me."

She shook her head and backed up. "I can't do that, Thatcher. I can't do that. I don't want that life."

"How do you know?"

Her brow furrowed. "You don't even want that life. Why would I want that kind of life?"

"Because you love me too."

He said it with hope, but he knew she was scared, and he was frantic. Everything was changing so fast.

"Thatcher... I can't. I just..." She turned to leave, but he stood in front of her, blocking her exit.

"You're going to run again?"

She glared at him. "I don't know you."

"You do know me. You're just afraid. Afraid to take a chance."

"I'm not the only one afraid," she snapped. "You're afraid of being alone. You come to Canada to hide away and lick your wounds, saying you want some kind of life in the north, but really you'll go back and become the

Duke of Weymouth because you can't stand up to your father and tell him that you don't want your birthright."

"You don't understand what you're talking about."

"I understand. You lashed out at me because you need someone to blame."

Her words stung like a slap. "And what about you? You're so afraid of anything. You say that you're envious of my plans, that I know where I'm going. Well, you have the whole world open to you. You can do whatever you want, be whoever you want, but you don't do that. You just follow your parents around blindly."

"Get out of my way." Her voice quivered, and he hated hurting her, but he was angry. Kathleen had only wanted him when he was going to be a duke, and Lacey didn't want him for the same reason.

The thing was, Thatcher wasn't even sure that she would want him if he didn't take his title. Even if he went to the Yukon and pursued his plan, he wasn't sure that she would follow him. Once again, he'd put his heart on the line, and the woman he'd fallen for had crushed it.

He'd been a fool thinking that Lacey was different; he should've known better when he first laid eyes on her in that wedding dress, fresh from jilting her ex-fiancé.

She couldn't even deal with her hurt from that.

She had locked away all her emotions. Like he should've done.

Thatcher stepped to the side. Lacey opened the door and left the infirmary, slamming the door behind her.

All he could do was stand there.

He was angry at himself for falling in love again and for putting his heart on the line. Thatcher understood what he had to do, now that the world knew exactly where he was. He picked up the phone and made a call.

It would be six in the evening, and he hoped that Michael would be there.

"Weymouth Manor," the butler's voice said over the crackling line.

"Heath, it's Edward. I would like to speak to Michael."

"Very good, my lord. Please hold the line."

Thatcher waited, his pulse thundering in his ears.

"Edward?" Michael asked in amazement.

"Yes."

"You actually called."

"Well, since the secret is out, there is no need to hide."

"You're coming home?" Michael asked.

"I am. Can you arrange a flight for me out of Anchorage?"

"Anchorage? You're not in Vancouver?"

"No. I'm going to disembark here in Anchorage after I speak to the captain, but I'm sure it will be fine. The world knows where I am, and I'm sure there will be press waiting in Vancouver. If I fly from Anchorage, I may be able to avoid all that."

"I'll arrange a car to come to the port in about an hour," Michael said.

"Tell me one thing," Thatcher said, his voice breaking slightly. "Is Father really dying?"

Michael sighed. "It doesn't look good. He's emailed you several times. He thought you might never come home and wants to make amends."

"Well, tell him I'm on the next flight out of Anchorage."

"Tickets will be waiting at the airport," Michael said. "I'll have a car meet you at Heathrow when you arrive."

"Thank you."

"I'll see you soon."

Thatcher ended the call. When he woke up this morning, he'd thought that he would have another week with Lacey, and a part of him had hoped he could convince her to spend her life with him.

For one brief moment, he'd felt like there was hope and that he could put his heart in the hands of another.

How wrong he'd been.

Lacey paced in her room, trying to process everything that had happened in the infirmary.

He says he loves me.

Only, she couldn't quite believe that, and she felt a dread inside her, because she knew she loved him too. She was terrified by that prospect.

How could he love her?

It felt like her heart was going to burst.

Why did she let this go so far?

Why did she open up her heart when she didn't even know what she wanted? She felt like crying, and there was a knot deep in the pit of her stomach she couldn't shake.

She hated herself. She hated that she was so afraid.

Even too afraid to open the numerous messages from Will.

It would be so simple. Why couldn't she face it?

Maybe Thatcher was right. She was just running away from all of her problems.

He says he loves me.

But being with him might mean packing up and moving to England to become a duchess. She might not know what she wanted, but she knew she didn't want that. She took this job to have an adventure and to clear her head so that she could figure out what she wanted in life. Instead, she ran smack-dab into a Prince Charming of sorts. Tears welled up in her eyes as she thought about him. She had gone to the infirmary to console him because his secret was out and it was partly her fault—it was because of her he was on the train over the White Pass and got spotted—but it had all gone horribly wrong.

She shook her head.

She had been so afraid for so long to put real trust in someone or something else.

What if Thatcher took her to England, and she wasn't good enough? What if they got married, but she hated it there and their marriage ended? What if she couldn't have children for the lineage?

There were so many things she was uncertain about. And then she remembered what Thatcher had said about things not growing in a comfort zone.

She saw now how true those words were.

The thing was, she'd never asked these questions when she was with Will, because it really never mattered. Not the way it did with Thatcher.

A tear slid down her cheek as it hit her.

She was really in love with Thatcher. She had liked Will well enough; what they had was comfortable, and she was willing to marry him because he was stable. But with Thatcher, there was this level of the unknown, and she was terrified about what the future might hold. It was a risk. One she had never been willing to take a chance on because she was afraid of all the ups and downs of love.

She was so afraid of having her heart broken in the process of trying to find someone she would be truly happy with, that she had actually broken her own heart. Lacey had pushed away love with Thatcher because she didn't know what the future held, and she was so scared of losing him.

Lacey broke down crying.

Something she hadn't done in so long.

Everything she had been holding on to came out in a flood of tears.

Her life flashed before her eyes, and she mourned her friends up north, her home, each move her family had made. She had swallowed all of that pain away until she was so full she was numb.

Now the only way to deal with it was to let it out.

Tears transitioned into great heaving sobs, and when her storm of emotion finally subsided, she wiped her tears away and picked up her phone to read the email messages from Will.

He asked for her forgiveness and said everything that she had come to realize for herself. That they hadn't really been in love, that marriage just seemed like the right thing to do, and when Lacey was so distant with him, because they had no real connection, he took solace in Beth's company. They had connected and eventually fallen in love.

He apologized for her finding them like that, said it wasn't supposed to happen and he was on his way to end the marriage when she'd walked in. He had planned to leave her at the altar, but she got there first.

Lacey swallowed the lump in her throat and replied that she forgave him and agreed with him. She let Will know that it was okay. And then emailed Beth to say the same.

And it was.

That's why she'd been numb to what happened, because it didn't hurt. She didn't care.

She did care about someone, though, and she'd just

turned down his offer of a happiness she'd never thought she'd find.

Not that she wanted to live in England, but Lacey realized it wasn't a place that was home; home was the person that you loved. That was why she'd followed her parents for so long—she'd found her home in their love.

But now she needed to move on. She needed to put down her own roots—make her own home—and she wanted to do that with Thatcher.

She quickly washed her face and headed out into the hall just as the ship started to move, pulling away from Anchorage.

She made her way back to the infirmary, but when she got there, all of Thatcher's things were gone. His computer, his mug. Everything.

Her stomach knotted, and she left the infirmary, heading to his quarters. But when she got there, one of the housekeeping staff was inside, and she could see his room had been stripped.

"Where is Dr. Bell?"

The cleaner looked up. "He disembarked in Anchorage."

"What?" Lacey asked, panicked.

"He asked the captain if he could leave. Apparently his father is dying, and he's going to be the new Duke of Weymouth!" the woman said excitedly. "He was flying straight out."

Lacey nodded numbly and left his room, her heart breaking.

She'd ruined it.

Ruined her best chance at happiness.

Thatcher had left her.

And now she had no way to get a hold of him to tell him that she loved him too. She was stuck on this ship for a week, but she knew what she needed to do to make things right once she got to Vancouver.

She might not be able to stop him at the gate, but she was going to fly to England and tell him she loved him. Even if he rejected her, she would take a chance for once in her life, because her future was nothing without him.

CHAPTER FOURTEEN

Two weeks later, England

THATCHER SAT IN the study at Weymouth Manor, watching the drizzle outside through the window. If he squinted his eyes enough, he could pretend that he was on the ship going up the inside passage, except that it was manicured lawns and farmland beyond the stone fences of his father's manor.

He'd rather be back on the ship or in the Yukon.

That was a lie.

He'd rather be back in Lacey's arms than anywhere else. She might have rejected him and run scared, but he knew deep down that Lacey loved him. She was just afraid.

And he could be patient.

Except, he wasn't sure where she was. He'd tried calling the only Greenwoods listed in Vancouver, but there had been no response, and he didn't leave a message.

There was a knock at the door.

"Come," Thatcher said, swiveling in his chair.

Michael came into the study. "Your letter was received, renouncing your title."

Thatcher took a deep breath. "And Father is okay with this?"

Michael nodded. "He just wants you in his life. I know he was absent when we were kids, but he's changed. He's trying to make amends. You've just been too stubborn to listen the last couple of years."

Thatcher smiled. "I know."

He'd been stubborn about a lot of things. When he'd arrived back at Weymouth Manor a couple of weeks ago, brokenhearted and tired from his trip, he'd been shocked at how warmly he'd been received and the apologies his father had been making.

Thatcher had always thought he was so different from his father, but he wasn't.

They were cut from the same cloth.

In stubbornness, anyhow.

And it was that stubborn streak that may have cost him the love of his life. He'd been a fool, but there was nothing he could do about it just yet. He was stuck here because he had to wait until the title was officially renounced before he could go to the Yukon. The thing was, he wasn't sure he wanted to go to the Yukon alone.

Ultimately, he wanted Lacey and would do anything to have her in his life.

"Are you sure this is what you want?" Michael asked, his hands in his pockets.

"Yes," Thatcher said. "I want to be a physician. I've never wanted to manage land or attend functions or have a seat in the House of Lords. All that bores me to tears, but you...you love that. And what's more, you are good at it. You were born to be the duke. Not me."

Michael nodded. "Well, I'm happy to take it on. Weymouth Manor has always meant so much to me. As have you. These last five years without you in my life—and me wondering where in the bloody hell you've been—have been awful."

"I'm sorry, Michael."

Michael cocked his eyebrow and sternly looked down his nose at Thatcher, which seemed to be a trait for all successful dukes in this family.

"Well, you better come back and visit from time to time. Don't expect me to go to the Yukon. I have no idea why you love it there so much."

"Neither do I." Thatcher sighed. "But I do."

There was another knock at the door, and Heath entered the room. "I'm sorry, my lords. There is a young lady from Canada here to see you," he said, addressing Thatcher.

His heart skipped a beat, and he stood up.

"What?"

Heath looked at him. "A young lady from Canada, or more importantly, someone by the name of Lacey, sir."

Michael looked back at him. "Is this the girl you were moping about?"

Thatcher ignored him. "Show her to the sitting room, Heath, and I'll be there in a moment."

"Very good, my lord." Heath left.

"Is this the woman you fell in love with?" Michael asked.

"Yes. Although I'm worried she's changed her mind and wants to be a duchess. Like Kathleen."

Michael gave him a look. "I seriously doubt that, if she's anything like the way you've described her."

"Well, she doesn't know that I rescinded the title."

"I don't think she's here for a title. If she's the woman you said she is, then she's here for you. You are worthy of love, Thatcher. With or without a title. You're an honorable and decent man. Kathleen was a gold digger. Go find out why your Canadian is here and take your chance."

Thatcher nodded and left the study.

His stomach was in knots as he made his way to the sitting room.

Heath had left the door open, and he saw she was standing in the middle of the room, her mouth open as she looked at his father's paintings adorning the walls, some from the masters.

"Lacey," he said, taking a step into the room.

She spun around. Her cheeks bloomed with pink. "Thatcher."

"What're you doing here?"

Lacey had been so nervous. When she got off the cruise ship in Vancouver, she'd declined continuing with the job and made her way over to her parents' to collect herself and pack. She was going to England, but first she had to do some reconnaissance and figure out where in England he was.

She found out where Weymouth Manor was and then packed for her trip, getting the earliest flight she could.

After a couple of connections and a delayed flight, she landed in England, rented a car, had a quick lesson about driving on the left and then made her way to Weymouth Manor to tell Thatcher that she wanted him.

If that meant she had to live in England, then fine.

All she wanted and needed was Thatcher.

She was so in love with him, and though she'd been scared to let herself love him—because she wasn't sure that she could handle the pain if she ever lost him—she also knew she couldn't spend the rest of her life living in fear and not taking chances.

So here she was, standing in a sitting room that was a bit overwhelming, her heart pounding in her throat. She suddenly felt like that movie she'd watched a long time ago where the heroine had said something about a girl being in front of a boy... She couldn't remember the words exactly, but she suddenly understood how that girl felt.

"I've come to apologize," she said, finally finding her voice.

"For what?" he asked.

"For saying that you were wrong, and for saying that I don't love you, because you were absolutely right. I was afraid. I was running away and...and I love you." She tried to swallow past the lump in her throat, her hands shaking as she waited for his response.

He turned and shut the door to the sitting room behind him. "You love me?"

"I do. And if we have to live here so you can take your title, then okay."

He paused. "Are you only back here because of my title? Do you only want me because of that?"

"No. I honestly would hate being a duchess, and I would make the worst duchess ever. You don't know how many people in this country already hate me— I'm sure I probably pissed off a dozen of your tenants driving on the right accidentally a few times and almost hitting a sheep or two on the way here. I would not be good at this life, but I know one thing."

"What's that?" he asked, the hint of a smile appearing on his face.

"My life wouldn't be whole without you. I love you, Thatcher. My life isn't complete without you in it."

He smiled and closed the gap between them, taking her in his arms and kissing her. The kiss seared her blood and made her heart sing.

"I love you, Lacey Greenwood, even if you would

make a lousy duchess. But you don't have to worry about that."

"I don't?" she asked.

"I gave up my title. My brother, Michael, who is much more suited to the task, is going to take over the title when my father dies…which won't be for a while yet. He's doing much better."

"You're not going to be the duke?"

"No," he said seriously, his arms around her. "Do you still want me? Do you think that you could live a life with just a simple physician?"

She sighed and smiled. "Yes. I think I can. You know I love the north."

"It doesn't have to be the Yukon. I can go anywhere."

Lacey shook her head. "No, the Yukon. That's where you wanted to go, and I would love to live back in the north. As long as you'll have me as your nurse practitioner and midwife still, then I'll follow you anywhere. I can't live without you. You are my home, Thatcher. It's not a place that makes a home or roots. It's the person you share your life with."

He smiled and picked her up, spinning her around. "I love you, Lacey. Marry me. Now. Before you decide to run away on me."

She laughed. "Fine, but isn't it kind of hard to get married quickly here? I mean, don't we need a special license or something…"

"My father can handle it. He has some connections with the archbishop. We'll get married here. Then, as soon as my visa comes in, we'll go to Vancouver, get your things and drive up to the Yukon. Does that sound like a future you can live with?"

Lacey smiled. "Yes, my lord. I think I can handle a future like that."

Thatcher kissed her again, and it felt like her heart was going to burst.

"Let's go tell my father and brother. Oh, and I'll let him know there are a few tenants he'll have to buy off."

Lacey laughed and took his hand. They left the sitting room to make their way up the stairs so that she could meet her future father-in-law, the Duke of Weymouth.

She'd always been afraid of her future, but with Thatcher by her side, she was no longer scared about what that future held.

For the first time ever, she was looking forward to finding out.

EPILOGUE

One year later, Stewart River, Yukon Territory

LACEY STEPPED OUTSIDE onto the deck of the log cabin she'd helped Thatcher build in a small town that was nestled between Dawson City and Whitehorse. The summer breeze felt good; it had been unusually hot for late August.

The clinic had been busy, and she would have to make her way into the small town soon to do a couple of home checks on some pregnant patients.

Thatcher was chopping wood to get ready for the winter, which was coming fast, and Lacey smiled, watching him.

She had just finished cleaning their guest room for her parents' arrival in a week.

She had something exciting to tell them, but first she had to let Thatcher know. It was something they had talked about, but hadn't really planned for yet.

"Do you have a minute?" Lacey asked, walking down the steps.

"Yes." He sank his ax into the log. "You leaving soon for town?"

"Soon, but not yet." She smiled and found she was just as nervous as that day when she'd shown up at Weymouth Manor and bared her heart to him. "I need to show you something."

"Sure."

She handed him a sheet of paper that had her blood results on it. She'd run the test herself, sending it off to the lab as it was hard to come by a simple pregnancy test up here.

"You took a blood test?" he asked, confused.

"Yes, take a look and tell me what you think."

He cocked an eyebrow and glanced at the sheet. "Cholesterol looks good."

"Yes, but look closer."

He was scanning the paper, and she knew the moment he saw it, because his eyes opened wide and he stared at it closer. "HcG?"

"Yes." She laughed nervously. "About eight weeks."

"Are you serious?" he asked in disbelief.

"Yes. Are you happy?"

"More than happy." He scooped her up in his arms and kissed her.

"Well, now you can see why I'm so anxious for my parents to come. I want to tell them in person that they'll be grandparents. We'll have to video chat your father soon too and let him know."

Thatcher kissed her again. "We will, but first I plan to take you in that cabin and show you just how happy you've made me."

"What about the firewood?"

"Who cares?" he said huskily.

"I have patients."

"Not until later. For the next couple of hours, you're mine, Nurse Bell."

He kissed her, and she laughed as he carried her over the threshold into their happy-ever-after.

* * * * *

COMING SOON!

We really hope you enjoyed reading this book. If you're looking for more romance, be sure to head to the shops when new books are available on

Thursday 28th October

To see which titles are coming soon, please visit
millsandboon.co.uk/nextmonth

MILLS & BOON

Coming next month

CHRISTMAS MIRACLE IN JAMAICA
Ann McIntosh

Chloe took a deep, audible breath and then said, "I'm pregnant."

The words made no sense to him. And yet they must have, because his heart stumbled and an icy pit opened up in his stomach.

"And before you ask, yes, the baby is yours. If it isn't, then we'll need to contact the Vatican about a miracle, because you're the only man I've been with since I left my husband two years ago."

Her words came at him as though from a distance. The frigid sensation had spread from his belly to form a band around his chest, causing the fleeting thought that perhaps he was having a myocardial infarction.

Then Chloe's face softened into an expression so beatific, all other thoughts flew from his head at the sight.

"It's actually a true miracle to me," she said, her voice low and so full of joy it melted the ice in his torso. "I was told I wasn't able to conceive because of endometriosis. So—" She paused, her chin tilting up to that pugnacious angle he'd come to know so well. "So what I wanted you to know is that I'm keeping this baby, and if you don't want to be involved in his or her life, I can assure you my child will lack for nothing."

He knew he should say something, but try as he might, nothing came out. And it felt as though he'd been turned to stone. All he could do was watch as Chloe gave him a small smile and stood up.

"I'll let you get on with your afternoon," she said, and then she was gone.

Pregnant? With my child?

Sam's brain couldn't seem to grasp the concept, and he finally staggered to his feet, not knowing where exactly he planned to go.

Endometriosis…

His heart stopped, and a wave of nausea had him swallowing against the thickness rising in his throat.

Chloe's pregnancy was high-risk.

His legs gave way again, and he plopped back into his chair, momentarily overcome by fear so strong it dulled the edges of his sight to darkness.

What would be worse, he wondered dully: losing a child you never knew existed until it was gone or a second one you suddenly realized you wanted almost too much?

Because, just then, Sam realized the baby growing in Chloe Bailey's womb meant more to him than he'd have ever expected.

That baby—his child—was as much a miracle for him as it was for its mother.

Continue reading
CHRISTMAS MIRACLE IN JAMAICA
Ann McIntosh

Available next month
www.millsandboon.co.uk

MILLS & BOON

Desire

Indulge in secrets and scandal, intense drama and plenty of sizzling hot action with powerful and passionate heroes who have it all: wealth, status, good looks…everything but the right woman.